A Song for Somme
By: Jennifer Malech

Books

A Song for Somme is a work of historical fiction. Though based upon real historical settings, all characters and story incidents are a product of the author's imagination.

First Editing Published Edition. For any information, email
editors@firstediting.com
TS N.Woodward Ave. #85151
Tallahassee, FL 32313 USA
USA/Canada 1(321)251-6977
UK 44(0) 20 3006 28 86

ISBN-13: 978-0-692-97576-3
Printed in the United States of America

In honour of the life of C. S Lewis, this book is dedicated to his writings that have transcended the way people, including myself, understand suffering in our world.

A SONG FOR SOMME

Contents

Part 3

JENNIFER MALECH

Part 1 Autumn 1922

JENNIFER MALECH

Chapter 1
A Return to Oxford

It was unfamiliar, yet at the same time, invigorating. Bach's Concerto for Two Violins danced between the intricate designs of the startling light's ceilings. I checked the scribbled handwriting on the piece of paper to make sure that I was in the right building. Of course, the concerto piece was evidence enough, but all the same, I didn't know if changes had been made since the war.

"Lloyd, there you are old chap." Charles's excitement collided with the stagnant walls.

"It's about time you showed up." I slapped his chest with his musical scores.

"Who would have thought? A couple of war veterans in pursuit of a music education, huh, old chap?"

"It's a miracle they let you in," I replied.

"And, now you are being daft. The king sent me here on recommendation himself."

"The next best thing to the king," I smiled.

"My father almost didn't allow it," he responded.

"Yes, it is a mystery as to why your father almost didn't allow you into the programme," I replied without a change of tone.

"I promised him I was serious this time," he said, but then proceeded to laugh, indicating that he had convinced his father to let him back into the programme, even though he most likely would not take it seriously at all, no matter how bloody talented he was.

"Even a war can't change Charles Atwood's habits," I said, before walking towards our first class for the day.

He smoothed his midnight black hair and replied, "Perhaps you are right, but it will be much more fun this time around."

"I'm serious, Charles. You know my rules. No parties, no girls. Not this time around."

"You're on your own, Lloyd."

"War taught you nothing."

"Sure it did. Life is shorter than I thought," he smiled. "Might as well have fun."

"Music comes first, Charles."

"Oh, lighten up. You're always so serious."

"If you aren't careful, your father will remove you from the programme, and then what? You'll be subject to the authority of the aristocracy. Is that what you want?"

"I haven't been subject to their formalities in years, old chap."

"You deny your privileges." I was annoyed.

"Of all people, you talking to me about *my* life being a privilege!" He laughed harshly and added, "You are always the one saying the aristocracy is a life of great restriction."

"I am not talking about your position in society. I only meant that you don't have to worry a day about spending a pence on your education. Do you know how many fellows would long to be in your trousers?"

He laughed and shook his head. "Tell that to my father, old chap."

I ignored him.

Charles shook his head and then changed subject. "What courses are you taking this time around?"

"Chamber Music Performance, Seminar in Composition, Vocal Instruction and some other composition course. I can't remember the name of it now."

"Crikey. You aren't thinking of doing this for a living, old chap?"

"Don't call me old chap."

"You already know you've lost that battle."

"I, unlike others with privileges, have to make a living some way or another."

"So, that's what this talk of the aristocracy is all about, old chap?"

"Let's focus on finding the classroom, shall we?"

While Charles was one of my closest friends, he was also a real pain at times. We were both in our first semester at Oxford when Great Britain entered the Great War. It was shortly after Britain had declared war on Germany when both Charles and I had made the decision to go to the warfront. We had served under the same regiment, and somehow had both gone unscathed, except for a few scars here and there. Most of our friends didn't make it, and as a result, my nickname came about. I was already the oldest amongst our friends at the start of war and now, eight years later, every time Charles mentioned that bloody nickname, it reminded me that I should have been dead with the rest of them. I was an old bloke now.

Half of the students in the programme were at least a decade younger and most certainly not as committed to the art. I knew I shouldn't judge those eager faces sitting in their chairs filled with hopes and dreams, but I couldn't help it. I judged them because I knew them; I had been in their shoes eight years ago. Sometimes, it seemed like it belonged to a different lifetime and other times, it felt as familiar as yesterday's supper.

I let my thoughts drift and realised that I had forgotten to ask what courses he was taking. "How about you, Charles? Anything interesting this semester?"

"Music Theory and Vocal Instruction for the hell of it."

"That's it?" I asked in shock.

"Crikey, you think I could get away with that, old chap? You know why I'm here."

I admitted that I really didn't and made some remorseful remark about the girls he had hung around with before the war.

"No, Charles, why are you here, really?"

"Why, do you think my old man would send me back to school if he thought I would mess around the whole time?"

"It's good to hear you admit it."

"I like the music just as much as you do, old chap."

It didn't seem worth it, to throw away all that money for only a course or two, but of course, Charles didn't have to worry about such. His father was president of the university's music programme and Charles was the heir to his father's land. His father was re-making a name for himself in society, and thought it best that his son invest in a worthwhile education for their family's sake. Charles had been born into the British aristocracy, but unfortunate circumstances had moved their family from their affluent estate in Manchester to the outskirts of Oxford.

I never learnt the details of why they had lost their estate and why Charles' father had chosen university to remake himself. The less I knew, the better. Besides, despite all of it, their family still had a bloody lot of money.

If it wasn't for Mr. Atwood's loss of their estate in Manchester, I believed that education would have never been a consideration for his son. If that was the case,

Charles and I would have never met. Sometimes, I
wondered if it would have been better that way, but war
changed that. We had been through things together; he
was the only person alive who could understand how
those circumstances had changed me.

I stopped the brisk walk and realised that I was indeed
lost. Rubbing my forehead and taking the sheet of paper,
I asked a young man walking on by to direct me in the
right direction of the classroom where we were to take
Vocal Instruction. Charles didn't seem to care that we
were already late.

After receiving directions from the student, who looked
as though his mum still dressed him every morning,
Charles bluntly commented.

"Jazz is going to revolutionise the way we ever thought
about music."

"You are a trumpet player who belongs in an orchestra,
not some jazz club band. You wouldn't be here
otherwise."

"That's where I think you are wrong, old chap. You are
too old-fashioned. Classical music had its day. It's time
for some new rhythms to shape our world. Jazz is already
revolutionizing the music scene in America."

"Classical music will never die. If it was able to do so, it
should have died with King George VI," I stated.

"I'm not saying it will, but it is going to change, whether
you want it to or not."

"You're too good for that scene," I replied.

"What was that, old chap?" A huge grin crossed his face.
"I love to hear you say it."

Charles knew he was good, and I always hated to
admit it out loud. He was the best trumpet player I had
ever known, and I'm not just saying so because he was
my friend.

"You heard me. That's all I have left to say on the matter."

I sighed in relief as the classroom that we were approaching was the room number scribbled on the paper in hand.

Upon entrance, I apologised for the both of us as we made our way to the back of the room.

"As I was saying, tardiness is prohibited." The instructor's voice was high pitched. I wondered if he had fast-forwarded his speech to prick us underneath our skin.

A blonde haired boy seated to our right let out a quiet laugh which informed me that my predictions had indeed been true. As I sat there in a room full of people, students whose lives had borne little experience, I envied them. I longed for their innocence, their naivety, and their indifference to what really took place on the battlefields in France. It wasn't their fault, and it was futile to make them understand, but all the same, I felt like a foreigner on new soil. Oxford wasn't as it used to be, no matter if the hallways and windows still groaned the same.

We had been back at our classes for a month now. Charles seemed to be taking his courses more seriously than before, which I attributed to Cherry's insistence that he not miss a class and play his trumpet for her. Cherry was the girl that Charles had been taking out as of late. She wasn't his girl really; I didn't know exactly what to call her, for Charles' parents certainly wouldn't approve of the match. It was the one thing that no one could be envious of: to be trapped in a system where position and money were the causes behind every familial decision.

Most English men were stilted to express human emotion, yet Charles wasn't like the rest of them. He wore his heart on his sleeve.

They met at the library, the Radcliffe Camera, of all places, Charles and Cherry that is. That would have never happened before the war, which made me realise that perhaps the war had really changed Charles after all. If anything, it had taught him discipline, and perhaps made him realise that his family's fortune should have never been taken for granted to begin with. Even though their family's name had been ruined, though not entirely, Charles parents still hoped that he would marry someone with a title. From what I knew, Cherry was far from such qualifications. Yet, Charles didn't care about these traditions, and truth be told, where his parents thought his education would be an entrance back into society, it truly was Charles' escape from a lifetime of rules and regulations.

He returned late to our flat, but I didn't mind it. I was working on a musical composition, despite my instructor's request that we not write anything until we completed this term's courses. I knew I was better than most of the kids there, at least that's what I called them, they were only kids. I tried not to judge them, for their innocence was not their fault, but no matter how hard I tried, prudence robbed their ability to make me think against it.

Ever since I had returned to England, I heard the music in my ears and I couldn't let it remain in my head for that much longer. Charles called me insane. I called him insensitive.

It was after the Battle of Somme, that's when I heard the notes scrape through my ears and down my spine. When I returned to English soil, it haunted me, reminding me that all of that blood was just as futile as explaining to one of the kids why it had been shed in the end.

Charles and I rarely talked about the war. I attributed this to the fact that most of our friends had been taken. You grow up as a boy reading about war stories, by hell, you romanticise it and worship those men in novels who took out dozens of chaps with their weaponry. I didn't know if Charles felt the same since the day we became victorious four years ago, but I can assure you that there is no romance in the trenches of war. None of us felt like heroes, and to those who did, their names belonged under the same list of men who truly died for cowardice, not like Victor. This is why I didn't share my thoughts with Charles; I knew he probably belonged on that list. "You home, old chap?" His voice made its way through the thin hallway and met me in my study room.

I didn't answer. He would find me soon enough. After a dozen steps, the echo of his footsteps came to a standstill.

"There you are! Did you hear me, old chap?"

I grunted.

"Well, what is Beethoven working on tonight?" He slapped my back and took a seat.

"Nothing that will interest you," I replied without a change in my tone.

"That might be the case, but I have something that will certainly interest you."

Charles placed a ticket on the desk and mischievously grinned. "What's this?" I held the ticket in my hand and read the print out loud.

"London Symphony Orchestra."

"Tickets for Saturday's show. Thought you'd be pleased." I turned the ticket over as though it was a trick of some kind.

"Is this a bribe?"

"Oh, come on, can't I do something nice for my friend?" he smiled.

"What is the timetable?"

"Can you read old chap? The bloody ticket says it will start just past eight."

"Who else did you invite?" I asked.

He rolled his eyes as he realised that I had caught onto his scheme.

"Come on, old chap, I just want you to have a little fun. And, I'd like you to meet Cherry. She's a decent girl."

"Far too decent for you," I replied bluntly.

I had yet to meet her. All I knew was that Cherry Walsh was studying Latin and French Literature and she was more intelligent than most girls Charles had ever met. She was fluent in at least three languages, at least that is what Charles said.

"She's bringing a friend, I believe her name is Charlotte. I don't know much about her, but if she's a friend of Cherry's, I'm sure she's just as decent a lady."

"I'll think about it," I replied. Placing the ticket next to my sheet music, I returned diligently to the notes that fluctuated in my head.

"A trip to London would do you good," Charles smiled and then left the room.

I stared at the composition piece before me, wrestling with what key to write it in. I couldn't let the notes remain in the Key of F# major, for it was too triumphant sounding and I felt far from it. F# minor was more fitting, a key of disarray. Although I had returned to Oxford, there was discontentment found in its cracks, a howling for the days before the war, of feet that trod upon their boards which no longer walked this earth. I knew I would not remain in this key, at least I was hopeful for such. Perhaps the evening at the Symphony would be a good thing after all. Perhaps the key would shift to G major then. God, I hoped so. It was a terrible thing feeling the way I did, and Charles' enthusiasm didn't make it any better. I sighed and got up from where I was sitting.

Charles was in the kitchen and had just put a pot of water on the cooker. His garter belts were hanging off his trousers. His ruffled hair made him appear to be a man who had just returned from a day at Gran's farmland. "Alright, I'll go," I said, splitting the silence of the flat.

Charles immediately turned around with a grin about his face, a grin that I wanted to wipe off. I was bitter that he foolishly enjoyed life, while I still couldn't understand why I still had breath in my lungs and was sharing a London flat with Charles instead of Victor. He was doing me a favour, though, for I probably couldn't afford this place on my own, and he had wanted an escape. Charles had even told me that he had to beg his valet not to follow him to Oxford. I couldn't imagine having a man dress me every day.

"Cherry thinks it'll be a marvellous time for you. She's been worried about you, old chap," Charles' enthusiasm never failed.

I was surprised that Cherry even thought about me, for I hadn't even met her yet.

"Then, I'm certain she's right."

"She always is."

And, with such an agreement, my hands felt as though they were hovering over the ivories, unsure as to whether or not I should return to F# Major. Someone other than Charles held concern for my well-being, and that was something to play about.

Chapter 2
A Secret Cherry

"Lloyd, how splendid to finally meet Charles' flatmate! It isn't a figment of his imagination after all."

"No ma'am. I am flesh and blood, much more than pure imagination."

Cherry, as enthusiastic a girl as ever there was one, laughed at my response and startled me by planting a kiss on the cheek. She took my arm and allowed me to escort her into the hall. Her independent eagerness wiped away both my cynicism and dab hand all at the same time. I had determined that I liked Cherry, for she was different from all of the other girls Charles had seen before the war. Of course, I felt that I had already determined that from conversations that Charles and I had about her, but meeting her in person validated my presumptions altogether.

As we entered the concert hall, I realised for the first time that I hadn't been here since before the war. Queen's was the musical centre of England. While it's interior was outlandish, the acoustics were marvellous.

"Isn't it wonderful, Charles?" Cherry turned around to face him, her arm still wrapped in my own. He admitted that it was a spectacular sight to behold. I took another glance at Cherry and noticed that her pale skin, freckles, and short red curls fit her perfectly. Cherry admired the fixed walls that had been entirely unchanged over the years. Before the war, I always fancied the pure painting of the Paris Opera and knew that it was Cherry's first time at Queen's Hall when she gasped at the sight of the opera painting that spread across the Queen's ceiling.

As we entered the archaic room, and as its plush seats waited for the evenings guests to take their place, I enquired about Cherry's friend who was supposed to be joining us for the evening.

"Oh, I forgot to mention, old chap, Charlotte had a family engagement to attend to. She telephoned us just before we left," Charles replied.

"I thought you knew," Cherry turned and apologised, her arm still in mine.

I brushed her concerns aside and told her that it was perfectly alright.

"Well, shall we take our seats?" Charles asked.

"Yes, it'd be best before the first movement begins," I commented.

With such, I handed her off to Charles and watched the dashing couple make their way towards our seats. I admired them from afar and as much as Charles got on my nerves, I understood why Cherry had an eye for him. He came from somewhat of a respectable family, played the trumpet like it was the last day of his life, and was a great conversationalist. He never failed to make sure everyone was included in conversation and he was very intelligent, even though he never let on that he was.

If I was a stranger gazing in from the outside, I would not understand the match, but of course, Charles never wanted outsiders to know just how intelligent he was. It was infuriating at times, for he was bloody brilliant at everything he did and yet he played it off as though everyone was just as brilliant. While his smile appeared coy to the outside world, I knew such demonstrations to be quite different. He was far from modest, and Cherry knew it. She was allured by his confidence, and yet, she too, remained a mystery to the outside world.

I usually prided myself in my ability to read people as easily as a fairy book, but I could not read Cherry quite yet. If I had not known Charles my entire life, undoubtedly he would belong in the same category of books as Cherry.

Now, as we walked to our seats, I smiled as I thought of the look that crossed Charles' face when he had entered our flat the evening before last.

It was at a dinner party, in which Charles accompanied Cherry to Brighton, an event in which I wondered if Cherry might change his beliefs about marital commitment after all.

When he spoke of her, he reminded me of myself before the war.

He had looked me in the eyes and said, "She was simply fearless. An Irish girl speaking her mind to a room full of English aristocrats and dukes. There's something you would never see before the war, huh, old chap?"

I could tell that Charles was gobsmacked by the entire evening so I asked about the food. He didn't hear me, though.

"Did you know she had a brother who died in the Irish War of Independence?"

I shook my head. I wasn't going to be a know-all and explain that there would be no possibility of me knowing something that he had not known.

"She's a firecracker, old chap."

"You need a firecracker to keep your trousers on," I replied.

"Are you jealous, old chap?" he smiled.

"You better treat her right, Charles, that's all."

"I've never felt this way about a girl before. She's mysterious and entirely unpredictable."

"You never were predictable yourself."

"Perhaps we aren't well balanced for one another after all," he laughed.

"You really like her?" I asked, knowing that he was half drunk and it was the only way I could ever get him to talk about his feelings. He would probably deny it all the next morning.

"She's different."

"So, you've said."

I took a swish from my glass and offered him some old scotch that had been hidden in the cabinets for who knows how long.

"She doesn't come from a lot of money, but you would never know it. I'm the one who fought in the war, old chap. Yet, she seems to know more about it than I do."

"Is she a socialist, then?" I asked.

"Don't go around saying that word," he grinned.

"I'm not one. Just asked if she was."

"Funny little thing. I don't know why she calls herself one."

"Well, why else did her brother fight in the War of Independence?"

"It was about fighting for their independence from us. They didn't want to pay their loyalty to our king."

"Yet, so many of them fought for the British army during the war," I uttered.

That I could not understand.

"They had no choice. Some of them refused to fight in the war, you know," Charles replied.

"Yes, that's true. Remember Richard Sullivan?"

"How could I forget the chap. He was too bloody brilliant for his own britches."

"I ran into him shortly before I left for America. He told me that he was returning to Ireland to make amends with his family."

I relieved my cigar with the ashes, while Charles breathed its fine smoke into the atmosphere.

"What happened?"

"His brothers joined the Irish Republic. He said it was foolish of them. He somehow got caught up in all the mess. He never returned to London."

The drink burned my throat and I took another swish, afraid that I had already shown Charles too much emotion.

"Poor chap."

I wondered once again if Charles ever thought about how we had been the ones to survive the war, but I never asked.

"Lloyd, has the ceiling left you in a trance?" Cherry's voice took me away from our flat as I remembered that I was at Queen's Hall. Charles and my conversation vanished altogether.

The Paris ceiling watched me as I took my steps, shadowed by the men whose voices filtered the air. *Ils sont fous.*

I shook my head and apologised.

"I fear anyone could become lost in the painter's efforts," she smiled.

As her voice trailed through the theatre seats, I have to admit, I was just as interested as Charles to learn more about her. She was a fascinating creature to behold, as though she had been raised on a different planet entirely. I followed Charles and Cherry to our seats, feeling terribly nostalgic all of a sudden.

Victor and I had seen the symphony the night before we left for France. He had told me that if it was going to be his last time to hear classical music for a while, we might as jolly well enjoy ourselves. He always enjoyed the music, although he never once played an instrument. I supposed that's what happens when you grow up in a household of musicians.   Queen's Hall was Victor's favourite place on earth. It's also where he had met Lindsay, a sensible girl and the only woman he had ever loved. I tried not to think of them both, it made me sick. "Are you going to try out for the Orchestra this Spring?" Cherry interrupted my thoughts as we took our place in the familiar seats.

I made eye contact with Charles as he shrugged. "I'd prefer to give the younger men a chance," I simply replied.

"Charles told me that you have a real knack for the piano. I don't believe he would lie about such a thing."

"We'll see." I turned my gaze towards Charles.

Her persistence made you question everything. She made you smile, that Cherry.

"I'm certain you must. Well, you must try out, at the very least," she said.

"Only if you insist," I replied with a smile.

"Oh, Lloyd, there must be someone else who inspires ambition within?" she seemed slightly exasperated.

"No, not really."

She pouted and turned to Charles. "Is Lloyd always so cynical?"

"Don't mind him. He's only that way because he's truthfully better than the rest of us."

I knew they knew perfectly well that I could hear them and wondered if Charles' previous comment was a compliment.

Within moments, the theatre filled with the eruption of strings as the orchestra took their position. Blast, I loved that sound. The dissonance that rung through your ears as the musicians calmly fine-tuned their instruments while the maestro made his way to the centre of the stage.

And, just like that, the dissonance turned into a quiet landscape. Everyone held their breath as the conductor lifted his baton into the air, the musicians' eyes glued to his, ready for that first chord to strike the audience with awe and wonder.

I was already on the edge of my seat. From the corner of my eye, I noticed Cherry glance my way as she tried not to laugh at the little boy I had then become. My composure didn't change; I didn't care what others thought. I was enraptured from the moment the concertmaster hit the E string with such melancholic vigour. I understood their heartbeat so well. That is why we have music. There are some emotions that will never be produced through words, for it can only be found in the mastermind of musical composition.

From the moment the maestro met the concertmaster's bow, the dynamics were exquisite, displaying perfectly well the motif of duality that was found in the overall composition. I resonated with the writing and wondered if the composer had served in the war. There was refrain and deep resonance that even depicted a sign of requiem, perhaps for the fallen that the composer could not deny. The incorporated bells sounded similar to that of church bells, which reminded me of when I was a boy. We attended mass services only a few times, once when our cook had unexpectedly passed away. Mum thought it our duty to attend the service, while Victor and I spent the hour counting the dust particles on the hymnals. That is until the choir sang.

I must have been only seven then, but I became the most captivated seven year old that all of Derbyshire had ever seen. Mum thought Victor had put something in my tea that morning; I merely nodded and Victor got a scolding later. The poor kid was but five years old. I shook my head at the memory. Victor should be here, not I.

The first movement ended and the theatre erupted with applause. Cherry's blue eyes shone in agreement with the composer's coda, a harmonious election of notes that left the listener in need of more.

I had almost forgotten what it was like to sit there, engulfed by the array of perfumes from all around the world as you listened to the medleys drift into the orchestral backdrop, a close depiction to the cathedrals we visited when we were young boys.

"Simply marvellous, wasn't it old chap? It could as well have been the end." Charles put an arm around Cherry.

"Marvellous isn't the right word," I replied.

"Sorry I'm not as eloquent as you," he teased.

"It sounded like a haunting church chorus," Cherry piped in.

"Exactly," I smiled and held my composure, for fear that they both would leave me to watch the second movement on my own.

She coyly smiled and pointed at the pianist on stage. "That should be you, Lloyd, that is if Charles hasn't exaggerated your musical ability."

"I'd be surprised if he exaggerated such words in my favour."

"I'd be equally surprised if you did the same," he laughed.

"Have I come to the opera hall with a bunch of schoolchildren?" She raised an eyebrow and both Charles and I shut up. "After all, I think you both should try out for Oxford's orchestra."

"You know I only want to play jazz music, darling,"
Charles responded.

My ears perked up. Did Cherry also disagree with
Charles' ambitions to take his talents to the jazz club?
"We made a deal." Cherry winked at me. I so desired to
ask them what that deal was, but realised it was in my best
interest to trust Cherry on this one.

We returned to the London flat after two more
movements, each one more intoxicating than the first.
Charles was bloody lucky to have his own place in
London, and while I did not envy the money from which
he came from, I did aspire to have a London flat of my
own someday. The interior collected dust during his
months at Oxford for he did not believe that he needed
paid staff to ensure the upkeep was grand enough for
weekend getaways. He believed those days were behind
us.

Cherry whistled a tune about the kitchen as she made
sarnies for us to eat. We were starving. I don't know
whose idea it had been to only have a few drinks and no
food before the show, for after the last movement had
come to a near end, I had begun to feel terrifically sick.
"This should help," Cherry plopped some ginger ale and
sarnies by my side.

I smiled and thanked her, while Charles stole a kiss
from her before she made her way back into the kitchen.
Her red dress still sparkled in the dim light. I wondered if
Charles paid attention to such things. I was not one for
fashion, by absolute no means, but the sleeveless dress
and diamonds around her neck had me even more

curious to know more about her family. All I knew was that she came from the Irish Highlands; I wondered what had brought her to England in the first place.

"Are you going to eat with us, darling?" Charles turned towards the red sparkles that brought life to our dull kitchen.

"After you stubborn calves agree to audition for the orchestra," she laughed.

Her persistency intrigued me, especially since we had only just met.

"Do you know much about music, Cherry?" I asked.

"Papa seems to think so."

"Is your father fond of music?" I was intrigued.

"Papa is fond of life itself," she mysteriously grinned and plopped onto the seat besides Charles.

"Do your parents still live in Ireland?" I asked.

"Papa does, yes."

"And, your mum?"

"Mam passed away when I was five years old."

"Oh, I am sorry to hear that." I took another swish of the scotch and felt quite fogey when I realised I couldn't take as many glasses as I did before the war.

"Oh, don't be. Mam lived a wonderful life."

Her smile became enchanting, taking me to the cliffs of the Roseland Heritage coast as she gazed in my eyes and continued with her thought.

"She used to sing *Mo Ghile Mear* to Tom and I before we fell asleep at night. Do you know of the Irish ballad?"

"I am not familiar with it," I replied softly.

"Would you sing it for us, love?" Charles was quick to ask. Cherry didn't even think twice. It was as though she set up the question expecting such a response.

She stood up then and brushed the dusty books that remained unread in Charles' parlour.

As soon as the first note hit the ceiling, I am certain the dust evaporated from the book's shelves. My posture quickened. I glanced over at Charles who sat aback; his leg criss-crossed atop the other and a boyish grin spread across his face. I knew then that he had already heard her sing. It was magical, though I am not fond of magic.

The words danced across my spine. My appetite fled as all I wanted was to hear Cherry sing some more.

She sang in the Irish language at first and then drifted the melody in a language that I could understand. Even if she had not done such, I would have been lost in her fluctuating voice.

Can you feel the river run?
Waves are dancing to the sun
Take the tide and face the sea
And find a way to follow me

Leave the field and leave the fire
And find the flame of your desire
Set your heart on this far shore
And sing your dream to me once more

He is my hero, my dashing darling
He is my Caesar, dashing darling
Rest or pleasure I did not get
Since he went far away, my darling

Now the time has come to leave
Keep the flame and still believe
Know that love will shine through darkness
One bright star to light the wave

The lyrics haunted me then. Lindsay's face came to

mind as we ran along the Cornwall shores. Did Cherry know what she was doing to me just then? I felt that she could.

With the last lyric, she sat down effortlessly besides Charles. He gave her a kiss on the cheek and remarked how splendid her song was.

"It's my only memory of her, really, but the most cherished that a daughter could ever have. Even when she was ill, she sang those words. She knew that her love shone through darkness, just as the lyrics say. There are few who come to discover that and Mam was one of them."

I imagined her mother to be some kind of Irish princess, a maiden whose inevitable fate made her soft whereas many others, including myself, could not make out life to be such.

"What do you have to say of Cherry's song, Lloyd?" he smiled.

"You have a strong voice," I simply replied.

I could not give in and tell her what the song did to me. It took me away to a life I had long forgotten, a life that I could never return to. I know I've said it, but I've envied the naivety that I once had.

"Mam had a stronger voice. As I said, I don't have very many memories of her, but Papa kept her alive through his painting."

"Your father paints?" I replied with a puzzled brow.

Her father was becoming just as curious as she. They were a family with old money who sat around painting the Irish countryside and singing folklore tunes with the servants. Cherry didn't say such, but I imagined so, although Charles had told me that she had come from no money at all. With such a voice, I couldn't be certain.

"Have you never heard of an Irish painter, Lloyd?" she

laughed.

"It was unexpected, that's all."

"And, what does your father do?" she mocked me.

Charles interrupted her then.

"Darling, did I tell you I have a surprise for you?"

Before Charles swept her away into the library, she peered into my soul, trying to understand the distance that suddenly cast its spell in my eyes.

I didn't want her to know about my father, not just yet. I didn't want his abandonment to ruin her song. For once, I was thankful that Charles was there.

Chapter 3
Jazz Electricity

The weekend in London had been rather enjoyable and Cherry's eager personality lightened the tension that had stood in the way of Charles and I for the past few months. We had been back in Oxford for two weeks, two weeks of which Cherry now seemed welcome to call on us at any hour, her spending more time at our flat than with her own sex.

"You will absolutely regret it if you don't come," Cherry stated.

"I thought you didn't like jazz music," I objected.

"Such a phrase has never been uttered from my lips."

"I have yet to determine how I feel on the whole matter," I replied.

"How can you determine something for which you've never even experienced?" she commented.

"What do you know about jazz?" I asked.

"A lot more than you, it seems. Shortly after the war ended, I went to see the Original Dixieland Jazz Band at the London Hippodrome. They were simply marvellous, Lloyd." She paused and stated once more, "Simply marvellous."

"So, this is why you support Charles and all of his wild imaginings?"

"Whether you realise it or not, music is changing just as

quickly as our timetables."

"You are Irish after all."

"Change in English society has to take place at some point. Did you not know that even King George requested their performance at Buckingham Palace?"

"No. I'm not knowledgeable on culture as you are," I responded. "Is that who's performing tonight?"

"No," she sighed. "They are touring in America, which I suppose isn't selfish of them since it is their homeland."

Cherry stood waiting for me to give an answer as to whether or not I would be joining her and Charles at the nightclub. Minutes prior, she had come knocking on our door insisting that I answer her before she strike down the door herself.

"Cherry, I may not be a man of high class, but I am still faithful to the classics. I am a respecter of technique and order, not syncopated improvisation."

"I promise good company." She was pertinent. "Charlotte is in town. She's staying at the Macdonald Randolph, so I believe she will fare well. Does a five-star dinner not entice you?"

"No, it certainly does not." I paused. "Are you certain Charlotte isn't a figment of your imagination to get me out of the flat?" I mocked.

"Charles was right. You can be impossibly stubborn sometimes," she retorted.

"I have my music to tend to, Cherry. I'd rather not spend the evening amongst intolerable music and unlikable company."

"Am I unlikable then?" she smirked.

"Only when you insist upon my presence with others that I wish not to be seen with."

"You insult Charlotte without having ever met her."

"I wasn't speaking of Charlotte."

Cherry stood with her hands on her hips while I stood hovering over the table, pages from my recent composition scattered in hand.

"Well, if I can't convince you, what is it that requires so much of your attention?"

Cherry picked up the score from the table.

"Does it have a name?" she asked.

"Does what have a name?"

"Your imaginary corgi, Lloyd. No, what else would I be talking about?"

I laughed. She had a wonderful sense of humour.

"It's in the beginning stages."

I turned towards the kitchen and asked if she'd like a drink.

"Do you have anything that doesn't contain alcohol?"

"I might be able to muster up something." I laughed and then remarked, "So, you are a true lady, then?"

"A lady that doesn't fancy alcohol?"

I shook my head.

"You are unattended in my flat, and yet you won't even take a drink from your host."

"It isn't that."

Cherry moved upward on the balls of her feet, holding her clutch, and switching her gaze to the bustling street life below the flat. I sat down and took a sip from the remaining scotch.

"I don't drink alcohol at all, on any occasion."

I refrained from spitting. Her slight smile made me curious as to how a phrase could ever be uttered from a woman's lips, especially a girl with Irish blood spilling through her veins.

"I told you my mother passed away when I was a girl."

"Yes, I was sorry to hear so. She sounded like a wonderful woman."

"She was an extraordinary woman. Her death nearly took Papa as well."

"The one who paints?" I smiled.

"No other father I know."

Cherry sat on Charles' love seat and smoothed her dress, complete confidence in her posture. I wondered if she would continue with her story for if she didn't, I knew it was not my place to ask and I might never come to find out just what she meant.

"Papa took to drinking after Mam's death, but not in the kind that most men take to. As much as my memories of my mother were stolen from my childhood, memories of Papa were also taken. Alcohol became his lover."

"I am sorry to hear such."

As the words spilled across the room, I longed to put the bottle of scotch down just then, realising that every time she gazed upon a bottle, it reminded her of what had been stolen from her childhood.

"He poisoned his blood and in turn, poisoned my brother's life and mine."

As she said it, I quinced.

Her gentle smile was found in her eyes. I suddenly knew what Charles meant when he said that Cherry seemed to know more about the world we fought for, even though we were the ones who had fought in it.

I knew then that she wanted more than my company tonight, she wanted someone with understanding. Charles wouldn't be able to give that to her; his father hadn't been the one who abandoned him and taken liquor to his death bed. Charles must have told Cherry or else she wouldn't have told me about her own father. I could see it in her eyes. It was incredible how someone could read someone so perfectly well by just gazing into their eyes. I felt that I could hold an entire conversation with Cherry without a single word.

"Do you really want me to go to the nightclub tonight?" She smiled. "Yes, Lloyd. I wasn't going to leave until you agreed."

We arrived at the nightclub, my arm in Cherry's. We were to meet Charles there, who I had later learned was on schedule to play that evening. I hadn't realised that over the past month that's how he had been spending his Wednesday evenings. He was an upper class English gentleman scheduled to play alongside a few black Americans. Cherry spoke of the jazz quartet as though they were already one of the most sought after bands in all of England. You would have thought that Charles and I didn't live together after all; we barely knew where the other was and what the other was doing. Perhaps it was best that way.

I was indifferent to it all, just as much as I was indifferent to the sudden change in women's roles in society. However, with my arm linked in Cherry's, I had begun to think that perhaps it was the best for society, a refreshing reform after the slaughter of war.

Cherry had dazzled herself in pearls and a cotton pink dress that made me believe that Cherry would never lose her youth. I smiled at her ability to draw the room's attention to herself without even trying.

Upon first impulse, the electricity in the air was invigorating to any individual who actually wanted to be there. It was much different from any concert hall that I had been to in London where the best of the romantics pleased our ears throughout the evening. Instead, we seemed to be confined to a secret affair, an Oxford basement that couldn't have seated more than two hundred people.

We entered to a room full of colour, a happiness that seemed to only be attained through these walls. The trumpet player counted off and the chase was on. Cigar smoke filled the confined space and laughter split the air, reminiscent of the parties that Charles, Victor, and I used to attend before the war.

"Come on, Lloyd, let me introduce you to Charlotte."

"Hasn't she already given you her condolences?" I shouted above the music.

Cherry merely laughed.

"Impossible, that should be your middle name, Lloyd."

She raised her voice, intertwined with the double-time composition. Pushing her way through the crowd, I followed her into the adjoining room where the jazz composition greeted one's ears with a glorious double-time feel. Perhaps Cherry was right, I hadn't really experienced the genre for myself; who was I to judge such an affair?

Classical music was irreplaceable, that I knew. My only hope was that the feelings that accompanied jazz composition would not replace the human need for a night at the opera theatre. I would not forgive Charles or his jazz companions if they replaced society's desire for classical music altogether. If Mendelssohn, Tchaikovsky and Debussy were to be replaced by Cherry's beloved Dixieland Jazz Band, then I'd have another reason to despise the war's after effects.

"Here we are. Charlotte, you look lovely, dear." Her pompous voice accompanied the jazz score equivocally.

Cherry gave her friend a hug. Dressed in a slimming yellow dress, her brown curls rested just above her shoulders, sporting a similar hairdo to Cherry. She was petite and taller than I had imagined, although not quite as tall as me. Her brown eyes brought about a warmth that made me feel as though we had met before even though I knew we hadn't.

"Charlotte, this is Lloyd."

"The classical enthusiast," she commented.

"I hope I'm known for more than just that," I replied and then added, "It's a pleasure to finally meet. I had begun to think you were Cherry's imaginary friend."

"Would you not put it past her?"

"Not at all," I smiled.

"Neither would I," she teased her friend.

"Neither would I," Cherry echoed Charlotte and then took a seat at the small round table where Charlotte had been seated.

"Have you been without company for the past hour?" I asked.

"I've been rather entertained. I am a creature of observance, Lloyd. Human noise silences reality."

I have to admit, from just a few words out of Charlotte's mouth, I was intrigued.

"Then, what am I silent about?" I tested her.

"Everyone in the room knows you don't want to be here. Even human noise can't silence such," she smiled while Cherry laughed.

I merely shook my head and summoned a waiter for a glass to drink.

"Then, I am right?" Charlotte smiled.

"You believe you have this world figured out, don't you?" There was slight harshness in my reply and while it usually was my initial reaction to apologise, I did not.

"The more I observe, the more I realise that I have figured out nothing," she objected.

"Then, you've learned well," I replied and took the drink

from the eager waiter.

"When's Charles to arrive?" Charlotte asked.

"Is he not here, yet?" I asked surprised.

"Oh, he's probably in the alley practising until they are called on stage," Cherry commented.

"That's rather uncivilised for a musician, especially for Charles."

"This is a different world here. It doesn't mean that it's any better, but it is different and that should be something to be excited about, not something to be apathetic about," Cherry replied.

"I assume you agree?" I asked Charlotte.

"Would it matter to you if I did?"

She smiled and I knew that she was only teasing me. At least, that is what I kept telling myself.

An eruption of applause filled our eardrums as the musicians took their bows and then returned to the dusky hallway where they would no doubt be treated to free drinks on the house.

Cherry's posture changed.

"Would you look at that handsome man?"

Her blue eyes glistened as Charles took the stage. I had never been with her when they didn't glisten, and wondered what one would have to do to possess such a quality.

After a few drinks, I was pleasantly surprised by how delightful the composition was to my ears; but I wasn't going to admit it to Charles. The pianist took to the stage with a number that could have been easily played by a first-year music student; however, the energy that the man brought to the room was one that could not be easily traded. Cherry commented that he had come over from America.

"Charles says there are quite a few African-Americans

who have come to England to expand their musical career," Charlotte commented.

"Charles' pianist is from New Orleans." Cherry seemed thrilled.

Perhaps I would be honest with Cherry if she asked how I enjoyed the evening in the end, for as soon as Charles hit those notes, I knew that he was right. Surrounded by intoxicating drink and annoying laughter, I became transported into the music that fled Charles' trumpet.

Chapter 4
The Bohemian Girl

The dreary weather outside painted even drearier prisms across the library's floors. I was seated beside Cherry, a routine that we had taken to every Wednesday and Friday. We rarely spoke of Charles who had just informed us that he had taken another new endeavour with the band from America. It stole his time away from Cherry, and even his studies, although she told me that she didn't mind.

My eyes glanced to her handwriting, her cursive not as eloquent as most, but lovely in its own way. She wrote frantically as though she only had a matter of minutes until the library was to catch on fire. I hadn't flipped a page of my book for quite some time to which she must have noticed for her frantic speed of writing came to a stop.

"Are you bored?" she smiled.

"Sometimes I wonder why I even came back to school in the first place," I said.

"To make our dreams come true, isn't that every one of our desires?" She raised her eyebrows.

"Do you enjoy your studies?" I whispered.

"Yes. Don't you?" she leaned in to where I could see every line in her face more clearly than ever before. I could count the freckles on her face if I wanted to.

"People say I take it too seriously," I replied.

"People like Charles?" she was on the verge of laughter.

"And others," I smiled.

"Do you think you take it all too seriously?" she asked with wide eyes.

"What do you think?"

"I think we need to leave this rubbish library." She slammed her book shut, drawing the attention of other students. We both tried not to laugh and I gathered her books for her while she put her coat on.

Walking outside, we were refreshed by the freedom of the air, not confined to the library's walls; no matter how much I enjoyed my studies, I wished it was all finished. All I wanted to do was compose, but I knew that my greatest opportunities for such would only come from my education at Oxford.

"I am fond of this dreary weather," she suddenly said. "Are you?"

"Yes, it reminds me of my mam. I loved the sunshine, always have." She paused and turned to face me. "When I was a little girl, my mam used to take me outside and tell me, 'My dear, there is no such thing as a dreary day. All you need to do is sing. It is song that brings the sunshine to this world.' I believed her. So, even after she passed away, I used to walk through our gardens and sing some of the Irish ballads she used to always sing to us."

"Do you still do it?"

"Sing on dreary days?"

I nodded.

"Yes. Would you like me to sing, Lloyd?" Her smile brought an inevitable smile to my own lips.

"Sing me an Irish Ballad that you used to sing when you were a girl."

She thought about it for a moment, our footsteps lightly chorusing the sounds of a metronome. There was hardly anyone else in the park that we were walking through, but I imagined that even if there were a plethora of others there, she still would have sung.

I dreamt that I dwelt in marble halls,
With vassals and serfs at my side,

And of all who assembled within those walls,
That I was the hope and the pride.

I had riches too great to count, could boast
Of a high ancestral name;
But I also dreamt, which pleased me most,
That you lov'd me still the same...

That you lov'd me, you lov'd me still the same,
That you lov'd me, you lov'd me still the same.

Then, she stopped singing altogether, although I wish she hadn't stopped for the ballad was brilliantly haunting. "Do you dream that you have riches too great to count?" I laughed.
"No, not riches, not that," she smiled and then asked, "Have you heard it before? The song, that is."
"No, I am afraid my knowledge of music is primarily in classical pieces that no one seems to remember nowadays."

"Would you like to know the story behind the song?"

"There seems to be a story behind every Irish ballad you sing."

"Of course there is."

"Well, then, by all means, tell me more."

"The piece comes from the opera *The Bohemian Girl*. It is well known in England. Mam saw it with Papa in London quite some time ago. She made the lyrics her own, turning words of text into ethereal melodies."

"What is *The Bohemian Girl* about?"

"It tells the story of a young girl who was kidnapped by gypsies. She became separated from her father, who was a wealthy count. The bohemian girl thought all of those experiences were mere dreams and would sing about them. Yet, in reality, these dreams were actually true events of her life."

"Does she ever come to know that it was not a dream?"

"She does. It is a happy ending, but I don't want to ruin it for you."

"I doubt I'll ever go see it."

"Perhaps we should one day." She smiled again and then asked me, "Do you ever feel like there are parts of your life that were just a dream, but in fact they might actually be true after all?"

"I think the older we get that statement may very well be true."

"Well, I most certainly do. Just like the bohemian girl, that is why I sing, to remind myself that my mam was more than just a dream."

I wondered if she was this vulnerable with Charles, but tried not to think about it. I knew what I was doing to myself by spending too much time with Cherry for she was the only one who seemed to understand my innermost thoughts. The war, more often than not, felt like a dream. Like Cherry, who sang about her mam to bring back the memory, I wrote about the war, to bring back Victor and everyone else who bloody lost their life in an event that I wish was just a dream.

After escorting Cherry back to her flat and arriving back to my own, I was surprised to find that Charles was there.

"Charlotte is in town for the entire weekend."

They were the first words out of his mouth and he seemed rather pleased.

"Am I to applaud this account?" I placed my books on the sofa.

I was surprised that Cherry had said nothing to me about it while we were at the library. For some reason, I felt as though this was Charles doing altogether.

"No need to frown. You will come out with us this weekend, won't you, old chap?"

"Yes, I'll go. You don't need to keep asking me every weekend. However, I cannot sacrifice Friday evening. I'll be there Saturday."

"You are taking this music composition too seriously. Are you planning on becoming a maestro?"

"You are no better. Does your ambition involve additions beyond your jazz band?" I asked.

"I don't need the money, Lloyd."

"Your inheritance gives you no right to sacrifice your work."

I was irritated that his father gave him a monthly sum without any consideration to the fact that Charles would never learn how to handle money appropriately.

We were seated together in our library, miniscule but comfortable enough. Rather than paying for housing at the university like we did before the war, Charles and I had decided to find a flat that was only a couple of blocks down the street. Charles could very well afford his own flat, but he spared me the insufferable costs and had decided to share the monthly rent with me. I knew it wasn't his own money that he was spending; regardless, it meant something. I knew he wasn't as selfish as I sometimes made him to be, but I still had a hard time trusting him. Of course, I had forgiven him years ago, or else we wouldn't even be living together.

There is something about a war that brings a man's enemies to agreeable terms when they are found fighting for the same cause. Charles and I had never been enemies to that extreme; rather, certain circumstances had created a barrier in our friendship.

I must have been staring off into space again, for Charles slapped me with one of the music compositions. "You alright, old chap?"

"For once in your life, can you call me, Lloyd?"

I was irritated with him now. However, I was more irritated with memories that had preyed upon my thoughts once again. Lindsay's deep green eyes and soft brown curls melted into the evening breeze. I hadn't been to Cornwall since Lindsay moved to Ireland.

"Have you thought about Cherry's request?" Charles asked.

"To audition for the Orchestra?"

"Yes, the very thing."

"It creeps into my thoughts occasionally. But, don't let my decision determine yours."

"It hasn't before, so it won't now." He smiled and slapped my back before returning to the kitchen.

I didn't want to make my decision based on his and knew I had enough time cut out for myself between university, my work shifts at the Eagle and Child, and my evenings spent composing music. As his footsteps echoed through the hall, I couldn't help but wonder what decision Charles had made for himself and whether or not I should do the same.

I had stayed up later than I had liked the night previous and was feeling a little groggy, even after drinking several coffees that morning. Charles and I were meeting the girls down at Oxford University Parks. It was the warmest of winter days; Cherry had insisted that since it was finally above 10 degrees Celsius, we had no other choice but to take a picnic in the park. She had made such remarks laughingly on behalf of the king and insisted that the fresh air would be good for us all.

Cherry was right, of course. It was a beautiful day, despite the winter temperatures. Of course, we were all bundled up in enough layers to make one comfortable even through a blustery storm. The girls wore funny little hats and pink scarfs that suited Cherry's complexion marvellously. I tried not to think about it while Charles and I carried the food and blankets in hand. Charlotte and Cherry walked on ahead of us, their laughter as charming as a schoolgirl chorus.

"Over here! Isn't it grand?" Cherry's voice in and of itself seemed to lift my sore spirit, for I hadn't really been looking forward to the day until now.

As we sat on tattered benches, Charles helped Cherry with the distribution of sarnies and crisps. The sparrow's song nearby greeted us as we sat in stillness, a refreshing retreat from the Bodleian walls.

"Well, Lloyd, are you trying out for the Orchestra after all?" Cherry asked.

"You make it sound as though I have no choice," I

replied.

"Perhaps that is exactly so," she laughed.

"Regardless of Charles' decision, I have decided that I am going to go ahead and audition."

"That's swell," Charles replied.

Cherry clapped her hands and Charlotte agreed that it was marvellous. I had almost forgotten that she was sitting beside me.

After some relentless teasing from Cherry, Charles admitted that he had already decided that he was going to try out as well.

"Although, I might as well already take my position on stage," he added.

His confidence could have been taken as cockiness by any other group, but we all understood that he was most certainly accurate in such a statement. He was by far the best trumpet player at Oxford, especially after choosing to spend more time in his studies this past autumn, thanks to Cherry, of course.

After wiping my fingers dry, I took a deep breath and allowed the afternoon air to refresh my aching bones. The night before, Charles had called me a dewdropper in which I had replied that laziness seen by the majority is usually genius seen by the extraordinary. He had laughed at the mockery in my statement that had once been uttered by he before we had gone to war. Those were the days when Charles was the very definition of a dewdropper. And, now, my attention to my music, in seclusion from the outside world, seemed to be a dose of laziness in his eyes. He didn't believe I actually did anything when he was gone, but I knew that one day I would prove him wrong, so I tried not to let his comments bother me that much.

Cherry and Charles then excused themselves, taking a

stroll through the park that was dusted in snow from last week's storm.

I realised then that Charlotte and I were left alone and I was drained at the thought that I would have to keep conversation with her to pass the time. I was certain that she was a decent girl, but she was too sensible for my liking. I could only hope then that we could find a topic that brought about mutual interest, rather than dull conversation.

"How is your music coming along?"

Well, that was a good topic. I half wondered if Cherry had instructed Charlotte beforehand on just the things to ask me. It felt as though it had been entirely planned. Whether it had been planned or not, her tone seemed genuine.

"Do you know anything of music?" I asked.

"I played the piano a little when I was a girl, but that was only because my mum insisted. When she realised how much I hated it, she finally let me pursue what I had wanted to all along."

"What was that?"

"Tennis."

"Tennis?"

"Don't be so surprised, it's a common sport." She laughed and continued, "My papa took me to Wimbledon when I was seven years old and ever since, it had planted this ridiculous idea in my head that I would one day compete there."

"Do you still play?"

"On occasion, but not competitively. Not anymore anyways."

"Why did you stop, then?"

"It's rather a long story."

"I'm fond of stories."

"Are you? Because from what I have gathered from Charles and Cherry, you seem to be some sort of recluse."

She must have noticed the defenciveness in my features and quickly apologised.

"I am sorry, I should not be prejudiced in anyway," she stated.

"I admit, neither should I. Well, then, what must I do to persuade you to tell me your entire tennis history?"

"Take me to dinner and dancing," she replied, reflecting the grin that had crossed my face.

I simply laughed. She wasn't as sensible as I had thought her to be.

"Must a man pay for conversation every time?"

"Just as much as a woman must pay for such through patience, a virtue that if not quickly learned will lead her to great misery."

"That sounds like a quote from a book."

"Might be. Now, how about your music?"

"So, you change the subject to leave me in complete curiosity about your tennis career?"

"I told you the terms, dinner and dancing," she smiled mischievously. "I will say that I am pleased that you are trying out for the orchestra. Of course, not as much as Cherry is pleased."

"Is she really?"

"Of course. Why would she have kept insisting that you and Charles audition?"

"To be quite frank, I don't understand Cherry half the time."

"Neither do any of us, but that is what makes her a true treasure of a friend. Besides, Cherry is by far the best violinist I have ever had the privilege of listening to."

"Cherry plays the violin?"

Charlotte was taken aback by the surprise in my tone of voice.

"Yes, she's rather remarkable," she responded without a change in tone.

"I knew that her mum was musical."

"Oh, yes. Very musical. I believe that is why she is able to play so well."

"Does Charles know?"

"I would be shocked if he didn't."

"Well, now I most certainly will tease her for not telling me."

"Lloyd, I learned a long time ago that Cherry leads quite the mysterious life. You can't expect her to give away all her secrets to everyone."

"I supposed you are now going to tell me that Cherry isn't Irish after all?"

"Nope, not that. Just stick around long enough, and I'm certain she will tell you a thing or two, perhaps even something she hasn't even yet told me."

"What has made her so—?"

I tried to find the right word.

"Enigmatic?" Charlotte replied.

"Exactly."

"Most people are fond of their childhoods. While Cherry grew up in an old castle in Ireland, she has few memories of such. Her mysterious persona is a reminder that no one can judge a book by its cover."

"A castle? I thought Cherry came from little money."

"Oh, yes. It's rather a gruesome tale."

"Am I supposed to be spared of that as well? Am I not allowed to know anything of Cherry's life?" I asked feeling a little deflated.

Her smile returned and then she turned her gaze towards the gardens where Charles and Cherry walked, arm in arm; a true couple of the century. They seemed to have escaped from an 18th century romance novel.

"If you must know, Cherry keeps that chapter of her life hidden away, like a treasure map that has been trapped in a chest to which no man is able to find the key."

"So, I am to never know of this mysterious castle." I had hoped that Charlotte would say more.

"I find that there is nothing wrong in leaving past chapters in the past. Don't you?"

"Yes, I rather agree with you there."

"Good. Now, when are you free for dinner? Your distracting conversation could not make me forget. Or, have you forgotten so soon?" she simpered.

"Are we to go without a chaperone and risk your good name?" I laughed.

"I am no longer sixteen, Lloyd," she smiled.

I had entirely underestimated her. She was a woman who had an opinion; perhaps, the women's right to vote was bringing about a real shift to the female race. I did not yet know if I entirely agreed with it all; regardless, I rather commended Charlotte for her forwardness.

"In a fortnight or so?" I smiled widely.

"Reprehend the army and find me there," she laughed.

I couldn't help but laugh at her enthusiasm. It was women like Cherry and Charlotte that made me believe I knew nothing at all about women, and I supposed it was best to keep it that way.

We were gathered together in Cherry's flat, the distant sound of students wandering in from a late night out. Upon my insistence, we decided to stay inside; besides, it was bloody cold out there.

I had confronted Cherry about her violin playing to which Charles had immediately confirmed Charlotte's assumptions.

"You should hear her sometime, old chap. She's bloody brilliant on the fiddle."

"Was I the only that didn't know you play?" I asked Cherry, a slight tone of hurt in my voice, though I did not mean it.

"You are a classical genius, Lloyd. I wouldn't want to bring your standards down to my own," she replied.

"Blast, I am certain you play well."

"Then, you will have patience to wait and determine that for yourself."

"Well, I very much look forward to it."

Cherry was seated beside Charles on the sofa, while Charlotte sat quietly in a chair across from me.

"What were you two talking of when we took a walk? Seemed to be rather serious," Cherry smiled.

"Charlotte's tennis playing," I was quick to respond.

"Yes, we must play sometime. When the weather gets better, perhaps?" Charles replied.

"That would be delightful. Would you gentlemen be interested in a trip to York this summer? After the spring term, perhaps?" Charlotte asked.

"What would take us to York?" I asked.

"My family has a summer estate there."

"A place where Charlotte would most certainly beat you both at a round of tennis," Cherry laughed.

"That sounds like a challenge too enticing to refuse," Charles added.

"Oh, I absolutely love England during the summertime," Cherry blurted.

They continued to talk about summer plans, while I only listened. I was not particularly excited about the idea, for I was lost in the mysterious layers of Cherry's past. I don't know why I cared, but I did.

As the trio laughed into the night, I offered a sentence or two to the conversation here and there, only to make it appear as though I was invested as they were. The only true time I partook in conversation for the night is when Cherry began to talk about England's politics.

If Charles had never told me, I would have never known that she was a full blooded Irish girl and certainly I would have never thought that her brother had died fighting for Ireland's independence. As she spoke of the changes to England's society, I gaped at her ability to believe in something so fiercely.

She was bright, that Cherry, which made me wonder if she really did love Charles, for I quickly realised that she was too smart to be taken advantage of by any man. While we had met not that long ago, I knew that Cherry felt neither superior or inferior to Charles, nor any man for that matter. Through Charles and my conversations and other observations, I discovered that Cherry never once shied away from letting her voice be heard, no matter the audience. She spoke her mind at political meetings in a room full of Republicans and never once feared overstaying her welcome.

Charles had told me such just a few days ago. I learnt everything about her through him and hoped that one day, Cherry would perhaps unveil some of her secrets to me, just as she had done with Charlotte and Charles. She captivated her audience like a swan on a glassy lake.

Charles was wrapped around her finger; his behaviour and facial expressions were evidence enough. It is a wondrous thing for a man to suddenly become enraptured by his female counterpart. It seemed that there would be no going back to the days before the war now. Perhaps I was wrong after all, about Charles being committed to one woman for the rest of his life, that is; Charles was strong willed, prideful, and independent to the bone, but Cherry was changing him in a way. I deemed it to be a rare quality of hers.

As we sat in the still evening, well after midnight, Cherry ended the evening conversation on the war's victory. She spoke of the change in women's rights with such fierceness, as she was equally convinced that parliament would keep employment rates at a higher rate as they had done during the war.

"Do you believe that the war was profitable, then?" I asked, coming out of my state of complacency.

"Do you not?" she defended herself.

"I base my thoughts on what I saw in France."

The smoke of my cigar melted any tension in the room as I realised I wasn't really listening to her entirely. I was stubborn, that I knew.

That's when I asked her, for I had been extremely curious, especially after learning from Charlotte that Cherry did not come from money after all.

"What did you do during the war, Cherry?"

"I worked at a munition factory, if you are curious."

"So, you feel that you contributed?" I sorely asked.

"Lloyd," Charles began, "that's rather—"

Cherry cut off Charles. "He means no disrespect." Then, turning towards me, she stated, "I understand your anger towards the repercussions of the war. But, what was done had to be done."

"Taking the lives of innocent men did not have to be done."

"Then, what would your solution have been? That we rebelled against the cause and sat at home twiddling our thumbs?" Her eyes widened as she asked the question.

"Nothing of the sorts. I went to war because I wanted to. It did not mean that I agreed with every order given and taken once I was there."

It was becoming a vulnerable hour. I knew we had better leave before I filled their hearts with pity and unrelenting grief.

"You may despise what took place in France, but you cannot despise the efforts of the men and women who fought for our freedom. If it wasn't for every one of them, including each of us in this room, we might have never had the privilege of such an enjoyable evening in the first place."

"Tell that to the men in the ground." I stared at her then and shook my head. "I'm sorry, Cherry, really, I've bloody had too much to drink."

"You have every right, as any of us, to be angry."

"I am not angry." I rejected her sentiment. "Sometimes, I just wonder if there was a better way, have not all of us ever wondered so?"

"Yes, you are not far off in that statement," Charlotte answered softly.

Both Charles and Cherry said nothing. Crikey, I really had drank too much. My anger billowed when such was the case. I only hoped that she did not see that my anger, for whatever it was worth, was directed at her.

"We cannot change what has already been done, Lloyd. Why did you fight in the war in the first place?" Cherry then asked, seeming to forget the first of the conversation altogether.

She spoke with such poise and in that moment, I both admired and despised her for it. She had caught me off guard by the sudden change in her mannerisms.

"I did what was the right thing to do, what we all thought, at the time, was the right thing to do."

"Exactly," she stated.

"Did I not already make that clear?"

"I needed you to say it again. I needed to hear that you truly believed such."

Charles smiled at Cherry's willingness, a willingness that would not allow her to sit down until she made her position known.

"What is the point in it? I do not sit here asking you why the Irish Republic fought the British patrols nor do I ask why several of the British intelligence were assassinated in Dublin. What's done is done. There is no point in going backwards now, is there?"

"Neither in conversation," she replied and smiled, a gesture that I didn't quite understand.

Did we agree with one another? For some reason, I felt as though we did.

It seemed that Charles and Charlotte had disappeared from the room and that it was just Cherry and I now, alone in the dim lit room, taken back to the haunting trenches of France. Her blue eyes took me there, for they were the same colour blue as Victor's had been. So honest and entirely unapologetic.

"You fought because it was the right thing to do. For king and country, every man for the man next to him, every woman for the woman next to her. Regardless of class, we all became one. Whether we agreed or not, we took our station and held on."

"The war is over now, old chap." Charles stated.

"Yes, I am forever reminded. I believe I have already made my point clear tonight."

I stood up hastily and felt quite nauseous. "Charles, it's best we leave now," I stated.

"Sober up a bit, old chap. Then, we make our leave."

"You know, you aren't much different from most of the

young boys at university," Cherry commented. Her hands were politely in her lap.

"How so?" I turned around and faced her, her eyes lifting to my own.

"You believe the war to be senseless in some regards. Yet, this is what astounds me. You are still very much a traditionalist."

"I am only traditional when it comes to music, not to the Edwardian values that most youth like to reason as being the main attribution to the war. Imperialism, not idealism, was the driving force behind the war."

"Then, our people should welcome the world of jazz with great approval," she grinned.

"Is that what this is all about? You hope that I will be equally ecstatic as you all towards jazz being the very thing that will break the traditional values that we had longed for before the war?"

"You said that you believe in change, did you not?" She raised an eyebrow.

"Yes, of course. When it comes to crossing the socioeconomic and racial lines, I do approve, and I am not ashamed to say such. However, I don't believe that jazz has to be the answer to bring about such societal change."

"Jazz is the very thing to do just that," Charles commented.

"Didn't you enjoy that time we went to the nightclub, Lloyd? Were you not enthusiastic?" Cherry asked with wide eyes.

Charlotte had been quiet nearly the entire time and Charles seemed as well to be enjoying himself by the conversation.

I couldn't help but laugh a little, though not kindly.

"I do not know what I think, but do not make me a lesser

man because of it."
"No one could ever be capable of such, not even
Charles," she smiled softly.

Cherry's red hair danced in the dim light, and I knew
that despite our conversation of misunderstanding, we
still understood one another. I realised that I felt
nauseous as, once again, I had had too much to drink and
not enough to eat.

Leaving their company and excusing myself from the
disagreeable evening, I walked outside and began the
brisk walk to our flat, only a couple blocks away.

It was a quiet evening, there were only a few students
here and there in the streets. Before I could even turn the
street corner, his voice greeted my ears.
"Lloyd!"

I hadn't heard him call me that in years. He must have
had too much to drink as well. I turned to see him
running across the wet pavement, his breath greeting the
thin air.
"You're a fool, old chap."
"It was rather stuffy in there. I told you that I had matters
to tend to."
"Not at this hour. Have you really become that foolish? I
fear I may have to deny Cherry more often and make sure
my mate isn't making a jump for the plank."

I didn't say anything. We just walked, our footsteps in
sync with one another. It was sometime before he finally
spoke.
"So, what do you think of Cherry, really, old chap?
You've gotten to know her quite well."
"She's intelligent, just as you said she was."
"That's for certain, she's more intelligent than I will ever
be," he commented.
"You better not let her through the strings, some other

chap will pick her up in no time."

"You don't mean you, old chap."

"No, most certainly not. I'm just saying that she's a rare one."

He smiled and patted me on the back before making our way into the front entrance of our muggy flat.

I was weary to the bone. While I wished to defer Cherry's queries elsewhere, I couldn't let them leave my mind. Her queries made me realise that she cared for me. While I did not respond gracefully, it seemed to me that she was only trying to rescue me from my cynicism, reminding me how fortunate I was to have returned to England. She was not indifferent to my feelings, which gave her every right to speak her mind and then beckon me to my own senses. It was easily forgiven.

Why, though, could I not appreciate life as they were all able to do so? And, so easily, nonetheless. Perhaps, I was the only one who voiced the aftermath of the war and wore it on my every day sleeve. I realised that I had been wrong, though, no matter how much I wanted to feel like I wasn't alone in my feelings. Although, I wasn't alone. Cherry, in her own way, told me that tonight.

Cherry's smile etched itself into my thoughts when I finally laid my head to rest in the early hours of the morning. Her difference is what drew men, an attraction sweeter than the latest perfume all the girls were wearing nowadays, something called Chanel. I had asked Cherry about the scent one time, it wasn't potent like the girls I had been around before the war. I told her I had liked it, to which she had laughed and replied that she wished she hadn't given into the popular game. When I asked her why, she explained that such an act made her too ordinary. That's when I knew Cherry would never be defined as one of those women in the catalogues. Once again, she had proven so tonight.

I had been truthful with all of them all night, except for one thing. Charles proposed I'd pursue Cherry if he let her through the strings. He was right. I most certainly would.

Spring 1923

Chapter 5
An Oxford Audition

The halls were romantically archaic. At Queen's College, the acoustics were vibrant enough to make anyone want to break out into song. It was the start of the spring term, which also meant that the day had arrived for Charles and I to audition for the Orchestra.

We had spent a lot of time together over these past couple of months. Charlotte seemed to be in town every weekend, and if she wasn't, then we would take a trip into London for a night or two. We had become our own club of the sorts, except I rarely went with the three of them to the jazz club, or whatever it was called. It was almost like a secret society, for I believed the rest of England deemed jazz music to be riotous. However, with an increase in American enrolment to the university, the sounds of jazz were beginning to make their way through Great Britain.

While I had enjoyed my evening at the underground jazz club in London, my weekends were usually spent taking supper at the Eagle and Child, the local pub just down the street from the libraries. I usually made my way to the pub after spending the day playing the ivories in our flat. I had sold my piano years ago and had just recently bought a Steinway & Sons model. She was absolutely gorgeous and barely fit in the parlour, but Charles didn't mind. He rarely spent his time in there anyways. For the most part, the tables were covered in a plethora of music compositions and tea stained cups that needed to transfer themselves to the kitchen. For the dishes alone, I considered hiring a maid, but realised that such a sum out of my pocket would be ludicrous. I barely had enough money to afford my daily expenses.

"Do you remember what room it's in?" Charles asked, his face a little puzzled from where we stood.

"I believe Cherry did say it would be at the very end of the hall."

That's when I heard them. The vibrant sound of strings being fine-tuned from the courtyard. A door to our right led to the courtyard where eager musicians awaited their turn on stage. It was at times like these that I wished I played a string or brass instrument, for at least I could act like I was preparing for the curtains, rather than sitting there nervously awaiting my turn.

Within a few minutes time, I immediately spied her. Charles was too busy polishing his second love. Cherry's ginger curls bounced up and down as she cheerfully made her way over. It was terrifically gloomy today, but Cherry's smile made it all the better.

"What are you two doing out here?" she asked.

"Awaiting for them to call the musicians in," I replied earnestly.

Charles came over and planted a kiss on her cheek. "I've arranged for you two to audition amongst the first," she piped up.

"You've arranged?" I asked.

"Yes, it's my last spring being a part of this grand ordeal and I was voted in as the vice president of this year's orchestra class. After all, they have had to put up with me for these past three years, so it is no surprise that they gave me some sort of position, especially being one of the only females aboard this ship."

"Why did you not tell us?" I laughed.

"I didn't want it to sway your decision on whether or not you would try out for the part," she smiled.

"Are you certain you had no hand in getting us here? I have a difficult time believing these positions are entirely earned," I smiled.

"That's for me to know and for you to choose whatever you'd like to think."

"Don't worry. I'll convince her to tell me the truth later, old chap." Charles winked at me.

Cherry led us into the main hall where we were to audition. It wasn't as grand in size as I had imagined, but it was charming nonetheless. There were four people seated up front, their faces as serious as any. After an oboe player took his last breath, Charles name was announced.

As Charles took his position on stage, I whispered in Cherry's ear, "Are you certain that we don't already have the part and that this is merely an act of traditional routine?"

"Well, you do like tradition, don't you?" she smiled. "Like I said, Lloyd Fox, thats for me to know and for you to believe whatever you'd like."

What else could I do but shake my head and grin at her teasing. There was no use in trying to get Cherry to tell me otherwise.

After a short audition from Charles, for he needn't play more than a few measures, I took to the piano stool. My fingers hovered above the keys. My eyes closed for a moment, as my heart searched for the notes. Within all but a few seconds, I opened my eyes and began to erupt the ceiling with B Flat Major. I felt my heart sore in a new way. I hadn't played in a room with such wondrous sound since before the war. It was strange, really. Most of the time, I felt as though I had no emotion, but when those black and white ivories nearly escaped from under my fingertips, something happened within me. Taking just one moment to lift my gaze from the keys to the audience, I watched, for just a moment, the intensity in Cherry's gaze, the illumination of her soft red curls, and the way her chest took deep breaths as she bit the end of her fingernails, hoping that such an act would allow all feelings to cease.

Ever since I had met Cherry, she had done something to me. She had awakened the music inside of me. Her folklore voice rang in the back of my mind, the sweetness so pure, almost as though it belonged to an entirely different world, a world that I had never had the privilege of entering into. That is what the music did for me, for it had begun to take on a new voice within myself, a voice that belonged in a different world almost.

I had to look away and return to the music. The resounding melody stirred my veins. And, then, the last note sounded. You could have heard a feather drop in the room, for it became hauntingly still.

"Thank you, Lloyd, we will be in contact with you soon," stated a greying gentleman dressed in a brown tweed suit and oval shaped glasses. He looked as though he would see his grave at any moment. I imagined myself in later years doing the same; living for the music, that is what we were doing after all, all of us musicians.

And just like that, the months of anticipation were gone within a moment's time.

"We must go out and celebrate tonight, old chap."
Charles was enthusiastic as ever.

"It's going to be a wonderful last term for myself, having you two join me for rehearsals and the spring concerts," Cherry commented. "I want you gentleman to firmly believe me when I say that the positions were fairly earned."

"So, what do you say?" Charles asked again.

"Actually, I'm going out with Charlotte tonight."

I had not kept my promise of taking Charlotte out within a fortnight as I had originally said, so I had decided that it would be best to take her out now. I had been rather busy the last few months and after a few attempts on Charlotte's part, I had finally accepted her invitation to dinner. My entire focus had been on my studies and the audition so I had excused myself many a time, reminding her and I both that I couldn't have any distractions, even though I knew Charlotte would not be that for me.

"Well, have a splendid time. Are you taking her to an extravagant dinner?" Cherry asked.

"A local favourite," I grinned. "The Eagle and Child."

"Charlotte agreed to this?" Cherry asked. "She's in town from London, and she agreed to a dinner at the pub of all places?"

"Yes, what's wrong with pub food?"

"Nothing. Charlotte has always had finer taste, but maybe us common folk, you and me, are changing her," Cherry smiled.

"Now, don't let Charles influence you the other way around. Us common folk stick together," I laughed.

"It might be too late for that, old chap," he laughed and

took her arm.

He whispered something into her ear to which her pure laughter then vibrated off the walls. Charles took a quick glance at me, Cherry's arm wrapped around his. He smiled slyly as though he held a secret that no man would ever come to know.

As soon as they had gone, I went to my room, searching for a suitable coat for the evening. Soon after I heard a knock at my door.

"Charlotte?" I was surprised to see her so soon.

"Is Cherry here?" she asked.

"No, what would make you think that?" I asked.

"My train arrived early, and I had ran into Charles shortly after my arrival. He insisted that I meet here a quarter past three, for that's when Cherry was to arrive."

"No, they just left moments ago. But, please, do come in."

As I closed the door behind Charlotte, I realised that Charles' glance just moments earlier had not been a look of disapproval after all. Rather, I felt that he had sensed how I had truly begun to feel about Cherry, and was working it in his power to bring another woman into my life. For if he succeeded, then there was no chance that Cherry would forsake him for another, for his best friend nonetheless. Charles could have any girl, and perhaps, his reason for being so enraptured by Cherry was due to the simple fact that she had not been so easy to get. I had learnt through Charlotte that there had been many men who had been interested in Cherry, but she had refused every last one of them, that is, until she met Charles.

Returning to the parlour, with my hands in my pockets, I apologised to Charlotte for the mess. I felt like a schoolboy who was apologising to his mum after a day in the mud. Charlotte's well practiced manners still made me feel uneasy from time to time. She had grown up dining with dukes and duchesses, yet here she was, agreeing to have dinner with me at a pub. Of course, it had been the other way around, hadn't it? She had asked me if we could go to the pub. She, like Cherry, had a certain curiosity about her.

"You never did tell me about your music," she remarked, seeming to find the fact that Charles had misled her perfectly alright.

Bent over my piano, she had been ruffling her fingers through the composition papers that had been scattered throughout the room.

I sat down and took a deep breath.

"No, I don't talk about my music with anyone."

"It's such a big part of your life, and I don't believe I would be far off in assuming that it is the biggest part of your life. So, why keep it all to yourself?"

"Does a mother share with the rest of the world the child she has hidden within her for nine months?"

She smiled marvelouslly at me and took a seat on the piano stool.

"Does your child have a name yet?" she asked.

"Cherry tried to pry the same information out of my hands," I replied.

"We are both stubborn women, what can I say?" she laughed.

"When the world is ready, that child will be introduced," I smiled.

We both sat there, her eyes gazing about the flat, while I merely studied her face from afar. I just realised that she had never been here before.

"Charming place," she finally said and then added, "Lloyd, should I return at a later time? I can run a few errands and then return later."

I was about to agree to her proposition, but then decided against it.

"I could use a walk. Why don't we take a stroll before heading over to the pub?"

"Sounds splendid," she smiled.

I returned to my bedroom where I quickly finished getting dressed, buttoning the many unruly buttons that made me quite uncomfortable if I was being quite frank.

When I made my way back into the parlour, I noticed Charlotte's blonde hair reflected the sunlight like a prism. She was the most cheerful thing. I supposed it was her gentle smile that frightened me most, which made me wonder why in the world I had agreed to take her to dinner. Well, there was no use feeling sorry for the both of us now.

Taking her arm, we made our way outside and walked through the park near Christ's Church. It looked more like a piece of farmland than anything, stretching further into a green sea of trees.

"It's much more pleasant than the last time I was here." Her smile greeted the gentle breeze, and I agreed that it was indeed more pleasant than when she had last been here in the winter.

"I was going to mention earlier. I heard that you and Charles are the newest members of the Oxford Orchestra now. I must congratulate you."

"It's nothing, really, but thank you, all the same." I was abrupt.

"So, are you to conduct at this year's Summer Extravaganza?" she asked.

"I do not know of it."

"Every summer, the fair comes into town. The orchestra and the band plays in the park. According to Cherry, some of the schoolgirls make the best lemon cake you ever had and there is plenty of time for festival games. Cherry insists that it's a marvellous time, and we can't argue with her, can we?"

"I am certain the pianist doesn't make his appearance at such an affair. Besides, you can't expect me to be ready to conduct an entire orchestra."

"Not an entire orchestra, just the summer band. I'm certain it wouldn't hurt a fly if you asked."

"We have yet to begin rehearsals, Charlotte. Although, I do appreciate your enthusiasm, all the same. It is no wonder you and Cherry are friends."

She sighed and walked on ahead of me. We walked past the River Cherwell where a plethora of voices could be heard through the trees. While the tulips were yet to bloom, the streets were adorned in a mass of shrubbery. It was what I loved most about Oxford; how the trees and ivory waterfalls isolated the colleges from the rest of the universe. Strolling through its magical streets, Oxford made me forget that life in London had ever existed.

"Well, if you won't partake in the music at the summer fair, will you at least join the gentlemen for a game of cricket?" she asked as we passed the golden walls of Christ's Church College, the largest of the colleges at Oxford. I thought it to be the most beautiful college, its windows resembled an 18th century church as the intertwining of red and green ivory painted a perfect frame for its many windows.

I lifted my gaze from the mesmerizing windows and took another look at Charlotte as we made a right onto the main street towards the pub. It was a rather long walk, and I was glad to find that Charlotte seemed not to mind, for her face glistened in the same way sunshine would greet the grey street puddles. Her soft brown eyes were so different from Cherry's piercing blue eyes. They made her older and wiser than she really was, yet at the same time, there was a youthfulness in them, that much I had determined.

"Do not beg me to join the University Cricket Club. Charles tried and did not succeed," I finally said.

She simply laughed. Whether it was at me or the idea that Charles did not succeed, I did not know. But, she laughed. And, as she did so, she made me realise, just as Cherry had done many a time, that I really knew nothing about women. Were they all so interested in watching men dressed in leisure white clothing, making them appear more pale than they already are, engage in a game of cricket?

The club had been around for years, well before the war in fact. Many of the fellows at university joined every year. For the universities in Britain, it was a wonderful game of competition and as Charlotte reminded me, an entertaining spectator sport.

"Should we swing by the pavilion so that I can convince you otherwise?" She seemed to be dancing on her feet, alluring me to join her side.

"I'm beginning to think that your early arrival in Oxford was not a mistake after all," I commented.

"Yes, it would not surprise us both if Cherry and Charles sent me on mission to ensure that you don't become some sort of recluse this summer. However, I am entirely on my own in this manner."

"Are you the social butterfly of the season?"

"To which my sole purpose is to get you to come out more," she stated.

"A rather dull task, I fear."

She shook her head and continued to walk beside me in complete silence. Before long, a light rain greeted the cobbled streets, and I remarked that there was nothing like a February day without a refreshing rain to ease us into spring. The church's bells echoed through the streets, indicating the top of the hour. Taking her hand, we ran through the underbrush of the trees and made our way past St. Adale's towards the Eagle and Child. It was only a light mist, nothing that we weren't used to. It took us no more than ten minutes before the familiar sight of Eagle and Child's sign greeted us. Stepping inside the quaint building, the smells of beer and fish n' chips greeted our senses.

"I hope you like pub food," I commented.

"Do you think I'm really that civilised that I can't enjoy a good pub meal?"

"I supposed you'll attribute that change to the war?"

We took the first seat next to the window on the left. Enclosed from view of the bar, it was a perfect spot for intimate conversation.

"Yes, the war changed a lot of things, as any war does." As she said so, a tall gentleman with fading curly hair came over to the table and gave me a handshake.

"You're not working tonight, eh? Brought your lady friend?" The spirited boy grinned and shook his head in approval.

"Charlotte, this is Andy, Eagle and Child's best bartender."

"It's a pleasure," she shook his hand.

"You're a dandy. At least that is what Lloyd says, don't you?"

I didn't have the heart to tell him that he was wrong in assuming that Charlotte was the girl I had spoken of on occasion. I must have never told him what she looked like, only that she was fiery by nature and more mysterious than any Arthur Conan Doyle story. Tonight was about Charlotte, not Cherry.

I simply smiled. It's all I could do.

"Well, drinks on the house, of course. No need to come order at the bar."

"Thank you, Andy."

When he left, Charlotte gazed about the dusky room. Its walls were unchanged. The ceiling was lower than probably any dining hall she had ever set foot in. The company was rowdy and the smells were far contrary to the gardens we had just walked through.

"I've never step foot in a pub before. Would you believe it?" she laughed.

"I would have been shocked if you had said otherwise," I confessed.

As she gazed about the room, I asked, "You are in London and Oxford most often. Where do you stay in London?"

"At my father's estate," she remarked.

"I thought your father's estate is all the way in York? You did recommend we go there during the summertime, if I am not mistaken."

A wide smile crossed her lips and she replied, "Oh, yes. But, Papa also has an estate in London, Hampstead to be precise. It belonged to my great uncle. He had never married and to my papa's utmost surprise, his inheritance, all of it, was given to Papa, an only child, you see."

"Remarkable. So, you stay in that grand house all by yourself?"

"I'd starve if that was the case," she laughed.

"Well, of course, you have kitchen staff, amongst others."

"Yes, the cook is my favourite, though do not tell." She smiled and added, "We also have distinguished guests that pass through. My aunt, my mum's sister, is rather intrusive, and comes to stay with me whenever she hears that I'm in London. Even in her flamboyancy, she is rather a delight."

"Why does your family remain in York?"

"You know how those old houses run." She gave me more credit than necessary.

"I confess, I do not." I wondered if she knew about my family's background.

She leaned forward and replied, "Once it's in your possession, it never leaves, unless you can no longer afford to upkeep the gardens. Papa had a friend that lost his entire estate during the war."

"Penny dreadful."

"If he had lost his life, too, then I would agree," she laughed most heartedly. "However, the gentleman moved to the Mediterranean. I'd say he's happier than he's been in years."

"Are you happy?"

"Most ardently." That big toothy smile spread across the table. "I am alone, away from my family, and free to spend as much time in London and Oxford as I please, without having someone to account for where I've gone." She was still young, I thought.

"Not even your lady's maid?" I asked.

"We are more like friends, really," she smiled.

"She knows you are here?"

"A lady's maid is like God, really. She knows everything." She laughed.

I couldn't help but smile at her comment.

"Will your family keep your uncle's property, then?"

"I imagine until the day I marry and Papa insists that I return to York."

"You hope for that?"

"I've no other choice."

"Forgive me, but you seem like the sort of woman that has a mind of her own, not bound by others' choices, not even your own family's."

"I am bound, though I do not object." She smiled again. "My family raised me with certain beliefs, and I must carry those out."

"Your family is intriguing."

"Not yours?" she asked.

"My family's story would be on the forgotten shelf, yours, more likely, requested by all of society."

"That's a rather bold statement given you've never met my family. You might take your statement back," she laughed.

"I've met you. That seems to be enough of an assessment," I replied.

"Are you an observant creature as well, Lloyd?"

"War made me more observant of people."

There was sympathy in her eyes. I decided that I wouldn't be a sorry sort for the night.

Andy brought us food and drink quite quickly to which I remarked that his service should be commended by King George. Charlotte laughed as he responded that he had been waiting three years' time for such a commence.

I had almost forgotten my manners as I dug into the fish with my hands, ale spilling from my fingertips. Gazing up at her, I wiped my mouth with my sleeve and quickly apologised.

"Well, if this is how you eat pub food, then I must do as the locals do," Charlotte smiled.

She dug in, the fish oil already climbing down her forearm.

"Here," I handed her a napkin and remarked that eating fish and mushy peas with a fork was perfectly acceptable.

She was a lady, not a farmland's daughter. I had to remind myself of such, yet she had seemed adventurous

enough to try it and for that, I commended her. I
wondered what her father would think if he knew where
she was now. He would probably request that she pack
her bags and leave his London estate at once, returning to
York where she would be imprisoned to its hundreds of
rooms, playing hide and seek with the estate's ghosts until
she was to be wed.

"Well, you asked what Cherry did during the war, but
Lloyd, you failed to ask one thing," she interrupted my
thoughts.

"Oh?"

"You never asked what I did during the war," she
grinned.

"Well, Charlotte, what did you during the war?" I
laughed.

"Prepare yourself, it may shock you."

"I may go into hysteria," I replied.

"Despite such remarks, I would have you know that I
worked with the farm tenants on our estate. I ploughed,
led the cart horses, fed the pigs, and made sure that every
home was taken enough rations."

"Did you ever?"

"Can you not imagine me sporting overalls and a shovel?"
her brown eyes softened that much more.

I wiped my fingers and called to Andy for another
round of drinks.

"With so many of the men away at war, someone had to
take care of the land. It was the very least I could do. My
sister went away to France as a nurse. You know, Cherry
had a good friend who got terribly ill from working at the
munition factory. There were quite a few cases of injury
and quite a few fatalities."

"Yes, from the toxins," I commented. "Did Cherry's
friend recover?"

"I'm sorry, I shouldn't have spoken of it. No, she did not recover."

She looked away then, and I felt sorry that I had probed her.

"I am sorry to hear that. Sometimes, I forget that it wasn't just us men at war or the lower class that saw the worst of it."

"That's alright. Sometimes, I quite forget as well. Sometimes, it feels as though it was part of another life altogether."

"You know, Charlotte, that is why I cannot make my mind up about the jazz sensation. I fear that it is trying to impose on our lives, making us forget everything that we left behind."

"Isn't it a good thing, though? It's a fresh start."

"Yes, I reckon that is how any normal individual would see it, but I find myself not normal, not since I returned to England. Crikey, I've said too much."

"No, I appreciate your honesty. It's refreshing to hear amongst my usual company of men." She paused. "Cherry appreciates it as well."

Why did she have to mention her name once more? I wondered if she had suspicions; perhaps, just as much as Charles did.

"Well, we don't need to entertain you with jazz, but I would very much like it if you would entertain with us this summer," she commented. "After Cherry graduates in June, and before she accompanies me to Scotland—"

"Cherry is going with you to Scotland?" I interrupted her, astonished at the very thing.

"We've only spoken of it. Of course, that is if Charles doesn't ask for Cherry's hand by then."

"In marriage?" I could feel the heat once again rising in my chest and throat. It was happening more often as of late.

"Yes, shouldn't you be pleased?"

"I don't think one can be so certain on such matters."

"When you are young and in love, the very last thing is certainty, but it is a chance worth taking, isn't it?"

"Crikey, the times really have changed." I cranked my neck in taking the last of my drink.

"With an increase of women in the workforce, there might be less of us who think of marriage, but the war hasn't quite yet changed that. Perhaps one day, we will think of it less, but you must know that men deal with a breed who desire the very thing. There is no wrong in not waiting if a woman loves a man and a man loves a woman."

She was a romantic after all. While she had surprised me with her war efforts, I could tell that she was still a traditionalist in values, yet, somewhere within, there was a carefree spirit that wanted to break free. Perhaps, in her own naivety, she thought marriage was the answer. I wanted to tell her then that it wasn't, but decided that I would end the evening on a happier note.

"Yes, you are right in such. Why should they wait?" I forced a smile. "Now, how many more drinks must you take before you tell me about your glorious tennis days."

"I'm satisfied. You kept your bargain, now I must keep mine."

"By all means," I lifted my hands and encouraged her to begin.

"After an agreement between my father and mum, they signed me up for tennis lessons with one of the best in the country. I probably was out on the courts more hours than I was locked away at school."

"Were you really that good?"

"Some would say," she smiled and took a bite of her

chips.

"So, what happened?"

"I competed all over and earned a slot at a women's bracket held at Wimbledon."

"Did you really?" I smiled.

"Yes, a lady doesn't make up things of the sorts. Papa was real proud."

"Did you win?"

"I never played there."

"Why not?"

"The war," she said without hesitation.

"Oh," that's all I could say.

"Lloyd, I know you think that none of us understand, but we do."

"Cherry keeps telling me the same thing," I said.

"That's because she likes you." She briefly smiled.

"And, do you like me?"

"As my companion, nothing more. I am entitled to nothing more."

"Because of my lack of a title?"

"Rightfully so."

"Yet, if you were to deny the expectations, would you still force me to be only your companion?"

"Probably not." She laughed softly.

"Did the end of the war give permission for women to be so blunt?" I stated.

"We are meant to be just friends."

It was as though she had forced the words out of her own mouth. I knew she didn't believe them, and perhaps I could have fought for her freedom from a life she had no other choice to abide by. But, I couldn't.

"I wish you would have said that sooner," I replied.

"Because you like Cherry," she replied honestly once again.

"I—"

"It's as clear as the sun rising in the east," she replied.

"How did I ever give such an impression?"

"Did you not learn from when we first met? I am a creature of observance, Lloyd."

"Say nothing to Charles." It was all I asked for.

She smiled at my agreement. I returned it, just before being swept away by Andy and another. They led me to the rugged piano to play some folklore tunes, a few favourites of the locals. Taking a glance in my peripheral vision to where Charlotte sat silhouetted by the doorway, I saw the largest smile to have ever crossed her face. Tonight, she bid adieu to all of the rules. I couldn't give her what she wanted, but I could give her this gift nonetheless. She was delighted by the music and company, she was my ally in all of this, though I knew not why. And, for some reason, I couldn't help but end the night in G Major. The acoustics made the wooden floors vibrate beneath us. Charlotte's smile reminded me that it was okay to feel happy, even if only for a moment.

Chapter 6
A Journal's Nightmares

The months had passed rather quickly. We had already had two performances and were approaching the last. Cherry was to graduate the following month. When Cherry had first played the violin, I was envious of the very thing. She was a mastermind, and yet humble as any. When she had taken her seat as second chair violinist, I had sat there amazed. Her vibrato was as effortless as walking through the park. Her transitions between the strings did not once bring about a dissonant note. And, her arpeggio was seamless.

At the last concert, Cherry had performed the concerto in G, a composition that was usually given to the first violinist, but had been graced instead by Cherry. When she played, the soft concert light transported you to the Scottish Highlands, then to the cliffs of Ireland, and down to the Cornish seaside, the voices of all of Britain intertwined together in a three-movement sonata wonder piece. She made me wish I played the violin instead. Of course, I had always wished that, but she made me believe in whatever it was that she was playing. It was as though there were mysterious layers behind her fingering.

Her col legno danced off the strings with such fluidity that I could almost imagine her dancing alongside the strings, getting lost in that castle of hers, the one where Cherry's music had to have come from. I had determined that I would find out about the secret castle that Cherry had never spoken of.

"Lloyd, have you ever considered joining the London Orchestra?" Allen interrupted my thoughts.

We had just finished our last rehearsal before the final spring concert and Allen Townshend, the infamous cellist and friend of mine, had been provoking me to entertain the thought. His father was well respected in society, and like Charles, his education in music was merely an interest to pass the time until he was to be married to some aristocratic daughter no doubt. Allen was the second of five children; his father's estate would be passed down to his older brother, a favourable fate according to Allen.

"After you graduate in the winter, it might be a good thing to tour for a while before settling down in the business of music composition. You have no other engagements, so why not consider it?" he asked me genuinely.

"I thought I would stay in Oxford after graduation."

"But you've been here for the past couple years," he commented.

"Yes, and what's a few more? This has become home for me."

"Lloyd, we are young. The move to London would be an easy one. We could room together, if that'd please you. I know that your finances are rubbish."

Allen was kind, but blunt. I might have been as blunt as him, but I was certainly not as vocal about it; thus, this quality caught me off guard at times.

"Ask me again after the summertime," I replied.

"Alright, as you please," he smiled.

"Allen, Lloyd, do you care to join us at the Eagle and

Child for some refreshments?" Ted Astair's voice rang down the hall.

"Why not?" I shrugged.

I was still working at the Eagle and Child in the evenings and while I usually chose to differentiate my pleasure from work, I felt that there was no wrong in blurring the lines from time to time.

We were immediately welcomed by a large group of friends from university. It was only a few hours after noon, yet it was surprisingly busy, especially being a weekday and all.

"Come, I got us a small table away from the crowd." Ted beckoned us through the narrow hallway towards the back of the pub where it was just as crowded as the two rooms at the front entrance.

It was a small, yet cozy joint. Feeling claustrophobic from the dark walls that caved in around us, I leaned back in my chair and sighed.

"What's the matter, Lloyd? Mr. Anderson working your fingers dry again?" Ted asked.

"They've past the dry stage," I replied. "I admit his strive for perfectionism is of worthy remark."

"That it is," Ted replied.

Ted was a short fellow from Kidlington. Oxford was as cultured as he had ever been. I wondered if Allen had proposed to Ted about making the transfer to London after our winter term was over this coming December. For some reason, I had a feeling that he hadn't. Ted was a queer fellow; he took to the countryside as though it was his own child and talked of botany in a way that left the rest of us scrambling to find a topic of conversation that would deter us away from such talk.

"Old faithful, she is, the Eagle and Child," Allen commented.

"Yes, although I'll probably never step in here again after we graduate in the winter," Ted replied.

"Do you have plans for after graduation, Ted?" I asked.

"I can't say I do," he quickly reacted.

We didn't probe him and left it with the dust that collected on the bookshelves above our heads.

Shortly after we had received our tin drinks, Ted then greeted an older gentleman that had just taken a seat to the left of us.

"Reverend Thomas, I didn't know you paid visit to the Eagle and Child." He firmly shook his hand, to which the rosy cheeked man received it well and asked to be introduced to the table.

"Would you like to take a seat?" Ted asked.

"If you don't mind dining with a clergyman," his eyes twinkled.

"It might do us good," Allen laughed.

Taking a chair and placing it beside me, Reverend Thomas took his seat. Ted quickly made introductions to the table, for it was only Allen and I, apart from himself.

"What are you gents up to on this beautiful day?" the reverend asked.

"Just as much as you are, sir," Allen replied.

"After a long day being trapped by Oxford's towers, it is good to grab a drink with friends," I commented.

"A rare pleasure, isn't it?' he smiled and took a drink from his glass.

I was not delighted to be engaged in conversation, especially with a clergyman. My body was already weary, for Mr. Anderson, our beloved maestro, had been cunningly working us to the brim.

"Thomas is a practising vicar at St. Andrew," Ted commented.

"As opposed to a neglectful one?" I asked, taking the last

of my drink in one gulp.

Ted's lanky body seemed to shrivel at my comment and quickly apologised for my behaviour.

Instead, Reverend Thomas seemed rather amused.

"Are you a musician as well?" he asked me with an intense gaze, one from which I would not be able to break if I tried. His gaze then softened. He smiled, immediately showing the ageing wrinkles around his eyes.

"I am, sir."

"Are you a practising musician?" he enquired.

I moistened my lips and before I could reply, he laughed.

"I'm just giving you a hard time, lad. No reason to become sour about the mouth," he smiled.

"How is the congregation doing? Well, I hope." Ted drew the vicar's attention away from my dejected comments.

"Yes, however, it's been more empty as of late. Man's attention might be more diverted nowadays," he simply replied with no indication as to what he meant, although I for certain felt he was alluding to the loosening of society's values.

The three of them, Allen, Ted, and the reverend continued to talk of university studies and the upcoming concert, including the opportunities that lay around the corner for us musicians upon the new year. Sitting there, still as stick and bones, I played with my tin cup like a child who had suddenly grown great interest in a beetle bug.

"Have you thought anymore about joining the clergy?" the vicar asked Ted honestly.

"Yes, I'm going to speak to mother about it."

"You still need your mum's opinion?" I laughed, not kindly, however.

"Is it so wrong for a man to ask of his mum's advice?" Ted replied.

"No, I suppose not." I leaned back and gazed at the opposite wall, realising that I was really gazing upon nothing. I really didn't feel like conversing today. Crikey, I felt warm about the head.

"Don't mind, Lloyd. He lives in a state of contradiction." Allen grinned and patted my shoulder with the greatest enthusiasm.

"Ahh, well, we all live in contradiction with ourselves, do we not? We despise the world we live in, and try to find a way out of our own unhappiness, but it cannot be found, at least by man alone," Reverend Thomas retorted.

My head slowly turned towards the fogey gentleman. Was he playing games with my mind now? Why did he feel he had the authority to speak on my current state of unhappiness? We all sat in silence as the tips of his fingers met. Taking them, he pointed at me and expanded on his previous comment.

"You remind me of myself when I was your age. I speak from a knowing heart, that is all. I will not probe any further. I'll leave Ted in charge of those matters."

He winked at Ted and all three of them broke into laughter. I did not break from my resting face. My mood had grown suddenly worse, and I wished that I had returned to the flat, instead of the pub. Crikey, I didn't feel good.

We returned not an hour later to my flat, to which Ted and Allen took biscuits that Cherry had brought over just that morning. They then took liberty of planting themselves on the sofa, hoping to stay awhile.

"Rather a peculiar fellow, wasn't he?" Allen stated.

"Oh, he's a rather kind man. I've been down to the old church and heard him speak. His rhetoric is superb," Ted commented.

"Are you really going to sacrifice your music for the

church?" Allen let out a whoop of laughter.

I was quiet.

"Lloyd, you alright? You seem not yourself since we took to the pub." Ted ignored Allen's question. "Must I add, you were rather unforgiving with Reverend Thomas."

"I didn't mean the things I said," I simply stated, although I really meant otherwise.

Sulking into the overstuffed chair, Ted was concerned over my lack of conversation.

"In all actuality, I'm rather not feeling too well, gentlemen. I think I'm going to go lie down for a moment. You are welcome to stay until Charles arrives back from the library."

"No, it's rather best we be going anyways," Ted replied.

"Right you are," Allen quickly followed his command.

After they left, I collapsed onto my stiff bed as my body melted into the messy sheets. Within moments, my eyes drifted into a heavy sleep, a sleep that I had not experienced since before returning to Oxford.

It was a repeated dream that I had most often, a nightmare. The rain was so heavy outside that we could barely see the man's face in front of us. My boots were covered in mud making each step heavier than the first. There was hope that the rains would relent for it wasn't working in our favour.

"I've never seen such batty weather," Victor commented.

"Live long enough and you might see worse," I smiled.

"Is that a bet?"

"If you are brave enough to try," I laughed. Offering him my lighter, we smoked underneath one of the gutters.

"I got a letter from Lindsay," he said with a grin on his face, allowing the smoke to greet the rain like brothers lost at sea.

"Is she well?" I asked.

"I know what you mean to ask," he replied.

"I only mean—"

Victor interrupted me. "I know she's peculiar, but that's why I like her. Her family has tried to warn me, but I can't end it, Lloyd. Lindsay wrote in hopes that I ignored all their comments during my last leave. She was afraid I'd never call again, nor any man for that matter."

"You aren't any man," I grinned.

"No, I'm bloody not," he smiled and closed his eyes. However, it was only a brief second for there were shouts coming from the northern end of the trench. An unexpected ceasefire took over, right in the middle of the storm.

I don't remember much of anything else that took place after that, for amidst the debris and the rains, I saw them both, Charles and Victor, still as statues about 50 metres away.

"Victor!" I shouted above the winds. There was no reply. "Victor! Charles!" My cries were desperate as I instructed a few men to my right to make the move to where the bodies lay.

When I awoke, my forehead was beaten with sweat. I frantically grabbed for the blankets and wondered where my commander had taken me. Had he transferred me to the officer's dugout? My heartrate was beating itself through the roof and I wondered why it was so quiet outside. Then, it hit me. I had been dreaming, blast, I had never been so excited to wake from sleep.

Pulling the covers off the bed, I reached into my bag

and found the notebook that I had kept during the war. The leather journal was worn, its pages filled, the words rarely read since they had first been written. After lighting a candle, I pushed a chair next to the window and opened it. The breeze felt refreshing through my hair, ridding of any sweat that remained creased on my forehead. Taking the journal after lighting a cigarette, I opened it with quick hesitation.

1 July 1916

The boys were eager and restless all night before the attack. In the day, we had loaded the wagons with field artillery ammunition, ready at any moment's notice. The East Yorkshire Regiment, what a sight we all were. None of us knew it would be like this, how do you prepare a man for such?

7 July 1916

We advanced at La Boissele, yet a pool of blood ran between us. The barbed wire put up by the Germans was difficult to get through, but we somehow made the advance. I barely remember it; it could as of well been a dream. A considerable number of guns and material have fallen to the Allies. An officer announced that it seemed that there were well over 6,000 prisoners that were captured by the French alone. Several of the German bombproof shelters have been destroyed; they were bloody foolish for believing that their forts were indestructible.

9 July 1916

We had felt some success. Our regiment, alongside some Northerners, has seized many German prisoners, including many of their materials, which has made most of the men happy. However, shortly after the siege, a torrential rain overtook the land, filling the trenches quickly and making the journey quite slippery which of course only impeded our advance. Yesterday, in terrible cloudy weather might I add, we bombed some of the German materials. In advancing through the Valley of Somme, the goal has not only been to kills as many of the Germans as possible, but also to collect as much as their artillery as possible. Machine guns, bomb throwers, searchlights, and minenwerfer, all of it, whatever we could get our hands on.

14 July 1916

Victor's forearm was smashed in a bomb. Charles has been badly injured in the blow. They are both alive and have been taken by some fellows from the Red Cross to some facility nearby where other casualties remain. The fighting is ruthless; I can only hope that Victor makes it out alive. I will not forgive myself, nor God, if he doesn't.

17 July 1916

Fighting continues to take place in the ruins of Ovillers. No word about Victor. We've lost many of our men, I try not to think about it. We take roll call in the trenches as though we are all schoolboys again, except the roll is always changing. War is never a concrete thing, it surprises you all the time. One moment we've made advances, the next we have found that others have been taken as prisoners of war.

27 July 1916

Charles saved Victor's life, they've both returned to the regiment. Charles showed me his scar after the others had gone to bed. I wonder if he will show his mum when we return to England. Crikey, I hoped we would return. It has been incredibly rainy as of late, making the journey through the land quite unbearable. The trench walls reverberate at night when a surprise invasion occurs. If only there was an answer to how many more days this was supposed to go on. I haven't slept in days. I doubt I'll ever sleep again.

I closed the journal suddenly. It was the last entry; I never wrote again. The day after, Victor was reported dead.

Cherry was as charming as ever. I couldn't help but smile as Cherry and Charles gathered together for a picture. The camera man's flash greeted us all like a lightning bolt. She had done what very few had done at her age, let alone her sex. While I was indifferent to many matters of the women's rights movement, I did, however, commend the women who were breaking the social norms. It was no surprise, though, for normalcy was becoming something of the past, and what could be defined as normal nowadays anyways?

Cherry graduated with honours in Latin and Greek with a major in history. On several occasions, I had asked Charles what she intended to do with such a degree to which he had replied that with Cherry, there was no definite answer. All the same, I had wondered about her interest in the subject matter and asked her about it one day while we were all studying at the Bodleian Libraries.

It had been bitterly quiet. Hushed voices murmured in the row next to us. The sunlight streamed in through the large glass windows, reminding us that spring had finally arrived.

"What intrigues you so much about the Latin and Greek languages? Is it the linguistics?" I asked.

"Do you find Shakespeare interesting?" she asked with a certain depth in her eyes. "Or, do you find it difficult to understand? And, if you answer to the latter, is your lack of interest due to your lack of understanding?"

"So, you study Latin and Greek so that you may read the original texts as they were intended to be read."

"Yes, exactly that. I find it exciting that I have entrance into a world that probably three fourths of this room never will find themselves in."

No wonder she lived her life full of so many secrets. It brought her a certain kind of joy, one that not many could identify with, myself included.

"You can read a rendition of Romeo and Juliet or you can read the original text. They will both evoke different emotions. It is the same when I read Greek mythology or any ancient text for that matter. Besides, Papa always told me that I have always been keen on history, ever since I was a girl. Of course, that comes as no surprise..."

And, then, she just stopped talking altogether, leaving me to wonder if her interest in history had anything to do with the castle that she had grown up in. I desperately wanted to ask her, but then again, I didn't want to break Cherry's trust in Charlotte.

"Lloyd, today is not a day to be a recluse. Come stand by me." The memory vanished as her voice greeted the wind.

Cherry squinted, her face brightened by the glowing sunshine, Charles' arm still wrapped about her waist, both of them begging for me to take a picture with them. I had almost forgotten for a moment that I was no longer in the library, but was surrounded by too enthusiastic of a crowd outside Somerville Hall. If it was anyone else but Cherry, I would have said no. How could I explain it to anybody? The blinding light brought me back to the warfront and it took everything within me to ignore the terrible sensation. It felt as though I was drowning in the voices surrounding me, the debris of the trenches suddenly filling the dresses that swirled around me. Years had passed but the nightmares had come back in such a profound way that I knew not how to break free from their memory. Yet, there she stood, her blazing red hair breaking through the thoughts that resurfaced, pushing them back into a world that was far away. Somehow, it seemed as though she had entrance into my world, a world that no one else did.

"Lloyd, you alright, old chap? You look as though you've just reunited with your worst enemy," Charles laughed.

"Yes, it must be the sun," I quickly commented.

"Charles, you better not let him disappear while I'm away in Scotland," she commented.

"So, you are going then?" I asked.

"Yes, it will be rather good for me. Of course, we won't be leaving until August. Charlotte's father has some business in York until then, so we will leave shortly after."

The blue in her dress complimented her so well. I wondered if she knew just how pretty she looked.

"Will you perform at the Extravaganza in July?" I asked her.

"Of course, Lloyd. I wouldn't miss my last hurrah with Oxford for the world. That following weekend, that's when we'd agree to making the trip to York, isn't it?"

"Yes, I believe so. I'm looking forward to it immensely," Charles replied.

"As am I." I smiled.

I really meant it. I hadn't been to the north east countryside in years. The countryside was a wondrous place, the estates stricken with such beauty that you felt as though the estates themselves belonged in museums in London. Victor and I used to spend our summers in York with our Uncle William when we were boys, that of course was during the time when our mum had been taken real ill.

"Charlotte, you came after all." Cherry ran towards her friend and linked arms with her.

That's when I noticed that Allen was with her. I felt nothing towards Charlotte, so I did not try to think twice about it, but I wondered all the same how they had met. It must have been through Cherry, of course. It did not surprise me. The two of them were compatible in every way. I had enjoyed our dinner together, and I liked her very much, but had made no attempt to call on her again for we had made it clear between the two of us; although Charles and Cherry kept asking about it, thinking otherwise. Did they not understand that it would never work out between us? Charlotte thought she longed for a life outside the rules, but she really didn't. I spent enough time with her to realise that she needed a suitable match, suitable meaning one with position and money. I couldn't have her come to despise me years later.

So, the five of us joined together and walked through University Parks, greeted by a plethora of smiles and summertime air that made it appear as though nothing horrible could ever happen again in our world.

"Allen, what are you to do with your summer?" Cherry asked, her voice filled with such care that I feel I would never be able to find such sentiment in simple queries.

"Is this your attempt to persuade me to come to York after the Extravaganza?" he asked, indicating by his smile that he already had an answer.

"Charlotte isn't as forward as I am." Cherry laughed gaily.

"I'd beg to differ," I said, inserting my opinion.

The four of them turned to me in surprise, for I had been quiet this entire time.

Charlotte laughed and brushed the comment aside. Inserting her arm in Allen's, she exclaimed, "It would be

wonderful for you to spend more time with Papa and
Mummy. And, with Charles and Lloyd as your
combatants, what more could you ask for?"

"Then, we shall win the war." He returned her smile and
followed Charles and Cherry down the path back towards
the university.

If Allen had met Charlotte's parents before, it must
have meant that they had previously known each other.
Perhaps, their acquaintance wasn't of Cherry's doing after
all. I couldn't keep up with all of their connections, and
simply accepted the fact that Charlotte's smile would now
occupy Allen's peripheral vision.

Standing still for a moment, my hands in my pockets, I
watched the four of them, envious once again of
something I felt that I would never be able to achieve for
as long as I walked this earth. Their laughter
revolutionised the gardens, reminding me that I was still
stuck in the past with Mozart's Don Giovani to
accompany my lament.

However, when she turned, the wind blowing her hair
in her face, I couldn't help but smile. Perhaps it was
because she reminded me so much of Lindsay, maybe
that is what Cherry's smile was all about. Whatever it was,
it was enough to pick up my two feet and join them for a
celebratory evening.

Summer 1923

JENNIFER MALECH

Chapter 7
Confessions of Chatsmoore

We arrived at Charlotte's parents estate Tuesday afternoon. The Extravaganza had been as marvellous as an event as Charlotte had said it would be. It seemed as though the entire county had arrived in Oxford for the weekend.

I had chosen not to perform for the occasion, but enthusiastically watched Allen perform with the outlandish quartet. Charlotte had been rather amused by his performance, and I half wished once again that I played a string instrument.

We had enjoyed knickerbocker glories while wandering about the park's grounds; from tent to tent, we watched eager children and adults alike flood the carnival games in hope of winning a fancy prize.

"I wouldn't spend my last nor my first pound on one of those games," Allen remarked as we had wandered through the tents.

"Why not? Are you a sore loser?" Charlotte laughed.

"They are rigged, I tell you," he stated simply.

"Rigged or not, they are meant for fun. No more different than gambling on the horses," Charles commented.

Taking Cherry's hand, Charles ran over to the ring toss and by all means, the rules of riggidy did not apply to his hand. By golly, he won her a prize. Later, he proved Allen wrong once again when he won a separate prize for Charlotte.

Now, a week later, as we walked across the front lawn towards Charlotte's home, I dreaded that this weekend would be an even more social one than the last. Charlotte had asked me if I would be able to bear it; I assured her that I rather enjoyed the countryside.

The gardens were more extravagant than I had imagined them to be. In the front gardens, there was a fountain that stood a couple stories high, surrounded by marble statues that seemed to be like goddesses bowing to the water. I could only imagine how many gardeners were employed to take care of the land.

Chatsmoore's butler greeted us with kind eyes; a stout maid took our bags from us once we arrived in the main hall. Their entire staff welcomed us to Chatsmoore Estate, which made me awkwardly uncomfortable, as though I was already wearing my dinner jacket.

Charlotte twirled in her white garden dress, ushering us to a grander room than the first. The vast open windows were embellished in lace curtains that quietly matched Charlotte's own aurora. Her hand glistened in the sunlight as she stretched it forth and beckoned for us to follow her into the back gardens where we were to join her mother and father for afternoon tea. She informed us that they had wanted to give us all a formal welcome at the front gate, but she had insisted against it.

"What do I call them?" I whispered in Cherry's ear.

"Charlotte's parents?" she asked to which I nodded.

"Lord and Lady Branston, and if you come to familial terms, you might be able to call his Lordship, Matthew," she teasingly smiled.

"I still don't understand all of the titles."

"I will explain it to you sometime later. It took me quite some time to understand it all myself. Charlotte's father, Matthew Carnegie, is the 8th Earl of Branston."

"Judging by this estate, I knew his title must be of great nobility," I commented, admiring the vast halls.

Allen had arrived on the earlier train and was seated beside Charlotte's kind looking father. They had both been poured a cuppa. I wondered how long Allen had already been here.

"Papa, the rest of our company."

She introduced Charles and I after he had planted a kiss on Cherry's cheek and remarked how good it was to see her again. Charlotte had told me that ever since she had met Cherry, Mr. Carnegie had become the father that Cherry had always longed for. It seemed to be that Cherry rarely kept in touch with her own papa. She was quiet about her private life and even though we had many moments alone over the past several months, I never once probed her about it.

Cherry stood with one hand on her face and the other on her hip; she basked in the glorious sunshine as the winds made her appear to be ten years younger than she really was. While she was in her mid-twenties, in that moment, she could have easily been passed for a teenager.

"Matthew, this is Charles, whom I have written about." Cherry then inserted her arm in his, patted his hand and showed him off as though he was something to be admired by everyone else there.

"Yes, yes, I could not forget. Mrs. Carnegie would not allow such." He smiled most heartedly and shook his hand. As their hands firmly embraced, I realised that Lord Branston knew exactly whom Charles was, yet it was respectable for them all not to talk about the Atwood's past.

We all took our seats and welcomed tea from the under butler. He most certainly wasn't the head butler, for he was too young for the position. I only knew these things because of Uncle William, and thankfully, I would now have Cherry to be my reference guide all weekend long.

I continued to remain quiet, nothing short of the normal, while Cherry and Charlotte babbled on like two birds locked away in the saplings.

"We are sorry we couldn't make it to the Extravaganza," Lady Branston remarked.

"Was it a good crowd?" Lord Branston asked.

"The best we've seen in years," Charlotte chimed in.

"Cherry says you are finishing up your schooling at Oxford. She made mention that you are all musicians." Lord Branston directed his attention towards us men.

We nodded that we were while Charles remarked that he was rather sorry that Cherry would not be there in the autumn.

"What ever will you do?" the man chuckled.

Cherry smiled and took a sip from her tea, "If he can't manage without me, then I'm afraid he won't be able to manage with me either."

"Well stated." Lady Branston fanned herself with a fan that was probably worth more than my life savings.

"You all served in the war?" Lord Branston asked. "What about afterwards? What did you do during the in-between time before returning to Oxford?"

"My father became president of the music department soon after the war ended, so I managed to help him with home affairs while he took on the new transition," Charles replied.

"Your father manages an estate in Oxford now?" Lord Branston asked.

"Yes, just north of Oxford," Charles replied steadily.

It was a good thing he had nothing to drink during the trip over; he had to earn a good repertoire with the Carnegies, especially if they were like a second set of parents to Cherry.

"What about you, Lloyd?" Lord Branston was earnest and sincere in his queries. His white moustache reminded me of one of my commanders from the war. "I feel as though I've already learnt everything there is to know about Allen here."

They must have had a good talk; that would have pleased Charlotte, of course. Allen would ensure that Charlotte could keep the estate if they ever married, something that was not in my power to do so. The politics of the aristocracy would always be a peculiar thing to me.

"I travelled to America for a few years after the war." I realised that I had never told Charlotte of such while Cherry had learnt of such information within one of our first few encounters.

"Why, you never told me that you went to America," Allen interjected.

I had almost forgotten that he was there. I guess I had forgotten to tell him as well.

"Yes, I spent some time in Chicago, travelled with a fellow comrade who was engaged to a girl from there. They are married now with a child, funny little family."

"Was America a land of too much change?" Lord Branston laughed. "Is that why you came back?"

"I will say that it's a few years ahead of England, that is for certain. For the better, I cannot say."

"So, what made you return to England?" Lady Branston

asked, still fanning herself.

"After they had married, I realised that the only thing I really wanted in life was back here in England. I hoped to finish my studies at Oxford. So, I sent a letter to Charles asking for accommodation and I'm glad that he hadn't already married off himself."

Cherry and I exchanged glances; I had not meant to look at her when I had uttered the statement.

"Aren't we all glad?" Charlotte piped up.

After a morning game of cricket with a few of Lord Branston's friends, we agreed that after lunch, we would meet in the back gardens and then take to the river for a swim.

After freshening up after lunch, I scurried down the long flight of stairs and made my way towards the gardens. When I arrived, I realised that I was the first to find myself lost among the bluebells and dog roses. That is until I spied her.

"Cherry!" I yelled her name, but she hadn't heard me.

Her red hair was adorned by honeysuckles and her yellow dress floated in the grass; it appeared as though she truly was the fair maiden that I had imagined when I had first heard her sing.

I picked up my pace and ran towards her, realising, as I neared, that her eyes were closed and she was humming another Irish ballad that I was not familiar with.

"Cherry!" I said her name again, a little more quietly this time.

"Lloyd, are you not fond of instructions?"

"No more than you," I laughed.

"Why wait in the gardens when you can enjoy all of this?"

she spread out her arms towards the fields that surrounded us.

"Do you not care for a swim, then?" I asked Cherry.

"I find floating around in a body of water too intimate of an act."

I couldn't tell if she was joking until the slightest smirk emerged from her rosy lips.

"I'm only teasing."

And, with that, she took off her outer garments, exposing her swimming costume that had been hidden underneath and turned towards me.

"I'll race you down to the river," she nearly squealed.

She was certainly not the daughter of an earl. I could only smile as I threw my shirt beside her clothes and raced her, surprised to find that she was more athletic than I would have ever thought. She arrived just ahead of me to which she teased me.

"Lloyd Fox, you don't play fair, now do you? You didn't have to let me win. Perhaps a swim to the other side of the river bend?"

I wanted to admit that her rare beauty in the sunlight is what slowed me down, but I realised that wouldn't be fair to anyone. We had only known one another for eight months and yet, I felt as though I had known her for my entire life. Perhaps, it felt so because she had Lindsay's smile; I had finally come to realise that at Cherry's graduation, and in a way, it was a comforting thought.

It was the first time, since arriving in York, that we had found ourselves alone together. I knew it a dangerous thing; for the past few months, even though her arm was enraptured by Charles, her glances had indicated elsewise. I had tried to justify them and reminded myself that it could all just be a figment of my imagination; however, I had a terrible imagination, so if Cherry was the one to awaken it, then I felt I must congratulate her for such a feat. If she was to break out into a folklore tune, I knew I would not be able to stand it anymore.

Her smile, the way her nose crinkled when she fully exposed her slightly crooked teeth, and the glisten on the ridge of her blue eyes made me wonder about her more and more.

"Did you forget to wait for me?" Charles emerged from the woods, only dressed in his white shorts. With a splash into the river, my fantasies were overcome and washed away by the rippling tide of the waves.

"A woman doesn't need permission to wait on her man," Cherry laughed.

"Is that so?" He splashed water in her face and she returned the same.

Crikey, where were Allen and Charlotte? I don't know how much more I could stand it. To pass the time, I found myself searching for the notes in the whistling trees, trying to write the next measurements to my failing composition.

Then, within seconds, their voices entered our tracks. Allen and Charlotte's laughter erupted any tranquillity that had been present just minutes prior when Cherry and I were the only ones to have occupied this magical place, a moment that I would not soon forget.

After a full English breakfast, Cherry asked if I would like to join her for a walk to visit the horses in the stables. I had agreed, not knowing that it would only be her and me.

"Where is Charles?" I asked when she showed up alone.

"Are you disappointed that he's not joining us?" she

asked.

"No, I, well…"

"No need to get tongue tied, Lloyd," she smiled.

I couldn't play games with her. Did she know how I felt? She had to, she most certainly had to.

When we arrived at the stables, she immediately took to a horse named Constantine. Her face rested gently on his midnight black mane. Constantine's coarseness became softened just by her touch.

"Hello, old friend," she whispered.

I was transfixed by the affair, the ways in which Cherry could bring any creature into submission by her honeyed voice.

We stayed only a moment longer before taking the path behind the stable.

"Charles better be careful, you might have stolen Constantine's heart," I stated.

"Is it he that Charles must be concerned about?" she was soft spoken.

Did she mean what I thought she had meant? I stood still in my tracks, for I was transfixed by her figure; she was a creature that graced the ground from which she walked upon. Within the depths of my mind, I could hear her singsong voice fluctuate like the ocean's waves coming in with the tide.

Before I talked myself out of it, I slowly walked towards the place where she stood, only five metres in front of me, the shadows of the trees surrounded her, but she stood, entirely still, in the middle of the path where the sun had made its home.

Without a moment's waste, I kissed her; at first, her gentle lips were hesitant, but then, not a second later, they relaxed and submitted to the act.

"I'm terribly sorry," I drew away from her.

"No, you aren't," she smiled softly.

"Are you?" My voice was tremulous, a tone of voice that I was not familiar with. I was desperate to know if she felt any affection towards me.

She only smiled and didn't answer the question. She may be revolutionary, but she was traditional in some sense. To give away that she was not the least bit sorry would prove to demean her character.

"Perhaps we should join the others, Lloyd." She inserted her arm in mine and took a deep breath as our stride greeted the afternoon birds.

However, I could not ignore it. She found her way into my heart and instantly broke it with her ease to insert ourselves back into the reality where she and Charles were together. I couldn't understand why she remained with him if she returned the affection towards me. I was certain she did; her facial expressions said it all, they had the entire time we had been in York.

I knew I was foolish. But, would I regret it? That moment, like many others, would not leave my mind. As soon as our footsteps turned around the corner of the underbrush, the trees gradually disappearing to illuminate the Chatsmoore Estate, Cherry let go of my arm and began to skip along the trail. In that moment, I was reminded that she had not grown up a lady in the same ways that Charlotte had.

Whereas Charlotte adorned herself with pearls and a velvet hat that hid half of her face, Cherry's face was adorned by the subtle wisps of her misplaced hair, entirely aware that society could not place her within a box.

We had returned to the others and joined Lord and Lady Branston for an extravagant dinner, but I did not find myself in the least bit peckish. I sat there, simply mesmerised by the ways in which Cherry was able to act as though nothing had happened, as though this weekend was something that I would have to forget altogether. Their laughter erupted the statuesque ceilings, reminding me that this was an affair that I would never grow accustomed to, a lifestyle of which I could not come to acknowledge as my own. Everything we breathed upon was old money; how had Cherry now accepted it as her own? She had admitted to being a socialist, yet she drank and dined with the very people that caused a chill to creep down her bones. Where had I gone amiss? And, crikey, why had I kissed her?

Somehow, I had allowed myself to break from the party and walk with Cherry once again through the estate's gardens. I knew that I needed to talk to her again, to clarify things, if anything.

An iridescent display of butterflies fluttered on by, bumblebees drifted in and out of the berry bushes, and we ourselves, were enjoying the fruits of nature with refreshing glasses of lemonade in hand.

For the past day, my thoughts had been all over the place. Surely, Cherry had given what I had done more thought. The silence that stood between us once again spoke of such.

"Should we sit here?" Cherry asked, taking a seat at the trunk of an overgrown tree. I sat beside her, the bitter lemonade still in hand.

"So, Charlotte tells me that you have decided to remain in London come Autumn," I finally said.

"Yes." She said nothing else.

"I asked her what you were to do, but she told me that it was not her news to tell."

"Well, are you going to ask me?" She raised an eyebrow. I couldn't help but laugh.

"What awaits Cherry in the delightful city of London?"

"You said that rather unamusingly. Do you not care for London? I thought you liked it there. Queen's Hall, now isn't that one of your favourite places to attend?"

"Yes, I do like Queen's Hall, but I prefer the people in Oxford over London any day."

"Are there too many posh people there? How have you survived this weekend?" she grinned.

"With great self-restraint." I took a sip from the cool glass of lemonade.

"Well, you must congratulate me then, Lloyd. I am going to teach Latin and violin at one of the primary schools in London."

"Why, that's marvellous! Just what you had hoped for," I replied and returned her smile.

"Yes, everything I could hope for," she sighed. "Charlotte can't understand how I can lower myself to teaching for a living, but then again I am not an earl's daughter."

"No, that you aren't. A job isn't necessary for their likes." I took a sip of lemonade. "But, it is a grand estate, isn't it? I can still admire it."

"The Chatsmoore Estate will always have a place in my heart," she smiled.

"Has the estate been in the family for many years?"

"Oh, yes. The estate belonged to Mr. Carnegie's father, and before that, it belonged to his grandfather."

"Do they plan to keep it?"

"While a lot of families are choosing smaller estates these days, I believe Chatsmoore will live on. Besides, Charlotte couldn't bear to part from it."

I wondered if Cherry actually believed that about Charlotte.

"Will the estate go to her?"

"Since the Carnegies didn't have a son, none of his children will become the heir. It does bother me so that English women have to stand back and watch as their father's estate goes to another. Of course, the Married Women's Property Act of 1882 ended that, but not in Charlotte's favour. The herability of Chatsmoore will go to the entail. If, however, Charlotte is to marry the entail and have a son, than the estate will one day go to her son. Now, you see, why marriage is so important for people of their kind."

"Which is why Lord Branston insists upon Charlotte's marriage to Allen," I replied. "Blimey, Allen is the entail." I had put the puzzle pieces together.

"Yes, so you know now," Cherry said.

"It's surprising to me that they've gone their whole lives without ever meeting."

"There was no reason for them to meet. Lord Branston's heir, once Charlotte's fiancé, died in the war."

"She was engaged?"

"To Lord Branston's heir, yes. It was an arranged marriage, really. Although arranged, Charlotte loved him very much. She was devastated when the news of his death reached the family. More tragic than anything else, it was at the very end of the war, just days before the Armistice was signed. I didn't hear from her for many weeks after."

I didn't know what to say and merely sat there with my hands folded together.

"I think the thought of being forced upon the next heir was too much for her to bear," Cherry continued. "That's when she thought of giving it all up and marrying another."

Her eye's focus was so direct. It all made sense now.

"Me? She said that she wanted nothing but to remain friends," I replied in my defence.

Cherry let out a sigh. "Oh, Lloyd. Don't you know that a woman never speaks her mind?"

"It's an unfair game you play," I replied.

"To which we often outsmart our counterpart. It's such a shame," she smiled.

"So, Charlotte has given into the game of the aristocracy?"

"I think she likes Allen and Allen absolutely adores her," she defended Charlotte.

"Not just her money?" I couldn't help but ask.

"That's rather shallow thinking, even for Lloyd Fox." She raised an eyebrow and gave me one of her sensational grins. "Besides, if Lord Branston didn't like Allen, I imagine he nor Lady Branston would encourage their courtship."

"Lord Branston seems keen on the idea," I replied.

"Yes, I think he rather likes him, don't you?"

I nodded and we sat there, avoiding the very thing that we both knew we must speak about.

"Cherry, I hope you didn't misunderstand me yesterday," I spoke softly.

"I believe I understood you perfectly well," her voice flattened.

"It had been so long since I…" I couldn't finish the sentence.

"Do you have your eyes on anyone?" Cherry enquired, her sweet smile interrupted my confession. I couldn't understand why she did it. She most certainly wasn't an earl's daughter.

Furthermore, was she really going to tease me after the day that I had just kissed her? It was entirely unfair, but then again, she wasn't like any of the girls that I had ever been with before the war.

"Just my music, Cherry. You already know that."

That's when it occurred to me.

"Has Charlotte said anything to you?" I asked.

"Only that you are not a man of commitment."

"I am committed to my music."

"You don't need to cry us a river. We are all very aware of your lover."

"I didn't mean to push Charlotte out like that. Without so much as even saying a word, she knew that it would never work."

"Did she?" she asked. "It isn't always about money with them, you know."

"You said it yourself. Allen will give her a position and they will be able to keep the estate. I think it very much is about position and money."

"Oh, don't worry. I received that the feelings between you two were quite mutual. Charlotte told me so, anyways," she smiled.

"It has to be. Charlotte is right. If she wants to keep Chatsmoore, we can't be any more than friends," I commented.

We sat listening to the wind rustling in the trees. The system that Charlotte was a part of was something that my name did not bear.

"What was Lindsay like?" she suddenly asked with great cheer.

I almost spilled the drink all over myself from such an outlandish statement.

"What?"

"Lindsay? What was she like?"

"Who told you about her?"

"It's just Charles said you haven't been interested in anyone since Lindsay."

Cherry certainly wasn't English. Didn't she know that this kind of talk was forbidden?

"He's right, but that isn't for you to know. Don't ever mention her name again."

I didn't mean to, but anger quickly arose in my throat. Cherry didn't mean anything by it, but at just the mere mention of Lindsay's name, it haunted me and made me long for France's trenches; what a terrible thing to long for.

"I asked because I care about you," she stated.

Cherry reached for my arm and at her touch, I knew I would cave; I knew I would tell her the secret that I had carried with me for years. Even Charles didn't know the full truth.

"Lindsay was my brother's girl."

"Victor, your younger brother?"

"Yes, the only brother I have. Well, had."

Before I could tell her the secret that still haunted me from time to time, gallivant Charles came to the rescue. With the largest grin about his face, he announced that it had been arranged for us to go hunting with Charlotte's father in the morning.

I quickly got up and wiped my mouth of the lemonade stains. We had been seated underneath a large elm tree, shielding us from the afternoon sun that had made its way in the summer blue skies.

"Thought you'd be pleased, Lloyd. Where are you running off to?"

"Sometimes I wonder if you hear anything I say. You know how I despise hunting," I stated.

Glancing at Cherry, I could tell that she had wished I would tell her more, but I couldn't, not with Charles there. Taking my empty glass, I told them to enjoy the rare sunshine without me and retreated back to the house, making my way quickly across the broad lawn.

Slamming the door behind me, I arrived in the front library, entirely unaware that Charlotte had been seated there, reading a paper by Sigmund Freud. Philosophy had become her new obsession.

"Oh, you startled me." I had interrupted her afternoon reading.

"Is it a rare sighting to find a woman locked away in a library, Lloyd?" she teased.

"On such a fine day as today, I would think so. Where's Allen?"

"He's gone to look at some of our tenant's estates with Papa." She acted as though I should have known such. Taking a seat across from her, I couldn't help but ask.

"So, is it serious between you two?"

"We like one another very much." Her brown eyes felt sorry for me.

"Why did you not say anything sooner?" I asked.

"Cherry told you of Peter's death, I take it." There was defeat in her voice, as though she had been found out by the bobbies. I merely nodded. She took a deep breath and straightened her posture.

"Then I supposed you've now suspected that my visits to Oxford were not only to entertain Cherry in that boring place, but were also visits driven by a curiosity, a thought encouraged by Papa's sly remarks at dinner. The persistence to be married to another was unbearable to me. I thought if I met Papa's heir and learned of what a terrible man he was, I could silence my family's pleas forever."

"So, you came to Oxford to spy on Allen?" I asked with amusement in my voice.

"I wouldn't claim to be a spy. Don't you remember when we first met? I'm a creature of observation, Lloyd."

"You were pleased by your observation then?"

"My parents always wanted it. There was no other choice, really." She chose not to answer my questions directly.

"You'll be happy at Chatsmoore?"

"The rebellious heart remains until our youthful days are through. Mummy would say I've made the most of life before signing away to settlement."

"Why did you never say anything to me about Allen, though?" I asked her the question again.

"Our silence is a hope to deny the inevitable, isn't it? I learned that the first day I met you, Lloyd."

"A triumphant observation."

"Allen is lovely, don't get me wrong."

I don't know what my face looked like for she then added, "Don't look so surprised, Lloyd."

"It's not that I'm surprised by your relationship. I am only surprised that I had never heard a word from you after our time together."

"It took you two months to even return your promise of dinner and dancing. If we kept that up, I'd expect a promissory note of an engagement for about the time we were fifty years old," she laughed softly. " I thought we had been very clear with one another that night at the pub."

"Yes, we had. You have now chosen Chatsmoore and I have chosen my music—"

"Yes, Lloyd. We all know about your music. May I be frank with you?" There was a fierceness in her voice that must have been influenced by Cherry. Or, was it the other way around?

"By all means."

"If you aren't careful, your love affair with your music will be the very thing that drives away the ones you love the most."

I gulped; Charlotte couldn't understand, not entirely. There was nothing that I could say.

"Your stubbornness is a fault of your pride. I would advise you to be careful." She closed the book she had been reading and placed it on the table beside her.

"You know, when I first met you, I thought you were a sensible and quiet creature." I felt deflated.

"Quiet, no. Sensible, yes," she said quietly.

She came over to where I sat and planted a kiss on my cheek.

"Lloyd, you are a genius. It would be a shame not to live your life because of it."

Then, like a firefly passing through the darkness, she disappeared behind the corridors. Taking a deep breath, I leaned back in the chair and closed my eyes. Charlotte didn't want to spend the rest of her life at this estate. She had hoped for something from me, but I couldn't give it to her, she bloody knew that. I had my music.

When we were at the pub, she was doing her best to convince herself that the aristocratic life she had been born into was exactly what she wanted. She finally had come to realise that there was no other life for her. After our night together, that is why she so quickly agreed to finally meeting Allen, it had to be.

Autumn 1923

JENNIFER MALECH

Chapter 8
Kidlington's Song

They had somehow convinced me to wear a black tie to blend in with the rest of them. Allen, Ted, and I had agreed to join Charles in London for the week. It was our last hurrah before the school year was to begin, our very last term until we were free men; Charles and Allen had women at their left and estates at their right. A degree was just a hobby, a way to pass the time. As for Ted, he seemed to be more confidant in his plans, though none of us knew what they were just yet. I dreaded what life lay ahead of me after Oxford. The Bohedian Libraries had become, just as Charlotte had indicated, my lover. It was the birth place of my music, and I feared departing from their safety.

My summer had been surprisingly enjoyable, with a few trips here and there to get me through the long shifts at the Eagle and Child. I was working overtime, in hopes to put a little money away if I was to make the decision to board with Allen in London come January. The rent was more expensive there and I had yet to determine if I would be able to afford it or not.

The weekend previous, Ted had taken me to visit his family in Kidlington. We had taken a boat ride along the canal and met up with his two jovial sisters, who were both at least a decade younger. Spirited things they were;

they were both Ted's pride and joy.

After much debate, I had agreed to attend church with his family and had found that the hymns were no different from when I was a boy. It was dull as ever, yet Ted was happy and what right had I to comment on how redundant the organ chords sounded throughout the archaic steeple. The church building was near the water and I must admit that it was a charming place, covered in vines that were overgrown with a masterpiece of colourful flowers.

Afterwards, we had taken the girls horseback riding through Kidlington's countryside. Sally, the oldest of the two girls accompanied me on the horse and Georgie, with more freckles than skin and two long braids that reached past her waist, clung onto Ted as though she would face her death within a moment's time. While I had somewhat enjoyed the weekend that I had spent in York earlier that month, that particular weekend with Ted's family had been something different, a reminder of the roots from which I had come from. I had not wanted the weekend in Kidlington to end and admitted to Ted that his mum's lamb and mint pie was the best that I had ever tasted. "She won a blue ribbon for it for the entire county," he had replied.

"I don't doubt it." I smiled at him and then took to conversation with his mum, reminding me of my own mother. It was a comfort, really.

And, now, just a week later, here we were in the bustling city of London, greeted by car horns and endless chatter, so very different from the peacefulness of Kidlington.

It was strange, really, for as we approached a building that was more striking than the church steeple, with music that doubled most of the guests over with excitement, it was not as charming of an invitation. I glanced over at Ted and noticed that his smile was not as genuine as it had been last weekend. Perhaps, he would always be a home fellow and wouldn't stir far from Oxfordshire, just as I hoped would be the case with me come January.

Ted and I quietly followed Allen and Charles into the dark and damp building. Both Cherry and Charlotte had already taken to dancing. After only one round of drinks, Charlotte quickly stole Allen away from us, while Cherry made mention that she was not in a particular mood for more dancing.

"Why ever not?" Allen asked right before they hit the dance floor.

"Perhaps if Ted here takes you for a swing, you'll change your mind," I commented, my voice rising ever so slightly above the music.

"Do you dance, Ted? You don't strike me as one for dancing," Cherry remarked.

"No, ma'am." He was firm in his reply.

"Oh, come on. You danced the foxtrot with what's her face. Shelly, wasn't it?" Charles chuckled.

"The foxtrot, you know of it?" Cherry perked up then.

"Only a little. I beg you, I'm not one for dancing."

Cherry didn't hear him. As though her mood shifted entirely at the prospect of dancing with Ted, she took him by the hand and practically pulled him out of his chair. Charles was amused, I was amazed.

Ted quickly turned back, like a lad who didn't want to be taken to the schoolhouse, yet found himself with no other choice, being pulled into a crowd of people whose values were far different from Ted's own. That was Cherry, though. She seemed to always get her way.

As I watched him awkwardly take her by the waist, I

couldn't help but laugh. Perhaps, Reverend Thomas was right after all; the church was where Ted belonged.

"She's charming," Charles gloated.

"Most charming," I reassured him.

"I think I'm going to ask her to marry me, old chap." He said the words smoothly.

So, Charlotte was right after all. Of course, they had talked of marriage. I had tried to deny it until now.

"Do your parents approve?"

"To marry without a title?" he asked.

"Yes."

A grin emerged from his unclouded face. "I told you that I've already slipped from society's expectations, that includes my parents."

He had been raised to know that he could only marry into certain families. Despite all that, he planned to go against the expectations. He would get away with it, just as he always had.

"Are you sure, Charles? One woman for the rest of your life? It doesn't seem like you."

Cherry deserved better. Even though Charles was a decent man she deserved better.

"Money and love. Two things you will never have, old chap," he toasted to such.

"Why would you say such a thing?" I wanted to spit in his face, even though he was only teasing.

"You are pursuing the dream of a 19th century man and haven't laid eyes on one woman since returning home from the war," he retaliated.

Well, he was wrong there. I had, and it happened to be his beloved Cherry. What a terrible game of coincidence.

"Perhaps, you should go out with Charlotte again sometime."

"She's practically engaged to Allen. Look at the two of

them, they might as well be wed." I pointed towards
Allen, whose oval shaped face with the childhood scar
above his left lip had gone unnoticed amidst the crowd.

"That means nothing, at least that's what my father
used to say," Charles chuckled.
"Do you speak the same for yourself?" I asked with no
amusement in my voice.
"No, you wouldn't dare chase after Cherry." Charles
smiled mischievously.
"How do you know that?" My tone did not change.
It was as though he was challenging me.
"Because Cherry said so," he remarked.
"Cherry said so?" I placed my cup on the table and leaned
forward, looking him more direct in the eyes now.
"Do you really think that I hadn't taken notice to all the
time you two were spending together when we were in
York? And, what's more, the many months before that.
I'm not naive, old chap."
"You and I both know that Cherry isn't like any other
girl. She speaks her own mind, just as much as you do. I
like her, but...."

I paused, uncertain if I should be upright with him,
make him aware of how I really felt about Cherry and
how I truly felt about the ways in which she felt in return.
"Cherry likes you, too, but not enough to marry you." A
long breath of smoke escaped his lips. He grinned, that
sly smile of his that said *'You won't ever be like me, Lloyd.'*

We sat there in complete reticence. Charles' foot
lightly tapped to the same rhythm as the bass. Before I
could say anything more, Cherry skipped over and swept
Charles off his feet, returning Ted to sit beside me, his
face quite flushed from a few minutes of dancing. Charles
took a quick glance at me and then proceeded to take his
hand and slowly move it down Cherry's back, indicating

that there was no chance for me. He knew exactly what he was doing and I bloody despised him for it.

Ted had been rather quiet, as though he held a great secret and would be sentenced if he spared one word of what was troubling him. We were seated in his mum's kitchen, a quaint country home with only one wood table and one fireplace to keep the entire cottage warm. Ted had six younger siblings, which had Mrs. Astair dancing about her toes all day long.

The green hedges outside were perfectly trimmed, the golden cobblestone had been recently tended to, and the primroses were as fine as ever as they stretched from the front door of the cottage to the stables in the very back gardens.

I had agreed to accompany Ted to Kidlington for the night as there were a few things that he needed to retrieve from home before returning to Oxford for the school year. While most of our colleagues did not spare much of their time with Ted, for I admit that he was a little strange: he never had straight posture, and constantly played with his spectacles as though he had just started wearing them for the first time that day, I didn't mind his company as much as I had originally detested. For whatever reason, when I had first agreed to visit his family in Kidlington, Allen thought that I was not in my right mind; I thought the same. However, after an evening's time with his sisters, Georgie and Sally, I had realised how very much I had missed being around a family, a true family; it was an antidote in a way. "Would you like anything else?" Mrs. Astair asked in a soft manner, a tenderness that I imagined had to have come from raising seven children in such a small place. "No, thank you, ma'am. This cuppa taste marvellous."

She smiled, pleased with my answer, and returned to cutting carrots and potatoes for an evening stew, still glowing from the bluebells that we had picked up for her on our way into town.

We remained in the kitchen for only a few minutes longer, grabbed our hats and returned to the stables. Ted checked in on the horses while I remained outside the stables, marvelling at the countryside of Kidlington, it's vastness that spread before my eyes like a painting that hung from the ceiling of Chastsmoore Estate. In the distance, an archaic bridge over the River Chertwell greeted a collection of sheep that roamed and grazed the fields with a quiet manner. The sunshine's rays greeted the afternoon mist like a child's hand playing with cotton; it was playful and wonderful, a display that seemed too picturesque, straight out of a novel that evoked beauty instead of wrath.

"Lloyd, would you like to take a walk to the church?" Ted asked sheepishly.

I shrugged my shoulders.

"Nothing else to do," I commented.

While I was not interested in attending another church service, I was interested in the architecture and the ways in which the acoustics sounded in such a place. The walk was a short one and it was a good thing, too, for we barely spoke. We didn't have much to talk about.

Upon arriving at the church's graveyard, we walked up the secluded path that led to the wood-framed doors which greeted us with the most noble intentions. The church must have been built in the 16th century. No wonder Ted had wanted to show me the place; it was a different church from the one that we had attended during my last visit. I gazed at the exterior and remarked that it was extraordinary.

Following Ted inside, we walked past fifteen church pews before we made our way to the centre of the old church. The ceilings were low. The sun found its way in through one stained glass window; it stood just behind the church organ which sat at the centre of the stage. "The stain glass dates back to before the French Revolution," Ted finally said.

"It's exquisite," I replied.

"Would you care to take a seat?" Ted asked.

I joined him on the front church pew. We both sat there, staring up at the stained glass, the array of colours truly bewitching. The features in Ted's face softened as I waited for him to speak.

"I supposed you think I'm a fool, Lloyd." Ted glanced at me and then returned his gaze to the glass window.

"What would give you that idea?"

"I believe I'm going to give my word to Reverend Thomas and join the clergy in Oxford, after we finish the term, of course. Maybe I'll come back to Kidlington and join the teachings here."

I briefly smiled and patted him lightly on the shoulder. "It's your life, Ted. I am not one to say whether your choice or my choice is better than any other."

"Yes, of course not, but I don't think you understand me. No one understands me at university. I've rarely found a man who wants to converse with me, especially those who fought in the war, and that's the majority, isn't it?"

Ted had never fought in the war, of course he was younger when the war first broke out, and he had been asked by his mum to remain at home and take care of the groundwork while his father fought at war instead. His father had returned, that was a relief, for I don't know if

Ted would have ever been allowed to leave home and pursue his education had the opposite occurred.

"You see, Lloyd, you are the only one who talks to me like I am a man of twenty two, rather than a man of sixteen. I am no longer a boy, yet I feel like I am. You and Allen both have been good to me, and I thank you for that."

"We all fought our own battles during the war, you included," I replied.

"That's not the way any of them see it. There's no convincing them otherwise."

I thought of Charles then and the comments he had once made about Ted, in the company of a few of our other colleagues, and I brushed the thought aside. It wasn't worth repeating.

"I imagine you told Reverend Thomas all of these things," I stated.

"Yes, and he would agree with you - my battle was taking care of the land at home. I partially returned here this weekend hoping that there would be something to persuade me not to join the church, that there was work for me here, just like it was so during the war. Or, that maybe I could join you and Allen in London come January, that perhaps that would be a better life."

So, Allen had talked to him. I didn't yet know the answer to my own decision and just sat there.

"You know what they call clergymen." He sounded deflated.

I knew exactly what they called clergymen at university. There was a low respect for them, for most did not see the need for deacons and priests when we were old enough to have ourselves to teach in the ways we should go. We were grown men after all.

"Yes, but that doesn't make it right," I stated.

"So, you'll support my decision, then?"

He was so desperate for someone in the world to understand. I realised we were both so similar, and perhaps it was the same for all of us at Oxford. We sought the approval of our peers, hoping that by such, we would gain greater pleasure out of the very thing we were pursuing.

Chapter 9
Lindsay's Story

Ever since Charles had told me that he and Cherry were to be married, I could not stop thinking about it. I knew that I had to see Cherry before they made their vows to one another.

We were now seated in her parlour, Cherry and I that is. After making the journey from Oxford to London, I supposed I had hoped for something more, but I quickly realised that my efforts to try to postpone their wedding would be futile.

"You will always be a good friend to me, Lloyd. It must always remain the way it was before we went away to York. I am truly sorry that I led your feelings astray. What else do you expect me to say? Lloyd, don't look at me that way."

"Then, why do you ever request my company or why did you secretly enjoy a kiss from me?"

"I am certain that you and I could take a stroll through London and point out at least three women that you find yourself attracted to."

She sounded exasperated. If she admitted her feelings to me, it would ruin everything for her music career. Charles could give her a real chance at musical success I saw that now. Yet, it didn't necessarily make it the right choice.

"Attraction and feelings are two entirely different things,

Cherry."

"Lloyd, I am sorry, but I have made my decision."

Cherry didn't understand. She aroused something inside of me that no other person had been able to do, no one since Lindsay.

"You don't have to marry him, you know."

I knew it was unfair of me to say to her, but she needed to see that she at least had a choice.

"I can't explain my decision to you, Lloyd. You wouldn't understand."

"I thought Charles was always the one who didn't understand," I replied bitterly.

I didn't even try to cover up my feelings. She needed to know how I felt. And, then, as though we had been having an entirely different conversation altogether, Cherry brought her memory into the room.

"Did you love her?"

"Who?"

"Lindsay? Did you love her?"

If I didn't care so much for Cherry, I would have been furious at her for bringing up her name in the first place, and most likely would have acted upon my anger.

"I don't know what love is. Do you?"

She was silent. "Was it so wrong of me to ask?"

"Do you love Charles?" I asked her, hesitant at first.

"I do." She paused and continued. "He is willing to give up his position for me, Lloyd."

"Then, I am glad for you both." I forced a smile.

"Charles said I won't have to work anymore, that a job isn't necessary and all of that, but I told him that teaching violin and the languages doesn't feel like a job. He respects me for that."

"Have you met his parents, then?"

"Yes, they are pleased."

"You are remarkable to earn their blessing." I forced another smile.

"They are kind people, and remind me very much of the Carnegies," she smiled.

There was nothing more to say on the matter. She had made up her mind. For some reason, I knew not why, I knew I had to tell her. I had to tell Cherry about Lindsay, for she was the one who had brought it up in the first place. Charles couldn't interfere this time.

"I know I asked of you to never mention her name again, but I want you to know. I feel you ought to know."

I don't know why I felt like I should tell her, but Cherry was my closest friend, and I didn't really have many who I could call a true friend. Maybe I thought Lindsay's haunting story would leave me once I finally gave voice to it. What a lie to believe.

"Know what, Lloyd?"

"Lindsay's story."

"Go on then."

She perked up then and gently urged me to speak.

"Lindsay wasn't my girl as you have thought her to be, although I discovered that I loved her in the end. She was Victor's girl and always would be."

"Sounds like a tragic romance novel. The pursuit of your brother's girl."

I smiled as she laughed at the thought. I let her have it.

"Victor and Lindsay met at Queen's Hall. As soon as he set eyes on her, I knew him well enough to know that he was smitten. Over the course of a year, all of us spent time together. Victor and I attended our classes at Oxford while Lindsay came into town on the weekends when we remained in Oxford. We often visited London solely because of Victor's courtship with Lindsay."

"What was Victor like?" Cherry interrupted me.

"Victor was a quiet chap. He never had the gift of the arts like the rest of us. From the time he was in primary school, his mind worked numbers like the back of his hand. He was extremely intelligent and took to mathematics at Oxford. He was loyal and wouldn't touch a fly, which is why the war was such an awful experience for him. I believe Lindsay noticed the change in him each time he came home from France, and through her inquisitiveness, she tried to understand what he was holding back from her, for he had always been an honest man."

"So, what happened?"

"When Victor died, he didn't even receive proper recognition. He died for cowardice."

"Oh." Her voice was soft and touched a hidden part of me.

"When news of Victor's death reached Lindsay, she went on holiday to Fowey. She had family there and remained there for the next year. When I was away at war, I wrote letters to Lindsay constantly. I never had a girl like my fellow comrades had, but I had Lindsay. And, Lindsay had me. I returned on leave to England a few times and went to visit Lindsay in Cornwall."

As I told the story, it became as familiar as yesterday's supper. I could hear the men giving orders in the harbour, the salty air running through my hair, Lindsay's laughter greeting the seagulls and the smell of fish n' chips greeting us at our favourite pub. We used to walk down to the cove after lunch and greet the locals who were also taking an afternoon stroll. Lindsay used to gather her arm in mine during our walks alongside the burrowing cliffs. There was no other place like it. I was comforted by her touch, which was probably why I beckoned her to take walks with me so often during my visits. She cared very little about her appearance, yet she was effortlessly beautiful. Perhaps it was her free spirit that had initially drawn Victor and then equally so myself.

I hadn't realised that I had stopped talking.

"What were your visits like, to Fowey that is? I've never been before. Is it a pleasant city?"

"It is the perfect combination of the country and the sea."

"Sounds like a scene from a fairy story. Well, how about Lindsay? Is that where you learned to love her?"

"I valued her as my friend, Cherry. Nothing more. However, between my first and second trip to Fowey, something terrible happened."

"What?"

Her posture straightened as she became captivated by my every word, unable to break her gaze from mine. Those blue eyes of her pierced through my own which made me think she knew the end of the story before I ever said it. I had never told Charles the true reason for Lindsay's move to Ireland. My heart wanted no one else to view her as the county of Cornwall did.

"She became ill, not physically speaking. It is almost unexplainable, but perhaps the truth about Victor's death had finally reached her ears, for she hadn't known at first that he had died for cowardice. I believe they returned some of his things to her and maybe that is what did it."

"Did what? What kind of illness, then?"

"A depression that cannot be explained. I was there once when she lost her mind. It was a terrible thing. She was rolling on the ground, screaming. The servants were told to remain outside. It was as though she was trapped and we were on the outside, only able to look in, yet unable to rescue her from the despair that she then wrestled with."

"How dreadful," Cherry whispered, gently grabbing my

arm.

I did not refuse her touch and longed for a drink then. The memory would remain with me forever, for I could not understand why someone so beautiful and with so much potential would have to suffer so.

"These episodes were unexpected. I learnt through her mother that they came as quickly as an unexpected storm at sea. It became too much for her own family to handle. It wasn't fair, but they knew not else to do. They followed the advice of the vicar."

"Which was?"

Cherry's voice was so quiet, I had almost not heard her ask the question.

"They sent her to an asylum."

"Dear God." Cherry drew a hand to her mouth.

"I visited her at the asylum."

"I thought visitors weren't allowed."

"Any man can break the law if it brings justice to an innocent life."

"You thought her innocent then?"

I knew she did not agree with me, and sometimes I wondered if I myself agreed with my actions for the memories of that visit were intolerable. It began with a visit to Lindsay's parents. Her father was unwilling to offer information about where Lindsay had gone, but I received the information in the end. Showing up to the asylum, I had broken past the nurses and found the poor girl in a room with ten other women. The smells were repugnant, which had me wondering how much attention the girls were truly receiving. Gathering Lindsay in my arms, I reported to the nurse that I had civil instruction to remove her from the property. Showing up unannounced and in this manner was uncivilised on my part, but I could not live with myself if Lindsay was to die in such a place. The repercussions were minimum with only a few fees that had to be paid to the county.

"She by no means was in a right place of mind, but I knew that it would be better if she at least had an opportunity to find life again on the days that she was not mentally gone."

"Charles said that Lindsay moved to Ireland and confessed that she did not return your feelings. I would not have teased you so if I had known the truth. Lloyd, I am so sorry."

"I never wanted Charles to know. It is a terrible thing, Cherry. It is as though she was locked in her own world and no matter what you tried to do or say, she could not escape."

"Do you know how she is now? Has Ireland treated her well?"

"Her family arranged for her to stay with a great aunt after much debate. It was decided it would be best if she lived in seclusion at her aunt's cottage in Fanore, off the coast of Ireland. From what I know, she sees no one apart from her aunt and the servants."

"Have you ever visited her?"

"Never."

I stood up then and tried to find a bottle of something.

"Do you never think to visit her? I do not know of her mental condition as you do, but it might help. To see someone she loves, I am certain that could bring meaning to her life that no longer appears to have any value."

"That is the most difficult part, Cherry. Not even the ones who love her most can save her."

Silence settled on our conversation as I reached for the port that sat on the parlour's table. It must have been there for Charles.

Staring through the baroque windows, I realised that nothing had been achieved in telling Cherry the truth. I had hoped that the thoughts of Lindsay would leave me altogether, but instead they had an adverse effect.

"Lloyd, I feel that I owe you a truth for sharing with me a secret to your past that I am entirely undeserving to know."

"I am not exchanging my own for another. It feels good that someone other than myself knows of what really happened to Lindsay."

"Then, perhaps it's time you knew."

"Oh?"

"Lloyd, my name isn't Cherry."

"What?" I turned towards her, thinking that she was playing a joke on me, but her face said otherwise.

"My true name is Rose. Rose Ellis," she said without hesitancy.

"Why ever?"

"It was Papa's advice."

I thought she would start crying then, and perhaps, if it was someone other than her, she would have, but not Cherry. Or, Rose. Whatever her name was. What was I to call her now?

"Cherry, I mean, Rose—"

I would never get used to saying Rose, at least that's what I thought.

"Please, let me explain. I want to explain, you, of all people, deserve that," she interrupted me.

My hands were dry; I could hear my heart beating, for whatever she was to tell me had to be the answer to what I had wondered over these last couple of months.

"As you know, my brother died fighting in the Irish War for Independence."

"Yes." I did not press her to say anymore.

Her hair had been gathered in a large braid, dangling over her left shoulder. As she began to speak, she slowly began to unbraid it, making her voice all the more mesmerizing.

"When I first heard from Tom that their initial target was that of Dublin Castle, I became terribly afraid, certain that the rebels would be after other Irish Royalties, in hopes to warn all of Westminster's government."

"Did you not agree with the war, then? I thought you supported it."

"Let me tell you my story first, and then, I reckon these musings will make more sense. I hope you have some time, I've already wasted so much of your afternoon."

"No, I've nowhere to be," I lied. I had agreed to meet with Charles at St. James Square within the hour. We had agreed to dine together before making our way to Queen's Hall with Cherry and the rest of his friends. He could wait, by certain he might arrive at Cherry's door any minute. Crikey, her name was Rose.

She continued. Quietly, at first. But, as the words began to overflow, she became more animated, for it was as though she was reading a book about her life for the very first time.

"As you know, my mother died when I was a girl. She died giving birth to Tom. The doctor said that there was nothing that could be done for the epilepsy was uncontrollable. For years, Papa had taken out his anger on little Tom. We had a maid who took care of both Tom and me, and she let me take care of him as well. I was ten years old."

"I remember you mentioning that your mother died when you were young," I said quietly.

She stood up and asked if I cared for a cuppa, getting rid of the rubbish that had been scattered on the table.

"No, it's rather early for such," I commented.

"Yes, of course, you are right."

She glanced at the clock and tapped her hand on the edge of the chair in perfect sync with the clock's hand. She continued speaking while tapping.

"I told you that Papa painted beautiful paintings. He always spent his time wandering our gardens, what little they were, but proud of them he was. Anyhow, one day, he stumbled upon a young girl, only a year younger than me with soft brown eyes just like Mam. She was beautiful and somehow, she had agreed to Papa painting a portrait of her. When he had finished, a quick sketch is all it was, he had welcomed her into our home. After simple enquiry, we discovered that she lived in a castle nearby, although she would not tell us anything more."

"What was her name?" I interrupted her.

"Caitríona."

"An Irish name, if I've ever heard one," I smiled.

"Oh, yes. Did you ever watch the Countess Cathleen?"

"The play by W.B. Yeatts?" I asked.

"Yes, the very one."

"No, I've just heard of it. Victor knew of every play written in all of Great Britain." I then realised that a cuppa sounded swell after all.

"Well, the play was inspired by an old Irish folktale. The tale was always a childhood favourite of my own, even more so when I met Caitríona. Anyways, as the story goes, an entire Irish village faced great famine in their land and the only way to a promised harvest would be if they sold their souls to the devil."

"What a predicament." I tried my best not to smile as her eyes lit up.

"So, the people of Ireland were left in, as you said, quite a predicament. That is when Cathleen steps in and saves the day. She offered her soul to the devil so that her people might live. As she departed to meet with the devil, God rescued her, reminding her that such sacrifice could not, and should not ever, lead to such evil consequence."

"Did Caitríona sacrifice her soul?" I took a deep breath, wondering if in anyway the folktale had anything to do with the castle that she had mentioned. That is why she was telling the story, wasn't it?

"She did the courageous thing, just like Cathleen."

Now, I was entirely intrigued.

"Caitríona became a dear friend of mine, my best friend, you see."

"Where is she now?"

"She is no longer alive," Cherry looked away.

Now, she had entirely piqued my interest, for she was opening herself up to the past, a past that Charlotte had said would rather not remember. With each word that proceeded out of her mouth, it was as though I came to know Cherry, crikey, Rose, with a new understanding.

"We were poor, of course that is what happens when you have a drunk father who puts all of his hopes in his paintings. So, Papa did what anyone would do to provide for his children. He invited Caitríona into our home most often, and she, entirely unaware of his intentions, agreed."

"What were his intentions?"

"I'm sure you can guess. We had little land and Caitríona's family had a good harvest of wild animals."

"You father was a poacher?" I asked astonishingly.

"Yes, he swore Caitríona to secrecy. In addition to such, she brought us fruits and vegetables and fresh bread from the castle's kitchen."

"Courageous girl, yet stupid at the same time," I replied. She was about to object my statement and her lips slightly stammered, but she quickly closed them, her head slightly tilting towards the ground as though to acknowledge my statement in full.

"Well, Papa had sternly taken me aside many a time and said I was to never visit Caitríona in her castle. I had asked of it so often, even prayed that I may visit."

"I thought you weren't religious," I grinned.

"I never said I was, but Papa kept to some Protestant ways, must I remind you. Anyways, my prayer came true one day, for when Caitríona and I were picking wildflowers just beyond our meadow, she grabbed my hand and we took off running. I remember it so vividly. There was a hill that we had to climb, and she practically dragged me up the slope. It was quite a trek, and I wondered why I had never come across her castle before, but of course by this time, I was only twelve years old."

"Caitríona visited you for two years?"

"Yes, nearly every month, and Papa had never been suspected during that time. Now, that day, when Caitríona took me to the castle, a beastly thing it was, not as pretty as I had imagined, but it was magnificent all the same, I asked of Caitríona if she ever got lost in such a place, to which she laughed and only replied, 'Oh, Rose. You know hardly anything at all.' To which I, even as a young child, did not want anyone to think of such. So, I asked of her to teach me everything she knew. Even though she was younger than me, I wanted to be like her, anyone would have."

"Did you meet Caitríona's parents?"

Cherry's story seemed like it had come from a fairy tale itself.

"Yes, but by accident. Caitríona had been taken off guard and thought nothing else but to introduce me as her meadow friend. They asked simple queries and were quite pleasant folk, draped in fabrics that seemed to have cost the entire county their fortune." She paused and then asked, "Are you sure you don't want tea?"

"Actually, I'll take a cuppa," I met her eyes and hesitantly looked away.

She placed a kettle on the cooker and hummed a tune as she did so. The kettle sounded and she placed two steaming cups of tea and biscuits before us.

"I only visited the castle once more, for there would be no possible return. Papa was caught red-handed by one of the watchmen from the castle. Somehow, though I knew not how, Papa got away from the guards. Even at such a young age, I knew that the repercussions of poaching were grand, a large sum that Papa would never be able to pay which would of course put him in jail for perhaps the rest of his life. Thus, we moved from the village that night, Tom's screaming wailing throughout the majority of the night. As we groped our way through the woodlands on horseback, Papa whispered in my ear, 'You must go by a new name, Rose, and you must never again address me as your Papa.' I didn't ask questions but knew that it had something to do with Caitríona's castle."

"What a long journey," I replied.

"The longest. We finally arrived in Killarney and Papa had enough aside to find us a small cottage to take to. We were fortunate that no one asked queries, even if they had thought them." She paused.

"I supposed you wonder if I ever returned to the castle?" she asked pleasantly.

"I hadn't thought such, but now that you mentioned it, I do."

"Well, I did return, quite a few years later. Caitríona's mam answered the door, no servant, just her mam. I do not know what directed me to the castle that day, perhaps it was St. Catherine herself, but when I arrived, Caitríona was quite ill. It was something incurable, that is what the doctor had said. I did not ask questions, but remained there and held her hand. Her papa said that Caitríona had spoken of me all the time, that they were sorry that my own papa had gotten into trouble with the government and had fled. 'God bless his soul,' Caitríona's mam had said when I told her of his outcome. And, then, he, Caitríona's papa, gave me a considerable sum of money, though I did not ask for it."

"What happened to Caitríona?"

"I do not know, for when I returned to the castle a year later, they were all gone."

"You never heard of Caitríona's parents again?"

"No, never," she seemed a little deflated. "When I was sixteen, father became terribly ill from the alcohol. I sent Tom away to boarding school, from the money that Caitríona's papa had given me. Papa never queried my actions and simply obliged when the liquor had violently taken his mind. It was that autumn, when Tom was sent away to school, that I met the Carnegies. Their family had a holiday home in Killarney, although it seemed odd to want to holiday in such a place when they had come from old money for so long. I spent more nights dining at their home than my own."

"When did you start playing the violin, then?" I was curious.

"Lord Branston gave me his old fiddle that autumn. He taught me, and was patient as ever, the most patient of men if I ever knew one," she smiled

"I would have never thought so. You play as though you've been playing since you were a little girl," I softly replied.

"Lord Branston calls me his prodigy princess." Her upper lip curved, which displayed in a second how she revered him as her own father.

"He was wise to take you under his wing." I leaned forward in the chair, hoping that she would tell me more, inviting her in to tell me more. She blew away a feather of her hair and then proceeded, my hopes fulfilled.

"To return to the beginning of my story, Tom and I kept in touch through letters. He was only seventeen when the fight for independence broke out. When he wrote that they were to target the **Royal Irish Constabulary**, that is the UK police force that mainly remained in Dublin, my thoughts immediately were taken to my times spent with Caitríona and her family. I loved her family, more than my own, and I did not want harm to come upon those who believed that Ireland and England should all remain together, for this was Caitríona's belief. I knew that it would not benefit their family if an Irish Republic was to emerge. I learnt no matter how much I tried to insert myself into another world, however much I tried to become civilised like the Carnegies, I could not abandon my heart. It is why I supported the causes of the revolution, only praying, for perhaps only the second time in my life, that Caitríona and her family would be safe."

"But, of course, they would be safe. From what I know, the IRA did not target anyone apart from the police force," I commented.

"Yes, well, I couldn't have known that at the time and Tom was silent about what they were going to do. I sometimes imagined that he would take to that old castle and kill everyone inside, for he despised them, said it was their fault Papa was the way he was. Nothing I said made any sense to him, for Papa stopped painting shortly after our move to Killarney. He destroyed all of his paintings in a fire, and didn't start painting again until Tom had been away at boarding school for two years."

"Did Tom resent your father?"

"He resented the world we lived in. It made me terribly sad."

With such words, that is where it occurred to me. In some ways, I must have reminded her of Tom, my cynicism being the bloody driving force behind this life that we were all unfortunately blessed by. Crikey, I felt sorry for her then, sorry for myself.

"I supposed you wonder if I've seen my father again?"

Her question broke through the sombre shadows that had entered the room. I shook my head, indicating that in no way had I thought of such.

"Just as you said, not even the ones who love him most could save him. I had to say goodbye to him."

She spoke with such poise as the mysterious layers began to unravel, yet even then, there were still parts of Cherry that I knew I would never learn about. We sat in silence.

"If I didn't know you better, I would say that you made all of this up," I finally said.

"I supposed it does sound like a fairy story, doesn't it?" She smiled that irresistible smile of hers. "Now, you see why I never wanted to go by Rose again, for it was a secret that I hoped dead, a part of a life that I never wanted to think of again. You must understand *now* why I want to marry Charles. He is the first stable and certain thing in my life with a vivacity that reminds me very much of Caitríona."

"I don't think Charles would take kindly to you calling him vivacious," I laughed.

"No, but then again, Charles is like no one else I have ever met."

There was nothing left to say, for Cherry Rose had made her decision. She, herself, was like no one else I had ever met or would ever meet again.

Winter 1923

JENNIFER MALECH

Chapter 10
An Irish Rose + Her Musician

I couldn't stop thinking about what Rose had said. Her words were imprinted in my memory, like black ink possessed by a typewriter. I still couldn't fathom it, for the Cherry that I knew seemed like a creature that I had never known. While I now knew the secret to Charlotte's castle tale, I still did not know what to make of it all. What's more it made me believe that I was not the only one who knew of Cherry's real name. Charlotte had to know. Of course she did; especially if she knew of the castle. In my heart, I hoped Charlotte knew. I couldn't bear it if I was the only one who knew Rose's secret, but then again, it made me slightly possessive of a piece of Rose that even Charles did not have. It was terrible, for I wanted her. She stirred something within me, something that had been dead since Lindsay had returned to Ireland. Yet, I knew such would never be the case.

They were to be married in December, as soon as Charles finished his studies. Since Rose had taken the teaching job in London, they had decided to move into the flat that she was currently living in, close to the local nightclubs that Charles regularly attended whenever he visited Rose. It was evident that Charles would continue with his jazz career after graduation, taking with the band that he had played with on occasion. What a different life from the one he had grown up knowing.

They were a far decent band, the one Charles played with. They had travelled to England, all the way from New Orleans. Rose told me how much she loved their American accents and hoped that Charles and she could travel to America sometime, following in close pursuit of James, Tony, and Gerald, the threesome members of the band who had slowly inched their way into her own musical heart. She had asked me about America, desiring so much to know everything there was to know about such a country, a country far different from our own. I rarely spoke of it, though, for there seemed to be nothing really to say about it. I rarely spoke of anything of the past, of the war and my time in America, and my childhood, most certainly not.

Yet, Cherry, in her own way, was able to break down the walls that I had built, in a way no one else could.

We were at the jazz club again; it was nearly the end of the term, and Mr. Anderson was working the Orchestra as though our entire life depended upon it.

"It is a shame Charles didn't remain in the Orchestra," Cherry commented.

"Yes, but I think that has to entirely do with your leaving," I grinned.

"Perhaps. He is a man after the jazz business, a business that doesn't involve stiff company and overpriced drinks," she laughed.

After taking a drink, she turned to where I was seated and asked, "How is your lover?"

"You mean my composition?" I asked.

"Yes, Lloyd's lover, a mysterious woman of whom we shall never meet, or to whom the world will meet once we are all dead."

"It is coming along." I tried not to receive her teasing too well.

"Mr. Anderson really is turning you into a stiff neck," she stated.

"You know that I was already a stiff neck."

"But, not when you're with me." She flashed her eyelids at me and crinkled her nose, reminding me that she was right about such; however, whenever Charles was in the room as well, I retreated to my defence barrier, a mechanism that had allowed me to survive childhood.

"Well, then, since you won't talk about your composition, what does the future hold for Lloyd Fox?"

I was about to respond unfavourably, but changed my tone of voice.

"Limitless possibilities." I forced a smile, most likely a sorrowful one, for her red hair glowed in the dim lighting in such a pulchritudinous way. I thought her to be angelic.

"As for us all." She raised her glass and we toasted to such.

After taking another sip and admiring the band's ease to brighten up the entire room, I hoped to ask her a question. Perhaps the safest place to ask would be the dance floor. Standing up then, I shook my head and held out my hand.

"Does the princess prodigy care to dance with this hopeless bloke?"

She tilted her head, closed her eyes as though to think about it, and seconds later jumped up gleefully.

"If your smile faints not," she laughed.

I smiled as she grabbed my hand and joined me on the dance floor where Charles stood on stage playing with the rest of the band. He winked at me from the platform and would continue to entertain the crowd through the early hours of the morning. It was as though he was reminding me who still had Cherry.

The music's time signature then changed to a slower beat. As Cherry and I equally slowed our movements with the paced notes, I asked her quietly.

"Cherry, I know you don't like going by Rose, but may I ask you something? May I call you Rose?"

She seemed confused as to why I was asking such a thing.

"It's just that no one else does, and I find it wonderful, in a peculiar way, that I know something that only your father knows."

"How do you not know that there wasn't another Lloyd before you?" she laughed.

"Then, you aren't opposed to it?"

"It's funny rather, no, I'm not opposed to being called Rose again, especially if it's by you."

I smiled and thanked her.

It was strange. We invited one another into one another's pasts, the most vulnerable thing to ever do, and it was there that I realised that Rose was trying to heal me, and I, although not in any way fit for the part, was hoping to do the same for her. It was the strangest friendship, yet the one that I valued above all else. Every time I sat down to write new music, it had made my recent nightmares all the more real with only Rose's and then interchangeably Lindsay's face to mend my fingers and my ears anew.

I had to accept the fact, although I could not bear it; Rose would marry Charles, for I had already wed my music.

She was radiant, but of course, I could not expect anything less. The white dress, although simple in design, fit her like a glove. It was different from the latest fashions, that's what Rose had said anyways; she didn't want to spend a lot of money on a wedding dress, nor did she want a grand ceremony or reception.

They had decided to get married at St. Ebbe's church in Oxford after all. Located at the centre of the city in Pennyfarthing Place, the Anglican church seated more guests than Charles and Rose had even invited, which was quite a lot of people, might I add. The old stone and stained glass, the towers that marked the aisle and arched above us, the worn floor that had stood the test of time, and the monstrous doors at the centre back of the church enveloped us all into what society would call a joyful occasion of celebration.

All I could do was stand beside Charles and Rose as he took her hand, as they repeated their vows to one another, and as they took the holy communion, my thoughts wandering far from where I stood.

Then, as they proceeded towards those monstrous doors in the back, the sunlight's rays illuminated the smiles on their faces, welcomed by bagpipes in the front courtyard at Rose's request.

The same photographer who had been at Rose's graduation, as well as Charles and my own just last month, clicked away with his camera. I stood afar off, not wanting to be in any of their wedding photographs.

Carrying a small bouquet of purple flowers, Rose quickly made her way over to where I stood, dropping a few flowers in doing so.

"How do I look?" she smiled.

They were the first words that proceeded out of her mouth to me that day. I kissed her hand and remarked that she was stunning, but I needn't say that for her to know such.

"Lloyd, I know you will object, but today, I'd very much like for you to enjoy yourself."

"Do I not appear to be enjoying myself? No, you are right; perhaps, it was the lengthy vows that I had to stand through."

She lightly hit me on the shoulder, which reminded me once again that she wasn't a true lady of the 20th century.

"So, are you going to take a photograph with me?" she asked.

"Just you?"

"Yes, it's my wedding day and the photographer has an entire roll of film. We wouldn't want it to be wasted, now would we?" she glowed, by ever did she bloom like a dog rose herself.

"No, Rose, we wouldn't want that," I softly said and followed her to where the eccentric photographer stood. By golly did he love his job.

"Just a little over, yes, no, that's right. Splendid! Dashing. Oh, yes, marvellous indeed!" The photographer danced on his tip toes.

I turned towards Rose and whispered, "Must I tell him that he isn't paid a tip for his exuberance?"

Rose smiled incandescently and then broke out into quiet laughter, my laughter equally returned. Her blue eyes shone like the Cornish sea, unafraid by the cliffs that stood near off. Whatever was to come her way, she welcomed with grace, and she made me forget that the world around us even existed. Then, the camera flashed.

For the slightest moment, I forgot that it was not I who had wed her. Charles who had been standing off in the distance, talking to Allen and Charlotte, came over to retrieve his bride.

"Lloyd, you wouldn't dare think to run off with my bride," Charles laughed.

"Not in a hundred years." I lied for the sake of the occasion.

We all returned the laughter, though mine not genuine. I longingly looked forward to the reception where I could catch myself a glass of something to drink.

After they finished taking photographs, we only had to walk a couple blocks to Mr. Anderson's house where the reception was to be held, seeing as Rose had insisted on not having it at Charles' parents estate. Mr. Anderson's house was of comfortable size which meant that not all the invited guests to the wedding were welcomed to the reception. Rose did not care to celebrate with people she did not know, but agreed to a long list of guests at their wedding as an affair of society, a tradition that Charles was endeared by, although not her.

We arrived at Mr. Anderson's quaint place. The front entrance led to a music room about twice the size of my flat and the joint room was a whimsical library filled with, I imagined, music compositions of an astounding number.

I followed Charles and Rose's footsteps into the back gardens, and suddenly, the memory came. I had not asked for it, but it did. When Charles ducked his head underneath the garland that had been hung at the back entryway, I remembered the way that Victor had done the same; leaving our bunker, we entered the trench and walked through the mud, our trousers and caps already dampened by the rain that had swept over the battlefield. Victor had turned towards me, his face stricken with fear, as though he already knew that he wasn't going to survive the battle, for there was nothing that I could do or say that would have warned him against what he had already decided that morning. He died for cowardice, but they didn't take into bloody account the many battles that he had fought beforehand, the men that he had saved with his own body, and the wounds that he had suffered from such cases, to which he had then been forced to return after a quick recovery at hospital. Victor deserved his medals, his dignity, his family pride, and his wedding; he should have been wed to Lindsay in a similar wedding celebration to this one.

"There they are!" A similar phrase that had once been uttered by my commander and made me jilt back a little, only to find that it was Mr. Anderson himself, wearing an exuberant smile, to greet the bride and her groom as they walked into the gardens and greeted their guests, which included the Atwoods, the Carnegies, and an array of friends from university.

There she stood, Mr. Anderson's piano, one of two pianos that he owned. I had wondered if he had hired a crew to transfer the Steinway to sit at the centre of the gardens for just the wedding reception itself.

The dashing couple greeted Mr. Anderson, exclaiming how very kind it was to offer his home, gratitude that had been offered many a time already. Mr. Anderson came and shook my hand, asking me how things were turning out.

"I think it a wonderful thing that you are continuing with your music, beyond just writing, of course."

"I am aware that not many are given the opportunity," I replied, completely surprised by the new door that had been opened to me.

"So, when do you start performing at the infamous Café Royal?" he asked.

"Next week. I'll be playing at the dining hall in the evenings."

"The finest jewel of London's dining rooms, a wonderful opportunity."

"Yes, I must admit that the prospect of playing in a room where Oscar Wilde dined so often is an invigorating thought."

I took a sip from the drink that he had offered.

"Does it pay well?" his smile could be seen just beneath his moustache.

I was startled by the question.

"Surprisingly well. What's more is they have offered a room for me to stay in."

"Good, good. It is heart-warming to see that your talent isn't being wasted with only your own ears to hear for." He patted me on the shoulder and beckoned for me to take a seat at the piano.

I had agreed that I would play for the evening, to which I was glad I had agreed for it sickened me to do anything else while the reception took place. Rose's smile was enough, but to distract the reason for that smile, the music brought about a peace to my throat.

My fingers painted the portrait that stood in Queen's Hall, the melody returning instantaneously. Laughter split the air as the guests continued to converse, congratulate, and eat various delectable dishes that had been displayed rather wonderfully by Mr. Anderson's cook. All I could do was play.

After a while, Allen placed a glass of champagne on the piano's breast and remarked that the music was splendid; Charlotte then echoed how charming it all was and hinted that she hoped to have a celebration of her own someday, both Allen and I knowing that she hoped Allen would ask her sooner, rather than later. She was growing impatient, even though they had just starting taking to one another since only last summer.

An applause arose to the surface as Mr. Anderson gave a speech of some remark, welcoming all of his guests to his home, and reminding us all of how music, the greatest gift to us all, could bring two people together like nothing else. It was a moving speech, and I would have better received it had the address not been given to Charles and Rose.

"Now, it does me a great honour to see many of my students here tonight, both old and new, one of whom has graced us with some of the finest classical compositions of the 18th century."

He winked at me and the crowd drew another applause. "Without further ado, I believe Lloyd has something for the happy couple."

Rose and Charles looked at one another, surprised by the latter of Mr. Anderson's speech. I unbuttoned my suit jacket and cleared my throat. Taking the glass of champagne that Allen had placed at my side, I picked it up and began the short speech that I had not prepared whatsoever.

"I am not one who gives speeches often, which could be said of any musician. We would rather hide behind our music than address a crowd, so it is rather abrasive of Mr. Anderson to expect one of his students to deliver such a speech, following such a fine one as his own."

There was laughter from the crowd which eased the tension that stood between me and their expectant smiles. "All the same, I have chosen, once again, my music over a speech. To be performed, for the very first time, in front of you all, in honour of Charles and Cherry, I present a sonata called *An Irish Rose + Her Musician*."

Rose's eyes met with mine as it felt as though a sword had been pierced through my own words. The heaviness in our gaze lifted and I looked away, turning my attention to the rest of the crowd.

"But, first, I propose a toast, to Charles and Cherry, may your own music continue to leave its mark on this world as you enter this new chapter of marriage."

"Bravo!" Charlotte remarked and several others responded with great spirits.

When I said the words, I watched as Rose's chest took a deep breath in the same way when I had first performed at the music hall at Oxford. Her eyes locked with mine in a language that cannot be explained and her lips searched for the right response that we knew she would not be able to give.

She then looked at Charles and he gave her a kiss, pleased by my speech and my gift to them both.

For the past couple of months, ever since I had realised that the wedding was indeed to take place, I had begun to write the piece, transferring everything that Rose had become to me in the past year. She hadn't realised how much hope she had given me, for I do not know if I truly would have accepted the offer to become the Café Royal's main pianist if it had not been for her insistence.

I took to the piano bench and began to allow the words to take shape through two movements. The first was rather sullen, more similar to Beethoven's Moonlight Sonata than anything else, but then, as I evoked the emotions of the Irish Rose upon meeting her musician, the music crescendoed into an upbeat manner, for I blended the dynamics in a way that reminded me of the Irish folk tunes. It is difficult to capture such a sound on the piano, but after several nights of lost sleep, in the process of writing this sonata, I felt that I had found it.

When I glanced up and watched as Rose's eyes lit up and danced with the music, I knew that all of the time spent working on this piece was worth it. While it wasn't the first sonata that I had written, it was my very first that I had played in front of people, let alone an entire crowd of people.

As the last note ended with a resounding G allegro, Rose, with tears in her eyes, came over and planted a kiss on my cheek while Charles shook my hand and thanked me for the only gift that they could have ever asked for. All of us were about to begin a new life in London. I had already made the decision that I would rarely call on them, and perhaps, had it not been for Allen's persistency, I don't know if I would have agreed to the many dinner parties that were to come. For now, I did my best to smile and enjoy the evening, reminding myself how perfect of an Irish Rose she really was; one who had entrusted me with the truth behind her story, her smile, and more so, her own music.

Part 2

Spring 1924

JENNIFER MALECH

Chapter 11
The Heartbeat of Thames

I was in my hotel room adjusting my bow tie, a task that had become a part of my regular routine every evening. I didn't take one night off, for I didn't fancy it, and besides, I had the mornings all to myself to take rest. Even so, Mr. Abbey, the hotel manager, had insisted I at least take Sunday evenings for myself, perhaps take a nice girl out for cocktails he suggested, to which I told him that there were mornings for that. He simply responded that all the young girls nowadays weren't too eager for small talk and tea. They preferred the night life, most of them anyways; and, it was true.

Most of our guests in the evenings, especially as of late, had been one of an older crowd as the jazz nightclubs were quickly drawing almost the entirety of the younger generation; however, I rather didn't mind it, for the older generation was always so receptive to whatever I played. I stuck to the classics, sometimes wondering if I should play any of my original music, but at the end of the night, I somehow always decided against it.

There was then a knock at my door. I quickly finished adjusting my bow tie before receiving the caller on the other end of the door. Upon answering it, I was surprisingly pleased by the familiar face. Allen stood at the doorstep, dressed quite smart. He had taken a job as a bank teller at the Bank of England and was living with his aristocratic parents in St. James. Though he didn't necessarily need the job, he said he wanted to learn everything there was to know about banking in hopes to be of additional help to his agent for his future estate one day. Allen's eyes were both on Charlotte and Chatsmoore now.

When I had first accepted the job at the hotel, Allen realised that he'd rather move back in with his parents, for they had a large enough place, and there was no point to him living elsewhere if his own work was only a few blocks away from St. James; his class standing reminding me once again why Charlotte would have never been a greater interest of mine, no matter what Charles said on the side to convince me otherwise. They, Charlotte, Allen, and Charles, didn't understand us in the ways that Rose and I understood one another for we were a class so different from the one I entertained every night. Yet, now, I had to remind myself that Rose in some way belonged to them. It was a difficult acceptance and I knew it to be rather unfair to those of us who would never belong to an upper class society.

"Lloyd, I had begun to wonder if you had gone off on all of us," Allen laughed.

"I've been rather busy here at the hotel," I stated.

"Too busy to pay a visit to your old friends?" he asked.

"I don't have time for dinner parties," I responded steadily.

He tapped his foot and glanced about the hotel room, large enough for any single gentleman living in London. While the drapes were older and the Victorian paintings not to my taste, it was a decent place. I could not complain, for the room was entirely free of charge.

"You have a nice place here, Lloyd. No wonder you haven't come to see us," he smiled.

Since Rose and Charles' wedding, I hadn't bothered to get together with anyone from university. I had made one visit to Oxford to visit Ted, but that was it. Charlotte and Rose were both right: I had chosen my music instead. "How did you find me here?" I asked.

"Well, Lloyd, it's no secret that you're working here. All one has to do is ask the concierge where you are located." "Isn't that a violation of privacy?"

"Told him I was your entourage for the evening," he grinned.

"Well, I don't need one."

"When you are famous, you will."

"That day won't..."

"Look, Lloyd, if you believed in your music as half as much as   Charles believed in his talents, you'd find yourself touring with the London Symphony come autumn." He was serious in his interruption.

"I want to compose, not play, you already know that," I replied.

"Did you not receive my invitation to dine with my family next weekend?" Allen asked, changing the subject.

"No. Did you send it here to the hotel?"

"Yes, I must have mis-addressed it."

"Why the special occasion?" I asked.

"You haven't heard? No, of course not. You've been rather a recluse lately."

"Well?"

"Charlotte and I are to be married."

I was not surprised by the news; I was only surprised that he wanted me there at their engagement dinner.

"Oh, well, congratulations," I shook his hand, my face not changed by the news.

"Charlotte and I would both like it if you could be there."

"I supposed you are going to ask for me to play for the evening?"

"No, never that, but if you would like, we won't stop you. I know you prefer playing the piano over conversation."

"Then, yes, I'll accept."

"The invitation to dinner?"

"The invitation to play at your engagement dinner," I remarked.

He stood there, shook his head, and laughed.

"It is no wonder Cherry calls you impossible."

"Does she still associate my name with the word? I'm surprised she talks about me at all."

He turned and looked at me, evaluating the lines on my face, trying to determine whether or not he would say what he was wanting to say.

"Lloyd, I say this as your friend, and don't take it the wrong way, but you must let go of her."

I had been gathering pieces of music that were scattered about my table. Nothing had changed; my messiness, my inability to organise my thoughts together, and my lack for joy when her name was mentioned. Yet, now, Allen's words stilted me.

"I know that's why you don't come around anymore. Refusing to join us at the nightclubs, that I understand, but refusing invitations to cricket, hunting, and whatever else has been sent your way is beyond me. You couldn't make it any more obvious. Cherry has married Charles, and you must get on with your life."

"I have, I am. Is it not obvious? Must I shout it in the streets or request the king to make a public announcement about such?" I had raised my voice and spread my hands to showcase the hotel room, indicating that the very thing that I was doing was getting on with my life.

"Not by shutting out your friends, that won't get you anywhere."

"I visited Oxford last weekend," I replied.

"Who is there in Oxford that we still know?"

"Ted."

He looked blankly at me. "Ted? Ted, don't know how to tie my own shoes, Ted?"

"Allen, he's… ahh, forget it." I was irritated and grabbed my dinner jacket. "I really must make my way to the dining hall now."

"I will see you there, then. Charlotte and I have reservations for eight. We are meeting Charles and Cherry for dinner. I thought I would come tell you before everyone arrives."

At first, I thought he was kidding, but then realised that he wasn't. He sadly smiled; we both knew that it was going to be a difficult night for me. The woman I loved, the one who had redeemed a part of me that the war had stolen, would never be mine. She had written me, I failed to mention that to Allen, for I knew it would only justify his cause. Rose had asked me to dine with them several times, to which I replied that I never had a night off.

I knew this had to be Rose's doing, coming to the hotel for dinner that is, for she longed to see me as much as I longed to see her. And, now, there was no way around it. For Mr. Abbey's sake and every hotel guest that was to walk through our doors that evening, I would have to do my best to put on a smile and act as though everything was right in the world.   What a daunting task. It was strange, for in that moment I wished that Lindsay was here; she would, in her own way, know exactly what to say.

I took my seat at the piano stool just past seven. The ticking of the clock on the adjacent wall stared at me reminding me of the way my watch used to tick so loudly before a commenced battle at war. It had only been three months since I had seen Rose, but it had felt like an eternity. I still hadn't decided if I would leave the piano stool to go say hello once they arrived. With each minute that passed by, my palms became incredibly sweaty. Supposed Allen had lied? No, he was too straightforward for that.

Mr. Abbey greeted his guests as they walked into the dining hall. The chandeliers lit the white linen tables with an effect that made one truly feel that they were floating amongst the stars. As usual, the guests were of an older audience with a few tables of my age that I imagined had all come from St. James. Centrally located in Westminster, St. James square was home to some of Britain's finest aristocrats. I knew that Allen's family had a home that dated back to the 17th century there, belonging first to his great grandfather's father, although I imagined it not to be as wondrous as Charlotte's family estate in York.

I glanced away from the guests and continued to allow the music to erupt from within. As the notes crescendoed off the guests vermicelli soufflés and watercress salads, my daydream took me to the first time that Rose and I had played together. We had all been seated in Charles and my flat, at the time, conversing about our upcoming concert, when Rose had suddenly stood up and beckoned for us not to talk about it anymore.

"Lloyd, do you have anything that we could play? Something that isn't one of Mr. Anderson's compositions," she pleaded.

"Nothing that's finished," I stated.

"Well, perhaps, I can help you finish it, then? Don't they say that an artist paints best with friends?"

"Don't be ridiculous, I've never heard such a thing, and I really, well, you see, I just haven't..." I had stumbled with my words before she quickly interrupted me with that sensational grin about her face.

"How do you expect to have an entire orchestra one day play your music if you can't even allow some of your closest friends a taste of it in the beginning stages?" Her eyes had smiled, by golly did they smile.

"Alright."

She had me convinced. As soon as I said alright, she grabbed her violin and danced over to where I sat at the piano. Within minutes, we were playing the piece that I had called *The Heartbeat of Thames*. I had named it after River Thames, the river that flows through most of Southern England, right past Oxford and all the way to London. The memory lifted as my conscious returned to the dining hall.

However, I continued to think about the composition as I filled the room with a suite by Bach. No matter where life led people, in the interchanging winds and seasons of it all, the river's heartbeat remained the same, unchanged, vigorous, and hopeful for each city that it intersected, something that I very much envied. Crikey, I envied that very hope that people were somehow able to find.

During my time at Oxford, even though I could not see the flowing river in London, I knew that it was there, that the vibrant waters flowed in places that I had never been or would ever see in my lifetime. In a way, that is what Rose was to me. She was like a river that flowed into my thoughts, just like tonight, touching places that I had never been nor thought I would ever see or feel again.

Lifting my gaze from the sheet music to the dining hall, my heart seemed to come to a standstill. Crikey. Allen was right. They really had all come to dinner at the hotel.

I was glad to see her, but at the same time, I was not. Rose was dressed in the same red dress that she had worn on the first night I had met her. Her hair was dazzled in jewels and feathers, a white headband that fit her red locks like any jewelled crown.

My fingers were no longer sweaty, but my heart was beating through my chest. The staccato in my fingers resembled the rain that pattered outside. My heartbeat, like a staccato in and of itself, did its best to return to the calmness that I had felt for the past several weeks since taking the job. There had been nothing here to remind me of Rose, and now, here she was, dining at the hotel, dining in a room that would now bear her memory forever. Crikey, I wanted to ask Mr. Abbey for a glass of something, anything, to drink.

I didn't leave my piano stool until just after ten. They had stayed; the entire time, they had stayed. Of course, I shouldn't have expected anything less for three of them were musicians. By all means, they were some of the last people in the room that night; they were surrounded by empty tables like they were the last ones aboard the Titanic.

As I neared the table, Charles was the first to stand up. He walked a few feet to meet me before I found my way to the table.

"Lloyd, this hotel thing really has worked out. You look dapper!"

"It's good to see you, Charles."

It's all I could say. Allen and Charlotte smiled at me while Rose's spunkiness tore down any walls that I, and perhaps, Charles, had tried to build up over the past few months. She made me forget things that I thought I could never forget. She made war and terror seem as though they had never existed, and while I was aware that this was an exaggerated claim to be attributed to a woman who was by no means more than just a friend, I truly felt such claims to be accurate in that moment.

"Lloyd, you finally finished *The Heartbeat of Thames*." She smiled that cheerful smile of hers. The chandelier light reflected the sparkles of her dress, which made it seem as though there was a tint of fire in her blue eyes.

"Yes, thanks to you," I smiled. And, it was genuine.

Before I had finished my set for the night, something had aroused within me to play the piece; I had never played it in public before and it felt good to allow the notes to transcend beyond the black and white printed sheet music. It was the first time that I had played my own music in the dining hall and it was all thanks to her, to the Irish rose that could make me do anything really.

"Would you care to take a drink with us?" Allen asked.

There was an extra seat beside him and I accepted. The dining room was almost empty. Music no longer filled the silence, and the evening rain could be heard from inside.

"They will be closing the dining hall soon," I stated.

"So soon?" Charlotte asked with disdain in her reply.

"It is the middle of the week, not everyone is as lively as you," I grinned.

"I take it most of the hotel guests have already gone to bed, such a shame," Charlotte stated.

"Did you all find the food agreeable?" I asked.

"Of the utmost. It is no wonder you haven't left these walls," Charlotte replied.

"I've told you, I've been rather busy, just as you all have been."

"Did I tell you we are now living at Belgrave Square, old chap?" Charles asked.

"No, Cherry failed to mention that in her last letters." I emphasised that the statement was a plural one, for even though I knew it futile, I hoped he knew that his wife still wrote me. I avoided Allen's judgmental glance.

There would be nothing that could disintegrate my friendship with Rose. The look that crossed his face made me realise that he hadn't known, which meant he had made no effort to ask if I would like to dine with them both. That was all Rose's doing.

"Yes, it's a charming place." They were the first words out of Rose's mouth since I had sat down with them. She paused and looked at her husband. "It's a little too extravagant for my taste, but Charles insisted that we stay at Belgrave for at least a year. I'm giving it a chance."

I would have never given her the chance, for I would have given her what she wanted in the first place. I slightly wondered if she did enjoy it, or if she dreaded coming home to such a large home.

"What about your London flat?" I asked her.

"We couldn't have lived in that place forever, old chap," Charles laughed.

Charles explained that his parents had gifted them with one of the homes at Sefton when they had returned from their honeymoon. Charles had been well pleased, for it met his taste; apparently, it was far more comfortable than the small place that Rose had been residing at since last autumn.

"Allen told us that you agreed to play at our engagement party," Charlotte then stated. "I am well pleased by such news."

"I still have to talk to Mr. Abbey about it. He might not give me the night off."

"Of course he will! You never get a break, it seems," Allen replied.

As we conversed, I caught Rose staring at me. I could feel the slight pain on my lips for my heartbeat was irregular, that I was certain.

"Rose." I closed my eyes. "Crikey, a Rose wine sounds good."

Rose took a deep breath. I can't believe that I had come so close to giving her secret away; however, Rose was quick on her feet, so if I had not redeemed myself, I am sure she would have done so.

"I thought you don't like Rose wines," Charles queried me with a confused brow.

"A few months at the Café Royal and your taste buds will change." I did my best to smile.

"Perhaps, your political beliefs as well," Charles laughed.

"Never that," I smiled and finished off the first drink that a waiter had brought when I first sat down with all of them. I had always denied being a socialist, yet Charles knew otherwise, despite my rubbish of claims against the party.

"Will you play that piece at our engagement dinner?" Charlotte asked.

"Yes, the river one," Allen stated.

"*The Heartbeat of Thames*," Rose firmly corrected him.

"Of course. I am your piano player, whatever you wish," I replied.

What else could I do but smile in their company, drinking a rose wine that I absolutely detested.

I arrived at the Townshend's terrace, the lace curtains illuminating the shadows of guests that were already conversing and taking pleasure in one another's company for quite some time. It was just past eight in the evening. I loosened the bow tie around my neck and held onto the sheet music in my left hand. Crikey, it was going to be a long evening.

The front door was unlocked and I opened it with ease. The chatter was music in and of itself, although not pleasant. Before anyone else was there to greet me, a tall, slender woman with more pearls than I had ever seen in one place greeted me with kisses on the cheek. Allen was right at her feet, which made me realise that this enthusiastic woman was indeed Allen's mum. She was French and even though she had moved to Great Britain when she was in her teenage years, she radiated *la vie de France.*

"Lloyd, Maman was persistent that you had bailed on the occasion." Allen greeted me with a handshake.

"*C'est vrai.*" She touched Allen's cheek in a mothering way, and made her way past the grand hall towards a room that must have emerged from the Italian Renaissance.

"Mother is still French in many ways," Allen commented.

"I didn't know you spoke French," I replied.

"*Oui, monsieur,*" he laughed.

He then reached his hand out, beckoning for me to follow him into the music room where I had been greeted by endless laughter, like a record player that was unable to reproduce any other song.

Green velvet curtains hung midway over mirrored portraits as gold embellishments painted their way across all four walls. The ceiling itself was extravagant; although not as spectacular as Queen's Hall, it was well designed. A fireplace, although not lit, centred at the south wing of the room, while another mirror, double in size to the ones of the west wing, illuminated the bobbling heads that danced and conversed about the room. My feet brushed the marble floors, reminiscent of my time at the Chatsmoore Estate.

"Your parents have an exquisite house," I proclaimed. "She's father's pride," he smiled. "Of course, second to Maman."

Near the south end of the room, next to the inoperative fireplace, I spotted my date for the evening. A beautiful Steinway, quite similar to my own.

"Will she do?" Allen asked.

I smiled and he returned the smile, especially so as his wife to be joined us around the piano.

"You are so good to come." Charlotte's brown eyes softened.

"I'd be playing anyways tonight. Might as well play in the company of friends." I was half joking.

Although I did consider the two of them my friends, I was not fond of social parties like this one. I think I rather preferred fogey gentlemen picking at their pies than pot belly gentlemen engaged in political conversation far more dull than an evening spent at parliament.

I thanked them for their hospitality and took a seat at the piano stool. Within minutes, I filled the music room with Charlotte and Allen's request, *The Heartbeat of Thames*. As though the music itself emerged herself from the crowd, like a dog rose that had blossomed overnight, there she was, dressed in a dashing navy blue dress, the valiant Rose.

"Do you need a violin accompanist?" She greeted me with a smile as I continued to play the piece. We had barely spoken during our last encounter, and now, even with my conflicted feelings, I was glad to see her.

She leaned against the soundboard and stood there, transfixed by my rough fingertips, a roughness that had emerged from the war. They had never gone back to how they had once been, nor would they ever.

After finishing the piece, a quiet applause filled the room.

"Who are all these people?" I asked quietly.

"Friends of the Carnegies and the Townshends. I must admit I don't know anyone apart from the Carnegies. I was glad to see you when you walked into the room."

"And I, you. Your dress is stunning." I wasn't one who gave compliments often and even stumbled with the words.

"Thank you. Charles bought it for me when we were in Paris on our honeymoon."

"He has good taste." I looked away and cleared my throat. "Where is Charles?"

"He is performing with the American trio," she stated.

"He couldn't pay his congratulations to his friends? For certain, this seems like a social affair that Charles couldn't afford to miss." I did my best not to laugh, yet she caught my smile anyways.

"Lloyd, you always said he would go far with his trumpet and right now is a crucial time for his career. They are touring all through Southern England and by the end of it, he might be offered, well, we might be offered, a ticket to America."

"To America?"

"Yes, it's rather exciting, isn't it?"

"What about your home in Belgrave Square? Your family? Your friends? Isn't this where you belong?"

"I don't believe I belong in one place, Lloyd. I believe I could make anyplace my home. It's rather an exciting prospect."

I was silent until she asked me once again.

"Would you like a violin accompanist? I brought my violin tonight, hoping you would not object if you made your appearance. No one said you would come, but I did. I had faith in you, Lloyd Fox. I will always have faith in you, no matter what they say."

She didn't even wait for me to answer, but left the room, the last of her words still ringing in my head. For some reason, she made me have faith in myself, too.

My fingers digested her words as they danced across the ivories, my heart trying everything to disconnect itself from her world. Yet, I knew not how. I knew it would be awhile until I would be able to for when she returned, the layers of her blue dress sweeping beneath the piano, like the low tide waves coming in at dusk, I was stricken once again by her mystery that allured people everywhere to know more about the world from which she came.

She didn't say anything, but only begun to play, her fingers gracing the strings of the violin like a mother who gently touches her child's face to display deep affection. As though it was the first time I had ever heard such music erupt the air, I watched as her eyes fluttered and her body's movements became intertwined with the ascending notes. Every other body in that room disappeared as the waves of her dress made my fingers float in perfect harmony with her own fingers. It seemed that there was no one else in the room as she stood there and played alongside me. If this is what happiness felt like, than I hoped it would never leave.

The strands of her red hair fell about her face like a perfect waterfall as her eyelashes seemed like birds fluttering about the top of the waters. She was perfect, crikey, she was wonderful. I didn't have words to describe her or her music. I wouldn't mind attending the social affairs of society if I was able to sit and hear her play all night. After a few minutes, she finally opened her eyes and smiled at me, my thoughts being transmitted deep beyond her gaze. Rose was absolutely irreplaceable.

Chapter 12
Charles and the American Trio

The sensation that had come with my last visit to
London's jazz nightclub had been one that I could not
deny. No matter where the music would lead, I would
always prefer reading from a musical score over unique
improvisation that sometimes didn't even sound like
music at all. However, there was something about the
music that was so different that would make anyone
appreciate its intentions, although I was still firm in my
opinion of its overall place in society. After I had played
with Rose all through the night at Charlotte and Allen's
engagement dinner, I had agreed that I would come to
one of Charles performances and meet her for cocktails
one evening. She knew that I wasn't coming to see him
play as much as I had accepted because I longed to spend
time with her. I had missed her.

When I arrived at the building, a gentleman led me to
the backroom of which I had become familiar with from
my last two visits. Even in the dim light, her figure was
immediately recognisable. Naturally, it was that flaming
hair that drew me towards her.

Charles stood beside her. His posture made him
appear more lean and tall than he was.

"So, you really are still playing with the American Trio. I

thought Cherry was covering for you." I grinned as I greeted the man who I both despised and admired at the same time.

"Had you thought I joined the Communist Party?" he laughed.

"Oh, yes. Something of the sorts," I replied.

"Oh, that's my cue. Must return to the stage now before our guests are disappointed," Charles leaned back and took one last sip of whatever he was drinking. He then smiled and gave Rose a kiss before announcing that he had to return to the band.

"Keep your eye on her, old chap."

Charles winked and returned to the stage.

As soon as he did and the syncopations filled the air, I turned towards Rose and shook my head.

"What have you done to your hair?" I raised my voice above the music.

"Do you not like it?" Rose amazed me with her confidence and ability to change with the times, yet remain herself entirely. She would have sported such a look before the war, I'm certain.

"They call it the Castle Bob."

"I thought you weren't one to join the trend," I smiled.

"No, but it's rather more fitting for dancing. Besides, I admire Irene Castle, the one who pioneered the way for women to break away from those awful Victorian and Edwardian style haircuts."

"It suits you well," I smiled.

"Charles isn't as fond of it. I went to the barber without his knowing."

"Of course you did." I couldn't help but smile at her independence that had not been robbed by marriage.

"He was furious at first, even went so far as to say that we would never be invited by Queen Mary to any court function or royal ceremony."

"Has he ever been invited to the palace?" I laughed.

"No, he was only talking rubbish. However, his sister had been presented before the court when she made an appearance at her debutante ball. That was, of course, before the war."

I remembered such. His sister had received the monarch blessing just three years before Charles' family had given up their mansion in Manchester and moved to Oxford. It was shortly after Mr. Atwood had accepted the position at the university. It was a change for their family, not often made by those in their class, but then again, they had lost their estate, though not many knew that fact; I doubted even Rose knew.

"We all know that if you were offered the choice, you would have refused the whole ludicrousness of it all," I grinned.

"While I would never be found in such a setting, I think it's rather admirable. Don't you find it fascinating?"

"Find what fascinating?"

"The London social season. It's rather a peculiar part of aristocratic society that I don't think I'll ever come to understand."

"That is something I have to agree with you on."

She then laughed. "To earn the monarch's blessing for marriage, can you imagine if I had to do the same?"

"Would you not earn it?" I grinned.

"I probably would be adorned in too many feathers and would be summoned out of the building." She laughed and continued, "Charlotte came into season, you know. It happened shortly after we met. Of course, at the time, I was enchanted by the whole affair. Picking your own potatoes and taking care of the chickens and cows was certainly not as exciting as scrolling through the catalogue of dresses that Charlotte had been given. I voiced that it was silly, even though it was more exciting than my ordinary life. Charlotte was quick to protest the importance of the occasion so I made sure never to offend her again on the matter."

"For the best," I smiled. "Have you ever met Charles' sister?"

"Gabrielle? Oh, yes. We travelled to Italy shortly after our trip to Paris."

"Yes, she was always ambitious. I am glad she has made a life for herself in Italy. She always liked the country as a girl."

"She's to be married in the autumn. We met him, Leonardo, a very nice fellow. Charles approved, and you know how hard it is to seek his approval."

"Then, I am glad for her," I commented. "Lindsay and Gabrielle were good friends, you know?"

"No, I did not know," she stated.

I remained silent and turned my gaze towards the stage where the grins on those African American faces were as large as the room itself. They were the kind of gentlemen that I feel could become friends with anyone; it made me want to know more about their stories.

"We will go to the wedding, of course. I rather liked Italy," she said.

"I haven't been there since the war." I was short with my reply.

"You fought in Italy?"

"No, the Austrians mainly fought there. A few commanders and I went on leave to Rome once."

"It is a charming city, although I preferred Paris," she smiled.

"Marriage life has been treating you well. You have been rather busy. Thus, I need not be blamed for refusing your invitations to dinner." I took a sip from the warm drink in hand.

"Lloyd, you make is sound as though we have been travelling the countryside every weekend. Such is not the case and you know, it can get so lonesome in that large house sometimes. I had hoped you would come. I thought you would, but you didn't."

"So, you came to the hotel instead?"

"Yes, I miss you."

I wish she hadn't said so, although it was good to hear her say it.

"Do you enjoy playing at the hotel?" she asked.

"Yes," I smiled. "I told you the future has limitless possibilities."

"That it does. For us all, really." She paused, "Did Charles tell you that their band appeared in the Melody Maker?"

"The music newspaper?" I asked.

"Yes. Charles had an interview with some journalist a couple weeks ago. I believe it's going to open a new door for jazz throughout all of Great Britain." She seemed well pleased by the idea.

"Will you still go to America?" I asked sullenly.

"Perhaps. Although with the rise of American jazz artists, there is a great appeal for it here in England. I know I said I would love to travel to America, and the idea still allures me, but I would prefer to stay here for at least a few more years. Charles said there were even rumours that representatives from the British Broadcasting Corporation were interested in the American Trio. That would surely open up a new door here, that is if the article in the Melody Maker has not already done so."

"What a prospect. They will make a name for themselves," I replied.

"Charles believes so. It has made it all the more real, the

fact that this truly will be Charles' career. It is no longer a hobby."

"And, you were the one who pushed him to get there," I smiled.

"Yes, I know talent when I see it. That's why I could not stay away from the Café Royal for long," she grinned.

"What about your music? You can't let Charles overshadow your abilities, you are too genius for that."

"I teach my students and that brings me great happiness, more than any recognition on stage will ever do."

I shook my head. "You belong on the stage, just as we all do. We are musicians, Rose."

She took a deep breath and gazed at her husband as he improvised the trumpet's notes into mid-air.

"Then, let us agree on one thing."

"Hmm?"

"We are both too genius to allow Charles to overshadow our art. Let's agree not to let it be so. I'll play if you never give up on composition."

She reached out her hand and I shook it to which we both broke out into the largest of smiles before making our way to the dance floor. Perhaps, this is how life would always be, and I would have to be okay with it.

It was another night at the hotel, more lively than previous nights, and I was comforted by the thought that people truly did enjoy the music that I played. As I entered the hotel lobby, moving my way towards the dining hall, Mr. Abbey approached me.

"Lloyd, I failed to mention that you will be sharing the stage tonight."

"Oh?"

"Yes, you will only have to play for the first couple hours."

"Does this mean I'm to receive a pay deduction?" I asked earnestly.

"No, not yet. It depends on the outcome of tonight."

"Well, who is this band that is supposed to replace me?" I refrained from rough laughter.

"Lloyd, you will not be replaced."

The gentleman was skittish and emphasised with his hands that I was still his pianist. He seemed nervous, his short stature overwhelmed by me standing there. I had never seen him act in such a peculiar manner, for he was always so quiet.

"Well?" I asked him once again.

"After careful consideration, I agreed."

"Agreed on what?" I was growing impatient.

"Showcasing a new band here at the hotel, up and coming, really. One of the band members has dined here quite a few times, so I felt that it would be a good draw for the hotel overall. A good business investment, don't you think?"

It seemed as though he was trying to justify his decision to me. If he wasn't going to tell me now, well, I would find out within the next couple of hours. He stood there, his hands folded in front of him, and moistened his lips, but nothing came forth.

"I am going to go entertain our guests with music now, Mr. Abbey," I smiled, although not politely.

My patience had run out, so I exasperatedly made my way to the stage. It was six o'clock now, which meant the follow up band was to arrive around eight that evening.

The two hours passed rather quickly. I gazed about the room, watching as guests indulged in overly priced cocktails, attracted to the chandelier lights like moths that had nowhere else to go. As my gaze continued about the room, I became stricken with surprise when I watched Rose walk into the room, adorned in a slenderizing black dress, her headpiece matching the white pearls that dangled from her neck. It was the middle of the week, so I was surprised to see her at the hotel. A waiter led her to her seat and offered her some champagne to which, of course, she didn't accept. She was always graceful in her reply and I still forgot that she didn't drink at all. I thought that being married to Charles would change such, but it did not.

Then, it occurred to me. *Charles and The American Trio.* Crikey, of course. How could I not have realised it when Mr. Abbey became feverish at the prospect of having to tell me that my dear fellow was to outshine me in his pride of a dining hall. Charles was bloody brave to do such a thing.

I controlled my thoughts and continued to play when I spotted the arrival of their eager faces, the threesome entirely unaware what position Charles had put me in. This hotel and this platform was the one thing that had been mine and now, he wanted to take that away as well.

Before I knew it, I could see him moving in his things to my hotel room, claiming that was his as well. I knew that I was taking things to an extreme, but it reminded me of the days before the war, of the root as to why I could never trust him again. If it had not been for the war and what he had done for Victor in the end, than I am certain that we would have never been friends again.

When I finished playing the last piano note for my allotted time, I didn't even bother to look at Charles and certainly took no detour to go and greet his beloved wife. I simply grabbed my music and coat, leaving the guests

behind, them completely unaware of my association with
the second act. The hotel's front doors slammed shut
behind me. There was already a chill in the air so I was
glad that I grabbed my coat, even though I had already
been dressed in a full suit for the evening.

"Lloyd!" her sweet voice entered the brisk evening air.

She was the only one I couldn't run away from when
she called my name, no matter how furious I could get. I
stopped in my tracks and turned towards where she
stood; barefoot, her heels dangled from her right hand.

"It isn't proper for a lady to be barefoot in this kind of
weather or any for that matter," I teased.

"Lloyd, you left without even saying hello or goodbye."
She sounded sincere and concerned.

I remained quiet and only looked at her, completely
aware that I longed to kiss her, and hoped that Charles
would catch the very act. I wondered if she knew that, for
she stood at arm's length.

"You must be proud of him," I stated. "Oh, yes, it takes
quite some nerve to steal your friend's stage and fame."

"He doesn't mean to, Lloyd."

"Did you know of this when we last spoke? You thought
not to mention it to me?"

"It was not my position to say anything."

"Since when have you been concerned about position?"

"Lloyd, please don't do this. Charles cares about your
career, as much as I."

"Really? If you knew him before the war, you would agree
with me," I said through gritted teeth.

"I know of what he did before the war, what harmed your
friendship. But wasn't it you who said what's done is
done and that there is no point going backwards? The life
we live is in forward motion, not backward, unless we are
living in a parallel universe of which I am entirely

unaware."

"No, you don't understand, Rose. Charles is retreating to the ways of the past, and I warn you, as your friend, that it is a very dangerous game to play. No one can have that which he envies, for such a man will do anything to take it away from you."

"Then tell me your side of the story," she pleaded.

She couldn't afford to lose my friendship, and I couldn't afford to lose hers so after taking a few minutes to allow my anger to simmer down, I told her.

"Must you really know?"

"I've heard Charles' side of the story, so wouldn't it benefit us both if you told yours?" She remained standing in the same place.

"Was he truthful?"

"I'd like to think so."

She was patient with me, and her posture straightened, indicating that she would not allow me to move forward or backward until I told my side of the story. There was no point in wasting either of our time. I got straight to the point.

"It was our second year at Oxford. We went into town to visit my Uncle William, meeting with Victor at a party near University of London. Victor had just started his first year there in the autumn. At the party, that's where Charles met Lindsay, the girl that Victor had told us all about."

"Your Lindsay?"

"Not at that moment in time, but yes." I paused.

"Continue," she urged.

"She was a rare beauty and it was no wonder that Charles was attracted to her as any other man. I am sorry, I shouldn't…"

"No, go on," she urged with wide-eyes.

"She was Victor's girl and Charles knew it, but he still had eyes for her. He got real drunk that night and rallied up a group of men to go beat up Victor. His efforts were futile, for no man or woman in either their right or sane mind could accept Charles' actions as tolerable."

"Where were you when this happened?"

"I was playing cards with some friends in another room, probably gambling money that wasn't even my own." I felt ashamed by the memories. Crikey, I was just a boy then.

"One of our friends from Oxford found Victor all bloody in an alley, only a couple blocks from the party. He wasn't even conscious, but after a bath and treatment from Uncle William's doctor, he came around in the early hours of the next morning. It was my uncle that told me not to report it for it would bring a bad name to both our families. We returned to Oxford that following week and I moved to a different dormitory hall. Charles and I didn't see one another again until later that year when we had landed ourselves in the same military training class."

My hands were in my pockets and my gaze so far from Rose's as I told the story.

"But he saved Victor's life in the war, the first time that is, before he took his own life into his hands."

"Yes, I know about the incident. Charles has a terrible scar on his stomach."

"He was lucky to survive," I replied steadily.

"What a world it would be without advanced medicine." She paused and then insisted, "Tell me more."

"Charles fought in the same regiment as Victor and I. Of course, I was still resentful towards Charles, but he took Victor under his wing, and I couldn't scold a man for such. Whether it was done from guilt or compassion, I do not know, nor do I really care to know now. We all knew

Victor wasn't cut out for the war, Charles especially. So, in a way, I was grateful that Charles was there, for none of the other men understood that. I may had not yet forgiven Charles for what he did to Victor at university, but I gave him a second chance. When Charles helped Victor and saved his life, that first time at war, I felt I owed Charles everything. It seemed that everything of the past no longer mattered. Our friendship was given a new sheet of paper, a blank one."

We could hear the whistling in the trees as I stopped talking altogether.

"Lloyd, I am sorry, but I believe Charles meant to do right in the end. Men make foolish decisions when they are under the spell of alcohol. You of all people should understand that. You can't hold onto offenses. It will destroy you."

"I am not offended anymore."

"Then, why should what's happening now matter?"

"You are right. It doesn't matter. However, I thought I had moved past it all. But his recent actions have only stirred up old wounds. That is all."

"Can't you see that this will be a good thing for jazz music and for black musicians?" She was so earnest.

"Oh, so you are turning this into a political matter now, are you?"

"What are you trying to prove? Are you trying to amount to something due to your father's belief that you would be of no asset to the family? Because from my experience, that will get you nowhere, Lloyd."

She spoke of my father as though she knew him, and now, she was the one who was re-surfacing wounds that went far beyond the physical battle scars of war.

"No, that is not what I am doing." I stumbled with my words.

"Yes, Lloyd. Yes, it is exactly that."

"You despise my music, then?"

"You and Charles are so similar, after all."

Now, I was angry.

"You think that fame will wipe away everything from your childhood, that it will give you a new life, when in fact, it will not. I, most certainly, know of this to be true." She was almost in tears.

"How so?" I was angry with her; I had never been angry with Rose before, at least not in this way.

"My father thought the very same thing."

She took a deep breath, her blue eyes more piercing than ever. After taking a couple steps toward me, she lowered her voice.

"Charles was the first man I came across that played his instrument for pleasure, rather than for money. But, now, with a sudden demand for his playing, he's begun to chase after fame instead. I do not oppose fame, Lloyd. What I oppose is when the quest for fame overrules all other things, including that which matters most of all. My father was different. He never painted for pleasure. He did not enjoy it, said such things most often. When I asked why he spent so much time painting, he replied that it would get his name known throughout all of Great Britain."

I stepped aside and allowed the fumes between us to cease.

"Did Charles tell you about my father?" I asked roughly.

"Yes, he was kind and had gentle intentions, for when I told Charles of my own father, it must have created a sense of power within himself, a power to show me that I was not alone in a world where I often felt very much so. It was comforting, really, and I am glad he did."

We both stood there in silence, her still clutching her

heels and me, my music.

I thought of my mum and father then. My mum died when Victor and I were just boys, my father not long after. He had been a man who had tried to earn power and success through gambling, a practice that I, too, had taken up before the war. He had given away everything, his land, his sheep, his prospects, everything. I was only a boy, but I knew it was a terrible thing when he had returned from business *with the gentlemen in town* as he used to always tell us, making it sound as though it was a matter of simplicity and nothing to be concerned about.

I barely saw my father after that, for he had taken to heavy drinking. My mum's brother, Uncle William, who was a middle-class solicitor living in London at the time, had taken Victor and I in as his own. Shortly afterwards, we had learned of my father's death. The most tragic part was that I had not felt grief in anyway, for how do you mourn something that had caused so much pain in your life?

"Lloyd, you may have found my words to be harsh, but I speak of them from an understanding. You see, we aren't so different after all. We are survivors, we have learned how to survive in a world that hasn't taken care of us. And, in the process, we try to become that of which are parents never were for us and yet along the way, we will find that if we are not careful, we are leading ourselves to the same destruction that they found themselves in."

I stood completely mesmerised by her wisdom.

"Do you play for pleasure or do you play for fear that you will become just like your father?"

She said the words with the sweetest composure. I looked away and ignored the lump that had found its way in my throat.

"I admit, at first, it was a little bit of both. But, not

anymore. No, I play because it is the one thing in this world that erases my childhood and every memory from the war." I added, "There is joy in the music, entirely explanatory. Like your mam told you, music will always bring light to the downtrodden."

"Then, you will succeed," she gently smiled.

"But, Charles?" I asked. "Do you fear that he is too prideful?"

"At times, but I can't make decisions for him, just as much as he can't make them for me. Hence, the hair." She twirled her finger through a loose strand and let out a giggle, slightly forced at first, but then her smile became genuine.

"Not even the king can make decisions for you," I laughed quietly.

"Please, don't be angry with Charles. Be angry with me, but not Charles."

"I could never be angry with you, not for longer than five minutes that is," I smiled.

"Come on, Lloyd. I have a dinner table for two. I would hate to sit there alone."

What else was I to say? I returned to the dining hall, ready to face the reality of my future career head on. I supposed it was slowly sinking in. I would never go on to travel the world and compose for the most sought after symphony in all of Europe. Perhaps Rose, and even Charles on occasion, had been right all along. Perhaps, I had been chasing fame and success this whole time, hoping that it would erase all of the pain and grief I had felt since Victor's death.

As we returned to our seats, and watched as Charles took to the stage with great enthusiasm, I found that the tension had remained.

Chapter 13
Oxford's Towers

Charles' band had been successful, although, they had yet to make a name for themselves. The guests at the hotel had been complimenting the music, asking for that one American band with the trumpet player. That is all they knew, and it is all they wanted. Once the elderly left the dining hall at around eight o'clock every evening, it became an entirely new atmosphere. No longer did the youth desire classical music, no longer did it seem to have its place in a post-war world. Charles had been right, although not entirely.

To spare the blow, I decided to take the weekend off, something that I hadn't done in months. I had called Ted, asking if it would be okay for me to stay with him for the weekend, for I needed some peace and quiet away from the city. He had agreed wholeheartedly and welcomed me with a peculiar enthusiasm.

It was a pleasant journey from London, although not one that I would recommend making often. Ted was now living in the countryside of Kidlington. He had taken over duties at the church, just as he had hoped. While he was no longer living at home and had his own cottage in the village, he seemed to be quite happy with the life that, as he had told me, been blessed by. I was uncertain as to what he meant by it, but didn't question his enthusiasm.

Upon my arrival, Ted insisted that he give me a small tour of the place. It was a one story cottage with a barn in the back gardens, although there were no horses to be tended to. Ted mentioned that he hoped to buy a horse soon, for he missed horse riding. For now, he walked to the church, which was only a short twenty minute walk from his charming village.

"I've only one bedroom, so I fear you will have to stay in the seating parlour," Ted commented as we entered the cottage.

"That's okay, Ted. It's comfortable and it will do. I've slept in much more atrocious places," I smiled.

"Oh, yes. I am certain you have." He shook his head and then asked if I would like tea. "I can put a kettle on the cooker?"

"Why not?" I set my hat on the tableside and took a deep breath as I sat down.

It felt good to be away from the hustle of London, the syncopations of improvised piano notes replaced by the consistent chirps of birds outside. The day was a pretty one; Ted had left the windows open, allowing the cool breeze to refresh my mind, thoughts that had been all over the place as of late. The fog that rested above the gentle hills looked like icy frosting, the feet of sheep softly strolling through the morning.

I stared out at the countryside, reflecting on the first night that *Charles and the American Trio* had made their entrance at the Café Royal. After I had agreed to return to the dining hall with Rose, we had sat there and barely talked. We listened to the music and watched as laughter and smiles filled the room with bubbling champagne.

Charles had greeted me afterwards, and even introduced me to the rest of the band, asking if I'd like to get drinks with them at a local pub afterwards. Rose had given me the lifted eyebrow, and I accepted. Within those hours, I forgot everything. For a moment, it seemed as though Charles and I were two friends at a pub before our first days at Oxford. It felt strange, but I enjoyed myself, nonetheless. Rose's voice was always in the back of my mind.

"I thought we'd take my parent's car into Oxford tomorrow afternoon." Ted placed a cup of tea on the table, leaving my thoughts to scatter elsewhere for the moment.

"To visit the old stomping grounds?" I asked puzzled.

"I'm meeting with Reverend Thomas at St. Ebbe's church. I gave Reverend Thomas my word. I hadn't realised it until after you called." He fumbled with his hands, worried that his words had upset me.

A day spent at the very church from which Rose and Charles were wed, what an idea. However, I could not show my lack of approval to Ted in anyway.

"Reverend Thomas, what a fellow! What's on the agenda then?"

"Reverend Thomas and I are meeting to discuss the epistles of St. John. Probably won't interest you, so you could wander the grounds or do as you please. Then, afterwards, we could all take to lunch in town."

"The epistles of St. John. You do sound like a vicar," I smiled.

"You mock me." He blinked and tapped his fingers on the table.

I had never heard any tone of anger in his voice before. "No, not at all. Ted, you must understand me. You could quote child's scripture and it would be very eloquent to me. I only meant that you sound as though you're coming along quite nicely. It's a compliment. If it did not sound as so, take it as one, please."

"Yes, well, very well then. So, you aren't opposed to the idea?"

"No, I'm not a child, Ted. I will find something to do while you and Reverend Thomas talk."

I was about to make another remark, but stopped before I said anything to upset him again. He was a real sensitive fellow.

"Good. Reverend Thomas will be glad to see you."

"And, God knows, I, him."

While they remained at the church, I wondered around Oxford thinking of how it had not been too long ago since Charles, Rose, Charlotte, and I had been wandering through these gardens. It is where I first learnt that Rose truly was a beautiful enigma, a mystery that I had hoped to solve. I knew I hadn't managed to do so, but in a way, I had come close. Didn't she say that we were both survivors in this world? She seemed to have our situation figured out, while I couldn't even begin to identify where it had all began.

Ted and Reverend Thomas hadn't taken as long as I had thought they would at the church. I must have only been walking for an hour or so when I spotted them coming across the lawn. After little conversation, we agreed that there was no better place for fish n' chips than the Eagle and Child. You would have thought that we would have grown tired of it, but we hadn't.

We ordered drinks and fish n' chips around the table,

sitting near the back of the pub like how we used to.
"So, Ted tells me you've made quite an occupation for
yourself." Reverend Thomas looked at me with cheerful
eyes.
"Yes, they feed me and give me a roof over my head, so
there's no complaint in that," I remarked.
"None whatsoever. You are kind to have accompanied
Ted to Oxford today."
"I'd be feeding the imaginary horses in Ted's stable had I
remained in Kidlington," I commented.
"You've still no horses?" Reverend Thomas turned his
attention towards Ted.
"Not yet. The church can't pay for one and I've not
enough saved for one. It was kind of my father to lend
me the car."
I didn't understand how Ted's parents could afford such
luxuries, crikey, especially in Kidlington.
"I am glad they are making good use of the car," he
smiled, well pleased at Ted's reply. "But, you should have
told me sooner about the horse. We'll go looking this
week."

It occurred to me that Reverend Thomas was more
than a vicar, he was the benefactor to Ted's family.
However, it seemed ridiculous to me for him to provide a
car when Ted's family could gain more use out of
livestock. Reverend Thomas seemed to be reading my
mind, the quizzical lines in my forehead trying to piece
the puzzle pieces together.
"The car makes for easier transportation, doesn't it?"
Reverend Thomas directed the question at me.
"We took the car here today. A real beauty," I
commented.
"I won it at an auction. Would you believe it?"
"Honestly, not at all." I tried not to laugh.

"It's proved to be of great help to Ted's mother, although she was very opposed to the idea of it all. Ted taught her to drive the thing, what a hoot that was," he laughed.

"And, your father?" I asked Ted.

"Funny, Mum prefers to drive it," he laughed.

"Has she really gotten great use out of it?" I asked.

"Yes, Mother has been rather ambitious with selling her craftsman work to the local markets in town. She has even travelled to see my aunt and uncle," Ted replied.

"And your siblings?" I asked.

"When they aren't at school, they ride along with her, that is if Sally isn't home. They all feel like royalty, Lloyd. You should see their faces."

"Not that I don't think it a wonderful thing, but I don't understand why you didn't keep the car for yourself?" I asked Reverend Thomas.

"What good is our human existence if it is not used to better another?" Reverend Thomas smiled, the same wise smile that had crossed Rose's lips from time to time.

"I cannot argue with you there." I took a sip of the cool drink, thinking of Lindsay, especially more as of late.

Ever since Rose had mentioned attending Gabrielle's wedding in Italy, I thought of their laugh that seemed one and the same. Lindsay and Gabrielle had carried themselves across the meadow fields, like two little girls who knew no difference about the rules in society. They had been free then.

During the last dinner that I had agreed to accompany Rose at, she had made mention of how I should visit Lindsay. I couldn't understand why she was so persistent and hoped that she would soon let it go. Reverend Thomas's words rung in my mind as the grease of the fish spread across my rough hands. I had already bettered Lindsay's life. There was nothing more that I could do, no matter how adamant Rose was about such.

"Ted, we'd be wondering when you'd come around again." A kind looking man interrupted our conversation and shook Ted's hand.

"Matthew, this is Reverend Thomas and my friend, Lloyd Fox."

"Pleased to meet you." I shook his hand while Reverend Thomas asked how the gentlemen knew one another.

"We grew up together, but I moved away to Scotland a few years ago."

"Are you back now?" Ted asked.

"Yes, at least until the crow tells me to go elsewhere," he laughed. "Why don't you join us at the music hall later?"

"Lloyd, what do you think?" Ted asked.

"Nice offer, but I'd rather stay here," I replied. "You go on."

My weekend of relaxation was not going to be spent at my old stomping grounds, at the place that bore memories of Rose around every corner. I came here to get away from all of that. After a few minutes more, Ted excused himself and said he would meet me at the car at six this evening, if I didn't mind.

"Not at all. Enjoy yourself, Ted. Meet a girl, why don't you?" I laughed.

He ignored my comment and joined Matthew outside.

"Reverend Thomas, you really don't have to stay now. You've already spent more money than you bargained for."

"Oh, I don't mind."

"Reverend…"

"Call me Thomas. That's what Ted calls me anyhow. Don't worry, the clergy won't hang your neck for such."

I sat there, transfixed by his comment, wondering if it'd be okay for me to laugh.

"Take a joke, Lloyd," he laughed. I returned his sentiment.

"I didn't know Ted called you Thomas."

"Only when we spend time together one-on-one," he replied.

"Thomas, I owe you an apology. When we last met, I was not in my right state of mind. Crikey, it seems like forever ago."

"A man is allowed a foul day here and there. We are human after all. When a man is accused of the intolerable within him, he usually responds in a manner that is not always graceful." He smiled; his wrinkles were the same as I had remembered them to be.

Thomas waited for me to speak. I knew I was taking a leap when I asked him my next question, for it was somewhere out of the depth of the sea, although I knew it had to have come from when Rose and I had stood outside the hotel when I was angered by the prospect of Charles taking my place at the hotel.

"Is man on quest for something that can never be found?" I looked at the empty glass in hand.

I was almost surprised that I had asked the question, for ever since Thomas had spoken of the matter when we had first met, I had often replayed the very conversation in my head and had imagined how I would approach him on the subject if we were ever to meet again. I imagined that he had answers that I longed for, yet didn't yet know if I longed to know his answers in return. That is why I hesitated on whether or not I would ask.

"I hope I am not out of place when I ask, but are you a religious man?" Thomas asked.

"I am not," I stated.

"Well, perhaps, you can understand this example, then." He paused. "Lloyd, when I was a child, I used to run to gaze upon the towers at Oxford. I was in awe of the architecture and of the thrill that it must be to be a student walking through those halls. I made it a point in my mind that I would one day go to school there and that it would give me everything that I ever hoped for, a happiness that my life at home could not."

"Well, did it?"

"No, it did not."

I was perplexed by his story and asked what he meant by it.

"I told you that happiness cannot be found by man alone."

"Then, by what can it be found? Another man?" I asked with genuine concern.

"No, but I wonder if you are ready for my answer. If I told you, you most likely wouldn't listen to me. Perhaps one day you shall."

He was a religious man, so of course I realised that he most certainly was right. I would not listen, for his answers probably came from the same hymnals that Victor and I had played with in the church when we were boys.

Before I could stop myself, I spoke. There was something about Thomas, a trust that seemed to be buried in his breast coat pocket and passed along to any man who sat beside him.

"In all truth, the shadows of the war haunt me. It makes me wish that I had never returned. What a bloody thing to wish," I finally said.

He remained silent while I babbled on.

"My brother never returned from the war. I will never forgive myself for that."

"What was his name?"

"Victor, Victor Fox. From time to time, I wish I was him.

What a terrible thought."

"No, not terrible." He paused and then continued. "When I studied history at university, that was the worst of it. My own human mind could not understand the cyclical patterns of life. It seemed to me that war, crime, disease, and financial ruin outweighed any dose of happiness."

"I, have, at times, seen happiness and beauty, but then I wonder if all of it is not some sort of illusion. Sometimes, when I play the piano, it seems as though the music is dulling us all to sleep, to ignore the realities that exist outside this world. And, what's more is the very thing on earth that I had once thought most beautiful, has been destroyed by nature's unfortunate hand."

"Am I to guess what you speak of? Or, should I not enquire?"

So, I told him. I told him about Lindsay. He did not probe or ask any queries, but simply listened. At the end of it all, he left me with one simple question.

"Do you believe that loss of beauty equals loss of hope?"

"I don't believe I can be the determiner of such an answer."

"In due time, you shall. For now, keep composing music. Ted told me you are marvellous, more marvellous than I take it you let on."

And, with that, Thomas left the pub, leaving me with more queries than answers; I remained there until six o'clock as a familiar heavy rain had taken over Oxford.

In the end, Rose had been right. The British Broadcasting Corporation had come to the hotel the weekend that I was away in Kidlington, recording *Charles and the American Trio* for the entire countryside to hear. Within the week, they had been contacted by some royal family in Northern England who hoped that they would be the music performers for their next dinner event. Of course, they had accepted. While the Café Royal would be their main headlining place for the near future, they agreed as a group that they would definitely seize every opportunity to travel, giving me and my classical music more hours in the evenings to entertain.

Tonight was one of those nights for *Charles and the American Trio* had been requested to entertain in Manchester. I took to my station at a quarter past six and began to play an adagio movement, the graceful notes flowing with such legato that could ease any conversation in the room. I must have only been performing for an hour when one of the hotel waiters came to the stage and told me that there was a call waiting for me in the hotel lobby.

"Can you ask the caller to leave a message?" I asked, frazzled by the interruption.

"I am afraid not, sir. The caller said it was a matter of urgency," the waiter said with wide eyes.

"I suppose you will be the one to entertain us for the rest of the evening?" I asked annoyed.

"Sir?"

"I am sorry. My anger is not directed at you."

For once, I wished that *Charles and the American Trio* were here to fill the silence in the dining hall. The last thing we wanted was to lose regular guests, especially since some had been disappointed that the American jazz band and their trumpet player hadn't taken the stage for five days now.

I left the stage and followed the waiter into the hotel

lobby where the concierge directed me to the phone line.
"Lloyd, can you hear me?"
"Why, Charlotte? Whatever is the matter?"

The girl seemed entirely frazzled on the other line. I could sense the trembling in her voice, and knew immediately that something terrible had occurred.
"Cherry has been in an accident," she said through tears.
"What sort of an accident?"
"She took Charles' new beauty out for a spin and…"
"She's been in a car accident. God, is she badly hurt?" I asked, my thoughts immediately imagining the worst.
"Cherry has suffered a terrible blow. I'm here at the hospital now. Charles is in Manchester until the end of the week."
"Yes, yes I know."
"I've tried getting hold of him, but have failed to do so. I didn't know who else to call."
"Is she alive?" I took a deep breath.
"Yes, but Lloyd, I fear her life will never be the same again."
"Why would you say that?"

There was silence on the other end to which I wondered for a moment if her time had been cut short on the other line.
"The doctor thinks that Cherry has lost her sight."

I thought I had misheard her.
"Lloyd, are you there? Have I lost you?" Her voice grew fainter with each passing minute.
"Yes, I'm sorry."
"No, I am sorry to be the messenger of such dreadful news."
"What hospital are you at?"
"St. Mary's."
"I will catch the next bus."

"There's no point in that now. Cherry hasn't been conscious for hours. She is just now coming around."

"No, I've already made up my mind. Charles is practically in another country and she needs someone to be there by her side."

"Lloyd, you mustn't trouble yourself. Besides, I am here for her now. I won't leave her."

After a few moments of silence, I replied, "Alright, but I will make my way to hospital tomorrow morning."

When the clicker sounded on the other line, I placed the telephone back in its slot and stood there, my eyes closed and head bent, my hands digging into the table beside me.

There was no use in arguing with Charlotte; she was more sensible than Rose, but just as stubborn. I wouldn't have been able to get her to disagree with me even if I had made a proposal for familial peace between Charles and me.

Glancing at the clock on the wall, I realised that Mr. Abbey expected for me to play for the next couple hours. I was torn, caught in a dilemma over what to do. But, she was alive. And, she wasn't going to die from the blow. That I found comforting. Perhaps it wasn't as bad as it seemed, for I knew Charlotte to be one who could easily exaggerate matters.

Alright, I decided that I would entertain until ten and then immediately make my way over to the hospital. Besides, I wouldn't be getting much sleep tonight anyways. There was no telling where my thoughts would be.

I arrived at St. Mary's shortly after ten. Charlotte was in the lobby when I arrived. Her eyes were red and puffy from crying as she sat there clutching a handkerchief. When she saw me, she seemed as though she would start crying all over again. She immediately fled from her seat and gave me a hug.

"You didn't have to come, but how good of you to do so."

"Did you notify Allen?" I asked.

"Yes, he was here earlier, but had to leave just a short while ago. He told me to go home, but I couldn't, not yet."

My eyes drifted from the hard walls to Charlotte's soft face. I realised that I hadn't been to any kind of hospital since the war. I hated hospitals; they were so much like prison cells. St. Mary's was not that extreme, but in a way, it still gave off the same aura no matter how cheery the nurses appeared to be.

"He could have it all wrong. Doctors aren't always accurate. Our childhood doctor thought my cousin was dying of the measles, but he had misdiagnosed the symptoms. This could be the very same," she remarked with great hope in her voice.

I beckoned for her to take a seat and sat beside her, knowing all too well the similar speech that mothers would give as they visited their sons in hospital during and after the war. For always being so calm, I was surprised by Charlotte's state of shock. It made me wonder if she had known of someone else who had suffered a terrible blow in a car accident.

"Did the doctor give any update since we last talked?"

"He only told me that Cherry's skull had hit both the steering wheel and the windshield upon impact. They are letting her rest now and will do further examinations in the morning."

"Is she conscious?"

"Yes, she gained consciousness right before I called you. She couldn't see a thing, that's what the doctor said."

"May I talk to the doctor?" I asked.

"I don't see why not."

We asked the nurse at the front table if we could speak to the doctor that was tending to Cherry Atwood. She said it was too late for callers, but informed us that she would see what could be done. We returned to our seats and waited in silence. Charlotte was exhausted while I couldn't think clearly whatsoever. Then, Charlotte's posture changed as she looked beyond where I sat. I turned my head and saw a man, younger than most doctors I had come across. His posture had seen better days, but he walked with great confidence, almost like a god who could rescue any mistress lost at sea. It must have been his coat that made me think such thoughts, for his white coat pierced through the dim yellow lighting of the vast room, making one hopeful that he could be the deliverer of good news.

Charlotte and I stood up as the gentleman introduced himself to both of us as Dr. Levitt.

"I expect you hope to hear an update about Cherry?" the gentleman asked.

"Yes, and please don't spare us our feelings," I replied. "If it is the worst, we would prefer not to remain in the dark." Charlotte nodded, agreeing with me.

The doctor took a moment to take a deep breath and responded, "It might be too early to tell, but I believe that Cherry has lost her sight for good."

"So, there will be no recovery? It could just be temporary blindness." I queried the doctor as though I knew more than him.

"Again, it is too early to tell, but I am certain that Cherry is experiencing trauma to the brain."

"But, if it is the brain, how could she go blind?" Charlotte asked.

"There are many factors, but the most likely explanation is that the optic nerve was damaged upon impact. When pressure on the skull is heightened, especially in an accident like Cherry's, the pressure can cut off all blood circulation, damaging the optic nerve for—"

"Forever?" Charlotte interrupted. She had calmed herself down now and asked with poise that would have represented her class of society well.

"Well, yes. My dear, there is no other way to put it."

"There are no treatments?" I asked.

"No, none whatsoever."

"Blimey." I placed a hand over my mouth and allowed the doctor's words to penetrate my mind.

"Cherry will live a normal, healthy life," the doctor comforted us.

A life blinded from all beauty, I thought.

"I have cared for patients with vision loss before, and I must tell you that while it is not something that I would hope for even my worst enemy, I can say that my patients have learned how to live normal lives."

"I appreciate the sentiment, but it won't be as dandy as you say," I replied.

"Lloyd…" Charlotte touched my arm, indicating that it was time for me to stop speaking.

"I understand how you feel right now. But, I will tell you both this. Cherry is the first patient I have ever had that has been in an accident to such a degree and survived. Whatever your beliefs are, I believe Cherry is a miracle."

I said nothing, while Charlotte remarked that she believed that the doctor spoke the truth. Dr. Levitt then commented that he must return to the surgery room to tend to another patient and reminded us that we would know more in the morning.

"Thank you, Dr. Levitt," Charlotte softly said.

I merely nodded and said nothing more. I knew it wasn't his fault, but I was angry all the same. Hadn't there been advancements in medicine? There had been many during the war. Despite how I felt in that moment, I knew that Charles had to be contacted immediately. Charlotte said she had no way to know where he was, but I assured her that I could find out from Mr. Abbey at the hotel. I hated that I had to be the one to tell him.

As we left hospital, all I could think of was Thomas's words from when we had met at the Eagle and Child. Perhaps our conversation had been some sort of coincidence in and of itself, for his words were the only thing that brought me any sort of hope. Just as Lindsay had found new life, so would Rose. She would have no other choice.

Chapter 14
The Dissonance of Belgrave Square

It had been two weeks since Rose's accident. She had now been transferred to her home in Belgrave Square to face her new life. Now, it wouldn't matter whether or not she didn't like the colour of the lace curtains that hung in the window. For now, Charles had every right to decorate the place as he pleased. Dr. Levitt had been accurate in his first assessment of Rose's condition.

Charles had caught the first train to London after he had received my call the night of Rose's accident. I had gone in to see Rose that next morning, alongside Charlotte and Allen. When we had arrived, Rose still hadn't yet known about the state of her condition. Her entire head had been bandaged and her face, although it had been cleansed, had been clearly wounded. It was a terrible thing to witness, to sit there and hold her hand as she slept, her scarred face making me feel so hopeless. When she finally came around, she asked in a gentle voice, "Charles, is that you?"

"No, Rose, it's me," I whispered.

There was no one in the vicinity to hear my words or to question why I had called her Rose, for Charlotte and Allen had left the room for only a quick moment. She opened her eyes, and was silent. It was as though her blue eyes, in and of themselves, had not only lost their life, but had lost their bright colour.

"Am I dreaming?" she finally spoke.

"No, it's really me," I replied without a change in my voice.

"Where are we?" she asked. "It's terribly dark."

Touching her own face then, she felt the jagged lines in her cheeks and the bandages around her forehead.

"Lloyd, what's happened?" she asked steadily.

I couldn't be the one to tell her, not all of it, not yet.

"We are at a hospital. You were in a car accident."

There was a lump in my throat. Rose had already been told that very thing the previous night when she had become conscious in the presence of Charlotte, Dr. Levitt, and a few nurses.

"No, I didn't think it was real. I must still be dreaming," she stated.

Just then, Dr. Levitt had come to the bedside, a sense of relief entering my lungs. I couldn't be the one to tell her, that was a task too daunting for my own heart to make. But, I watched. I watched from afar as Dr. Levitt told Rose what had happened to her the day before. There was an understanding in her face and a quiver in her lips. She could not take silence for an answer. She asked many questions, the last being where Charles was.

"I phoned him last night. He's on this morning's first train from Manchester to London," I replied from where I stood.

There was no reply, but then it hit her. She clenched her left fist, trying to hold it all in; it was only moments later when she broke, realising that the news was not some imaginative dream in which she had been caught. Tears spilled down her cheeks as Charlotte took over any duty I had taken upon myself just an hour prior. She and

Allen had been standing next to me, giving the doctor and nurses their space.

I knew not what to say. I had seen worse on the battlefield, but this was something different.

When Charles had arrived later that afternoon, he was incredibly quiet. I believe he was in a similar state of shock as we all were, and not until he saw Rose did my phone call become tangibly real.

Shortly after, Dr. Levitt asked that we all leave the room, giving time for Cherry to rest and time for Charles to process with her what their lives were to look like now. We respected their wishes and left the hospital, all three of us incredibly quiet.

Now, two weeks after the accident, I found myself from time to time exploring those same emotions of that dreadful morning.

Charles and the American Trio hadn't performed in three weeks and our guests were becoming anxious and curious as to what had happened to the group. I could sense it, and had even been asked more than once about the matter. I admitted to our guests that there was a family emergency with one of the members to which condolences were then offered. They were always quick to add that they enjoyed my music, though. However, I could see it in their eyes. London wanted jazz music. And, I had begun to agree with them.

Rose had strictly asked for no visitors at this time, and as much as I longed to see her, I knew that it would do no good me showing up to their estate uninvited. Blimey, I wished I had accepted to dine with them all those months ago.

On this particular evening, Charlotte and Allen had invited me over for dinner at the Townshends. I admitted that it would indeed be good to get away from the hotel and had managed to get the night off.

When I arrived at their home, Mrs. Townshend greeted me with kisses, the French way that no one dare tell her was not customary to English tradition. She was real spirited, and I oddly found that I rather liked her.

I was surprised when I arrived, though I shouldn't have been, to have found a few other families dining there for the evening as well. I felt like a fish out of water, entirely unsure as to what to do with myself. Thankfully, I had dined a few times at the Atwoods and would at least know how to differentiate the salad fork from the dinner fork.

"You didn't tell me that others would be here," I said to Allen before joining British nobility in the dining room.

"My mother never entertains in small numbers. It's as though she competes with Buckingham Palace," he laughed.

"An admirable ambition."

"Just be yourself," Allen commented.

"I'm afraid that would have your mother asking for me to leave if such was the case."

He merely shook his head and told me that there was nothing wrong in dining with the British aristocracy.

I had gotten used to the stiff necked collars and white ties at dinner parties, but it didn't mean that I necessarily enjoyed it. It was a hindrance to sit at a long enough table to where you couldn't even see the other guests. I was not fond of conversation led solely by the turn of the hostess.

Charlotte had already gone ahead of the two of us and I sorrowfully wished that Charles and Rose were here. It hit me in waves, the reality of their circumstance, like the high tides that came in at dusk.

"Have you heard from Charles?" I asked Allen as we walked into the room and took our seats.

"Actually, he contacted me yesterday. They are considering going to York for a little while, to stay with the Carnegies until Cherry feels well enough to return to life in London."

"Wouldn't that be escaping the problem?" I asked.

"*Charles and the American Trio* are to return to your hotel, so it would only be Cherry going to stay with the Carnegies. In the end, she needs to be cared for, and Charles can't afford to do so right now, with his career and all."

"Yes, for it is far more important," I roughly commented.

"Lloyd, we don't know that we wouldn't do the same if we were in his shoes. Besides, it will give him extra time to hire a maid for Cherry, to look after her for her remaining days."

"You make it sound as though she is on her death bed. She is blind, not dying, Allen." I was sober and angry.

"Don't put words in my mouth. You know what I mean. Don't deny Cherry's need of a maid."

"Does she not already have a maid? It seems rather odd, especially as they live in such a grand house."

"He doesn't have a valet and she doesn't have a lady's maid. They, of course, have a full kitchen staff, but that is all. Cherry was very adamant that if they were to live in Belgrave Square, they would live ordinary lives as any other. So, Charles agreed."

"Like a good man." I was not sincere in my reply, but I supposed Charles only wanted what was best for his family now. I couldn't judge him for that.

Before he or I could say anything more, Mr. Townshend stood up and raised a glass. The room came to a quiet as all eyes became focused on the gentleman, still handsome in his later years.

"Before long, my son will be the one giving these speeches, so I must cherish the attention."

All heads turned towards Allen's older brother as the whole ordeal seemed like a rehearsal musical number. Laughter spilled across the room as I wondered why I had agreed to come.

"It is wonderful to take the stage together again," Charles commented.

"Not together," I corrected him.

"You can't disagree that you missed me," he smiled.

"I admit, it will be good not to answer on your behalf anymore."

We were at the bar, taking a couple drinks before the entertainment was to begin for the night. It was quiet at this hour, and it was my favourite time to come, to sit and not have to be bothered by others. Charles knew I came to the bar before entertaining the hotel guests for the evening and had decided to join me for a cocktail.

"How is Cherry?" I finally asked.

"The Carnegies are taking good care of her. You always know how much Cherry loved a good holiday."

"We'd be fooling ourselves if we'd believe that she was enjoying it this time," I stated.

"Crème brûlée and port for the gentlemen?" A waiter interrupted us.

We both brushed the gentleman aside, assuring him that we were more than satisfied with the drink that had already been offered.

"You know, old chap, in all honesty, I really sent Cherry away because I don't know what to do." He shook his head. "I miss her vibrancy, her…" He choked up, showing more emotion than he had ever shown me before. I wondered what was in the port.

"Her vibrancy will return," I reassured him, although not so certain myself.

"Probably. But our marriage is a lie."

"Why ever would you say that?" I asked.

"You were right. She never loved me, she's always loved you."

And, with that, he smacked down the glass that was now empty and took his coat, leaving the bar as though we were enemies that had just made a peace agreement. I didn't know for certain if it was him or the alcohol that was talking, but all the same, it was the most honest Charles Atwood had ever been.

That's when my assumptions were confirmed true. The lady dined at the hotel only a few days after Charles and I had first had that conversation at the bar. I wondered if she knew, that he was married and that his wife was locked away in a mansion in York, only waiting for her husband to return her to a house that she had never wanted in the first place, to a maid that would solve all of their problems.

Her fine black hair was like magic, for the style and colour seemed to change every time she came to dine at the hotel. I wondered how they had met, but didn't care to know. From where I sat on stage, I watched as Charles would take his seat beside her, but only for long enough so as not to draw any suspicions. She always stayed until *Charles and the American Trio* performed their last movement for the night.

I had been tempted to take a seat beside her for the past week, make myself known, ask her a load of questions to see if she was suitable for a lying cheater like Charles. I was not traditional so to speak, but I believed in the covenant of marriage, no matter if you no longer loved your wife or if your wife had gone mad or ended up disabled for life.

Still debating with my inner man, I finally decided that it would do me no good asking myself the queries that I longed to know the answers to. It seemed as though we were all imperfect humans trying to figure out the answers to life through the will and fragility of the human heart.

There was an empty chair to her left and I took it; the evening candles were already lit. Charles and the band had just taken the stage.

"Is this seat taken?" I asked politely.

"No, sir," she replied plainly.

"Wonderful band, don't you think?" I smiled and turned my gaze towards Charles and his trumpet.

"Yes." She was rather not open for conversation.

"Do you dine here often?" I asked.

"You should know. You are the hotel's pianist, aren't you?" She raised an eyebrow.

"Yes, but you must know that musicians pay little attention to the room which they play in," I smiled.

"Unless, of course, you are Charles Atwood. In that case, he pays the greatest attention to his audience."

"Do you know him well?" she enquired.

"I supposed you could say that," I was finding myself taking great delight in this conversation. "Of course, that's what most people could say after they've known one another their entire lives."

"Oh? So, you are friends."

"Friends, perhaps," I replied.

This lady was mysterious and if I was to receive any information, I would have to be mysterious in return.

"There's not another trumpet player that plays like he does," she stated.

"Are you educated in music?" I enquired.

"What's it your interest if I am or am not?"

And, this is where I could make my stance known. I wasn't going to back off now. I had already made the bet with myself before I sat down.

"If a woman is brave enough to take Charles Atwood on, she must know her music intricately."

I smiled and stood up, adjusted my tie and left the table. The lady, of whom I had never asked her name, and to whom she would have probably given me a false alias anyways, for she seemed the type, would probably tell Charles about the encounter. Charles would most likely accuse me of falsity and ask outrageously how I could ever believe such a thing. And, if he did, so be it. I had seen them together the night before last. While Rose couldn't stand up for herself, you'd better bloody believe that I was going to stand up for her now.

Chapter 15
A Queen's Hall Miracle

Mr. Abbey had given me the evening off, even though it was the middle of the week. *Charles and the American Trio* would be performing all evening long. I wondered how much longer it would be until I was to be replaced entirely. I had begun to worry and wondered if I should start looking into another job, perhaps a teaching job somewhere.

I had even considered paying a visit to the Carnegies, uninvited, to give Rose all the latest London news. It was then that it dawned on me, for I didn't understand why it hadn't occurred to me beforehand. Rose had not only lost her sight, but had lost her ability to teach the violin and Latin courses at the school in London. She had always spoken of how much happiness it had given her, which made me all the more terribly sad for her. I couldn't bear to imagine the possibility of never being graced with a Steinway again. But, perhaps, she could teach again one day.

It wasn't the end. Dr. Levitt had even said so, for it was the start of a new life. Maybe that is why I had returned to Queen's Hall for the evening, hoping to find the magic that Rose Cherry Ellis had first revived within me. Or, the most likely reason was that I returned to avoid the realities that lay behind closed doors at the hotel.

Ever since my encounter with the lady at the Café Royal, I couldn't let the memory of her and Charles escape. Crikey, I hated the thought. In his own way, Charles had gone batty, and supposed every artist goes mad every once in a while. Perhaps, it was a one-time thing and maybe he had too much to drink. However, I did not condone it, no man could.

Not purchasing a ticket in advance, I was surprised by the short queues and quickly found my seat at Queen's Hall, manoeuvring my way through the crowd and the dim lighting that had already fallen across the grand stage. I arrived a few minutes late, on purpose, for I had decided to dress down for the evening and didn't want to hear any remarks from any passersby. They might have thought I was in the wrong location and I didn't want to have to explain myself.

When I had taken my seat, the maestro had just arrived on stage as the last of the strings filled the air with a plethora of E chords. Blimey, I loved how the fine tuning echoed off the walls. And, then, as though the music itself had resurfaced the memory, her smile appeared; Lindsay's smile shot through the dim lighting.

It had been sometime since I had thought about Lindsay. Her smile filled the empty seat next to me, and then her smile was replaced by Rose's for wasn't it here I had first heard her enchanting voice and had asked of Charles who was this woman that had entered our lives. Yet, her smile had disappeared since her accident, in the same way that Lindsay's had. What I would give to go back to the naivety of that moment, not knowing all that was to come.

I thought it ironic that Vivaldi's *Four Seasons* was the composition for the night. As of late, I had felt that life was like a never ending winter, where spring never dawned upon us and where a harvest was never enjoyed from the spring rains and the summer winds. Instead, the ice had decided to stay. Perhaps the music could break it, or even just the thought of Rose playing the violin again could do so. There was hope in the music and I realised what a good thing it was to come after all, no matter the filtered memories that found their way in between the key changes.

The music had been marvellous as always, the very thing that I had needed. After the concert, I tried to leave unnoticed, but when I saw a glimmer of red hair just down the hall, I broke out into a light sprint. She was still in York, I thought for sure she was still there. I hadn't seen her since that morning at the hospital, which seemed like ages ago now. It couldn't be her, for perhaps my mind was merely playing a game with me.

When I turned the corner, I realised I had been right. What was more is that Charlotte stood beside her, supporting her each step of the way. Rose clung to her arm like a child clinging to their mum at the fair.
"Charlotte!" I said her name with such happiness in my lungs.
She immediately turned around, and Rose, alongside her, asked who had called.
"Why, it's Lloyd Fox, darling." Charlotte spoke to her in almost a mothering tone.

My smile was wide, I couldn't hide it. It was so good to see Rose. There was a soft scar above her left eye, but other than that, she looked perfectly wonderful. Of course, she still looked perfect with the scar. If it wasn't for it, I might have thought that I had imagined Rose's accident altogether.
"Did you come to the concert by yourself?" Charlotte asked, taking a deep breath.

"Yes, is it still rare for a man to do so nowadays?" I teased.

"No, of course not. I—"

"Cherry, you look lovely. I thought you were still in York," I interrupted Charlotte, desperate to get a word in with Rose.

"I returned to London last week," she replied.

"Ahhh. I only wish someone had told me," I commented.

"News doesn't always travel fast," Charlotte inserted.

"Doesn't it?" I asked, wondering if they had all been aware of   Rose's return to London and had kept the news from me on purpose. Did Charles finally realise the truth about his marriage to Rose, the girl whom he only knew as Cherry?

"Charles has taken the Café Royal by a storm. They ask for an encore nearly every night. You should be proud," I said, directing my words at Rose.

"Yes, he's real good, just like you always believed."

"No different from you. We fairly judge," I replied.

"I'm going to go check on the car. Lloyd, would you mind escorting Cherry to where the cars are parked out front. Our chauffeur will meet us there."

I nodded and she flittered off. Taking Rose's arm in my own, I wondered what it was like to be Rose. I wondered if she still sang and if she still desired to teach Latin. Answers to those questions would come in time; they need not to be addressed here at Queen's Hall.

We walked, side by side, the entire world around us entirely unaware of Rose's reality.

"So, you will stay at Belgrave Square?" I asked.

"Yes, there's no point to move elsewhere."

"And, Charles? He's pleased with the idea, I'm certain."

"Charles has barely talked to me since the accident."

Her words stung.

"I'm certain Charles has just had a lot on his mind as of late. Of course, with the band travelling all throughout Great Britain…"

"You don't need to try and fool me, Lloyd." She was quiet.

Crikey, I wish there was something that I could do. Did she know about Charles' affair? There would have been no way for her to find out, surely. Or, perhaps, it had begun before the accident? I did not know, for that was Charles dealings, but how on earth could he have thought that it wouldn't have hurt Rose in anyway? I wanted to do something; I wanted to find a way to rescue her from her misery.

"Rose, do not think me inconsiderate when I ask, but why did you marry Charles?"

"Why else does one marry, Lloyd?" She was silent and then stated, "Charles is one of your dear friends. Why do you disapprove of him so?"

The question took me aback. Perhaps she didn't know after all, about Charles' affair that is. I didn't know which one made me more sad: her lack of knowing or the knowledge thereof.

"I don't disap—"

Before I could finish the sentence, Rose interrupted me.

"I did love the piece that you played for us at our wedding. It was such a gift to us both." She paused and then continued, I taken aback by her interrogation. "I've had a lot of time to think recently. Charles is my husband and you are one of my dearest friends. Apart from what happened to Victor, why do you disapprove of him so much, Lloyd?"

I had never said the words out loud; Rose made me say things that I had only ever thought.

"I envy him, I always have."

Charles was more handsome than the two of us, but it wasn't his looks that I envied, it was his ability to appreciate life after the war. We were partners in crime before the war, the life of the party, the entertainment for everyone in the room. I had songs in my head all the time, but now, after the war, I had only been able to write two songs, the one I played at Rose and Charles' wedding and *The Heartbeat of Thames*. Perhaps, I thought I would be further along in my career by now. The other piece, the one that both Rose and Charlotte had queried me about, had yet to be finished. Even though I played at the Café Royal, I sometimes doubted that the composition would ever be finished. Perhaps I was only meant to be a musician, and nothing more than that.

"You are the very last person who should envy him."

"Why do you say that?" I asked.

"For you know his flaws better than any of us, don't you? You tried to warn me, but I never listened."

"No one could ever make you listen, Rose."

"Yes." That perplexing smile greeted me once again. "And, now, I am defined by a life of listening."

"You are defined by much more than that," I replied.

"I know, I am sorry. I am still trying to get used to it all. It's been rather…"

"You are a miracle, Rose Ellis," I said the words, quite unaware of where they had come from.

"That is what Dr. Levitt believes, isn't it?"

"Yes."

"But, do you? Do you really believe that I am a living miracle?"

"You are a survivor and survivors don't give up easy. That's what I truly believe you are. You and me. We are survivors, aren't we?" I asked her the question quietly, although we both knew the answer.

"And, Charles?"

"Charles is one of Great Britain's most sought after artists," I stated.

"Yes," she sighed. "We all know what artists do with incapable wives."

I ignored her comment. Perhaps, she did know. I wondered if asking why I disapproved of Charles was a way for her to convince herself that he wasn't the man that she secretly thought.

"Does Charles know your real name?" I asked suddenly, trying to veer her away from whatever she suspected.

"No, let's keep that between us," she smiled.

That was Rose. She didn't want to be defined by society, she didn't even want to be defined by a name. I wondered sometimes if her name was even Rose, but decided I'd prefer her as such and didn't want to ever know.

Despite everything, that mischievous smile found its way to meet me with such complex curiosity. There was something she wasn't telling me, and I knew then that I never would come to know. Everyone was allowed secrets of their own, especially Rose.

Maybe seeing Rose last week had made it all the more real, it still felt strange calling her such, but I rather liked the name. It suited her well, just as much as the name Cherry did. Indeed, our reunion had made it all the more real. Her accident, her being blind, and her trying in the best way possible to make the most of the life she had now been given. She spoke of Charles and while there was distance in her tone, there was still some form of love and fidelity that could not be explained otherwise. I still wondered how she loved him.

I searched through my desk papers and found it. The composition piece that I had written for Rose and Charles. I had entitled it *An Irish Rose + Her Musician*, right after she had told me that I could call her by her first name, the only person, to my knowledge, who had the privilege of such.

Allen and Charlotte were to be married at St. Bride's Church that afternoon, quite a societal affair. Rose had told me that everyone of high importance would be there of which I asked if the Royal family would be in attendance as well. She only laughed at me making me realise that she had become much more accustomed to the British aristocracy than I ever would be. Of course, King George and his family would not be there. It was a foolish question. Even having grown up with my uncle, a middle-class solicitor, it still made me foreign to most politics even if I had flirted with high society on several occasions as of late. It was all for Rose, surely she knew that.

Everything I did seemed to be for her. I had been reluctant in pulling out the composition, for it spoke of a fonder time in Rose's life, yet all the same, I thought it would do some good for Rose to hear it again. Allen and Charlotte would be pleased, of course. I had once again agreed to attend to the Steinway piano as my date this evening, for there was to be a reception at the Townshends afterwards. I had little in common with dukes, marquis, and earls.

As I gathered the music, I glanced outside and thought what a remarkable day it was for sunshine. Charlotte was lucky for such. The church was quite a ways from their home in St. James, although I imagined they would be travelling by car. I had decided to travel on foot, although I knew I would have to catch a bus back, or perhaps get a lift from someone at the wedding.

Allen and Charlotte's engagement dinner seemed ages ago. I remember querying Charles as to why he hadn't gone to support his friends at their engagement dinner and of course, he had given me the same answer as Rose. It was a crucial time for their band, which it had been, of course.

"Congratulate them for me, will you old chap?" Charles had said.

"By all means," I had replied.

"It could have been you, but you lost your chance while you had it. Don't feel sorry for yourself by no means."

"You and I both know that if Allen had never come along, I would have never married Charlotte."

"Nor any woman, for that matter."

"You are wrong there." I had drowned my throat in scotch.

"It's a shame Lindsay didn't feel the same about you," Charles replied.

Was he really that insensitive?

"I'm sorry, old chap. I'm just stating the facts, didn't mean to bring about past hurts."

"Lindsay's business is none of yours," I had replied.

I brushed aside the memory and made my way to the church. It was a beautiful day for a wedding. A beautiful day, indeed.

The couple glowed with happiness as they made their way into the music hall at the Townshends home. I had left the ceremony a little early, so I could arrive at the

Steinway with my music setup for the evening. It was a good thing I had for when I had arrived, the kitchen staff had gone batty. There wasn't enough time to arrange the assortments of delicacies of all kinds on the tables. Lending my two extra hands, the task was taken care of with moments to spare. As the guests walked in, the staff scurried back to the kitchen below like mice who had gone unnoticed.

I greeted the couple, offering my congratulations and well wishes. Charlotte's parents conversed in a corner of the room with a couple that I had never seen before, and imagined would never come to know. Before long, Lord Branston welcomed all the guests to the jovial celebration, inviting everyone to enjoy the music and food with a further invitation to enjoy as much drink as they pleased. The guests were satisfied and returned to their stations, and I to my piano stool.

My fingers had yet to grace the piano when I first noticed Rose enter the room, accompanied by a woman I had never met. Allen stood close by the piano and before I took a seat, I leaned towards him and asked, "Who is the woman with Cherry?"
"That's her new lady's maid that Charles hired. I don't remember her name now. Rose couldn't make it to the ceremony, but I am glad to see her here at the reception."

Charles had been at the ceremony and I had wondered where Rose had been. It had worried me at first, so it was good to see her here at the reception, at least. Charles, on the other hand, had already taken to two drinks as his rough laughter entered the room from the west end, every young lady drawn to his handsome stature and endearing charisma. I couldn't help but think of the mysterious woman with the ever changing black hair from the hotel.

The maid, who seemed but a child, ushered Rose to

take a seat at the wall adjacent to where I sat at the piano. Excusing myself from where Allen stood, I walked over to the two women and introduced myself to Rose's lady maid.

"My name is Annabel, sir."

"Pretty name," I commented.

"Are you the entertainment once again?" Rose asked.

"How could you guess?"

"Annabel warned me that it appeared the pianist was coming to say hello." Rose smiled while Annabel quietly bowed her head.

"A smart observation," I smiled at the girl, meek faced and quiet by nature. Her gaze lifted and met mine. She was a little sore for the eyes, but had perfect manners. "Well, I must return to my post before your husband entertains us instead," I laughed.

"Yes, we wouldn't want to make war and peace at Charlotte and Allen's wedding, now would we?" she laughed.

How wonderful it was to hear her laugh. So, I took my post at the piano, playing the notes with a new refreshing spirit in their dance. As I glanced up at Rose ever so often, I knew I wanted to give her a gift, the gift of the song she so loved. There was no other thought that entered my mind, for I began to play the notes of *An Irish Rose + Her Musician* with a passion that reminded me of why I had first taken to the piano so many years ago.

I could see it then, there were tears in her eyes. That is when I was reminded of the time when she had told me that Lord Branston had called her *his princess prodigy*. The thought hit me. Surely, she could play again.

After playing for over an hour, I decided to give my fingers a break and found Charles in the card room. I was tired of feeling sorry for myself. I could only think of one thing that would help, a choice, like Thomas had said, that would bring me back to life. So, I approached Charles and asked him if I could speak to him for a moment.

"Do you believe Cherry will ever play the violin again?" I asked.

"I doubt it." He was honest.

"Do you think she would oppose violin lessons?" I asked eagerly.

"Who would you suggest would have great patience for such?" Charles lightly laughed.

"The obvious."

"You?"

"Yes." I kept my gaze entirely on his.

"Do you really think she'll agree to it?"

"The accident may have taken away her sight, but it didn't take away her personality and determination, at least I don't believe it has."

"She seems to be going mad, stuck in that large house all day with just her and Annabel. Kind girl, though. At least she has someone to converse with now."

"I don't think there will be much conversation taking place between the two of them," I replied. "She's quieter than a mouse."

"Perhaps, it would be good for her, the lessons that is. Should we suggest it to her?"

"Today? Now?"

"Why not? There seems like no better time to suggest an opportunity. It's a rather wonderful day for such, old chap. I like the way you think."

I followed him into the room where Rose had not moved since she had arrived. Annabel had gone to get her whatever she pleased as Charlotte had come over to sit beside her for a short while before being swept away by another important face in society.

"Cherry, darling, how are you enjoying the party?"
Charles asked his bride.

"As much as you, I imagine," she smiled.

"I have Lloyd with me. He has a wonderful suggestion
that I think will interest you." His enthusiasm was more
than I had bargained for.

After telling her about the violin lessons, I was feeling
disheartened when I realised that there was no change in
her facial features. Her face was gentle, the paleness more
light than I had remembered.

"I don't know, Lloyd. It's wonderfully kind of you, but I
don't know. You might be wasting your time."

"But, you are a musician. And, musicians don't need eyes
to play any form of music."

"The technique I have not lost, but you must remember,
I cannot play by ear."

I had almost forgotten. I had thought it first strange
when I had met her. A musician that didn't play by ear, it
seemed rather unheard of.

"Then, you will learn. I will teach you." I was persistent.
Now that the idea had been exposed, I knew that I would
not relent.

Charles reached for his wife's hand and held it gently,
"Darling, it would be wonderful to hear you play again.
I've missed that more than anything else."

"More than anything?" she asked with tears in her eyes.
He kissed her hand and replied, "More than anything."

I felt suddenly that I was intruding on an intimate
conversation between two lovers. However, I remained
standing there, waiting for Rose to give her answer.

"Alright, what am I to lose?" she smiled.

"I could toast to that!" Charles kissed her on the cheek.

There was something different in his eyes. There had

to be a reason why he was so enthusiastic at the prospect. He had changed since Rose's accident. Of course, part of it had to do with the affair. I had been right. He had told me that it was a one-time thing, that there was nothing more, that he hadn't known what else to do or whatever excuse he had made. However, with such enthusiasm, I did not believe him now. There was something so uncharacteristically distasteful about it.

Chapter 16
Forbidden Secrets

Rose and I had begun our violin lessons. It was only the second day, for on the first day, we had not gotten anything done, but had rather enjoyed tea and biscuits instead. Annabel had been as kind as ever and had even given me a tour of the home that I had never stepped foot in before. I told Rose that it was a charming home, although the curtains were distasteful. She had laughed, for she had always told me how much she hated the curtains and she had never gotten around to changing them. She saw no point in it now.

She was eager, but her eagerness also got in the way of her pride. I watched as the frustration in her face made her sulk at the ghastly prospect that she was to learn some of her beloved pieces all over again, note by note. I reassured her that it would indeed take time, but that it would be worth it in the end. The encouragement seemed to help, but I watched as her gentle rose petals fell for the second time, the first since her accident.

We were both too strong willed for one another, or perhaps I was too strong willed for anyone. As I taught, I also became frustrated, telling her to stop being so hard on herself, for she believed that she couldn't do it before she even struck the first note.

"Lloyd, don't treat me any different because I've lost my sight. I couldn't bear it. Charles already treats me like a child." Her frustration was now focused all on me.

I objected to her accusation to which she only replied with, "Just because I'm blind, it doesn't mean I can't hear the anger in your voice or the lack thereof as you try to teach."

She was terribly wise, and I felt that I had already made myself a fool; she always seemed to know how to do just so.

So, we took a break, she to relax her muscles and me to relax my mind. Rose allowed me to fiddle at their piano, one that had yet to be used. It had only been there for appearances as she had told me that all fine homes like these had them. Annabel then returned and asked if we'd like anymore tea to which I quickly objected.

"Would you like to stay for dinner?" Rose asked, before the maid returned to her duties.

"I have to be back at the hotel by seven tonight."

"Well, I'd like to take an early dinner. Please stay. I can ask Annabel to tell our cook to make enough for another."

"I really…"

"Please stay."

"Alright."

She seemed pleased and told Annabel to inform the cook that Mr. Fox would be joining them for dinner. When she had left the room, she took a deep breath and sighed.

"Why do you not have a footman bring the tea?" I asked.

"Annabel or our butler gets the job done." She smiled. "I thought you not one fond of aristocratic tradition."

"Oh, I don't care. However, if you entertain Lady Atwood, you might consider it."

"I already have." She raised her shoulders as though I should know the fact.

"You entertained the Atwoods without footmen to serve the dinner?"

"No, I am afraid I've let you down there. In marriage, there are some battles you have to choose to surrender before they even begin."

"Yet, on occasion, your lady's maid still answers the door."

"Only when Charles is away," she grinned. "Besides, she's not my lady's maid. She's too young for that."

"Then, what is Annabel to you?"

"A companion who has been forced duty due to my lack of sight. I will never play by society's rules. Charles mother gave me an almost intolerable speech during their last visit."

"You truly are a rebel, Rose Ellis," I laughed.

"I married a rebel," she replied. "Well, if I am attributed to be such due to different expectations in my staff, then whatever are you, Lloyd Fox?"

"I take it we might never know."

"We will once that composition of yours is born," she warmly smiled.

"Perhaps."

"It was beastly today, wasn't it?" she suddenly said.

"What? The biscuits and tea?" I asked.

"Our lessons. At this rate, I might be able to finally play a child rhyme by my 100th birthday."

"Your vibrato was excellent," I quickly replied.

"I wish I had learned by ear. Perhaps if I had played since I was a child."

"It's an acquired skill, one that you had never been forced to learn. You are educated and have classically trained yourself, better than most I've ever heard. But, now, you have to learn." "For I have been forced."

"I think it does us good to be forced every once in a while. If we weren't, perhaps we would never see our dreams achieved," I responded.

"And, yet others need not be forced at all."

"Yes, isn't it funny?"

"You are wonderfully patient," she stated.

"An attribute gained from the war, I suppose. Although, I fear I let you down one too many times today," I replied.

"You must ignore anything I say that is said in a state of frustration."

"I never knew that Rose Ellis was capable of frustration." I did my best to refrain from laughter. However, I seemed to have said the right thing for her mood lifted then.

"I've never been patient a day in my life. It must have been why father never told me about the castle when I was a girl," she laughed.

"I like your castle stories. Do you have anymore?"

"Yes, many," she mysteriously smiled. "Once you are sworn to secrecy and go through the ritual ceremony, perhaps then I will be able to tell you. But, only then."

"Must I chop off my right toe?"

"Something like that. But, you won't find out until midway through the ceremony."

I loved her enthusiasm for fairy tales and mythical stories, reminding me always that there was some truth in them.

"Lloyd, do you really believe I will play again? Or, is all of this done out of some sort of self-pity?" She asked the question with an abrupt honesty.

I had been standing by the piano, but now joined her on the sofa.

"You must know that I never perform an action out of

self-pity."

"Just like with Lindsay," she stated. "I would like to meet her one day."

I was silent. She made me question everything.

"And, maybe, one day you shall."

"And, you? Will you see her again?"

"Perhaps. Why do you care if I see her again?" I asked.

"She sounds like a charming girl. Your stories of her remind me of Caitríona, for she was never in her complete right mind."

"You never told me that."

"But, a beautiful mind. She was no different than I, even if her parents believed otherwise."

"You amaze me." I was enthralled by her gentle voice.

"How so?"

"You welcome adversity with such grace, whereas others would not even know what to do if they were suddenly told that the cook has run out and they must fend for themselves."

"Yet, I would have it no other way, Lloyd."

"Except for your sight?"

"But, I am one of the lucky few. Some grow up having never seen the bluebells in the fields or the ridges in the cliffs. Yet, I have those memories. So, even if dust and filth surround me, I can always take myself to the places I find the most lovely." Her voice grew quieter as she spoke.

I asked her the next question without even thinking. "What's it like?"

"To be blind?" she half smiled.

"You don't have to answer."

There was silence that stood between us and I half believed that she wouldn't answer me after all.

"It isn't as terrible as one might predict." Her enthusiasm

was returning.

"It just breaks my heart that those vibrant blue eyes have no life in them," I replied honestly.

"Not less life. I may be less stable on my feet, but I am still human. People think they understand, but they don't. The same with war, isn't it? That is why Charles doesn't speak of it."

"Yes, rather difficult for others to understand if you haven't been through it yourself."

"But, you wish they understood."

"Yes."

"It's why you compose and it's why I'm playing again."

"Exactly so."

"Then, we understand one another."

"We always have." I smiled wishing that she could see my display of affection for her. She did not respond but only lifted her gaze to her fingers, which played with her oversized frock, much different from what she used to wear at the jazz bars every night.

"We used to sing in the trenches," I suddenly said.

"Did you really?" She paused and quietly said, "Tell me about it, Lloyd."

"We sang because it was better for a man's last sound in his ears to be a hopeful melody rather than firing artillery."

"What did you sing?" she nearly whispered.

"It wasn't always decent," I laughed. "I'm certain you can only imagine the melodies leaving the tongues of rough officers."

"Rather evasive towards your enemies," she laughed.

"I often heard Lindsay's voice in those trenches, I'm sure Victor heard it too. We sang a couple of her favourite songs."

"Hopefully more appropriate than the others?" she

grinned.

"Every once in a while." I laughed and after pausing for a brief moment. "I wish we had met before the war."

"I think it's best we hadn't, for it was probably best that you were held captive by Lindsay's voice over mine."

Before I had time to even think, blimey, I wasn't thinking much before I said anything nowadays, the words came forth.

"Rose, I am sorry, but I love you."

"No, no you do not." She was soft in her reply.

"You know I do. I will not deny it."

I moved closer towards her and took her hand.

"No, Lloyd, I am weak."

"Your body? Are you unwell?" I became concerned.

"No, I mean, I am weak for your touch. I should not even admit such."

I desperately wanted her, but knew that her fidelity was still with Charles, even if he had already broken such, many a time in fact. I despised him for it. All I desired was one kiss. What was the harm in such? Yet, at the same time, I knew that if I kissed her, I might not be able to stop. Both her and I knew that Charles had been seen with other women, yet Rose herself had no justifiable reason by the law, except for suspicion, to divorce such a man. Unfortunately, her own suspicions would be invalid due to what society saw as her disability. I thought how cruel of a world it was that my heart belonged to a woman whose heart could never belong to mine in return, no matter if she felt the same.

"Alright," she whispered.

I thought I had misunderstood her.

Annabel had already left the grand parlour where we sat, so it was only the two of us now. So, I caressed her cheek, her face turning towards me, a gentle glaze of mist in her eyes. She loved me too.

Then, as our lips embraced, the sweetness of sweet peas returned, the feelings that I had felt when I had first kissed her during that summer long ago. When I went in for another kiss, she did not refuse me and I wondered had it not been for Annabel's light footsteps in the hallway, would she have gone any further? It was terrible; I had to control myself. I don't know what had gotten into me. I told myself I was a better man than that, even if her husband was cheating on her while enjoying the luxuries of the era.

"Lloyd," she sounded like a young girl.

"Don't say anything," I whispered in her ear.

And, she didn't. She said nothing more.

Rose had made considerable progress. It wasn't the playing part that was difficult, for any musician could play with closed eyes, but it was learning again that had frustrated Rose. She had been one of the only musicians I had known who had always played solely by reading music, for her memory was terrible. However, I believed that if I spoke aloud every note, and tried patience, she would not only play the music, but make it her own. And, that is exactly what she had begun to do.

She was bright and learned so quickly during the space of two months. She had taken to learning by ear so well that I couldn't help but take pride in all that she had accomplished. Charles had even commented one evening that his wife's playing had warmed his heart again. It was a peculiar conversation to have, and I feared he only made light conversation with me so as to keep my lips sealed from whatever affair had taken place between him and the mysterious lady at the hotel.

As for Rose and I, we had never spoken again of the time that we had let passion rule out all other things not too long ago. She told me that it must never happen again, and even though she suspected that Charles had remained unfaithful, he had made a promise to her that it would not happen again. I had asked her if she really believed that, and she replied that she believed it to be true. Rose told me that if she gave him what he wanted now, if she showed him that she was to live a perfectly ordinary life as before, then he would return to her, entirely forgetful of the past chapters that would never be spoken about ever again. I wondered if it was for this reason that Rose had become so determined to learn the violin by ear.

"Mistress plays all day long, thanks to you," Annabel smiled.   She had offered me tea and asked if I would like anything else before Rose made her way down to the library.

"Does she really play all day? Does it not drive you batty?" I laughed.

"Oh, no, never sir. I could listen to the mistress play every minute of my life and never go batty at such."

It was the most that I had ever talked with Annabel, and I must say that I rather enjoyed her spirit; although quiet, I could see it now, it was a perfect fit for Rose. "Mistress has the entire house memorised by now. Sometimes, I forget that she's blind, sir." It was strange for this quiet creature to talk of her mistress in such a way. "Forgive me, sir."

"There is nothing to forgive," I reassured her.

"She will be down shortly now. I've notified her that you are here, and she was just finishing up getting dressed."

"I am patient, Annabel, thank you."

She curtsied quickly and allowed her little feet to patter through the hallway, reminding me of our own maid when I was a little boy.

It wasn't much longer until she made her way into the library, Annabel directing her towards her seat.

"Annabel told me that you are here. You've come early today."

I walked towards her and took her hand, gave it a light kiss and replied, "I brought these for you." I placed a bouquet of dog roses in her hand. "Happy birthday, Rose."

Annabel smiled and then left the room.

"Oh, Lloyd, the sweet smell reminds me of home," she smiled.

"No lady should be left without flowers on her birthday," I replied.

"I've never heard that before."

"My father used to tell my mum that."

It was the only kind memory I had of him. Somewhere along the way, I determined that I would try to keep around at least one happy memory of those who had hurt me most.

"How did you find out that it was my birthday?" she then asked. "I tell no one when I was born."

"Charles," I replied.

"Charles?"

"Yes, your husband."

"What would make him bring about such a subject?"

"I dare say I'd be giving away a surprise if I said so," I laughed.

Charles had asked me two weeks previous what he could do for his wife's birthday. He wanted to make it very special, considering everything that had happened over the past year. After a few suggestions, he decided that he would take her away to Brighton for the weekend. Charles had managed to take a few days off from performing for the weekend. This surely would show Rose that Charles was trying to redeem himself.

They were to leave this evening, but she did not yet know. I was certain that she would enjoy herself. I could already hear her giddy laugh as she clung onto Charles, inching herself further out into the ocean as the waves met her toes.

"I am not one to ask for gifts, but may I ask of something from you? It is my birthday, so of course you must oblige," she smiled.

"Are not dog roses enough?" I laughed.

"It is no wonder you are still unmarried, Lloyd," she gently laughed and asked for me to follow her into the music parlour.   She loved to tease me so, even if she knew how I felt. I supposed it was her way to disregard our matters of affection with ease.

"Well, what is your request?" I asked, taking my usual seat at the piano stool.

"Will you play your composition?"

"Which one?"

"Why, the one you've been working on ever since we've met. Your lover of whom we shall never know her name," she teased.

"When it's finished, I will tell you the name of it."

"So, you will play it for me, then?"

"It's not finished," I replied.

"Just one part of it, perhaps the first movement?"

She was persistent and I knew I would give in. It wasn't that I didn't want to play it for her, it was that this particular piece required so much emotion, for it told the story of a time in my life from which I never hoped any man would ever have to return to.

"Alright, I'll play."

She squealed with happiness and rested her elbows on the arm of the chair. I turned to face the ivories and closed my eyes for a quick moment before brushing the black and white keys with the greatest effort.

With my eyes still closed, the debris surrounded me then, the rain heavier than I had ever experienced as the sight of bloody limbs in our trenches made any man remorseful that his family would never know about what actually took place on the battlefield. This was the first movement.

It was one of those moments where I was thankful that Rose's sight had left her, for she was unable to see the distress that had risen in my cheekbones as the last note breathed stillness into the room.

"Hauntingly sublime," she complimented me.

"It's a work in progress," I stressed.

"Well, will you teach me?" she perked up.

"There's no violin part," I replied.

"Then, we will write one, *together*," she insisted.

"Do you really want to?"

"You are a composer, and I am your humble musician." She saluted me, to which I couldn't help but break out into laughter. Rose was classy, and wild, and childish, and at times, entirely impalpable. It is what I loved about her, for there truly was no other like her.

"Then, we shall compose together," I replied.

"That is the best news I've received all year," she smiled.

Chapter 17
A Shattered Violin

I awoke to a banging on my door.

"Crikey, what time is it?"

I looked at my clock and realised that it was half past midnight. Grabbing my robe, I wearily walked to the front door and was quite astonished when I opened to a frantic look in Charles eyes.

"It's Cherry. Lloyd, I need your help."

"What's happened? Why did you come here and not call anyone?"

"She's hurt herself."

"On purpose?"

There was fear in his eyes, something that Charles Atwood never was to be found with.

"I didn't want to take her to hospital. I figured they would take her away to one of those mental hospitals. I can't lose her, Lloyd."

"No, chap, we can't have that."

"I know you think I'm a fool. I'm sorry for what I've done."

I was surprised at the height of concern that he had for Rose in that moment; perhaps, I had been foolish not to see it, that he really did love her, despite his infidelity. I could not think about that now; it would make me sick

and even more angry at him. Besides, he had sounded honest when he told me of their trip to Brighton, said the salt air refreshed his spirits,
and Rose's too.

I quickly got dressed and followed him out the door. When we had arrived at their flat, I didn't know what to expect, but when I saw her and what remained of her violin, I had to look away. The strings were no longer attached, the wood scattered throughout the floor's surface. Annabel had a wet cloth to her forehead, although I knew right away that wasn't helping whatsoever. At least, the kindness in her touch was there.

Kneeling beside Rose, I checked her pulse and realised it was quite faint.
"Rose, can you hear me?"

Charles looked at me with great confusion.
"It's late. Don't take any notice of anything that comes out of my mouth. Rose was the girl I was with in Paris," I lied.

He seemed not to have heard me at all. And, that's when I saw the cause of Rose's state of being. Nearby, in tune with a darkness that brought dissonance to Rose's violin, there was an empty bottle of brandy.
"Did Cherry drink the brandy?" I asked.
"She asked if there was any before I left for the hotel."
"Did you not think anything of it?"
"Why would I?" he raised his voice.
"Because Cherry doesn't drink brandy, she doesn't drink any alcohol at all." I spoke through gritted teeth when I realised that Charles had no idea.

How could a man not know that his wife didn't fancy alcohol? I realised I knew his wife more than he did; perhaps, I had always known it, but now it had been confirmed.

"Annabel hasn't left her side. What do I do, old chap?"

Charles' knuckles had gone pale. I thought for a moment that I might lose him, too, but decided that we could not have such, not tonight anyways.

"We must get her to hospital immediately."

Gathering Rose in my arms, I yelled for Annabel to grab Rose's coat.

"They will know that she tried to poison herself."

Charles' voice echoed through the hall behind me.

"We'll say it was an accident, we've no other choice." I was nearly on the verge of yelling at him. He had been a lieutenant in the war, and yet, here he was, completely helpless at the cost of his wife's life.

I thought of Lindsay then as I rushed through their home, carrying Rose's helpless body in my arms. Blimey, I couldn't lose her either.

Rose was human after all. It made me realise that sometimes the most perfect people can never show their hell to anyone else. They hide it to protect themselves and others, all the while, hurting themselves in the end. However, I could not understand it. She had shown no signs that would have ever allowed one to think that she would do such a thing, for she had begun to master the violin once more and had enjoyed a pleasant holiday in Brighton with her husband who was one of the most talked about musicians in London. How could she have harmed herself? It didn't add up.

I was seated in the hospital lobby with Charlotte, a familiar place that I was not at all pleased about getting used to. Charles was with the doctor, determining the causes and lasting effects of what had taken place the night previous.

A little while later, Charles arrived and sat beside us. "The doctor says it was alcohol poisoning. It seems she had broken out into a seizure before she grew faint," he said sullenly.

"Annabel said that she had been vomiting all evening long," I replied.

We sat there, knackered, confused and peckish. We hadn't slept all night, and I sincerely hoped that both Charles and I would get some sleep before performing tonight.

"At least that's all it was," Charles replied.

But, was it? Was that all it was? Her violin had been nearly shattered in pieces. Why had Rose done so? Charles and my eyes met. There was something that he knew that he wasn't telling me.

It had been a week since we had been at hospital, waiting to receive the news about Rose. I had yet to see her since that day, for I wanted to give Rose her time and space. I could only imagine how many people in the county had come to visit.

However, after much consideration, I decided that I couldn't wait another day to go see her. Arriving at their doorstep, I was welcomed by their butler. Annabel was quiet as usual, yet there was something different in her gaze towards me. I ignored the feeling that I received from her as I made my way to the library, one of which had become quite familiar; the tall bookshelves carved themselves into the room like towers protecting the fair maiden in Caitríona's castle.

"I would have come sooner, but I imagine your time has been well occupied," I spoke to Rose gently.

"Well, I am happy to finally be called upon by my dearest friend," she said, triumphantly.

As she took a seat on the sofa, I glanced about the room, wondering if part of Annabel's duties were to sit and read to Rose throughout the day, for she wasn't able to read now and had no desire to learn braille. Rose had said that learning the violin by ear was enough to master. Her brain could not handle both; although, we both knew she did not want to be put in a box, the box of the blind community that she did not want to define herself as. So, she had made a life for herself. Yet, my thoughts did wonder. She held onto her secrets so tightly.

"You must have questions," she finally said.

"None that you have to answer," I replied.

"No, I owe you an explanation," she finally stated.

Her blue eyes were lighter this morning, and her voice didn't have as much vibrancy as it had regained since we had taken to her violin lessons once more.

"That evening, I had gotten terribly sick all of a sudden. I had already been nauseous throughout the day and had been vomiting for quite some time before I finally asked Charles if there was any brandy. That's how much pain I was in, Lloyd."

"Charles told us of such."

"Charles and I got into a fight before he left. Did he tell you that?" she asked.

"No, he made no mention of it."

"We got into a fight about you."

"About me?"

"He thought I had been with you. I told him not ever."

"Why would he suggest such a thing when he has no right to talk?" There was anger in my voice.

"I swore I would never tell anyone, but swearing, it's all just a silly ritual that no one actually believes, isn't it?"

"What married couple doesn't get into a fight?" I asked.

"No, what I am to tell you next, that is what I swore not to tell anyone."

She took a deep breath.

"You see, he accused me of being with you when I told him that even though he, my husband, has been unfaithful to me, it didn't mean that I had the right to do the same. He was shocked that I knew and went off cursing your name about the room. Charles thought you had been the one to tell me about his affair, but of course, you never had, although our conversations had only confirmed them."

I remained silent.

"Now, it will probably not surprise you when I say that it was Charles who shattered my violin. He threw it against the wall when I told him how much I had enjoyed the violin lessons from you. That's when I swore that I would not speak of our argument to no one."

"You shouldn't have had any need to swear to such in the first place."

"I asked Annabel to fetch the bottle of brandy after he had left. She thought it not wise. I scolded her. I truly thought I was going to die. The pain had grown unbearable. I must have drunk more than I realised. I promise it wasn't on purpose. I would never do such a thing. I may be blind, but I'm not a lunatic. I would never take my own life. However, Charles doesn't believe me."

"Why doesn't he believe you?"

"He knows I never wanted a child. I never wanted to be a mother."

"You mean?"

"Yes, my body is not taking to the pregnancy kindly."

She reached for her stomach several times and began to cry. "Charles hopes it's a son. If it's a girl, what a terrible thing it will be."

"Why would that make a difference?"

"His inheritance goes to his son and I don't want to get pregnant again. I never wanted the child in the first place, Lloyd."

"You never wanted a child with Charles."

I didn't care that I had said it out loud. I don't know if she had ignored my statement, but she talked as though she hadn't heard me, confirming my suspicions once again. Sometimes, I wondered if Rose forgot that I had her figured out now. She wasn't as mysterious as the first few months that I had known her.

"Sometimes, I lie awake at night and wonder what would happen if I lost the baby. Would Charles leave me, his disabled wife who is good for nothing?"

"You won't lose the baby."

"I've already lost one," she spoke plainly.

And, now it all made sense. I was surprised, shocked really, that she spoke of the privacy of her health.

"I am terrified that I will miscarry again, Lloyd. And, then, Charles will surely hate me."

"You won't."

"You are always so certain, Lloyd," she sounded exasperated.

"And, you are always so hopeful," I replied. "I believe it's rubbed off on me."

"Don't joke, not now."

I could tell by the expression on her face that she was scared, scared of the baby that would either be unborn or change her life forever.

"You are brave, Rose," I said, softly.

"Charles doesn't think so."

Where was the Rose that had gaily danced with her husband in the jazz music halls, entirely hopeful for the future world to come? Where had that Rose gone? I needed her, I needed her for my own hope.

"You and I both know that isn't true. Besides, he is well pleased with the violin lessons. You've improved tremendously."

"I think it's his pride, Lloyd." She was so sullen.

"Well, he will be proud in a good way once he meets his son or daughter."

"I am afraid, Lloyd," she nearly whispered.

"Look, you are going to be a wonderful mother," I encouraged her.

"Am I?" she sighed. "I rather think not sometimes. I never wanted to be a mother."

"That's childish."

"Is it? It's the honest truth, Lloyd."

"You were destined to be a mother," I interjected.

"As were all women?" She raised an eyebrow as the Rose I knew was returning to the surface.

"I would prefer a woman, over a man, to give birth to a child. We'd be terrible at it."

Her thin laughter entered the room. Crikey, I had missed her laugh, even if it was thinner than before the accident. It was pleasant, all the same. My heart softened; each day spent with her became more difficult.

"Rose, maybe Charles is right. Maybe, it would be best if I found someone else to give you the violin lessons."

"Why ever so?"

"My feelings for you, Rose. Perhaps Charles is right. Perhaps, all of this was a warning of some kind. After the last time, I am afraid that the next time I will take things…" I couldn't finish the sentence.

"No." She was violent in her response.

After taking a deep breath, she replied, "I just mean, I can't lose you as my friend as well."

"I don't…"

"If you try anything, I will hurt you so bad you wished you'd never agreed to meeting Charles and I at Queen's Hall those few years ago."

"Is that a threat?" I laughed.

"The least of all," she smiled.

It was good to see her smile. I hadn't seen her smile so wide since the night she had been taken to hospital.

"How could you ever think I would allow you to get away so easily?" she laughed.

"Then, I will take my punishment with gratitude," I smiled.

"Surely, there are worse punishments than being held captive by a blind woman in a library far grander than either she or her teacher could have ever afforded as children." She smiled. Her red hair glistened as the sunlight danced upon her shoulders; the ends of her hair looked like the feet of a ballerina.

"It is not my captivity that punishes me," I stated. "It is the student's ability to captivate me."

"If you refuse me violin lessons, you may as well refuse me my life," she boldly stated.

That was Rose, though. I could never win an argument with her. I thought I would be helping us all by finding her another instructor, but perhaps she was right; of course she was right.

"Do you believe I would refuse my own life as well?" I asked her gently.

"Yes, you seem more alive when you play with just me as your audience than when you play to an entire room full of people at the hotel," she commented.

"Then, why don't you dine at the hotel?" I asked. "Surely,

it would be good to hear Charles play as well?"
"Charles prefers it if I stay at home, and poor Annabel
wouldn't know what to do if she accompanied me."
"Then take Charlotte with you, just like you used to," I
replied.
"Marriage doesn't free a woman at the drop of a
handkerchief," she stated, so able to freely express her
mind.
"For you, it does," I responded.
"What is it that we've always said, Lloyd? We aren't like
Charles and Charlotte. We don't allow society to define us
or give us a list of rules that we must abide by to
guarantee that we have satisfied the advertisements or our
parents for all it's worth."
"Yes, that is true."
"So, we've been rather lucky, wouldn't you say? We know
who we are more than most."
"I don't know if I can be as certain as you are," I replied.
"Yes, of course you can be. That is why you play the
piano. It is there that you know who you are more than
the people who listen to your music know who they are."
"Perhaps it is a mindset that makes it appear that we are
better than they."
"Of course, we aren't. And, neither are they. We need one
another. That is why I need Charles."
"So, you do still love him?"
"Yes, Lloyd, I will always choose to love Charles."
"Despite what he's done?" I didn't care that I had asked
the question.
"Yes, I think that night at the hospital, he realised what I
had already realised. Apart from the war, Charles has
never had to face grief and loss to such capacity."
"But, he was like this before your car accident." I stared
outside at the homes that all looked the same, resembling

the lives of those who resided within, all except for Cherry Rose.

To me, she was Rose Ellis. To the world, she was Cherry Walsh Atwood. Is that how life was behind the hideous looking curtains of each home that I passed by each day? Was it something that was entirely different from what I had always imagined? Rose interrupted my thoughts.

"Yes, he was, but something has changed within Charles. I think he is frightened that if he practices his free will too much, he will lose me too. It's strange, Lloyd, but I can't imagine my life without him, even if he does not think me brave or always suitable."

"He does. Charles just isn't vocal about his feelings, you should know that more than most." I tried to help the situation. There was no arguing with her, no matter what I believed.

"Yes, perhaps. The good outweighs the bad in a person, isn't that what they say?" she softly replied.

"Yet, you still don't want his child?"

"Nor any man's," she stated without a second thought.

I nodded, believing that what she said was very much true.

"Lloyd?"

I forgot that she couldn't see my silent agreement.

"Yes, I believe you are right. The good outweighs the bad in us all."

Just like any other marriage, it had tested them. While I did not know if Charles would entirely give up his unfaithful behaviour, I believed that he cared for Rose and didn't want to lose his wife.

I thought of that terrible night when Charles had shown up to my place, pale to the bones, frightened that he would lose his Irish Rose, the very girl that, although now bound to a life of dependency, had led him to be the successful musician that he was today.

"Well, what music should we work on today?" I finally asked.

"Would you teach me the melody of the song you played at our wedding?" she replied.

With her request, I knew that this is how it would have to always be. I would have to silently adore her.

"If that is your wish, of course."

And, so I taught her. Rose learned quickly the melody of *An Irish Rose + Her Musician*. For someone who had always been impatient, all of this was teaching her patience, as much as it was teaching me the very same. As the notes reached the high ceilings of their home, I only hoped that it could be the perfume that would mend Rose and Charles' marriage.

Winter 1924

JENNIFER MALECH

Chapter 18
Little Rose

I had taken a short holiday to Scotland to visit my Uncle William in Edinburgh. It had been a trip that I had been meaning to take for quite some time. After having lived in England for nearly his entire life, he had made the move to Edinburgh upon his decision to retire from the law. Uncle William now lived comfortably on the outskirts of the city, a charming countryside that reminded me a little of the countryside in Manchester. It was when I was in Edinburgh that I received the news that Rose had her baby, a little girl. Charlotte had called me, always eager to deliver the latest news.

After the three week holiday and a week's return in London, I decided to visit Rose and her child. Rose's child was now a month old. I would have paid a visit sooner, but I had always heard that it was best to give the mother and child time to themselves. I knew very little of these things, and if I was honest with myself, I imagined that I was nervous about meeting Rose's daughter. Life would certainly be different now.

"She's a pearl," I complimented Rose, a beaming mother as ever I had seen one. I was delighted to see that her daughter had her wild red hair.

"All of the nurses have swooned over her," she replied. "Be careful, all of England would swoon over her if you let them," I laughed.

Little Rose's finger was wrapped about my own, her soft fingers more soft than anything I had ever encountered.

"Charles can have his spotlight. I prefer the quieter crowds," she replied.

"You didn't always," I stated.

"Motherhood changes you."

"And, growing older?"

"Yes, that too."

Little Rose let out a small, playful cry and I watched as Rose smiled affectionately with her daughter wrapped in her arms. It was hard to believe that she had never wanted the child, a child that now evidently gave her a certain kind of happiness.

Annabel walked into the room and took the baby from Rose's arms.

"I will take her to her nanny now, ma'am," she stated.

"Yes, thank you, Annabel."

After Annabel left the room, Rose smiled and then said, "I'm going to a church now. I haven't been since I was a little girl. Their music isn't as pretty as the opera, but it will do."

"That's new."

What was I to say to that? Congratulate her? So, I played my part and asked her a question that anyone else would ask to such a statement.

"How long have you been going?"

"Since little Rose was born. Becoming the responsibility of another human life makes you question things you've never queried before."

"Is that so?"

"There was something the nurse had said to me when I was at hospital that made me wonder."

"Wonder about what?"

She hesitated, her thin lips manoeuvring how to put her thoughts into just the right words. Her piercing blue eyes shimmered like glass and I looked away entirely forgetful that now, her eyes function simply as a mirror for the one who gazes upon them.

I would always admire Rose; married to a man who tried to please her but continually retreated to his old ways to satisfy an appetite that never went away, with a child that she had never asked for, and with a disability that had left her imprisoned to her home. Did she think it all unfair? She had told me that she was lucky, that we were lucky. Yet, I still had a difficult time accepting this fact.

However, when I played those unforgiving ivories, I sensed that Rose was right in one regard. My music was the most honest thing that my life had to offer. That, and Rose's company. If I had the two of them for as long as I had breath, then I knew that I wouldn't remain as bitter as previous days. I no longer was as bitter as the day that I had first met her, and despite our fate, I would always be so grateful that we had met. And, now, there was little Rose.

"When you were at war, did you ever wonder about life beyond death?" she asked all of a sudden.

If it was anyone else who had asked the question, I would have despised them, but in this instance, I did not. The curiosity in her gaze reminded me that I had no other choice but to answer her.

"What soldier didn't think about such?" I answered.

"And, what was your conclusion?"

"I don't know."

"What a shame," she sighed.

"In what?"

"We live this life either believing in something better or we live this life not knowing what we think at all. And, if that is the case then, we know absolutely nothing. No education can help man find what he is looking for."

"Is that what the nurse told you?"

"In a way. We talked about church. Papa would have thought it nonsensical."

"Your father isn't a religious man, then?"

"He was raised in a Protestant home in a domineering Catholic nation. At school, he was an outcast, so I think he forsook his family's traditions long before his own papa ever knew."

Whenever she spoke of her father, I sensed a distance in her speech, something that made me think she was much more like her mum after all.

"Anyways, the nurse's voice was the most soothing voice that I had ever encountered. Can you believe such to be true?"

"If you said it was, then I believe so."

"Well, ever since I lost my sight, it seems that the human voice has become all the more sweet."

"And, music?"

"Yes. It's rather peculiar, Lloyd. Music seems to transport me to many places that I have been, almost as though I really can see it all again. Perhaps there's a beauty in it? I am able to travel anywhere at any time."

As hopeful as her answer was, I thought then of all the places that she hadn't yet been, and how she would never be able to experience them in the way that others would be able to.

"Are you downcast, Lloyd?"

Silence had entered the room, but only for a few minutes.

"No, I was just thinking about what you said."

"I cannot wish for my sight, something that I will never be able to retrieve, but I do wish again to perform. Is that silly?"

"No, why else have I been so persistent with your violin lessons?"

"Because you had no other choice," she stated.

As soon as the words left her mouth, a thought occurred to me. Besides, I was rather uncomfortable with all this talk about church, and decided that I would sway the conversation elsewhere.

"Rose, you know of the composition I have been working on?"

"Yes, your enigmatic lover."

Laughter found its way into the room.

"Yes, you have every right to say so."

"Well, what about it?"

"First, I would like to take your violin to a shoppe and have a man I know work on restoring the instrument. There is nothing like your own violin and while the one you have been using is grand, I'd like to do such for you."

"But, isn't that expensive?"

"It certainly will cost me more than a pound," I laughed.

"Of course I will repay you."

"No, that is not why I have told you. Accept it as a gift, a gift for your friendship."

"I suppose I must relent, even though you know how I despise it. This misfortune has stripped my pride in all its understanding."

"I don't think any circumstance could do entirely just that," I teased her.

"Now, you cannot just mention your mysterious lover and end it there."

"Of course not. Now, I have a proposition. Unless you

accept my gift, that is your restored violin, I will not tell you that of which you have always probed for."

"The name behind your composition?"

"Yes."

"Alright, I'm feeling rather easy today."

"Good," I smiled.

"Well, I don't have all day, Lloyd Fox."

"Neither do I. Now, you do realise that with such information you are being sworn to a secrecy that if confessed to another, even your husband, will result in the most intolerable of crimes."

"Did you not hear anything I said about swearing to things?"

"Must I word it differently?" I laughed.

"What would be my punishment if I broke your secret?" she grinned.

"When the time comes, if it comes, we shall see then, won't we?" I paused and took a deep breath.

A grin and a sparkle in her eye made me forget for a moment that she was married to Charles, that she had lost her eyesight, and that I, a hopeless old chap, had foolishly opened my heart to the only person I felt understood me. After all, she was the only one that I had ever told about Lindsay, apart from Thomas, which I still didn't understand why I had told him anything.

Despite my own resistance, Rose mentioned Lindsay's name every so often, and if her conditions weren't as dire as they were, I probably would have given her one too many unforgiving speeches. Then again, was it wrong of me to treat her different due to her condition? She was no less human, no less ordinary, and no less emotionless than me.

"The composition begins in the Key of D# minor and remains there for quite some time. When I was at war, and silence greeted us in the bunks, I could hear myself playing the minor chord progression. It was as though my fingers knew not what else to play, especially after that day," I said.

"What day?" she asked curiously.

"Did you ever hear about the Battle for Somme?"

"No," she quietly replied. "Will you tell me about it?"

"The song that I am writing is dedicated to that battle. It was the deadliest battle during the war. It had the highest number of casualties."

She was quiet and listened, waiting for me to say more.

"I'm surprised Charles has never said anything to you."

"Why would he?"

"It was in the Valley of Somme where Charles earned his valiant scar," I remarked with not great enthusiasm.

"It's a ghastly scar," she stated.

"A hero's scar," I said with slight hesitation.

"The song, then? It's a memoir?"

I nodded.

"Do you know what the Key of D# minor evokes?" I asked her, believing that she very well knew the answer, probably a much better answer than even I could give.

"Feelings of great despair. It is an unpleasant key and I believe it is the only key that captures the deepest condition of human pain. I felt that when you first played it for me."

"Yes, exactly that. Deep distress that cannot be put into words, but only found through a sombre melody, that is if the listener chooses to truly listen." I was so pleased that she understood the music as I did.

"But, it doesn't end there?" It was more like a statement than anything else. "There has to be a triumphant voice."

"Which leads us to the second movement."

"Yes, the notorious key of D major. The key that we

wrote for the violin solo," she smiled.

She understood music as I understood it, yet she could not play from memory. She amazed me.

"Yes, you are right."

"And, your third movement? Is it in the same key or a different one altogether?"

"It steps down a whole step to C minor."

"It ends there?"

"Yes, it has to end there."

"What does it all mean? I could listen and determine for myself."

"It's not entirely finished yet, and I have a rule that I never play a piece that isn't finished."

"Yet, you played the first and second movement for me."

"That was different. We were composing together."

"Well, you best play it one day. So, what about the third movement?"

"The third movement represents a soldier declaring love for his country and a girl that he would never return to how it had once been."

"Because of what took place at war?"

"Yes. It could never be the same again, for any of us. For both the men who died and lived, this song is for them," I replied.

"And, the third movement, it's about Victor, Lindsay, and you, isn't it?"

I always knew Rose was smart and as soon as I played this composition for her, I knew she would understand everything.   If I couldn't share it with Rose, how could I share it with the outside world? This song was my story. And, somehow, it was now her story as well. Maybe that's why I wrote the violin solo for her. It evoked redemption.

"Well, if you aren't going to play it just yet, what is the name of your composition?" She asked again the question that she had longed to know the answer to for years.

It was a beautiful winter's day. The snowdrops were in full bloom, the trees were barren, and after the storm from the previous night, the outside world appeared to be fragile, like glass porcelain. My thoughts drifted as much as the outside breeze drifted to and from the garden's edge. It was picturesque, as though the storm had never occurred. Sometimes, that is how I felt about the war. "A Song for Somme," I replied.

I had never said the words aloud, and as I did so, I felt that I would never again return to the trenches of France in the ways that I had held onto for so long. Life moved on.

"The battle that Victor died in?" she asked. Rose remembered and I replied with a yes.

"You know, they glorify war. They send off young boys thinking they are going to have an adventure of a lifetime, but there is absolutely nothing to prepare them for such. Victor died, yes, a death of cowardice, yet out there, there is no way to explain it. He had already almost lost his life and he just couldn't take it anymore. To have to endure that again, to have to face the reality of constantly being in a state of survival makes one go crazy. How do you explain that to someone? You can't."

"But, your music can," Rose said.

"Yes, it's written for the whole bloody lot of them."

"It's written for all of us." Rose smiled.

"You must understand now why it has taken so long to write. All of us have wounds. And, some, after being patched up, are forced to be taken to the battlefields once again where we are shot in the same wounded place. So, we endure it a second time. We get patched up again. By the third, we know how painful it is so we try everything we can to escape that battlefield once more."

"A metaphor for life."

"Yes. Yet, now, what is there to escape but my music?"

"Your music brings healing," she replied.

"So, you have come to understand it?"

"As much as anyone can."

"Then, you forgive Victor?"

"Victor doesn't need my forgiveness, Lloyd. How am I to forgive a man who fought in a war that I never fought in. I can't blame him for what he's done."

"There are others who think elsewise."

"Well, others form their opinions too quickly. They shouldn't matter to you."

"Aren't you the one who says all opinions matter?"

"They do, but some aren't worth having," she stated.

"You must ignore them, just as much as you always have. Why make mention of all of this now?"

"Because one day I will perform *A Song for Somme*."

"I hope you will invite me to such an occasion." A vibrancy had returned to her voice.

"Rose, I hadn't thought about it until just now."

"What's that?"

"A guest at the hotel, he asked if I'd perform at an upcoming concert in the summer."

"Where is it to be?"

"Queen's Hall."

"Lloyd, not ever?" She was surprised, yet delighted at the same time. "Of course you said yes!"

"He just asked me two days ago. I said I would give him my answer today for he told me that he was to dine with his wife there this evening."

"Well, of course you will say yes."

"He wants me to play my latest composition. I suppose that is why I wanted you to hear all about it first."

"*A Song for Somme*? You will finally play it for an actual

audience?"

"There is no evidence that there will actually be a real audience."

"Of course there will be. Jazz music hasn't taken down Queen's Hall just yet."

I paused and thought about it for a moment before replying. "I will accept if you accept."

"If I accept?"

"*A Song for Somme* is only complete if you agree to play the violin solo during the second movement," I stated.

"Well, I—"

"You are the one who said you would love to perform again."

"But, so soon?" she replied. "It was unexpected, that's all."

Rose titled her head, thinking of what to say next.

"Alright, but I will agree on one condition," she smiled.

I knew it before she even said the words.

"I am suggesting that you do the very thing that you have thought about long and hard, but have not yet done. You will finally face your fears and go visit Lindsay in Ireland."

"That isn't fair," I replied. "I can't see her."

"Because you still love her?" Rose asked.

"Not as much as I love you," I stated.

"Oh, Lloyd," she sighed.

"I am not ashamed of it and I will not hide it, not even from Charles."

"You've never hid it from anyone, Lloyd."

"What else am I to do?"

"Do you fear the opinions of others so much that you deny another a right to love? Are you afraid that going to Ireland would be like stepping onto the battlefield for a third time?"

"No, it's not that," I replied.

"But, you love her. I know you do. Every time you tell me a story about her, you fascinate me to the ends of the earth." She paused and then stated, "I will meet her, you know."

"How will you go about just doing so? You have no means of transportation."

"Lloyd, you know as well as I do that survivors do not take no for an answer."

"Is that so?"

"Yes, and I will prove you wrong."

"Why do you care so much about her?"

"Because you care about her and I care about the people you care about."

"I don't understand why."

"Then, Lloyd, you know nothing of love."

I thought about everything she said and stood up, walking over towards the windows that greeted a quiet life in the street below us.

"If it is the only way you will perform with me, then I will go," I finally said.

"You will thank me in the end, you shall see," she smiled.

Spring 1925

Chapter 19
Lindsay's Song for Somme

Lindsay lived with her Aunt Birgitta on the outskirts of the Cliffs of Moher in a small town called Fanore. Tucked away from the seaside, a tower of trees, as though they did not belong, fanned the cobblestone home that stood steady amidst the harsh winds.

A herd of sheep greeted me from a distance for it seemed that their welcome made me feel as though I truly had no choice but to go through with Rose's request. I had already tried to talk myself out of the matter several times.

All of it felt like a dream. The train ride, the meal that I had just eaten at a pub in the town of Ballyvaughn, and now, the walk up the gravel road towards the comforting cottage in the city of Fanore.

The surrounding fields were green as ever and you could taste the Irish salt in the air as the distant sound of the ocean, although not in sight from where I stood, brought memories of the days spent in Fowey. I wondered if that is why Lindsay liked it here, at least that is what it appeared to be so from her letters to Gabrielle. I had written to Gabrielle, asking of Lindsay, to which she gave a wonderful report. However, people could say things just to make others feel better, couldn't they? Well, regardless, perhaps Fanore reminded her of Cornwall, which made it not so dreadful to be away from home after all.

When I finally arrived to the front gate, of which the splintered wood snagged a piece of my coat, I was transfixed by the gardens that surrounded the cottage. It felt as though they belonged in the deep forests from which Rose had grown up in.

I had checked into the local pub in town, so I had nothing in hand, for I had left my bags in my room. However, there was one thing, apart from the clothes on my back: a letter from Rose. She had insisted I deliver the letter to Lindsay at the most convenient of times as she was quite adamant that I was not to wait until my last day there. I decided I would give it to her on my first day in Fanore, for if I didn't, I would most likely forget, not on purpose.

For some reason, it hadn't dawned on me until I stood in Aunt Birgitta's gardens, completely mesmerised by the reality that I was only a few steps away from Lindsay, that she might, in fact, not even be home.

However, that notion was soon washed away when Lindsay's eyes met mine. She sat by the window, a piece of cloth on her lap, which made it appear as though she was sewing. I thought Lindsay hated sewing, but perhaps, now, it was a way to pass the time, as she was alone all day.

When our eyes met, she became like frozen ice. Entirely still, perhaps drowned by the thought that she was dreaming; her fears began to melt as she realised after a long minute that I was not an illusion. I simply waved and smiled, although I did not show my teeth.

She stood suddenly, like a girl who was entirely overcome by what to do next. If it wasn't for Aunt Birgitta, I wondered if she would have ever actually opened the door. There was a certain chill in the air that had begun to breathe its way across the land, the marine layer fog growing thicker with each passing minute.

The large door finally opened and Lindsay just stood there, like a ghost that would never disappear.

Neither of us spoke. We both tried, but no words came forth. My heart both sang and broke at the same time. I couldn't understand this moment, but it was ours, for whatever it was worth.

"Lindsay, is someone at the door?" Aunt Birgitta's voice filled the silence that stood between us.

"Yes, Aunt B. It's Lloyd."

She said it so softly as though she didn't believe it to be true.

"Who, dear?" The scratchy voice filled my ears with despair.

"Lloyd Fox. Surely, you remember Lloyd?" She turned her head and yelled the question into the other room.

I still stood outside, while she held the door like her prisoner. I couldn't hear Aunt Birgitta's reply for it was muffled somewhere in the background. The older lady must have gone into another room.

"It's so cold out there. Please, come in."

I followed her into a cosy parlour, the sort of place that I would imagine Rose would have liked to live in.

"Are you passing through?" she asked, not knowing what else to say.

"No, I've come to see you."

"In that case, I'll make sure Aunt Birgitta puts a kettle on the cooker."

The lady with greying hair was not as old as I had

imagined her to be. Her voice, although not the most pleasant, was soothing and made me feel as though I had known her my entire life. We had only met once, but that was years ago now and I doubted that she would remember me, but for some reason, she had.

"My dear, we never receive visitors out here, now do we Lindsay? So good for you to come. Oh, you look well. Put on some weight since I last saw you, but you look well. You must stay the night."

"No need for that. I have a room in town, but that's kind of you, Aunt Birgitta" I replied politely.

"How long are you to stay?" Lindsay asked.

"For the week," I responded.

"What for?"

"I'm on holiday," I stated.

"I don't know of many people who spend their holiday in Fanore," she laughed.

"People like me do," I grinned.

"Which is why we never receive visitors," she smiled.

Aunt Birgitta announced that she would be in the kitchen and told me to make myself at home, more than once, I must state. Lindsay beckoned for me to take a seat. It seemed as though the walls enclosed around us, like a child being tucked into bed. Her smile hardened and then softened as we sat there after receiving tea from Aunt Birgitta.

"Oh, Lloyd, I thought I would never see you again," she gently spoke.

"Neither did I, you, but here we are."

There was surprise, yet joy in Lindsay's face. Aunt Birgitta smiled and said that she had some laundry that needed to be done and thought how lovely it would be for us to catch up on lost time. I thanked her as she left the room and gave the lady a kiss on the hand.

When she left, I glanced about the seating parlour. It was filled with books and only one painting on the east wall, though a beautiful painting it was. As I stared at the painting, I realised that the ocean's unrealistic turquoise blues had been painted by Lindsay herself. It was of the Cornwall coast, a masterful representation captured better than the human eye.

After taking the entirety of the room in, I turned my gaze towards Lindsay. Her eyes had been settled on my figure ever since I had entered the room. She examined me like a detective, and I in return, began to do the same. She had not changed one bit. She was as youthful as the day I had first met her; I determined that it must be the Irish air keeping her so young.

"I enjoyed your letters. Very much, I enjoyed them." She played with her fingers like a child.

She bit her lip and stared at me as though we were strangers. Then, she took her cup of tea and set it on the table beside her.

"I had meant to come sooner. Actually, Cherry is the one who insisted that I come see you."

"Cherry?"

"My violinist."

Her eyes danced in the Irish sunlight.

"Oh, she must be charming. I couldn't imagine you with someone who is not."

"She's married to Charles, not me. Cherry is only my violinist."

"Charles. Gabrielle's brother, Charles?" she asked.

I nodded.

"It's been so long since I've heard from Gabrielle. She wrote me before she married. Did you know that she married last summer?"

"Yes. Charles and Cherry attended the wedding."

"I wish I had been allowed to go."

"Aunt Birgitta didn't let you?"

The lines on her face shifted; her mood changed like that of a light switch which made me realise that perhaps just the mention of the word marriage brought back memories associated with Victor. Lindsay reached for the cup of tea, even though it was empty and then placed it back on the table, a repeated action that I had remembered from when I had visited her in Fowey. She performed the repetitive act as though she was entirely unaware of the process altogether. Her scattered eyes gazed elsewhere, and I felt that I was losing her.

I had to rescue her before she left us for the day, like how she used to. What could I distract her with?

Her hand timidly touched her face in the most unnerving way. I moved closer to where she sat and gently took her hand. Her eyes fluttered, her fingers locked up, and she hesitantly looked at me.

"Would you like to take a walk?" I asked in the same tone that I would use to ask a child the same question. She was sceptical and it took her a few moments to reply.

"Yes, but do you think Aunt Birgitta will agree to it?"

"Of course she will. Does she not permit you to walk the gardens?"

"Not without her."

"Why, I'm no stranger. I am certain she will allow it."

We called for the older woman, who was plump in the face from eating afternoon biscuits and told us through a half-filled mouth that we mustn't be gone too long.

"I just put the kettle on the cooker," she sighed.

"It will be water not wasted, Aunt Birgitta." I tipped my hat and followed Lindsay outside.

While there was despair hidden deep in Lindsay's eyes, her youthful spirit had not disappeared. Lindsay's sweetness was like the most alluring perfume.

Past the gardens, the trickling of wintertime flowers led our feet towards a secluded path from the main estate. As we pursued the path deeper still, Lindsay giggled, an unexpected surprise from the state she was in just moments prior.

"What is it?"

Her childlike joy, yet she herself not a child, brought an inevitable smile to my face. She reminded me of why I had taken to her so affectionately during my time in Cornwall.

"I've never been alone with a man. I don't think mum sent me here to Ireland for such."

It was true. She hadn't been alone like this with a man. We had always been surrounded by other company, except for the times we would run along the Cornwall oceanside.

"That's not true. Have you forgotten our time in Cornwall?"

"It was different then." She smiled mysteriously.

"How so?"

"We were always on a strict timetable. We could be gone for hours now and no one would question it."

"I don't believe Aunt Birgitta would advise it."

"She's rather carefree and cares more about what ends up in her tummy than whether or not I run off with a man."

So, she hadn't forgotten.

Lindsay had left the comfort of my arm and had then walked on ahead. Dressed in a simple white dress, she turned; her soft brown curls, a bit longer than in the past, rested just below her shoulders. She looked like an angel, yet the ripples in her forehead reminded me that I had to offer some sort of explanation.

"Why did you not come sooner?" Her smile disappeared.

"It was advised by the family."

"By my family?" She scoffed at the idea.

"Yes. You know that it was only for your good health."

"Am I really that dangerous?"

"Dangerous? No, darling, you could never be that."

She played with her fingers in the same way that Rose always did whenever we were trying to figure out the violin melodies together. In some way, they were so alike, although Rose was more vocal and a little more rebellious with a mind of her own. Lindsay, rather, was like a fair maiden that could harm no one, which made it all the more painful when the illness took her mind from her, throwing daggers through the human hearts that surrounded her. Yet, she knew not what she was doing. That is what made it so terrible.

"I almost forgot. This is for you."

Pulling a piece of paper from my coat pocket, I handed her a letter, the letter that Rose had given to me when she insisted that I write Lindsay or else she would not perform with me at Queen's Hall.

"Oh, it's a letter. From whom?"

"Cherry gave it to me before I left."

I must admit that I was just as curious as she. What could Rose have to say to Lindsay? The two had never met.

"Shall I open it now?"

"By all means."

I stared at her fingers as they delicately opened the envelope, then retrieved the papers within. My heartbeat could quite possibly be heard by the swallows that flew on by.

Drifting my gaze elsewhere, I allowed her to take her time as she read through the letter. And, then, as though a spell had been broken, she began to sing.

Seen
Though she is not seen
I just want her to know
That she's seen
Though she feel's not seen
I just need her to know
Hidden behind glass walls
Secrets buried deep
Tears gone unnoticed
And, fears never voiced

Seen
Though she is not seen
I just want her to know
That she's seen
Though she feels not seen
I just need her to know

Like weeds in her garden
Hurts buried deep
Prayers gone unnoticed
And, hopes never voiced

Seen
Though she is not seen
I just need her to know
That folklores
Sung a hundred times
Beat with hearts
Thousands miles apart

For we are seen
Though we feel not seen
May we never depart

When Lindsay's angelic voice allowed the last word to drift into the trees, along with the swallows who seemed to join her in song, I was entirely mesmerised. Rose had written her a song. Lindsay sang as though it was an old folk tune that she had known for years.

There were tears in Lindsay's eyes as she held the piece of paper in her hand, her eyes still fixated on the flowers we had trampled upon. She had become terribly still.

Moving towards her, I grabbed her hand and with the other, the letter that she held. Lindsay did not refuse me, but allowed me to read the words. I could hear Lindsay's heartbeat, which made me certain that she, too, could hear mine.

Dearest Lindsay,

I have heard so much about you from Lloyd. He speaks of you in such a way that lets me know that his love for you has never departed. While we have not met, I feel that I know you and I know that quite certainly we would be the most wonderful of friends. Do not seek Lloyd's forgiveness, but mine. I probed him far too often, and so he spared me not one detail of your friendship. But, I am glad that he did, for that is where I found that we are alike.

He told me that you are fond of music, specifically Irish folklore tunes. I, too, am fond of such, for the songs are a nostalgic reminder of my homeland, of our homeland. While I am not granted a trip to Ireland due to circumstances that are out of my control, I hoped that at least these words would find you. I have given the letter to Lloyd, and perhaps I was foolish in doing so, for to send it to the post office would have been a more wise bet. However, I hoped that if these words found you, then Lloyd had made the right choice after all. You see, you can't force a man to do anything, and I suppose it speaks to the same for us women.

Now, my dear Lindsay, I hope that you would do me a favour and find joy in this letter. May you see that you are very much not alone and that we are all very much one in the same. In this letter, there is a song that I have written for you. I do hope that we will meet someday soon.

After signing her name, there was the title of her song and the lyrics that Lindsay had just sung. A lump had found its way in my throat when I read the words: *Lindsay's Song for Somme.*
"Do you know the meaning to the name?"
Lindsay wrapped her fingers in my own and I thought how mysterious Rose was. She was doing everything in her power to bring Lindsay and I together again. For some reason, I felt that it had been her mission from the very first day that she had learned about Lindsay.
"Did your aunt tell you that I studied at Oxford?" I asked.
"No, no one tells me anything." She was sullen.
Lindsay was fond of people, yet due to her mental state, she had been deprived of the very thing that would give her life: friendships. Like many other times, I felt sad for her. However, things were going to change, they had to change.
"I studied music and started working on a composition piece during my studies there. I didn't finish it until just recently. The second and third movement includes a

violin solo, a solo that Cherry is going to play alongside me at Queen's Hall come summer."

"Queen's Hall? *The* Queen's Hall?" she asked, her childlike spirit returning.

"Yes, the only one."

"She is a writer as well as a violinist. How I envy her." Lindsay's voice was so gentle, like a dove fluttering in the trees.

"Cherry would never call herself a writer, not in a million years, but a violinist, yes, she is very much that."

"Does she play well?"

"Would I have her play on stage in front of hundreds had I thought elsewise? No, she is the most marvellous of violinists."

"I would love to hear her play. Do you think I could?"

"One day, yes."

"So, as you were saying. Your composition, then?"

"It is called *A Song for Somme*. I wrote it in honour of my time at war, for those who fought in it, and for the hope that we have today because of their sacrifices."

The wind blew through the trees as Lindsay stared directly into my eyes. Then, as though the words had finally evaporated into her heart, Lindsay's eyes glistened with tears; she grabbed my arm tightly and I thought for a moment that she would lose her balance.

"You know, I still miss him," she quietly whispered.

"Victor?"

She nodded.

"I miss him, too."

"You wrote a song for Victor and your Cherry has now written a song for me," she said. "It is only right that I meet her."

Lindsay looked at me, hoping I would say more about her, but I couldn't, not yet anyways. I took her arm and we walked in silence, the letter from Rose still in my hand.

"Has your family come to visit you at all?" I finally asked.

"Just once, before they left for America," she replied.

"Your father was kind to pay for my trip there," I commented.

"Father always spoke kindly of you."

I wondered how much she knew.

"They still write me letters. I am happy for them all," she then added.

"And, are you happy?" I asked.

"I am happy that you have come to visit me." She took my arm and we continued to walk, drifting closer to the shore.

Chapter 20
Idealised Love

"Has Lloyd come to visit us again, darling?" She spoke to her daughter in such a soothing tone, a tone far different than from when I had first met her. Rose truly was blossoming into a mother.

I had just returned from Ireland the night before and arrived at Belgrave Square hoping to see Rose before heading over to the hotel for the rest of the evening.

The nanny entered the room and took four-month-old Rose from Rose's arms. We were seated in the library, my favourite room in their home.

"So, you went and saw her?" Rose finally said.

"Yes, it doesn't change anything."

"Sure it does, it changes everything," she replied.

"My love for you has not changed. If you thought it would, it has not."

"Hasn't it?" she asked steadily.

"What are you doing, Rose?"

"Making you realise what you haven't been able to face since we first met."

"Which is?"

"You are afraid of getting hurt again. With me, there is a steadfast certainty that I will always care for you, Lloyd. You don't know if you can expect the same from Lindsay.

So, you are afraid to try."

"I am not certain you entirely understand."

"Sure I do. I married Charles with certainty, yet now I have discovered that certainty itself isn't actually certain. You can't base your heart upon such."

"What made you so wise?" I asked amazed.

"A childhood of uncertainty."

I folded my arms and looked across the library, wondering what was to be accomplished that afternoon. "I do not know Lindsay as you do, but I believe I am right when I say you still love her," Rose said.

"She loved the song you wrote her." I ignored her latter statement.

"I hoped she would."

"Does it have a written melody?" I asked.

Nearby, on the table beside her, she retrieved a piece of paper and began to write. I watched as she did, her other hand navigating the letters as she wrote them. It took her some time, and I watched with amazement. After handing me the piece of paper, she rung the bell and asked their butler if he would be so kind as to bring her violin into the room.

"Would you not like to move to the music parlour?" the butler asked.

"The library is just as suitable," Rose replied.

I read the music as we waited for the butler to return with the violin that I had made sure was refurbished for her by the best violinist expert in all of London. He had mended it within a week, remarking that we couldn't have Cherry Atwood without a violin for too long. I agreed with him wholeheartedly.

I read the notes of the melody that Rose had just handed me and began to hum the tune in my head.

Seen though she is not seen
   B A B D C# A

I just want her to know
   F# F# B A F# D

    Clark, their butler, returned with the violin and quietly left the room. Rose rosined her bow, the muscle memory never lost, and placed the violin atop her left shoulder. As she began to play, she sang the notes so effortlessly. It is one thing to sing perfectly or play perfectly, it is another to do them both at once.

"It's as though you never stopped playing," I applauded her.

"It's as though my violin never shattered. Thank you for getting it restored," she smiled.

"Has Charles been pleased with your playing again?" I asked, still not entirely sure by my visit to see Lindsay.

"Yes, he doesn't come home as late as he used to and he has taken to little Rose more so than before."

"He should be proud," I stated.

"He still wants a son." She seemed unhappy about it.

"We can't always get our way."

"Don't tell Charles Atwood that."

"No, I wouldn't dare," I grinned.

"Well, enough small talk or I'll go mad."

"More mad than you already are?"

    She laughed. When she did, her face lit up in ways that it hadn't before.

"Well, we must practise for this summer's concert. I've practiced nearly every day," she stated.

    The concert at Queen's Hall was to be in a short couple of months. Rose was growing in excitement over it and had applauded my efforts to keep my bargain as

much as she had.   Who would have ever thought those
years ago that her and I would be playing on stage
together at Queen's Hall? It seemed like something out of
a novel.

"Yes, that we must. I couldn't allow my violinist to forget
her notes," I teased her.

"Nor could I allow my pianist to be too staccato," she
laughed.

"Rose, I truly want you to know that my visit to go see
Lindsay has changed nothing," I repeated.

"We shall not argue now, for we have a concert to
practise for," she replied with a large grin about her face.

It had only been a month since our last violin lesson
and the concert was nearing closer with each passing day.
We were gathered in her parlour, taking tea after an
hour's practice. I thought of Lindsay ever so often, but
ignored anything that tried to make me believe that I had
been in the wrong in going to see her.

As I thought on these things during an afternoon visit
to Belgrave Square, Rose asked me another one of her
questions that entirely caught me off guard.

"I know I already asked you if you ever thought about life
after death."

"Yes, and I suppose you are going to ask me another
philosophical question. Has motherhood stolen your
mind and replaced it with the mind of Socrates?"

She sighed and ignored me.

"Do you believe in a higher power?"

"I don't think any man can answer such a question."

"The vicar seems to be able to do so. Do you not think

about it at all? Does the unknown of that question not haunt you? It has me."

"Is that why you started going to church?" I asked honestly.

Ever since she had told me that her and little Rose had been taking to church, I wondered what drew her back there each and every week. I had never probed Rose about her church attendance; however, I had asked Annabel a short few weeks ago about it to which the young girl admitted that she too, as well as the nanny, enjoyed the church choir and the pretty songs they sang. The four of them, together at church, they were a sight for society.

"The vicar seems certain that he can answer such a question," Rose said.

"Supposed he's making it all up? Perhaps it's just a figment of his imagination, just as much as a woman romanticises about a future with a man. I feel as though man idealises for something other than here, to make up for that which is miserable. He romanticises about a future which none will attain."

"Do you really believe that? What a ghastly prospect."

"We are all entitled to our beliefs," I replied.

"Then, it seems to me that you do know the answer to my question. Your speech sounds as though you have made up your mind on such matters."

"I still don't know, Rose. I already told you. I don't think any man can answer that question. There is nothing that is absolute in our world."

"I believe you are wrong."

My heart sunk. How would I be able to argue with Rose? I couldn't.

"What if it's the other way around?" she asked.

"What is?"

"Well, you say that man romanticises about the world to come, a certain hope that allows him to escape his existing condition, but what if instead, it is our present world that we idealise, something that will never be attainable."

"That's rather philosophical."

"No, really, Lloyd. We try to find happiness through so many things. I tried to find it through my music, through my marriage, and I even tried to find it through my own child. It makes me think that there's something more."

"And, us? Did you not find it there? Is that why you have tried to push Lindsay back into my life?"

"Lloyd, don't say such things. I won't permit it. You know that's not true."

"Do I?"

I didn't. However, I continued to listen to her.

"You don't have to understand where I am coming from, but I do hope you will hear me out. For it's when I sat in that church that I felt in some sense I had experienced something more. There just has to be."

"So, you are going to base your entire ideology on one experience?"

"No, not one experience, but I believe it is that experience that has made me realise what I've been missing all along. I can't go back to my normal routine of life, Lloyd."

"Your life is far from a routine of normalcy," I replied.

"That's not what I mean. It's something that I can't explain. I tried to explain it to Charles, but he didn't listen. I thought if anyone would understand, it would be you, but I guess I was wrong. I was entirely wrong." She had grown exasperated.

"Rose, I can try to understand," I replied, afraid that I had hurt her.

"No. You are still as cynical as the day I met you." She sighed heavily.

I fell silent. Is that really what she thought of me? After a few more minutes in silence, I finally spoke, realising her efforts from the past few months were attributed to the fact that she merely just cared for my well-being. There was no one like Rose, for she carried the weight of someone else's burden, without ever receiving permission to do so. As soon as I thought I had her figured out, her gentle and fierce heart had surprised me once again.

"You thought Lindsay would set me free," I said.

She said nothing.

"Rose, can I be honest with you?"

"I'd like to think our relationship is built on honesty," she stated.

"It hasn't always been," I replied.

"Even without saying anything, we can still be honest with one another."

"Rose, I am a better man because of you. I know it is not my respectable place to speak to you in this way, but I can't sit here and remain silent. Ever since—"

"You don't need to continue," she stated.

I took a seat beside her and took hold of her hand. She was hesitant at first, but I didn't let go. I had to say it or else I would never say it.

"Rose, I find myself, yes, cynical from time to time, because just as you said, you had an experience that has made you believe in something more, that has you hoping for a better life than the one granted to us here on earth. I, too, have had many an experience that has made me think the very opposite and perhaps that has made me a cynical man. But, when I'm with you, all of that fades away and the world is right again."

"Yet, for you, it still is not."

"Then, it is not." I quietly repeated the phrase.
She became still and her voice became heavy.

"Though beautiful, you use music as an escape. You can't outrun the past. It will come back to haunt you."

"So, what do you suggest I do?"

"I suggest you face the demons you've been trying to run away from: the war, Victor, Lindsay, all of them," she said, raising her voice.

"What about you?" I asked.

"What about me?"

"Did you face your demons?"

"Yes, and I am free because of it," she replied gently.

"Maybe we can't all be set free." I sighed.

"Then, what would be the point of living? That is what I have come to determine, Lloyd," she said softly.

My hand that had been resting on her own could not remain there. I knew she would most likely not forgive me, but then at the same time, I wondered if the honesty she spoke of was found in our inability to speak of our love for one another. Perhaps, she had asked for it.

She allowed me to touch her face and as I did so, a single tear fell down her cheek.

"No, Lloyd, you mustn't."

"Just one kiss, that's all I ask for."

"But, Lindsay?"

"You aren't Lindsay," I stated through gritted teeth and then softened my voice to almost a whisper. "You are my wild Rose."

"Is this what you were afraid of?" she asked.

"Is this what you are afraid of?" I tightened my grip on her hand.

"Don't Lloyd."

I closed my eyes and let go of her hand, Lindsay's laughter once again entering my mind. Then, little Rose's cries entered the room.

When Rose excused herself from the room to go pick up her daughter in the adjoining room, I gaped at her ability to get around her own house so easily and had almost forgotten for a moment about her loss of sight. If it hadn't been for her walking stick, I might have not been reminded. As I sat there, pondering such things, I still couldn't accept what she believed. That which we idealised for in this world could never be as real as we hoped, it seemed almost as cynical as the latter. Rose was right. I did idealise for something; I had idealised for her love. I still did. Would it make me happy? According to Rose, it would not, but I couldn't accept that fact.

Like the Cornish waves greeting my summertime toes, an unexpected curiosity that I had not asked for gripped my senses. All of this talk about facing our demons had me determined to ask of Rose one more thing.

Grabbing my hat, I returned to the room where Rose quieted her baby, singing her the same Irish ballad that she had sung on the first night I had met her. She was so different from any mother of her class, but then again, she wasn't raised an earl's daughter as she liked to remind me. Little Rose's nanny stood their awkwardly, not sure as to why, in that moment, her employer had taken over her job.

"Are you going to church this Sunday?" I asked Rose. The question almost seemed as though it had been asked by someone other than me.

"I believe so."

There was surprise in her reply and equally so when I responded.

"I'd like to come with you, that is if it's not a disturbance."

"Lloyd, you could never be that."

Annabel was right. The choir was hauntingly beautiful, in the same way that the orchestra at Queen's Hall had always been for me. While I had insisted that Annabel take the day for herself as I was more than able to manage watching little Rose and escorting the mistress to the church myself, Annabel insisted that she didn't want to miss the Sunday service.

The preaching wasn't as dull as I had heard in previous services, and Rose had remarked, more than once, how eloquent the preacher's rhetoric was. I had to agree with her.

After the service, we were greeted by other congregates before leaving the church building. More than once, Rose had to clarify that I was not her husband. By the third or fourth enquiry, I began to tell them that I was, to which Rose subtly laughed and hit me at the rib.

Rose's arm was wrapped around mine and the sweet smell of spring roses filled the crisp air as we walked. Annabel walked on ahead of us with little Rose about her waist. We quickly followed in their footsteps leaving the congregates behind.

"Did you enjoy yourself, Lloyd?" Rose asked.

"The music was pretty, although, the sermon rather daft."

She ignored my comment. The spring blossoms greeted our senses. Howling distantly, the wind reminded me how quickly life could change.

"I cannot get the words out of my head," Rose commented, although I knew not what exactly.

"The vicar's? Was he really that charming?"

"No," she laughed. "The hymn that they sung at the end of the service."

"Ahh, yes. The infamous *Amazing Grace*. Our kitchen maid used to hum the old tune as diligently as making sure the daily bread was baked."

"Oh, Lloyd. Do you really despise the hymns? All of them?"

"Perhaps if you sang the hymns I'd be more obliged to appreciate them. I admit, the melody is rather alluring," I stated.

"That's just it. But, for me, it is the words. I once was blind, but now I see. What an irony. I once could see, but now I'm blind, and yet, I have found myself singing the same words as the writer."

"You really believe in this stuff, then? What does Charles make of it all?"

"He doesn't even know I attend church, and I'd rather keep it that way. I don't want him to attend church like my dear papa, like a man who views sitting on a pew of legalistic routine, who sits there to give himself a pat on the back and scream to the world that he is a better man because of it."

I stopped in my tracks and reached for her face, trying to reveal, through her lack of sight, my deep affection and sorrow for the life that I felt she had been cursed by, yet somehow she saw it as the very opposite.

"Rose, I wish there was something that I could do."

"Your friendship is all I require, and nothing more. If I have that, then I am quite content."

We continued to walk and she asked me another question, a question that I feared she had been wanting to ask ever since our last lesson.

"Did you think that if you kissed me, it would make your love for Lindsay disappear?"

"Perhaps. I haven't been able to think straight since I've returned from Ireland."

When she asked the question, I thought of the ten days that I had spent in Fanore. Lindsay was younger than Rose, more playful and not as wise; yet, she had indeed grown smarter even if she had remained at a distance my entire time in Fanore. If it wasn't for the spirited company of Aunt Birgitta, I don't know if I would have remained for as long as I did.

I believe Lindsay created the distance due to the fear that I would leave both her company and her heart again, of which I had done. However, Lindsay's face and sweet voice was victim to my memory. And, perhaps, I was the same for her.

"Then, I think it's an easy solution." Rose interrupted my thoughts as we continued to walk together.

"To what?"

"Your uneasy mind. I believe I have a solution."

"Which is?"

"You must invite Lindsay to the concert at Queen's Hall. She can stay with Charles and me. Of course, we have so many rooms at our place and we never have visitors. We would all enjoy it, I especially."

"Are you sure? I don't know if she would come."

"Why would she not?"

"For your choice of husband," I replied.

"It's a large house and with Charles away nearly every weekend, they might not even cross paths. Besides, why should I be spared the acquaintance of a woman who had once enraptured my husband's attention?" she smiled. "And, nearly every man at Oxford, for that matter."

"And, you say that I am impossible?" I laughed.

"It is why we are friends," she commented.

"You will have to get the approval past her Aunt Birgitta. I don't believe Lindsay has left Ireland in years. She might be afraid to do so."

"Have you not learned anything, Lloyd? I don't take no for an answer."

"You are like Charles, then."

"Only in that regard," she replied.

"Perhaps," I stated.

"Perhaps I am right," she replied.

"As you always are." I tried to refrain from laughter until she returned the sentiment and walked with me, the nanny just ahead of us carrying little Rose, Annabel walking quietly beside her.

"Are you glad you came to the church?" she asked again.

"It was more enjoyable than I would probably care to admit aloud," I smiled.

"It has given me hope, Lloyd. In a world of uncertainty, I have this hope now."

I simply smiled and continued to walk with her arm in my own. It was a beautiful and strange day, all the same, for somewhere within, it seemed as though the tides of life were changing.

Rose believed that her faith gave her hope in a world of uncertainty. I doubted I would ever believe the same, but somehow, when I was with her, there was hope, hope for something that could not be explained.

Part 3

Summer 1925

Chapter 21
A Dinner Affair

Annabel welcomed me at the front door, my footsteps making their way towards the library. Before entering, I stopped in my tracks as my fingers brushed the door that led into the library. I overheard the two of them, speaking as though they had been long lost friends. Turning towards Annabel, I told her to return to her duties for I needn't be escorted into a room every time I entered it. She curtsied and hurriedly went on her way.

I don't know how long I remained there, although I knew that it had been for more than a few minutes. Lindsay's back was towards me and Rose stared me straight in the face, although she did not know it. Two women, bound to a different sickness in their own way, conversed as though nothing was wrong in their world. There was laughter, there was mention of Lindsay's stubborn dog, and there was talk of their childhoods in the Irish countryside.

After eavesdropping for longer than I should have been allowed, I entered the room with complete admiration for them both.

"Lloyd!" Lindsay jumped up nervously and smiled. "I

didn't see you standing there."

I gestured for her to sit back down and took a seat beside her.

"You've come just in time. We were going to ring Clark for tea." Rose smiled triumphantly.

"Are we to call for tea every afternoon I visit?" I asked.

"It's a tradition that is a part of our lives," Rose objected. She had begun to play her part well, to which I wondered what Lady Rose had done with the fiery Rose that I had met only a couple of years ago. I merely nodded my head and accepted her invitation for afternoon tea.

"Well, what have you ladies planned for the evening?" I asked.

"We are to dine with Allen and Charlotte at their home in Hampstead."

"Will it be just the four of you?" I asked.

"A few others, although I know not who will be in attendance," Rose replied.

"And, Charles?"

"Charles is gone for the weekend," she said quite abruptly, indicating that there was nothing more to say on the subject.

I realised that a dinner in Hampstead at an estate far grander than any that Lindsay had ever step foot in, for it was far noble than even Belgrave Square, would be an event that she would soon not forget.

"How about you, Lloyd? Do you have any dinner plans tonight?" Lindsay asked.

I wanted to lie and make something up, but I knew right away that Rose would know that I had plotted a tale only to avoid having to decline her invitation once offered.

"None whatsoever," I finally said.

"Then, it is settled. You will ride over with Lindsay and I.

Our chauffeur will pick us up at seven," Rose stated.

"Perhaps I'd prefer the fresh air?" I asked.

"Are you planning on riding over on horseback? This isn't the 18th century, Lloyd," Rose laughed.

"No, I only meant that I am capable of finding my own ride there."

"Too proud to be seen with Charles Atwood's wife in public?" she grinned.

"Quite the contrary. You already know that," I replied.

"What should I wear?" Lindsay suddenly blurted out.

"Oh, dear, you can borrow something of mine, of course," Rose paused and then realised that she assumed that they were both the petite size, growing suddenly red in the face. "That is if…"

"That's kind of you, thank you," Lindsay interrupted her before she could say anything more. Lindsay, of course, was the same size as Rose, if not smaller, which made me wonder if Aunt Birgitta was the only one who ate all of the meals that she cooked. But then again, Lindsay had always been petite.

"Are you ready for the concert?" Rose then asked me.

"Does one ever know if they are truly ready for anything?" I asked.

She did not respond to my question for Clark walked into the room with a pot of tea.

"Thank you, Clark." Rose commented. "Also, could you please send a message to Annabel for me? Later this afternoon, would she be as kind to help our guest find a gown for this evening?"

"Yes, my lady," Clark took a quick glance at me and then left the room. I always wondered what their butler thought of me, but of course, I would never know. We were never given the time to exchange more than a few words with one another.

"You see, there is no need to worry now," Rose commented.

It had grown warm in the room. Rose remarked that it would be good to crack a window to which I found the tools to do so. The gentle breeze eased my mind. I admit that when Rose had first proposed the idea of Lindsay staying with her and Charles, I thought it was unattainable, but now I could see that it was a gamble that Rose had thought was worthwhile. As much as it had been for Lindsay, loneliness had been a companion of Rose's which is why she had taken to our violin lessons with such delight for it truly had become the only companion that she could look forward to each day.

Of course, there was little Rose and I am certain the child eased any ache for friendship, but it was not the same thing, especially after Charlotte's marriage. Allen and Charlotte had been travelling quite frequently, not able to pay visits as much as Rose would like, so nevertheless, there was a reason for her request in the end. Rose longed to be surrounded by people who understood her, people like Lindsay and me.

I couldn't help but smile when I saw her. Lindsay glided down the stairs in Rose's yellow dress like a swan floating down the river bank. Her brown curls sat atop her head, laced through pearls that would have any woman envious. She smiled when she saw me and then proceeded down the stairwell like a child pretending to be an imaginary princess.

Tilting her chin, she wore an insatiable grin as the paintings followed her footsteps. Avoiding my gaze, she met me at the foot of the stairs and then, after a brief pause, finally made eye contact with me.

"Good evening, sir." She curtsied and then laughed.

"You are marvellous," I grinned.

"To be quite honest, I've never been more uncomfortable in all my life."

"Then, that makes two of us." I offered my arm and she accepted.

We were at Allen and Charlotte's estate; the Hampstead estate that would be their home until they took over Chatsmoore. It was rare for them not to already live at Chatsmoore, but then again, I feel that a newlywed couple, no matter their position, would prefer a London house over a secluded estate in England's old countryside. I had arranged my own means of transportation just as I had originally suggested. Lindsay, on the other hand, had been given a tour of the estate by Lord Branston, avoiding all the eyes that were glued to her figure as she walked about the lengthy halls adorned in paintings that most likely could have doubled any of our fortunes, including Charles and Rose. Before her marriage to Allen, I couldn't imagine what it was like for Charlotte to live here alone with only her flamboyant aunt. It must have been paradise.

Lindsay had been led astray, all on her own, through the rooms upstairs, Charlotte's father probably taken away by a prominent figure in society.

"Where is Cherry?" I asked as we walked.

"Charlotte took her from me once we arrived," Lindsay stated.

"Have you enjoyed yourself thus far?"

"It seems like something out of a fairy tale. I'm afraid I'll break anything I touch," she laughed.

"If you don't wander far from me, you should find

yourself in one piece once the evening is through," I grinned.

"Do I look like a doll?" she asked honestly.

"Less porcelain like," I smiled.

"Oh, Lloyd, I do appear foolish, don't I?"

"No, forgive me if I've said anything wrong. I'm not fond of parties."

"Nor I."

"Then, why were you so eager to come?" I asked.

"Cherry insisted, and I wouldn't dare say no to her."

"So, you aren't pleased to be here, then?"

"Oh, it's not that I'm not pleased. I just wish I could have worn something a little more friendly for the lungs. I am only grateful that I don't have to walk in a corset buried in frocks."

I laughed at her good humour. That was Lindsay, entirely unapologetic and unaware of how much more boring the dinner would be altogether once we were called into the dining hall.

As soon as it was announced, I whispered to Lindsay to be prepared to smile and wave all evening long.

"Like King George and Queen Mary?" she giggled.

"Just like so. And, the less you breathe during dinner, the greater chances of receiving another dinner invitation."

"Must I faint altogether to please the lady of the house?" she whispered gleefully, entirely in awe of the chandeliers that stood over the grand dining table.

"There is an art to perfect posture. It's of far more importance than whether or not the working class earns their wages," I remarked.

"Oh, Lloyd, now I must be the one to comment that you are being too harsh. Are you really not that glad to be here?" she whispered.

"You must know that I'm a peculiar breed. I prefer soup

in a solitude chamber over such company." I slightly smiled.

"But, they are your friends, are they not?"

"Charlotte and Allen, yes. However, their company, no not never," I grinned.

"Have you ever held a single conversation with them? Perhaps you judge too quickly," she replied steadily.

"Perhaps we should take our seats and determine that for ourselves."

She followed my lead and took her seat at the south end of the table. I watched as her pretty eyelashes fluttered to gaze at the intricately designed ceilings above. The centre of the table was lined with candles, intertwined with an immaculate floral arrangement that must have represented every flower in the county.

"How long did it take to arrange such a table?" she whispered.

"Since the end of the war," I smiled.

She continued to marvel at the table setting while I quietly reminded her not to put her gloves on the table nor lean back in her chair.

"I don't even know where to begin with the silverware," she whispered.

"Observe the expert and follow my lead." I smiled, charmed by her pure curiosity. She nodded and continued to admire the room's aesthetics. As she did so, Lindsay hadn't even noticed that Lord Branston had asked how she had been enjoying her stay at the Atwood's home.

"Lindsay?" I made her aware of Lord Branston's question.

She returned to our presence. "Oh, sir, I am very sorry."

"You were admiring the painted ceilings. How could I scold you for such?" he smiled.

"It's all very pretty." She didn't know what else to say.

"I'd dare say I would get lost in such a place. I almost did earlier."

The gentleman smiled and replied, "Yes, you would have thought we would have taken to smaller estates after the war."

Whenever the war was mentioned, Lindsay grew incredibly still, like a statue displayed in the Chatsmoore's gardens.

"Sir, how is your estate running?" I did not want the thought of war to linger in Lindsay's mind.

"Very well, indeed. I have even convinced my son-in-law to accompany me to York next weekend to examine the land."

"I am sure Allen is pleased that you are allowing him to take an interest in the affairs of your estate," I stated.

"Yes, well, he is very eloquent in speech, far more than I. With the prospect of repairing the farm buildings, it will do us good to have a financial voice for our tenants."

"Will they lose any of their livestock?" I asked.

"Not if I can help it," he replied.

"I heard rumours that some tenants were losing their farms at the Levinsons estate," I interjected. "Something about there not being enough capital. It's a shame that the farmers have to pay the price of an estate's failed investment."

"With Leonard as my agent and Allen who has the best interests of the people at heart, I can guarantee that will not be the case, Mr. Fox."

His agent, Leonard, was an older fellow who adhered to certain protocol. Perhaps, Allen would be their saviour in all of the tension that had been taking place between Lord Branston and his agent. I only knew these things because of Charlotte's free spitting mouth.

"It is better to go in prepared for what it might be," I

stated.

"Like war?" he replied, lifting his gaze so as to indicate that I knew absolutely nothing of what we were talking about.

Lindsay reached for her stomach and became lost by turning circles in her soup. I desperately wished that Rose wasn't so far away, for we could talk of the concert, anything really, for talk of agriculture and politics always brought my mood down. But, I supposed I had asked for it. Such conversation was not usually permitted at a dinner like this one. However, I truly did believe that Lord Branston meant what he said when he stated that he hoped to give the people of his land new opportunities. The thing was I knew of too many stories where this was not the case, and for that, I had a biased opinion on the matter, no matter the charisma of the headmaster involved.

"Do Allen and Charlotte have plans to move to Chatsmoore then?" I asked the question with a new understanding.

Lord Branston seemed to think that his land, which had survived the war, unlike many of his friend's estates, was in a position to survive. And, so it would.

"Yes, although they both informed us that they wanted to wait until after they have their first child." He smiled. "Charlotte has lived under Chatsmoore's roof all her life, so it does her good to manage her own home here until Chatsmoore becomes their life's responsibility."

I nodded, agreeing that such made perfect sense.

"Is the food to your satisfaction?" I asked Lindsay, doing my best to change the subject. I sounded like my own mother.

She forced a smile and replied, "Oh, yes. This is the best English meal I've ever had."

"We haven't even eaten the main course yet," Lord Branston laughed.

Lindsay and I exchanged looks, and I reassured her that her behaviour had been marvellous thus far. She began to relax as Lady Branston, who had been quietly seated beside her husband, began to talk with Lindsay of the Irish countryside. She was a charming lady with more dignity than most ladies of her class that I had ever met.

While the change in conversation had lightened everyone's mood, we were all grateful when Allen stood up suddenly and gave a toast to welcome us all into his home. It was the first dinner that he had held with such distinguished company, for a quick glance about the table had me in complete realisation that there were none, apart from Lindsay and I, that were of the middle or lower class. Allen had married into greater nobility, so his title and recognition had changed. He had welcomed it with grace just as Rose had done, and far better than I ever would have. As he ended his speech, I realised that Lord Branston was right. Allen was a fine spokesman. Taking a glance to the far end of the table where Lindsay and I sat, Allen then concluded his speech.

"I must also take this time to welcome a very special guest to our table this evening. She travelled all the way from Ireland and from rumours made way by my beloved wife, she has the voice of an angel. Dearest Lindsay, we toast to you."

Everyone raised their glasses and tipped them off, echoing Allen's welcome. From all of the attention, Lindsay became reddened in the face and did her best to smile, and what took me and everyone else in the room entirely by surprise, she waved.

The best part is that she didn't even realise that such a response was strange, for she, in her own mind, thought it was the same response that anyone would give at such a distinguished toast. To save the girl from any further embarrassment, although I thought it was entirely charming, Charlotte stood beside her husband and turned the guests attention away from Lindsay, to which Lindsay then let out a deep breath. My collar restricted me from letting out a good laugh.

"I can't breathe," Lindsay told me as we left the dining hall to make way towards the entertainment parlour.

"Then, you have succeeded."

"Have I? They have been staring at me all night."

"Their eyes don't know how to react to a creature that is different from their own."

"Yes, I am always different, aren't I?"

"Differently charming." I reassured her that no one would have known her class otherwise.

"I feel strange, perhaps it was best I didn't come," she remarked.

"No, I've been rather grateful for your company."

"I am not thinking in ways that I normally am," she replied. It was a comment that she made most often when something had disturbed her, taking her very far away from our present reality.

"I promise you that it will be okay." I squeezed her hand. As the women made their way into the drawing room and the men made their way to the room next door for a drink, I reassured Lindsay that Rose would take good care of her for the rest of the evening.

"Why can't I join you, Lloyd?"

"It isn't the proper thing to do," I replied.

"Am I one who prefers the proper thing to do?" she asked.

"No, but I guarantee you that you will not want to argue with me on this matter. The conversation is not suitable for delicate ears like yours." I touched her cheek affectionately and followed the other gentlemen into the card room.

Lindsay let go of my arm and like a nervous puppy, she followed Charlotte and Rose into the drawing room behind a sea of affluent silhouettes.

The gentlemen did not remain in the card room for very long, for after a glass of drink each, we decided to join the ladies in the drawing room. As soon as we did, Charlotte immediately stood up and came over towards me.

"Do you think Lindsay would sing for us?"

"She is a shy girl as it is. I don't think putting her on the spot would do anyone much good. You saw her at the dinner table."

"I thought it rather refreshing," she said.

"You don't need my permission, but by all means, please ask her in private."

She smiled and returned to where Lindsay was seated, sipping on a glass of some sort of champagne. I watched as Charlotte asked Lindsay the question. Despite her reluctance, she nodded, to which I was utterly surprised.

Charlotte clapped her hands and announced that Lindsay had been so kind as to offer us all a song. Lindsay then stood as her fatigued yet beautiful figure drew all eyes to her yellow bodice. She took a deep breath, her fingers interlocking with one another, playing as they always had when she became nervous or anxious about anything in life.

As she began to sing, I, so often like herself, became a statue in the grandeur room. One could have heard a feather drop as her voice fluctuated, the notes hitting the tip of the tallest chandelier in their estate. When the words fell over the seats and rippled through the coloured floor beneath us, my eyes were drawn towards Rose. It was inevitable for there were tears in her eyes.

Seen though she is not seen, I just want her to know...

The words flowed through the audience like a river sweeping through a dry desert. With the last word of the melody, a grander applause than sometimes even heard at the Queen's Hall erupted throughout the room. Rose joined in the applause and remarked how splendid of an angel she really was. Lindsay drew herself to where Rose sat and tenderly kissed her hand.

"Thank you," Lindsay said. That was all she said. It was all she needed to say.

Chapter 22
A Queen's Concert

"I've never been more nervous in all of my life," I commented. Rose and I were backstage, only a few minutes shy of taking Queen's Hall stage, something that I had only ever dreamt about. It truly felt surreal, like something that would soon grip me out of my senses at any moment. As we waited to receive our cue to take the stage, Rose held onto my arm, clutching her violin in the other hand. She was perfectly calm.

"You never gave up on your dream, even when others tried to discourage the very thing." It seemed as though she sang the words to me.

"You believed in me," I replied.

"Yes, even when you made it about yourself, I still believed in your dream."

"You were right, you know. I was pursuing success, but not anymore. I just want his story to be heard."

"Victor's story?"

"Yes, all of ours, really."

"He is there in the crowd you know."

"With Lindsay?"

"Yes, he will always be a part of her just like you will always be a part of me."

As soon as she said the words, I wondered if she had actually said them. Every single time that I had mentioned my affection for her, she had dismissed it. And, yet, right now, in perhaps one of the most important moments of my life, she admitted the very thing that I had repeatedly asked from her.

"Well, Lloyd, it's time to share *A Song for Somme* with the world," she said after a crewman told us to make our entrance. Both the orchestra and the maestro had made it to their own positions already.

"Are you sure you don't want your stick?" I asked.

"No, you will be my eyes tonight, though do not forget me on stage once the applause ends the night."

Her smile brightened my own. I could have kissed her.

I escorted Rose to her area on stage and took my own position at the piano stool. It was the first time that I had stood on a stage like this since I had performed at Oxford. For with every performance at the hotel, I was able to see the crowd perfectly well and was able to read every one of their faces. Now, I knew not if there was an audience at all. The lights glared on us and I wondered if Rose could sense just how bright it was up on stage.

I thought that had it not been for her persistence, she would not even be standing alongside me for the beginning movement. Over the past couple of months as we had practised together, she admitted to me that the violinist had to play a part in the first movement for she represented the soldier's lover. His song intertwined with hers, didn't it? That is what she had asked. And, now, as we shared the stage together, I was so glad that I had answered yes. To share all three movements with her was something that could not be put into words.

The composition began with a one minute piano solo before the full orchestra was to join behind me. As the

maestro and I made eye contact, I quickly turned towards
the black and white ties of an orchestra seated directly
behind me and thought how strange it was for an entire
orchestra to play the composition that had been in my
head for years. During rehearsal, it had felt like a dream,
just as much as it did now.

I closed my eyes and took the cue, painting the notes
across the black and white ivories with gentle care.

In a haunting manner, Rose joined in with me after
the first minute. Our fingers, in all of their pain and
dysfunction, met together in the air. The two lovers were
departing ways, one off to war and the other to spend her
grieving days in Cornwall. Within a matter of moments,
the eruption of the drumline brought us all into war. The
battlefield was gruelling, an explosion of strings blared the
shouts of officers as the endless ceasefire carried into the
night. It was an uproar as the brass instruments joined in
march with the strings, the attack absolutely seamless. As
the end of the battle neared, the strings joined in col
legno with the march of the drums. I lifted my head from
the music before me and watched as nearly the entire
orchestra came to a quiet end, like satisfied sharks
returning back into the deep sea. For all that remained
was the cry of a single violin as her vibrato reached the
furthest ear in that grand room. And, then, the room
became suddenly still.

An applause, far grander than I had even expected,
filled the room. I could not see their faces, but in my
heart, I thanked them for being there. Perhaps, with the
knowledge that nearly every seat had been filled in
Queen's Hall, I performed the next two movements as
though it was the last performance that I would ever be a
part of. For more often than not, the mastermind behind
the composition does not play alongside his musicians.

Hence, it most likely would be my last performance.
However, this music was more than a composition. It was
a tribute to the fallen and it was a goodbye to a past that I
had not been able to say goodbye to just yet. With this
song being out in the public, it became, just as Rose had
said, a memoir, something of the past, something that
never had to be lived again, but only remembered from
time to time. I did what should have been done years ago:
I finally said goodbye to Victor.

We were seated all together, enjoying drinks that Allen
had bought from Germany. He remarked that he had
their butler save it in their cellar for just an occasion.
Apparently, he had the butler bring it over to Belgrave
Square just before the concert, making sure that it was
offered with dessert at the end of the night as a toast of
celebration to *A Song for Somme*.

All of them were there, those who I would consider
my friends. Even Ted had made the journey from
Kidlington and Charles had invited James, Tony, and
Gerald of *Charles and the American Trio* to join the jubilee.
Little Rose sat upon Rose's lap for the mother said that
her nanny needn't take her away just yet, for this was a
night that we should all take pride in. Charlotte agreed
and took a seat beside her friend while Charles beamed
over his wife, the first time that I had truly seen him take
such attention to her in months.

Lindsay sat there, quiet and reserved, but clearly
satisfied to be in their company. I had insisted that no
one else be invited, for if there were guests that arrived at
their estate that were not on my invitation list, I replied
that I would turn in for the night and return to the

comfort of my hotel room. Thankfully, Charles and Rose had kept their word.

"I've never seen the Queen's Hall so full since before the war," Charlotte commented.

"How did you manage to get so many people there?" Allen asked me.

"I said nothing to no one. How was I to know that there would even be an audience there tonight?"

"Well, I did," Charles remarked.

I curiously looked at him to which he laughed and replied, "I didn't mind using my influence in London society to invite people to the concert of the season, old chap."

"That was so thoughtful of you, Charles," Rose smiled.

Did he do it for Rose or did he really do it for me? There was a sense in his tone of voice that he had done it for both of us.

"Word travels fast in London," he added.

"Isn't that the truth. Before long, you'll be invited by King George to perform at the palace," Allen remarked.

"I doubt it, but I appreciate the sentiment." I smiled at the always eager Allen and then turned my attention towards the band's ambitious pianist.

"When are you to go on tour again?" I asked James.

"We are hoping that our next tour will be in America, actually," Tony remarked. James was more quiet than the rest of the band members, although the apparent leader of the group.

I turned my gaze from James and Tony and fixated it upon Charles.

"Are you going to go with them?"

"Cherry and I have talked about it and we are considering it. America would provide a wonderful opportunity for us all and I'm not too sentimentally tied to this estate to depart from it."

"I think it would be a wonderful opportunity," Allen remarked.

There was a sudden shift in the room, for one simple question, on my part, was to change the course of the evening altogether. Everyone in the room seemed to know about it; even Lindsay seemed not to be shocked by the news.

"How long have you known about the prospect?" My eyes did not drift away from Charles. He placed a hand on his wife's shoulder and looked at me with great pride. "We've been talking about it for quite some time, but just received the paperwork last month to go through with the offer."

Rose had known for an entire month and during our many hours of practise, she hadn't thought to make mention of their move to America, not even once.

"I've always wanted to go to America." Lindsay smoothed the tension in the room with her sweet voice.

For the rest of the evening, in the presence of our guests, the conversation was dropped altogether, for everyone seemed to realise what I had realised upon Tony's first remarks about America. The only thing that I had known is that there had been some run ins at the jazz nightclub in central London. Both Tony and Gerald had gotten into an argy-bargy that had not ended in their favour, for the argument was aroused due to some regards to the colour of their skin. I had not asked Charles anymore questions about it when he had come to the hotel with the news, but began to imagine now that the troubles that had begun to stir up regarding their demographic of a band had suddenly stirred an urgency to find somewhere else to take off with their career. And, of course, the band had always wanted to return to their roots, yet it seemed so soon to do so; for despite the tensions that had been caused around town, *Charles and the American Trio* had been welcomed by most social circles. At least, that is what I thought.

Charlotte was the one to quickly change the subject as she always seemed to do so effortlessly well, keeping the mood upright as she always did. She learned well from her mother.

Laughter and conversation continued to flood the overly decorated room, a room that had not held such entertainment since Rose's accident, and a room that I had begun to imagine would be barren before long with no remembrance of the many times that Rose and I had filled it with music. No, I wasn't partial towards the estate, for it was far too grand for my tastes as well, but it was in fact the very place that I had learned to believe in my music in the very same way that Rose had believed in me all along. It was true that she had awakened something within me and I would always be grateful for that. Yet, the thought of us being an ocean apart was a thought that I was not fond of whatsoever.

I remained quiet for most of the evening. Lindsay was the only one who seemed to notice.

After the guests had departed, except for Lindsay and me, the four of us sat in the parlour, breathing in all that had taken place over the past several hours. Part of me wished that it was altogether a dream, that Rose and Charles weren't really serious about moving to America and raising their little Rose there.

"Before I forget, I must congratulate you, Lloyd. I thought you would never do it," Charles stated.

"Perform at Queen's Hall?" I asked.

"No, perform that bloody brilliant of a composition," he smiled.

Rose added, "Bravo! I thought the orchestra brought the music to life wonderfully."

"That might have been so, but you were the star of the show," I stated.

"Not so, but thank you, all the same."

"I thought you all were marvellous," Lindsay commented.

"You almost brought a tear to my eye, old chap," Charles laughed.

Lindsay grew quiet again and before anyone else could say anything, she remarked that she was feeling rather tired and decided it would be best to retire to her bed.

"Are you alright, dear?" Rose asked.

"It was a rather eventful day, and I'm just feeling tired, that's all."

"Of course." I remarked that it was perfectly alright for her to go to bed. Charles, too, commented that he was exhausted from the day for he had not gotten much sleep the night previous. I told Charles that he could inform his staff to go to bed now for they needn't wait for me to leave as I was more than capable of walking myself out.

"I will leave through the back door," I said.

"Yes, yes, that would be fine." He gave his wife a kiss on the cheek and departed the room, minutes after Lindsay had done so.

As soon as his footsteps faded down the hall, I didn't waste a moment of my time with Rose. I didn't know how much longer we had until she was to also remark that she was weary and rather looking forward to her bed.

"Why did you not tell me about leaving for America?" I asked without any hesitation.

"Nothing was for certain and nothing still is for certain. I didn't want to tell you until we knew for sure."

"It seems to me that things are quite certain, at least the whole band seems rather eager for the move."

"That's only because of the riots that have taken place, and you know, as well as I, that those sort of things die down after a while."

Her words made me think of her brother and the rebellious ways of the Irish Republic.

"Are you afraid that something will happen to Charles?"

"I do not know. He's taken quite some nasty remarks from old friends regarding his choice of band members."

"That doesn't sound like the definition of a friend."

"Then, what is your definition? For you and Charles don't agree on everything, but have remained true friends over the years."

"I would consider ourselves more acquaintances, rather than friends," I replied.

"You keep the peace because he is married to me," she remarked quietly.

"That is one way to look at it," I stated.

"You know what you must do if anything ever happens to me," Rose suddenly said after a brief moment in silence. She was playing with the necklace around her neck.

"Why would anything ever happen to you?" I asked.

"It isn't a matter of fact, it's just always good to think ahead," she smiled. "Of course, I would tell you to do so now, but you wouldn't listen."

"To what proposition?"

"Marriage. You should marry Lindsay."

"I don't think Lindsay would marry me. She always had her heart set on Victor."

"Must I be the bearer of bad news and remind you that your brother is dead," she stated without any hesitation or apology. It was rather out of character for her to say such a thing, but perhaps the length of the day had tired her mind.

"I do not mean to sound hideous, but I don't know what else to say to prove my point."

"I know you mean well. It's just Lindsay is stuck in the past. She has been for the past nine years."

"Sometimes, I think you don't see that you are no different from her," she replied, hesitatantly.

"Stuck in the past?"

"Exactly so."

"Rose, in previous times, I would have argued with you about such."

"Why not now? You don't feel sorry for me again?" she smiled.

"No, not that. It's because I believe you have spoken from a place of truth. I feel that I finally said goodbye to Victor tonight."

She reached for my hand, trying to find it and I took it from her.

"Oh, Lloyd. I believe you've been carrying things for far too long and have been too scared to let them go."

"And, Lindsay?"

"Lindsay isn't right in her mind," she whispered, afraid that others could hear us.

"No, she isn't. Perhaps taking her to your vicar could help," I smiled. Rose could sense the sarcasm in my voice.

"Don't joke about such things. Perhaps it would do you both good to go to the church."

"So, you could marry us without us even knowing," I laughed.

"No." She laughed. "You are entirely impossible."

"There are some things that will never change," I replied.

"No, but there are some things that need to change," she said. "I believe that you are the one who could help Lindsay move forward in life. Better so, it might just help you as well."

"Not even Queen Mary could get her to do so," I replied.

"Nor King George, you. Perhaps it would be good if she stayed with us for a while longer. I think Lindsay desperately needs a friend. Loneliness is the greatest loss of hope."

I thought about it for a few minutes before finally replying.

"I will write Aunt Birgitta in the morning."

"Oh, would you?"

"Yes, if it would make you that glad."

"It would."

"I don't understand why you care so much."

"If I told you, you wouldn't forgive me."

"Whatever does that mean? You must tell me."

"No, not now. You'd be better obliged by not knowing," she stated with great triumph in her voice.

"Am I to ever know?"

"There are some questions in life that are better left unanswered."

She was mysterious. I thought of the comment that Charlotte had made mention of those many years ago, how Rose was one who did not speak much of her past and had buried secrets that even those closest to her knew nothing of.

"Do you think she would like to go to the jazz club tomorrow?" Rose then asked, entirely dropping our conversation altogether.

"It might be overwhelming for her," I replied honestly.

"She's not a child, Lloyd. Don't treat her like such."

"I don't treat you like a child."

"You sometimes do, must I remind you?" she teased me.

"I don't mean to."

"I know you don't."

"What if you bring her by the hotel tomorrow night? She would like that," I replied.

"Why hadn't I already thought of that. Of course, she would. I will arrange for Charlotte to meet us there as well. Allen is going away on business."

"Yes, to York," I commented, remembering the conversation that I had with Charlotte's father at dinner.

"Perhaps we could all go to the church together on Sunday?" she asked hopefully.

I wondered what Rose was scheming. Was this her plan to make me move forward as well? Had it been her plan all along? There was no use in arguing with Rose any further.

"Lindsay always loved going to church," I replied steadily.

"Whatever the future holds, promise me one thing, Lloyd." I could tell that she was growing tired for her voice was disdained now.

"Hmm?"

"You will not give up on Lindsay, nor me, no matter what is to come."

Chapter 23
War's Roots

I had an hour before I was due on stage and decided to take a drink at the bar.

I was surprised to see the clergyman, for I hadn't seen him since the last time we had discussed man's pursuit of happiness. It seemed to be a century ago.

"Reverend Thomas, it's been a while. You look well." I shook the gentleman's hand.

"Did you not learn the last time we meant? Please, call me Thomas. I may be a clergyman, but I am still a common man."

"As the gentleman wishes," I remarked with a grin.

"What brings you to London?

"I am speaking at an event here in town."

"For the church?" I asked.

"Yes."

"Are you are staying here at the hotel?"

"I am. I decided upon such after Ted told me that you still play here in the evenings."

"Please, have a drink on me."

He accepted and took a seat beside me at the bar.

"Have you enjoyed performing here at the hotel?" he asked.

"Yes, I rather have."

"It's a beautiful building. I once dined here with Oscar Wilde."

"Did you really?"

"Yes, that was years ago, not long before he died."

"Did he dine here often?"

"All the time. Isn't it funny how men take to a particular spot for food and drink?"

"I must say, the Eagle and Child thanks you."

"That they do."

"How is life in Oxford?" I asked.

"No different from when you last left it," he responded.

"Have you visited Ted in Kidlington?"

"Yes, I dine with his family most often on weekends. They are pleasant folk. Ted's told me that you've been going to church."

"Oh, no, not in the way that your kind do." I realised the harshness in my reply, but he brushed it aside.

"So, you are still indifferent to the case for the church?"

"I have my opinions."

"Of course. I'd very much like to hear them."

He spoke like a friend, and was not judgmental in his tone in anyway. It was for that reason that I felt I could tell him what had bothered me most, for nearly all my life, but especially since the war. With the few times that I had gone to the church with Rose, there were queries that had boggled my mind, leaving me in a state of insomnia from time to time.

"Do you really wish to hear them, for I might turn you away."

"I can promise you that whatever you have to say, it is probably something that I have heard before." He smiled warmly.

"I do not know if I believe in this God of yours," I stated.

"Well, then," he smiled, waiting for me to say more.

"What I cannot come to understand is that a Greater Power who is sovereign and apparently desires the best for his creation, his children, whatever the theologian wants to call the human being, would allow evil to triumph. In war, in families, in financial ruin, in health, in heartbreak, there is no room for good. It seems to me that there is more loss than gain in our world nowadays. How then could I believe that there is a source behind it all? And, if I did, how could I say, with great pleasure and a smile across my face, that this creative being actually cared?"

Thomas looked at me and merely smiled. He was a madman, I thought to myself. I wanted nothing to do with his beliefs, yet I accepted his offer when he beckoned the bartender for hors d'oeuvres, this time on him.

"I once asked myself the same questions, Lloyd."

"For those who have triumphed, I am certain they can echo the writers of the Bible with great attribution, but I do not believe I can do the same, no matter your efforts to convince me otherwise," I replied.

"Have you ever read the Bible?" Thomas asked.

"Sure, a few stories here and there. When I was a boy, my mum made us attend mass a few times."

"I think that you would discover that life has treated you very similar to the biblical writers."

"In what way?"

"Why, everything you mentioned. When they chose to follow God, pain and loss did not get up and walk away, quite the contrary."

"Then, how would it benefit me to place my trust in a

God? According to your speculation, I would be no better off than I already am."

"That may appear to be so on a piece of paper, but it is not true of the heart."

We both sat there, the evening light disappearing through the windows, the chatter in the room becoming increasingly quiet, an indicator that the time was approaching for me to make my way towards the dining hall. Yet, here I was, entirely intrigued by this man's conversation.

"To explain war and misfortune in our world is something that cannot be attributed to God. It can only be attributed to the main fact that humanity has searched for something other than God to bring him the fulfilment of life that he yearns for," Thomas stated.

"Perhaps that fulfilment that we long for cannot be found, so that is why this greater being has been created. It is a figment of imagination, an illusion to bring hope amidst our suffering, just as much as a fair lady gets lost in a fairy story, waiting for the right man to come along and sweep her off her feet, her prince charming so to speak. Or, to the woman who has been denied love, due to her birth standing, finds herself in a miserable marriage against her own rights wishing for the happier marriage that is somewhere else. We have an imagination, do we not?"

"An imagination that could quite possibly be inspired to some degree by a greater being."

"How can you be certain? I don't believe I will ever be. And, even if that was the case, this greater being, why would I put my hope in him?"

"You ask the wrong questions, Lloyd."

"Crikey, what question am I supposed to ask, Thomas?"

"You have free will to do as you please, don't you?" he

asked.

"I would like to believe that I am my own man."

"Man's free will is what has brought evil into our world," he stated without hesitation.

"Then, why has God not intervened?"

"To the choices man makes, God would be intervening not on man's behalf, but would in fact be taking away his own free will. There will always be consequences for man's poor choices." Thomas took a breath to take a bite of food and then continued. "Think of this. If a father gives his child free will to explore the gardens, and when the child decides to climb up a tree to which he then breaks his arm, was the father wrong to allow him to explore the gardens to begin with? No, the child must pay the consequences for his choices."

"However, the father could have intervened, if he had watched his child that is."

"Yet, because he loves his child, he allows his child to roam the gardens on his own account."

"You mean to say that if there was no free will, there would be no such thing as love?"

"I mean exactly that. Our free will gives us the opportunity to love in the way God intended."

"Yet, free will also makes man love in the way God did not intend, if there is a God who intended any such thing."

I took another glass of scotch and let it wash my throat with a desirable numbness. The questions still lingered; they floated in my brain, just as much as Rose's commentary. He did not change how I felt towards God.

"Lloyd, I like your curiosity."

"No doubt you despise my beliefs."

"I never despise a man for his beliefs. Only when he takes those beliefs to harm another man do I then despise him."

I glanced up at the clock and realised that it was time for me to make my way towards the hall, where I was expected to entertain guests for the next couple of hours, including Lindsay and Rose.

"I must go now," I stated.

"It was a pleasure, as always, Lloyd." He toasted to me as I grabbed my coat and left the room.

He was the most curious of gentlemen. I could not understand his indifference to my opinions and thought to myself that it would most likely be the last time I ever had a conversation with the gentleman.

Walking through the sea of people, I made my way past the waiters offering hors d'oueveres to anticipated guests. My fists were clenched and with my heartbeat higher than usual, I arrived at the piano stool full of anticipation; I wanted the dialogue between Thomas and I to disappear through the ivories, through the black and white keys that would never depart from me, the one absolute truth that I had for my own.

Within moments, I allowed any anger and confusion to be filtered through a Bach concerto of which the notes echoed deep across the dining hall, nearly dancing off the chandeliers. It paved the way for others to feel exactly what I was feeling in that moment of time.

I did not care that my hair became loose around my face as it fell in front of my eyelids in such a fashion that would have probably had the Queen mother begging for new entertainment. However, I did not care.

From the corner of my eye, I saw the two of them. Rose, who I had thought once perfect, and Lindsay, who I had once thought unreachable, made their way to their reserved table, laughing together as though they had been friends all their lives.

"You played wonderfully tonight," Rose commented as soon as I took my seat beside her.

"You haven't yet had the privilege to hear *Charles and the American Trio*, have you?" I directed the question towards Lindsay.

"No, I've only heard tremendous things from Cherry," she stated.

"But, then again, Cherry is biased." I watched as Rose's smile gently met the room's aroma of fine taste.

As Charles took the stage, I wondered how many more nights he and the band were to take the stage before making their way to America. I knew Mr. Abbey would not be fond of the idea, just as much as I wasn't fond of it, for other reasons, of course.

"Why, they've got themselves a singer," I replied, entirely surprised by the new addition to the band.

"She is from New Orleans," Rose smiled.

"Where is that?" Lindsay asked.

"It is a city in America, a jazz sensation of a city," Rose replied.

"Is that where you will go when you move there?" Lindsay asked.

"No, the band has been offered a position in New York." Rose smiled once again.

I could tell that she was rather excited about the prospect of leaving England, although I could not understand her reasoning. Why she was so eager to leave all of her friends here was beyond me. She had told me that we both needed to start our own lives and perhaps the best way of doing so would be through means of separation. I had told her she didn't mean it to which she assured me that she was quite certain that it would be the best thing. I had told her that she was only trying to fool herself into believing so, to which she had only replied with an "Oh, Lloyd." This conversation had taken place earlier that morning when I had stopped by the house to take Lindsay to the market for the first time. While waiting for Lindsay to get dressed, we sat in the parlour discussing the future and everything that was to come. "It is only a matter of time," she had said. A matter of time until they would have their tickets to leave for America. "Lloyd, did you really tell Cherry that you have agreed to come with us to church on Sunday?" Lindsay seem most pleased by the idea, interrupting my thoughts from this morning.

It was in that moment that I became so terribly sad that I could not communicate to Rose with my eyes like we had done before Charles and her were married. I wanted to tell her, without saying a word, that I couldn't believe she allowed Lindsay to think such a thing. I had never given my answer and after my conversation with Thomas, I most certainly wanted to say that it wasn't even a question worth asking.

Yet, somewhere in the back of my mind, there was the memory of a little boy whose mother allowed him to roam the gardens, entirely on his own accord, the memory of Victor screaming at the top of his lungs and me running towards the creek, only to find that Victor had slipped in and nearly drowned. Had Victor not slipped in and fell, would I have been angry with my mum in the end? Of course not, no, that wasn't a rational thought.

"Yes," I finally stated quite monotonically. I took a sip from a drink that the waiter had brought to our table, free of charge on Mr. Abbey's account.

"I am very much looking forward to it. I've not been in years." Lindsay smiled, taking a small glance at her hands in her lap, perhaps feeling joyful for my reply. She then returned her gaze towards the white woman with short brown curls like her own, singing a tune that had enraptured every person at the Café Royal.

Charles and the American Trio were going far. I wondered if they would change the name of the band with their new star. Crikey, why had I agreed to go to church? I continued to gaze at Lindsay, who seemed to wear the biggest smile since arriving in London, and thought of Victor once again. Had I really agreed because of him?

They were like two angels, that I had already determined, but as we sat there in the rough church building, lightened by the stain glass windows, I thought that perhaps they really were. Maybe the two of them weren't even human after all. A man could think such a thing as he reflected on the curious happenings that had taken place over the past year.

Lindsay's alto voice and Rose's soprano voice harmonised together so perfectly. Apart from the colour of their hair, they appeared to be like two Irish sisters who had come to live two wonderful lives in such a peculiar way with such unwavering joy.

The service went rather quickly and I found that I rather enjoyed it more than previous times, but I believed that to be solely due to the company of Lindsay and Rose's harmonious voices.

After the last song ended, we left the church, Lindsay walking on ahead of us right beside Annabel. The maid had taken to going to church with Rose so often that even if others were to accompany her, she could not bear the thought of missing it. She was peculiar, too. We were all peculiar, really.

"What do you tell Charles when you go off to church with Annabel?" I asked out of curiosity, watching as the nanny took little Rose for a stroll. I could tell that Rose immediately disapproved of my comment.

"I don't tell him anything. He knows I like taking Sunday walks with little Rose."

I waited for her to continue but she said no more. So, we walked, her arm in mine, as Lindsay now skipped across the gardens with Annabel, occasionally looking back at the two of us. She looked as if she were ten years younger.

Closing my eyes, I tried to imagine the world that Rose now lived in, and yet, I could not find the hope that she somehow seemed to derive from nothing. As we walked, it occurred to me that perhaps Rose was right. I had to meet with Thomas again. Unknowingly to Rose, ever since my agreement to accompany them to church, I had spent the past few days at the London library looking up everything I could on New Testament theology. I wanted to understand the world from which Rose and Thomas had both found themselves in. I had searched the sciences section, the very place that I was certain to discover rational explanation for experiences that I could not understand. The church, all of it, I thought it to be a myth. I couldn't understand it in the way that Rose did, and in the same way that Thomas did. Then, out of nowhere, a thought occurred to me. I couldn't believe that I would ask the question, but it seemed that I would do anything against my own free will for the love of Rose. "Rose, would you like to meet Thomas?"

"The gentleman who dines at the Eagle and Child more than any Oxford student?" she laughed.

"The very one."

"Is he in London?"

"For a few days, yes. He's staying at the Café Royal. Perhaps we can get your chauffeur to take us over in an hour or so?"

"You should know better than to give a woman such short notice."

"You are no ordinary woman," I replied.

"Of course not."

"I mean, because…"

"Lloyd, no need to become defensive. You would have told me the very same thing before my accident."

"Then, you say yes?"

"I said yes," she corrected me.

I was right. The gentleman, after taking a drink at the bar, made his way to a reserved table in the dining hall. Unbeknownst to Thomas, I had asked Mr. Abbey, upon returning from the church, to arrange an extra three seats for Rose, Lindsay, and me at the table of Reverend Thomas.

Thomas immediately spied me walking towards him, quickly followed by Lindsay and Rose.

"We meet again, so soon." He shook my hand.

"I do work here, Thomas," I smiled.

"Who are the pretty ladies?"

I quickly introduced the three of them to which I then informed him that I had reserved a few extra seats for us all.

"That is very thoughtful of you, Lloyd."

"I am very interested in your work with the church," Rose commented.

"Well, then, I take it we will have much to speak about." He smiled looking at me with great curiosity. "Your friend, here, would not be so eager for such conversation." He winked at the girls to which Lindsay giggled, quickly covering her mouth to refrain from a judgmental eye from myself.

I excused myself, telling them that I had to perform for the next hour and would join them afterwards. I had asked Charles in advance if he and his band would take my normal second hour of performance. Charles had been rather pleased to entertain the hotels guests for longer than normal, many of whom were not his usual audience.

After I had finished performing, Charles approached me with a compliment of my performance.

"It will be a shame once you leave for America, Charles," I told him.

"I hope you mean it," he replied.

"Mr. Abbey and I both." I smiled and gave Charles a slap on the back before making my way to my seat, beside Rose, Lindsay, and Thomas. Charles laughed and then took the stage.

"You didn't tell us that Thomas was here when we dined here the other night," Rose remarked as I took my seat beside them.

"I had not thought to introduce the three of you then."

"Lloyd can be so inconsiderate sometimes," Rose laughed.

"As can all men, ma'am," Thomas smiled.

"I would have to agree with you," I laughed.

"Tell me, is it true that *Charles and the American Trio* have decided to leave for America?" Thomas asked Rose.

"You know how rumours spread so quickly," she replied.

"Yes, all people love a good gossip," Thomas stated.

"How else would we get people to pay for additional drinks if there wasn't good gossip to entertain evening conversation by?" I asked.

"You must be careful," Rose directed her words at me. "A mean gossip can get a man in troubled waters."

"I'm already a man in troubled waters," I replied.

The table ignored my sentiment and Thomas proceeded to ask Lindsay about her family's whereabouts.

"Oh, they left for America years ago. I'm living with an aunt in Fanore, a small town off the west coast of Ireland."

"Yes, in County Clare?"

"The very one," she replied politely.

"A quiet place of refuge, a most sacred place for prayer." He smiled, most likely reflecting on his travels there.

"Yes, indeed it is." She returned his smile.

We conversed about so many different things that evening to which I surprisingly found that I preferred the company rather than returning to my hotel room alone. I was drawn to Thomas because of his pleasant nature. Even Lindsay was entirely herself, not persuaded by possible triggers in the room to make her anxious. The pure joy in her laugh and conversation I attributed entirely to Thomas.

We stayed until the end of the first half of Charles' performance, remarking that jazz music, although irreplaceable of a full string symphony, had brought a vibrancy to Londoners who had still been paying the repercussions from the Great War. I hated to admit it, but I finally believed that it did. Perhaps Rose had softened my heart after all.

"I'm feeling rather tired and I'd like to visit with little Rose before I go to bed tonight," Rose suddenly remarked.

"Of course, should I call for the chauffeur?" Lindsay asked.

"Yes, dear, that would be marvellous."

"Are you unwell?" I stood up suddenly from my chair.

"No, Lloyd, just fatigued, that is all. Lindsay and I ran so many errands this morning, so it's been a rather long day."

"Are you tired?" I turned my gaze towards Lindsay.

"I'm younger and lighter on my feet, sir. So, I must remark that I am not as knackered, but it would probably be best if I return to the house with Cherry."

Lindsay had never addressed me as sir before and I found the address quite discomforting.

"Of course, you must." I followed them into the lobby, making sure that the chauffeur brought around the car in a timely manner.

"Will we be seeing one another again?" Rose asked Thomas before getting into the vehicle. The gentleman had followed me into the lobby, remarking that it was probably best for him to return to his room as well for he was catching the earliest train the next morning.

"I do hope so. If you are ever in Oxford, you must pay me a visit," he replied with a jolly smile on his face.

"That is an offer to enticing to refuse." She smiled as Thomas took her hand and gave it a kiss, offering the same farewell to Lindsay.

Chapter 24
The Quest for Happiness

After the girls had left the hotel, although he had first remarked that he should return to his bedroom, Thomas asked me if I would like to take a walk outside.

"It's a beautiful summer night," he stated.

"Why not?" I replied.

"Your friends were kind to dine with an old bloke like me," he remarked with slight laughter in his voice.

"I believe you are a man of affection, no lady could disagree such company."

"I am rather surprised that you arranged the evening altogether," he admitted.

"As am I."

"You seemed rather despondent when you left our last conversation."

"Yes, I am a hopeless man at times, Thomas. May I ask you something?" Our footsteps echoed on the pavement.

"Be my guest." His smile was illuminated by the dim street lamps.

"Thomas, pardon the personal question, but were you close to your father?"

"No, Lloyd, my father was an unlikable man. I barely knew him."

I took a deep breath; I barely had the energy to tell Thomas the story. I rarely spoke of my father. Charles was the only one who knew what had truly happened, well, and now Rose, thanks to Charles.

"I barely knew my father as well, Thomas."

I didn't understand how I was able to be so vulnerable with this man that I barely knew. Yet, in some way, he seemed like a grandfather that had all the answers, even if I did disagree with many of them.

"It is a shame for a child to have to grow up without knowing his father," he replied.

I thought of how my mum had been one of the most beautiful of women, more beautiful than the highest in the country, and yet, my father cheated on her many a time. He died a terrible death, took to the liqueur and wasn't even surrounded by his own family when he took his last breath. We learned through a letter, of his death that is, a terrible way for anyone to leave this world.

"Do you never think that perhaps your love for God is a desire for a father you never had?" I asked honestly.

I almost felt terrible for asking, but I felt that I was asking myself the same question. It is why I did not want to believe in such a God.

"Our fathers influence our understanding of God, do they not? If a child grows up with a father who never provides for his financial means, then that child will grow up unable to trust in a God whose sole interest is to provide the very best for his child. That child, now a grown man, will have a hard time accepting this biblical truth."

"In truth, I feel no need for an earthly or heavenly father. Even if I do believe that there is a greater being, I do not believe that I need him involved in my life."

"You've had to learn to manage on your own," he stated.

"Yes."

"It is a dreadful thing to be found alone with no family."

"Well, I have my music, at least." I tried to make a joke of the matter.

"Now, may I ask you something?" Thomas asked.

I nodded.

"Even though your father was an ill-tempered man, did you not desire a relationship with him as a child? Did you not once long for your father as your friends appeared to have?"

"I hate to admit it, but I did."

"That shouldn't be a statement birthed of hate. It is a part of our created nature. It is just as much the same in our desire for a relationship with the Creator of this Universe, although we often mistake it for other things here on earth, such as money, love, and power."

I felt in some way that I was making a conversion to theism, although I did not want it. However, the logical evidence before me and the need for something beyond my music created a curiosity.

To deny such seemed as logical as denying my own existence. I pondered his statements; somehow I could understand them.

I continued to ponder these thoughts as Thomas and I walked in silence, making our way back towards the hotel.

We returned to the hotel, the door to the dining hall slightly ajar. It was now entirely empty after *Charles and the American Trio* had finished their final round of songs. Taking a deep breath, I gazed at the elaborate embellishments in the ceiling above, the sculpted white flowers encompassing a breath-taking painting of kaleidoscopic wonder. The grand white fireplace in the hotel's lobby was warmly lit of which the gold walls seemed to dance to its soft light in memory of the music that just moments before had fled its halls. All that remained were a few waiters who cleaned up the aftermath of the extravagant evening, like washed-up cargo after a treacherous storm at sea.

Thomas stood beside me in the lobby, the chimes of the clock echoing in perfect rhythm to the waiter's movements in the room straight ahead.

"I love this hall," Thomas stated. He lifted his gaze to the stained-glass windows situated high above the hotel's front doors.

"Even at night, this room is more welcoming than the rest of them," he added.

I agreed.

"The windows remind me of something you would see in a church cathedral," he rambled on.

We were both silent as the fire crackled and the clock warned the ending of another day. With each second that passed, it was as though the chimes themselves encouraged me with what I was to ask Thomas next.

"I had once asked you if man is on the quest for something that cannot be found," I stated before making my way down the hall towards my room.

"Ahh, yes, a universal quest that I believe every man asks at one point."

"Sometimes, our conversations replay in my mind like a broken record," I replied.

"What a dreadful thing to have to endure," he laughed.

"In truth, I invited you here tonight because I don't understand what's been happening to me as of late," I said almost sullenly.

"Well, Lloyd, is man on quest for something that can never be found on his own account?"

His eyes sparkled; an insatiable grin spread across his face that made me realise that once again he had allowed me

to answer my own questions. He was remarkable for that.
"So, you claim God is the answer to that quest. You
sound just like Cherry," I replied.
"Cherry speaks from that which cannot be denied."
"I must confess that such a claim has stirred an interest."
"Which is why you have kept me longer than you had
intended," he smiled.
I felt that he knew everything that had taken place
between Rose and me.

I was never a man of confession, but I felt that in
order for me to move forward at all, like Rose had been
telling me, I needed to confess what I had held onto for
the past few years.
"I believe I've wronged Cherry," I stated suddenly.
"She's a wonderful character. Whatever would make you
say such?"

I bit my lip, wondering how to put it into words that I
loved another man's wife and was trying to find the right
way to let her go. Somehow, I found the right words and
began to tell him everything. He had beckoned for me to
take a seat in the lobby, and proceeded to take a seat
beside me, the place more deserted than a forgotten
island. After telling him things that I had told no other
man, he turned towards me, looking me directly in the
face, eager to end any guilt or misery I had tried my best
to overcome on my own.
"Lloyd, will you let me tell you something?"
"Of course, anything."
"You have asked me how could I believe in a higher
power that created us. Tonight, I believe you've answered
your own question."

I wondered what the gentleman had to drink with
dinner that evening, for I did not understand that which
he spoke of. I stared blankly at him and he continued.

"Who determines what is right from wrong?" he then asked me.

"We do."

"Yes, but we base our morals on something. Or, do you predict that this is something that has merely been acquired over time, an evolution of moral values?"

"I would determine the latter, sir."

"You have all the free will in the world to believe such, yet, you are wrong."

"It is the law of human nature, I believe."

"What makes one man's morals better than another? Who determines whether or not one man's morals are better?" he asked me. "You ask whether or not there is a power that influences and determines our actions. If there was not such, our behaviour might become very different. It is for the complete absence of God, that is consciously made by man, that we find a world that is turned upside down for evil."

"Do you believe that one's conscience is governed by a higher source than? Something that is outside of himself? No, I believe the law of man in and of itself differentiates right from wrong."

"You sit here, uninvited, curious by the law that you have broken. But, whose law have you broken? Cherry's? Your own? Or, some greater power that my fellow clergymen call God?"

"Well…" I stumbled with my words.

"It is a moral law that none are able to keep except God Himself, and that is why, in our own failing of such a law, we must come to God. It is only there that the answer is found."

"It can't be that simple."

"Lloyd, I understand your predicament. I once vowed myself to the same philosophy."

"Sir Thomas could not have been an atheist," I smiled.

"Oh, yes. But, then I came to realise that it took more work for me to believe in our existence by mere accident than to believe that there is a God who created us all."

"Then, who created God?"

He smiled then.

"You know, Lloyd, that was my greatest reason to deny a Higher Intelligence than I."

"What did you determine?"

"That if I knew the answer, I would be God Himself," he laughed.

"It is still not an answer," I responded.

"We can't find answers for everything, Lloyd."

"Just as much as I can't find the answer as to why some happily love and others do not. I am sorry I have said too much." I ran my hands through my hair.

The gentleman merely listened and smiled.

"Love is much more than we understand."

I rested my hands upon my head and came to the realisation that I truly never would be with Rose as I desired. And, wherever my moral code had come from, I knew for certain that Thomas was right, for such a choice would fit his definition of true love.

Fleeting, temporary, and fulfilling every desire within man's body, I had been enraptured by Rose and left with nothing in return but my own selfish ambition, in the same way that I had first pursued music. I had thought my love for her was sincere, but what did I know of love. Thomas made me believe that I really knew nothing at all.

As Thomas and I finished the last of our conversation, I found that while I would never have Rose as I desired, she wouldn't be the answer to my own life's existence. This thought, so contradictory to my feelings for the past few years, took me by complete surprise.

I had been invited to dine with Lindsay and Rose at Belgrave Square. It was two nights after our last dinner at the hotel. After a wonderful dinner, we had sat in the drawing room talking about little to none while lightly commenting on the rising success of *Charles and the American Trio*. Lindsay had then excused herself for bed shortly after the nanny had taken little Rose to bed.

"Are you tired? Should I call for Annabel?" I asked Rose who was more quiet this night than previous evenings.

"No, please stay, Lloyd. At least until Charles gets home."

I glanced at the clock. It was nearing midnight. The ruffled curtains were blowing at the far end of the room for a window had been left opened. The library was even more haunting at this hour, although I could not have imagined what such a place would have looked like before gas had made its way into such mansions.

"Where is Charles, anyways? Is he still at the hotel?"

"Yes." She was so quiet in her reply, I wondered at first if she had said no.

"Do they stay behind at the bars afterwards?" I asked.

"Yes, when the hour grows dim, he prefers their company over mine."

I couldn't tell if she was joking and after careful evaluation of her face, I realised that she was not joking in the slightest. "Rose, I—"

"Please don't say anything more on the matter. Our lives keep moving on and we must choose whether or not we will move with it."

"Do you think Charles will give more attention to his family once you move to America?"

"Perhaps. He is a kind man, Lloyd. When he wants to be, he is kind. What's more, he provides for his family."

"His inheritance provides for his family," I spoke roughly.

"Oh, Lloyd."

I realised that I was being unfair.

It was quiet, the only sounds of the clock chiming in the grand hallway. There were words I wanted to say and perhaps it was the distant chimes of the grandfather clock that encouraged me to do so. While I was finally letting go of Rose, there were things I wanted to ask her. I didn't know if it was a desire for closure in our relationship as it had once been, but I knew I had to ask her one last time.

"Why do you stay with him?"

There was no reply, at first.

"Why do you ask me again?"

"Because I'm trying to understand the unfathomable."

"I seem to be an unfathomable creature to you these days," she slightly smiled.

"I respect your religious beliefs now, Rose."

"Do you now share them?" she asked hopefully.

"In my own way. As I said, I'm still trying to understand the incomprehensible."

"My marriage? God's love?"

"Both," I replied steadily.

"I know that my marriage appears to be an unhappy one, but in all truth, I cannot bear the thought of parting from him. I cannot possibly expect you to understand for you aren't married."

"One day I shall."

"Shall you?" she asked, taken aback by my reply.

"I believe I might be able to love Lindsay as much as I love you," I whispered.

"Oh, Lloyd. Our love was based on mere passion, due to feelings, that at times, were beyond our own control. I love Charles because I do not know how not to. It is a by-product of love that no one could ever predict."

"So, you will recklessly disregard your happiness and remain faithful to your husband?"

"Always, yes. I used not to think in this way. I, at one point, even thought I would leave him."

"To be with me?"

"Yes," she sighed. "Oh, I can't believe I admitted that to you."

It occurred to me, just as it had occurred in the past, but I had tried not to believe it to be true. Now, I had the only chance I would ever have to ask her my next question.

"That is when you wrote to Lindsay, isn't it? An act to relieve the terror within your own mind to do that which you felt you had lost control of - your own free will to leave Charles."

"I do not deny that it was my intention. I am very fond of you, Lloyd, but Charles is my husband and the father of my daughter. I made a vow to Charles, a vow that I cannot break no matter how many times I have wanted to. Can you imagine if all vows were broken on the daily? Our world would be in a never ending war, expected to last forever."

"Yes, of course."

"Before you mock me, I must tell you. Ever since I started attending the church, I not only found something that I was not looking for, but I found the very thing that I had been searching for all along. And, I am happy, very very happy. I only want the same for you."

"You astound me."

"However so?"

"Life has been unkind, yet you see yourself as one of the most fortunate."

"Of course I do. What good is it to focus on that which I do not have? It only makes me miserable. If you can't change your life, you can change it by way of gratitude for the things that cannot be changed."

I remained silent, her lips pierced the air, waiting for me to answer, but I gave her none.

"I believe you, Lloyd Fox, are in search of it, too."

"Why do you say so?"

"You would not be here today if you were so indifferent. You care for people so deeply, yet you keep your heart buried so deep." She paused, "Are you afraid to love her?"

"In a way."

"Because of her sickness?"

"It's much more than that."

Rose knew me, she knew me like no one else, in the same ways that I understood Lindsay, a girl who locked her heart away in a small cottage in Ireland.

"You know, I've never once, since Victor died asked how she was and had her reply that she was well."

"It's dreadful, but she's eager to see a doctor." Rose's voice was soft in the dimly lit room.

"Did she tell you that?" I asked.

"Women are able to converse in ways that a man and a woman cannot," she stated.

I accepted her response and replied, "Victor would have rallied every doctor together in all of Great Britain until he found the cure."

"They say that sickness of the mind is incurable."

"Is that what they said of Caitríona?"

"Yes, it was the very thing that Caitríona's papa used to tell her all the time." Tears glistened in her eyes.

I didn't mean to upset Rose by asking so, but I had
wondered if Lindsay's presence in their home had
reminded her of the girl that had lived in the castle.
"I am sorry. Rose, I know I am cynical most often, but
when it comes to such matters, I have to disagree."
"Why so?"
She was honest. She didn't believe that Lindsay could be
cured, perhaps in the same way that her Caitríona had
never been cured.
"I never told you of my time in America." I said it
without thinking.
"No?"
"I went away because I was suffering terrible nightmares.
Charles had even considered admitting me himself but
knew that I would never forgive him for such."
"It was the war?"
"It was, it is, always the war. Shell shock, they called it. A
mild case."
She listened intently.
"It never left me. Not until I started writing composition
music again. Will it ever go away? I don't know. But,
when I write, it silences the silence."
"What encouraged you to compose again?" she asked
inquisitively.
"I was inspired after attending a musical on Broadway,
believe it or not."
"I've always wanted to go to Broadway. I must go when,
well, if, we ever go to America." She paused. "So, was the
Broadway musical the cure, then?"
"It reminded me that I was alive and to live in denial of
my life would be to deny the fallen's sacrifice altogether."
I exhaled deeply. "It was shortly after attending the
musical that my American doctor had suggested to me
that I return to Oxford. He thought that it would do me

good for it was the only time that I spoke of fond memories. He was a pleasant old man."

"So, that was your cure? A ticket back to England."

"No, it was a ticket to become a successful man. But, now I see that it was much more. My education gave me back all hope that had been lost in the trenches, just like the church has been that very thing for you."

She smiled for I was accepting the very thing that she had wanted me to see for months. They were the demons she had spoken of not so long ago.

"When I rescued Lindsay from the asylum, I never wanted to see her again, which was probably another reason for my hasty leave for America after returning from the war. It hurt too much to love someone who didn't want to receive any help as she thought that nothing was wrong with her. Yet, now, after my time in America and an improvement in my own mind, I believe that there is a cure, there has to be."

"Yes, there has to be," she whispered. "Besides, Lindsay knows *now* that something is wrong with her."

"It appears so. "

"You will love her, won't you?"

"In the same way I would have, you."

"I am glad that you have finally come to realise such."

"It was Thomas that made me realise so."

"Thomas?" She was surprised.

"I told him about you, about us. He did not condemn me."

"Why would he ever? Reverend Taylor says that forgiveness is ours, all of ours." She paused and stated, "You know, I cursed myself for allowing you to kiss me again."

"That wasn't your fault."

"But, I had given into temptation, hadn't I?"

"Yet, you stopped."

"That's the thing, Lloyd. I wondered if I would have, and that is what had made me at war with myself. I discovered my virtues not to be as strong as I thought. However, in that moment of fault, I found myself again and realised that any thoughts I had towards forsaking Charles were wrong. It was a moment of weakness, that of which we all have."

"Love is not weakness."

"Between a married woman and an unmarried man, love is the greatest of weaknesses."

"I knew it was wrong, however spending time with you had not been wrong by no means."

"It has not helped," she spoke to her defence.

"So, that is why you sent me away to see Lindsay?"

"Partially, but no, there was more. I truly believed you love her."

"And, now, what do you believe?"

"I believe it more than ever. And, I equally believe that Lindsay loves you."

"Has she said such to you?"

"I already told you that women converse of things that are not talked about amongst men," she smiled.

"I need not probe, of course." I paused, "Do you remember that time we talked of idealised love?"

"Yes, how could I forget it. You perhaps thought me an entirely different person, wondering who had stolen the real Rose."

"I believe that is what our love is, at least that is what it has to be."

"We do love each other, Lloyd. We always will. But, in this case, our choice to remain apart is a great choice to love."

"The greatest choice to love," I replied.

Reaching for her hand, I kissed it and then bid her goodnight.

Chapter 25
Friendship's Quarrel

We had all agreed to a picnic at Hyde Park. It was a lovely summer day and even Charles had finally made time to spend with his wife and little girl. I wondered if having Lindsay around made him feel entitled to duty so as not to appear to be a neglectful husband. Charlotte and Allen had also joined us for the afternoon, now expecting a child of their own, the announcement made to all of us just that morning.

Rose was pleased for her friend and Lindsay, too, offered her congratulations. I watched as Rose reached for Charlotte's hands, Charlotte quick to take them and leave her not standing there alone. The two of them walking together, arm in arm, reminded me of the early days at the Chatsmoore Estate. How different it all was then. Lindsay walked on ahead, grabbing little flowers as she did so, placing them in her hair like how she used to during our time in Cornwall. Staring at her, I thought that she truly was beautiful, a rare beauty that could not be described. As I watched her, I thought of her life in Ireland and of the loneliness she must have felt over the past few years.

I had heard from Aunt Birgitta just this morning, asking of how her little peach was doing to which I ensured her that she was the healthiest, full of wonderful colour and not in anticipation to return home, although she did make mention of how much she missed her aunt's cooking. Aunt Birgitta would be pleased by such a reply, as would Lindsay approve of such a letter, too. I knew that her aunt was eager for her return, but I wanted to postpone it for as long as possible.

"It is the most cheerful day," Rose commented as we spread forth the blankets and took our positions next to the baskets of food that Annabel and one of Allen's footmen had brought.

It was days like these, when her eyes glistened in the sun, that I entirely forgot that Rose had lost her sight. She never complained about it, at least not in front of anyone it seemed to be, and for that alone, we all had something to learn from Rose.

"Did you know that Cherry has been asked to play the violin at church?" Lindsay asked all of us as Annabel distributed the food.

"At the church?" Charles asked.

Lindsay, mid-way through eating a cherry, sat still, entirely forgetful that Rose did not tell Charles of their Sunday endeavours. In that instance, she remembered how much Charles would disapprove.

"I only meant that Cherry can play there any time she chooses. The acoustics are brilliant, far more than even Queen's Hall," she smiled.

Charles seemed pleased by her answer and asked how such a conversation had come about.

"As your wife, I am more recognised in society than you would dare to think," she laughed.

"As my wife, you best receive the attention you deserve." He held her hand.

I wondered why it was that Charles came and went,

only to really attend to his wife in a public manner; it seemed like a show for the British aristocracy just like any of their dinners that would be attended to at the Chatsmoore Estate or any other, addressing the man to the left and right of you as his grace.

"Do you have a name in mind for a child?" Rose asked Charlotte.

"I have not thought that far ahead. It is a terrible responsibility to have to hold, for what if your child grows to despise their name and thence forth, you?" Charlotte asked.

"I take it they could always change their name," Lindsay gently replied.

We all laughed and finished eating sarnies and fruit cakes, a well prepared meal by the finest of cooks.

"Do you have plans to teach your child tennis?" I asked Charlotte humorously.

"Yes, boy or girl," she smiled amusingly.

"No doubt to compete at Wimbledon one day," I replied.

"Are you still sore from that terrific loss?" Charlotte laughed.

"That was years ago, perhaps, we should play again," I stated.

"Even a blind woman could beat you," Rose replied without hesitancy.

"Stick to music, old chap," Charles smiled.

"Lloyd, are you to compose any other masterpieces?" Allen suddenly asked.

"If you had originally decided to room with me, instead of marrying Charlotte, you would have found that my entire room has been buried in compositions over the past several months. My feet can barely find the floor," I joked.

"Well, that's swell." Allen laughed as well as the others.

"But, really? Will you perform again?"

"I'll continue to write, that's for certain, but I am considering taking a new job."

"You'll be seventy and pursuing a new career, old chap. You are always looking for the next best thing," Charles commented. "Don't you think it's rather late in the game for that?"

"I meant that I will pursue a different aspect of music. The University of London has offered me a position to teach Piano and Music Composition in the fall. It turns out the head of the department was at the concert last month."

"That's splendid, Lloyd," Rose beamed. "You are a marvellous teacher. Of all people, I know this most certainly."

"How many classes?" Allen asked.

"Not entirely sure, but probably four to begin with."

"Well, you will certainly have your hands full, that's for sure," Allen replied.

I watched as Lindsay smiled and then stood up, apologising to us all that she needed to take a little walk before her feet went numb. No one else seemed to notice the shift in her manners except for me. After a few minutes, I also excused myself and ran towards Lindsay.

"Lindsay, darling, why did you leave so abruptly?"

"Don't call me darling," she said.

"Lindsay, are you alright?" I asked.

"Not entirely, but isn't that how it always is with me."

Something had upset her, something so harmless could set her down the wrong path; I couldn't understand it. Yet, it was entirely out of her control, which made me feel all the more out of control myself.

I reached for her hand and took it suddenly while gently wiping a tear that had fell down her face.

"I don't want to leave," she finally said.

"Well, why do you have to?"

"It will be just as before, won't it?" she asked.

"No, not as before. It will be different this time."

"You are to take a job at university and I am to return to Aunt Birgitta in Ireland," she said bitterly.

"Holidays don't last forever," I replied.

I didn't know how to say it, not yet anyways. It was as though an old wound was healing and replacing Lindsay with Rose, although Lindsay had been the first to occupy my heart those many years ago, it was all too sudden. It wasn't fair to Lindsay. However, I wanted to make myself clear to her, but before I could do so, Charles loud voice flooded through the park.

"Lindsay! Lloyd!"

We turned to see that Charles was frantically waving at us from afar. I grabbed Lindsay's hand and she took it, our feet scurrying through the grass, eager to find what it was that Charles had become so upset by.

As we drew closer, I was shocked to find that Annabel was being tended to by Rose and Charlotte.

"She was pouring the wine and suddenly fainted," Charles remarked.

"Should we get her to a doctor?" Charlotte looked up at Charles and Allen.

"No, there's no need for that," Lindsay commented. We all looked at her.

"Position her on her back and loosen her belt," Lindsay instructed Charlotte. "Now, take her legs and raise them, gently, please. Charlotte, if you could wet that piece of cloth with the drinking water, please?"

Lindsay checked Annabel's pulse and murmured that her breathing was fine and that all we could do was just wait for her to regain conscious.

"Oh, I hate this," Charlotte whispered. "There seemed to have been nothing wrong with her."

Charlotte, always accurate in observation, hated to think that she had wrongly observed the afternoon altogether.

The rest of the gentlemen and I stood around the scene, telling passersby to please continue on their afternoon journey. Lindsay seemed to know what she was doing, for a few moments later, the girl came around. "Will you pour me a glass of water, please?" Lindsay instructed Rose.

She did as was told and handed her the glass of water; Lindsay insisted that Annabel take the drink without hesitation.

"What do you think caused it?" Charlotte whispered to Rose.

"It is nothing more than dehydration," Lindsay replied, overhearing her just fine. "Give her ten minutes time and then I suggest that we return to the house. Annabel should take the remainder of the day to rest."

"Of course." Rose nodded and Charles stooped down to take the girl into her arms after the ten minutes were given.

Rose followed quickly behind her husband using the cane that Charles had made for her. It was an useful tool for getting around, although Rose was often stubborn in not using it around the house or when she went out for social parties.

Charlotte and Allen remained behind to help clean up the disrupted party.

"Do you need any help?" I asked while Lindsay still stood by my side.

"It is only a small picnic, not a lunch that needs an entire staff to clean up after," Allen laughed.

"I believe we will return home," Charlotte replied. "Perhaps you both would like to join us for dinner one evening?"

"Perhaps, but you know my rule," I grinned.

"No other guests invited," Allen shook my hand.

"Except for you, Lindsay," Charlotte smiled at the girl who had been Annabel's afternoon nurse.

Taking Lindsay by the arm, we left the serenity of the park, listening to the birds whistle through blossomed trees as the summer wind greeted our ears with its own song.

"How did you know what to do?" I asked Lindsay.

She hesitated and then spoke softly, "My little brother used to have fainting spells most often, very similar to Annabel's."

"I didn't know you had a little brother," I commented. "Did he leave for America with your parents?"

"No, he died during the war."

"I never met him?"

"No, not to my knowledge, anyways."

After the scene that had been caused in the park, I had taken Lindsay to the market and bought her a knickerbocker glory, a treat that I thought she deserved. Her smile lit up as she tried the delectable ice cream dish for the first time. We had made no mention of our conversation earlier, and I was rather glad that she had forgotten it, although there was something that made me believe she had not, for it was just like Lindsay to do so.

Arriving at Belgrave Square, I escorted Lindsay to the front door and replied that I'd like to come in as well to hear how Annabel was doing.

"We called our doctor," Rose informed us when we arrived at the front parlour.

"Is it anything to be concerned about?" I asked

"Thankfully, none whatsoever," she replied. "However, I am afraid that I am quite tired and will retire to bed early tonight."

"May I help you to your room?" Lindsay suddenly asked.

"Would you be a dear?" She extended her hand and Lindsay escorted her up the stairs towards her bedroom, their quiet laughter echoing through the opulent corridor. Charles and I stood there, entirely silent on the day's matters. "Have you considered investing in a one story house? It would be easier for her," I finally said.

"You and I both know how stubborn Cherry is. Besides, neither of us can imagine giving up this home just yet."

"But, you will when you leave for America?"

"I would like to keep the estate. It isn't a permanent move," he replied.

"So you will keep the place due to conveniency and tradition?" I asked.

"Yes, the very thing. Would you like some port?"

"No, I'd rather not."

"Denying a friend's hospitality. You know, that's the first step in the degradation of a friendship," he laughed

"Is it?" I asked, my eyes suddenly squinting and examining the movement in his own gaze, very carefully. "Because, I believe a lack of honesty is the first."

"When have I been dishonest with you, old chap?"

"Don't test me." I tried to get rid of the anger in my throat. Ever since Cherry had confirmed my suspicions, I was furious that he was still being unfaithful to his wife. I probably wouldn't have cared as much as I did had he been betrothed to another, but here it was.

We were going to have to confront this sooner or later. We had confronted it before, that one time at the hotel bar when he had made a promise to end it, but he hadn't done so, had he?

Charles offered me a glass of port anyways, and we took a seat, the wall's paintings of men and women from the 18th century gazing in on the scene.

"You will think me out of place to speak on such matters, but I believe you need to find the time to better attend to your wife," I finally said.

"Crikey, Lloyd. I can't just give up my dreams because my wife is blind."

I was absolutely repulsed by his response.

"Are you listening to yourself?"

"I only mean that I am doing everything I can to ensure that Cherry and I have a future worth having."

"Neglect is not so."

"Did I not spend the day with my wife, today?"

"The first in months. You've spent more time entertaining others than spending time with your own daughter." I didn't care that I spoke harshly.

Charles, who was pouring himself another glass of port, set the glass down and walked over to where I sat.

"How dare you, old chap." He squared me and asked me a question that I believed he had wanted to ask me for quite some time.

"Have you been with my wife?"

"How could you ever say such a thing?" I stood up rapidly. "You know that I would never take advantage of Cherry. I have morals, unlike you."

"Get out!" Charles spoke with a fierceness in his eyes that I had not seen since the war.

"Is that how we are going to address this?" I was disgusted. "Like little boys?"

Before I could say anything else, Charles' fist was in my face. Blood was already spilling from my nose and I returned the blow, knocking over a family vase upon doing so. As the porcelain pieces shattered across the floor, that is when I noticed her. I wondered how long she had been standing there.

"Lloyd?" she asked with great fear in her eyes.

"Lindsay, darling?" I shook off any anger that I had felt in that moment and made my way to where she stood.

"You are bleeding," she said quietly, looking beyond where I stood, her curious brow and fear in her eyes fixated entirely on Charles now.

"I thought you had gone to bed, Lindsay."

"I was on my way to select a new book from the library," she commented in her defence.

"What remarkable timing. The lovely Lindsay has come to rescue you from a terrible loss," Charles grinned.

I began to wonder how he even lived with himself.

"Lloyd can fight his own battles." She spoke in such an unfamiliar manner.

"As could Victor." Charles stared at her.

"Is that the same thing you told Victor as you let a group of men nearly beat him to death? And, what for? You never would have me." There was anger in her speech. I had never seen her confront or defend anyone on matters that concerned her.

"Is that what I told Victor?" Charles laughed quite abruptly. "It was a group of university students having a bit of fun. Did you forget that I bloody saved his life at war, Lindsay?"

"Victor died at war." Her posture altered as she spoke.

"But, I saved him and I have a nasty scar as a result."

"You should have let him die, then he would have never shot himself and be found with cowardice in the end," she stated quite boldly. "You consider yourself a high and mighty hero who does not fear things not going his way, because it always does, Charles Atwood."

I believe Charles was just as shocked as I was at such rhetoric.

"Lindsay, calm yourself. You will wake the rest of the household," I warned her.

"You don't care, you don't bloody care," she spoke through tears. "Neither do you bloody care for Cherry."

"Lindsay," I grabbed her arm and told her to calm down. She wasn't in her right mind.

"What makes you a good judge of other people's nature?" Charles challenged her. "Locked away in your castle…"

"Charles, stop!" she yelled.

"Charles, if you knew what was good for you, you would leave the room," I said, becoming more outraged at his behaviour by the minute.

"You have no right asking me to leave my own home," he sniggered.

"I didn't ask you to leave your home, just this room," I stated.

"I told you, get out." His eyes glared at me.

There was no way I could leave their home knowing that Lindsay could still be a prisoner to Charles' behaviour.

"You are coming with me," I looked at Lindsay without any hesitation.

"Lloyd…"

"You are coming with me."

"Where will I go?"

"I'll book you a room at the hotel."

Lindsay scurried out of the room and headed to the bedroom she had been staying in to retrieve her one and only suitcase. I didn't look at Charles again and left, slamming the front door behind me. It was only a few minutes more when Lindsay, who was now dressed in a hat and coat over her summer dress, came out the door.

Lindsay's eyes were entirely glued to my own as she shut the door, much quieter than I had done just moments prior.

She stood there, her silhouette dancing off the illuminating shadows of the grand house. The temperatures had dropped significantly since our excursion in the park.

"You didn't do anything wrong, Lindsay, do you hear me?"

I offered my hand and she accepted it. She was nervous for I could tell that her head was circulating in many directions.

"Oh, Lloyd, I never meant to bring any harm."

"He deserved every word," I spoke firmly.

We walked, I, careful not to say anything that would disturb her anymore.

"Will you and Charles ever make amends?"

"One day, we shall. These things die over, don't they?" I smiled briefly, but it faded quite as sudden as it had been forced.

"I don't know if I can be so certain," she replied.

Taking one of her hands, I kissed it and told her that it would all be for the better. She was not reassured by my remarks.

It wasn't long until we arrived at the hotel and booked Lindsay a room for the next few nights.

"Lloyd, I don't want to be alone, not right now," she said, suddenly afraid.

"You will be right down the hall from me."

"Do you have any tea? I'd really fancy a cup," she said suddenly.

"Yes, I supposed a cuppa won't hurt anyone."

After checking out the room that she had been given, only a few rooms down from my own, she knocked on my door. When she first entered, she appeared like a mouse, hesitant to walk any further into the room, alarmed by the mess that spread across the tables and floor. Her nerves were entirely on edge, especially so after watching the brawl that Charles and I had gotten into. I still couldn't believe the things that she had said to Charles; I admit, I was quite proud of her.

"It's only sheet music." I laughed at Lindsay, who remained at the edge of the room, like a child playing in the shallow ends of the sea.

Handing her a cuppa, she took it with great gratitude and began to examine the papers on the table, gliding her fingers atop the music, like a swan swimming on a glassy sea. Her movements reminded me of the first time Rose had first become alarmed by Charles and my flat in Oxford.

"Did you write all of these? Are they really all yours?" she asked, briefly taking a moment to lock eyes with mine.

"They all are mine."

"I thought *A Song for Somme* was the only composition piece that you had written."

She fluttered her eyelids shyly, almost afraid to admit that she didn't believe me capable to write more.

"No, I've locked them all away for so long. Rose said I should share them with the music department at the university."

"Would you be permitted?"

"If I am to teach music composition, I don't see why not. I may not be the one to play or even conduct them all, but it would be better than them sitting in a London hotel room."

She smiled faintly and continued to gaze upon it all,

sheet by sheet.

"I believe the world will be a better place because of it."
She smiled and returned to tending to the sheet music as
though it was her own flock of sheep.

It was the first time I realised that Lindsay was
changing me; she had been since I arrived in Ireland. It
was why I was so afraid to go in the first place, for aren't
we all afraid of it? Change. The very word makes us
cringe, yet the very word is what forces us to live for the
better.

Chapter 26
An Irish Goodbye

Lindsay stayed at the hotel for the next week, accompanying me to the University of London to walk the music halls and meet a few of my future colleagues in the mornings. In the afternoons, she would visit Rose when Charles was gone. That first day that she had gone to their home, after the quarrel that Charles and I had gotten into, I had asked Lindsay afterwards what Cherry had thought of her leaving unannounced.

"I simply told her that I wanted to learn what hotel life was like. She thought it perfectly endearing."

"Of course she did," I replied, taking a sip from a cup of coffee nonchalantly.

"Do you still have violin lessons with her?" she had asked.

"No, Cherry insisted that we take a break for a little while, something about wanting to spend more time with little Rose."

However, I got the feeling that Rose was creating distance between us so that Lindsay and I could cross our bridge together. She was smart and I couldn't put anything past her. Perhaps Rose couldn't have planned this any better, for a week at the hotel meant that Lindsay and I were spending the most time with one another since she had arrived in London. I knew how much Rose wanted us to be together. I wanted it, too, but at the right time.

In the evenings, Lindsay sat in the back of the dining hall observing the audience and listening to the music that I played. Each night, she told me that she never tired of the piano pieces. However, as soon as Charles took to the stage, she would depart, like a fairy that had the power to disappear in a moment's notice. I wondered if Lindsay had told Rose about the fight. It was a miracle that she hadn't been disturbed by the noise, but of course, her room was far enough away not to have heard anything, especially if she had already taken to sleep.

On this particular night, after I had finished performing, I found Lindsay in the hallway, sitting outside her hotel room, her face in her dress like a little girl. "Lindsay? Why are you sitting in the hall?"
"I rather didn't want to go inside my room, neither did I want to be in the dining room with the other guests," she said.
"It's a chilly night. Would you like a cup of coffee or tea?"

I reached out my hand and she stood up, the knees of her dress stained with tears. It was the most dreadful thing to see someone you care for be filled with such misery, even if only for a moment's time. Taking my hand, she followed me to my room and quietly took a seat on the sofa while I made my way to the kitchen.

After removing the kettle of hot water from the cooker and finding some biscuits that had been stored away in a cabinet, I joined Lindsay on the sofa. It was for this moment that I was glad to have one of the only rooms with a cooker. At first, I had told Mr. Abbey that I didn't need it, but he insisted that any musician living under his name should not be without an option to make himself a nice cup of tea every once in a while. He was a pleasant fellow.

As I drank the cup of coffee that I had prepared for myself, I watched as Lindsay didn't even take one sip from her cup. Instead, she stared into the distance, entirely oblivious to my company.

"I would like to return home, Lloyd," she finally said.

"Home to Aunt Birgitta?"

"Yes, it has been lovely being here, but it's also been difficult."

"But, I thought you said you couldn't bear the thought of leaving?"

"I can't bear it, but I also know now that it is time for me to return home."

"Have you not enjoyed your visits with Cherry and our excursions into town to see the church and the libraries? Am I more boring than you had thought?" I tried to get her to crack a smile, but she did not move a muscle.

"It's not that."

"Do you regret coming, then?"

"I regret being able to tell you that of which I wish I could tell you."

She was talking in mysteries, just as Rose had done in the past.

"You and Cherry are so similar," I laughingly remarked.

"Are we?" She shifted the weight of her feet that had been buried beneath her legs on the sofa.

"Lindsay? What is it that you aren't telling me?"

I set my cup on the table beside me and gently took her hand. She seemed not even to recognise the act for she continued to stare into the distance.

"Lloyd, she wouldn't forgive me and you wouldn't forgive

me." She said the words as though she was talking to herself.

"Who?"

She did not answer and I became angry.

"Who, Lindsay?" I raised my voice, waiting for her to answer me, afraid that I would do something to harm her if she continued to speak in such a manner. It was a feeling of helplessness outside of my own comfort or anyone's comfort for that matter.

"Rose," she said her name so quietly. My ears thought for sure I had misheard her.

"Rose?" I said her name, realising how strange it sounded to say the name to someone other than Rose herself.

Lindsay simply nodded, her brown curls hiding half of her face. I stood up slowly and walked about the room, her silence more harmful than her words. After a brief moment, I sat down again, my hands dangling in front of me, entirely unsure of what to say next. Lindsay failed to look at me beyond her veil of hair.

"How do you know Rose's name?" I finally asked.

"In very much the same way you do," she replied.

"No, there's something you aren't telling me. No one else knows."

"Except for Papa." She said it so quietly that I thought once again I had misheard her.

I tried to understand what she was saying and where my thoughts were going.

"Is Rose your sister?" I finally asked, sounding like a fool in asking such a question.

She lifted her head. Her eyes were filled with tears. They began to stream down her cheeks.

"Oh, Lloyd. We swore we would tell no one."

I stood up suddenly.

"Is this a joke? This makes no sense."

"We swore, Lloyd. We swore."

"Have you lost your mind?" I asked the frazzled girl.

"You spend the summer with her and suddenly you think you are sisters."

"No, we really are, by blood, we are sisters. I know it is a shock, but I didn't want to leave England without you knowing. I knew Rose would never tell you. In fact, I'm quite overcome with the fact that I have."

"You didn't think for one moment that I would care to know that you and Rose are sisters?"

"Do you not think it was a shock to me as well?"

"How long have you known?"

"Shortly after your visit to Ireland, I wrote back to Cherry, with the address that she had given me in her letter, thanking her for the song that she had written, not knowing at the time that it was Rose, for how could I? She returned my letter claiming that she thought us to be sisters, for she knew of information that no one else could possibly know."

"This is madness."

"It is the truth, you must believe me."

"How could I believe someone who isn't right in their mind? You say things, all too often, to gain a response from others in return. Whether it is for your own satisfaction, I do not know, but I will tell you that I am not satisfied nor pleased by such conversation."

She stood then, alarmed by my response. I didn't even realise that what I had said, as I was saying it, was harsh in manner.

"I am sorry, Lindsay. I am just trying to make sense of it all."

"Then, maybe you should ask her, ask the girl you still love, for you have shown me that you certainly do not trust me."

"I do trust you."

"You don't." She spoke with a tremble in her voice. "There were moments where I thought you did, where I thought that perhaps I could live a normal life. I was silly to think that you loved me, but it isn't like how it once was when we were in Cornwall. No, you see, whenever I thought for a moment that perhaps there was a future for us, I saw the way you admired or spoke of Rose and I knew that I could never be that for you…"

"Lindsay, you are so different from Rose. Surely, you must know that."

I reached for her hand, but she brushed it aside and stood up suddenly. There were tears in her eyes and her skin had reddened from both anger and fear.

"I have a terrible headache. Will you please excuse me?" She stood up suddenly and ran towards the door.

"Lindsay, please take a moment to calm down and we can continue this conversation. I promise—"

"I'd rather that we continue it in the morning."

As the door closed behind her, I felt like a fish out of water. I did not understand what had just happened and wondered if Lindsay had made up the story to capture my attention, to make me hear how she felt about the relationship between her and me. It was true that I had been distracted as of late, but my focus had been on my music and the upcoming opportunities. Was I any different from Charles?

No matter how many times I made myself think that it was a story of Lindsay's imagination, there was something in her tone of voice that made me believe that she really was speaking from a place of truth. There was nothing we could do now. It had been a rather eventful day and we were both tired. It would be better to address things in the morning.

Annabel opened the door, startled to see me standing there, especially after hearing of my last encounter at their estate. I was surprised to find that she was back to her normal self so quickly and equally so that Rose still allowed her maid to answer the front door. It went entirely against tradition, but then again, when had Rose ever followed tradition?

"Sir, I know it is out of my place to speak, but the master would not approve of you being here."

I wondered how much Charles had told her to persuade her that I not be welcomed in their home come any future calls like today.

"Your master has a mistress and I would like to speak to her," I replied steadily.

"The Mrs. has just gone to bed."

"At this hour? It's only an hour past noon."

I did not believe her.

"She isn't feeling well, sir, but I can take her a message."

"May I see her?"

"I don't believe Mr. Atwood would approve of that, sir."

Annabel guarded the door as though the Atwood Estate was her fortress. She must have been reading too many novels as of late.

I pushed through the door, and walked past the trembling girl.

"Cherry, are you home?"

My voice echoed through the hall.

"Where is she?"

I turned towards the girl who appeared that she would lay faint at any moment once again.

"Crikey, Annabel, I do not play games!"

I shouldn't have spoken to her in such a manner, especially after what had happened just last week. The heat was rising in my throat. Just weeks prior, I had been a welcomed guest at any hour, and now I was turned down like a child wanting a sweet from the market.

"Lloyd, is that you?"

Rose's voice greeted my ears like pure honey on a brisk day.

I glared at Annabel who scurried away, the both of us entirely aware that she had been given a nasty speech by her master about who was allowed to see his wife from now on. It was written clearly across the girl's face.

"You do know that Charles disapproves of you being here," Rose said as I neared her in the library.

"I do not care whether or not Charles approves or disapproves of me being here. Did he tell you what happened?"

"He said that you got in a fight and that Lindsay preferred to take accommodation at the hotel. It seems to have been rather good for her, perhaps make her think of Victor less."

"Do you use Victor as an excuse for everything?" I was angry now.

"Is Lindsay still at the hotel?" she asked, ignoring the anger in my request.

"No, she's left for Ireland, just this morning" I replied coolly.

"All on her own?" She was entirely shocked. "Without even saying goodbye? However did she manage such a thing and why did she leave, Lloyd?"

"She was upset by a conversation we had last night and when I went to her room this morning, she had gone. Mr. Atwood informed me that she had left a note at the front counter. The note said that she had taken the 7:00 train for Edinburgh."

"What kind of conversation would force her to leave in such great haste?"

"I think it's about time you told me the truth, Rose." I tried to remain calm.

"What truth is there to tell?" she asked, alarmed by my manners.

"As to who you really are." My eyes were fierce, yet she did not know.

"What has Lindsay said?" she asked alarmed.

I should have come over last night as soon as Lindsay had told me, but it had been too late of an hour to do so.

"I want you to answer just one question for me. When Lindsay first arrived here, was it the very first time that you had ever met in your lifetime?"

She was quiet and quite gobsmacked by such a question.

"No, it was not the first time," she finally said.

"At first, I thought Lindsay was mad, but now I think that perhaps she was telling me the truth. Crikey, Rose. When was the first time you had ever met?"

"We were little girls. Lloyd, it was so long ago, how can I remember?" She was nervous.

"There is no use in hiding behind your lips, Rose."

She was quiet, so quiet that we could hear little Rose's playful screams from upstairs.

"We've known one another our entire lives, but were just recently acquainted, all thanks to you."

"All your lives. How long, Rose?" I drew myself closer to her, to where she knew that if she reached her hand out, she would touch my chest.

"Since Lindsay was born."

"And, why is that?"

"Because we are sisters." She stated the words with such

ease as though it was a statement of fact that was obvious more than any other.

"Exactly." I let out a long breath. "I can't believe it."

"I can't believe she told you. If it was anyone, it would have been me."

"Why not tell me, though?"

"It is rather complicated."

"You lied to me." I was angry.

"I did not lie, but simply withheld information, that is all." I could tell that she was troubled by my manner.

"Is there anything else I need to know that you have not told me?"

"No, but even if there is, why would I have to tell you? You aren't my husband."

The words stung, even if I had come to determine that this truth would always be so.

Then, out of nowhere, the thought occurred to me. "Caitríona?"

"Yes, Lloyd. You've guessed right. Caitríona is Lindsay." It made much more sense now. Charles castle comment that had been directed at Lindsay on the night of our brawl confirmed that he, too, knew that Lindsay and Cherry were sisters.

"I know this is a great shock to you," she said steadily.

"I, I—"

"Lindsay was really sent away to a castle, she lived there with the Fitzgeralds, they were of high regard in the county."

"But, why was she sent away to a castle?"

"Lindsay and I both watched Mam die, but Lindsay went mad after it all. For some reason, Papa blamed her as well for Mam's death, and told her that he had never wanted more than two children. Papa sent her to the castle in hopes that it would help. Papa and Mr. Fitzgerald were good friends. Papa probably would have sent me away as well, but he needed me to cook and clean and take care of Tom, who was just a baby."

"At seven years old?" I didn't believe it.

"We had a kitchen maid, of course, so I mainly watched over Tom, but Papa needed me for when I grew older. He rid of our kitchen maid, said she was too great of an expense."

"So, you made it up, the story about meeting her in the meadow for the first time."

"I did not, not entirely. We did meet one another in the meadow, unknowingly to Papa."

"So, he never painted her?"

"He painted her memory. I believe he always loved her, and thought he was giving her a better life, the child that he never knew how to handle since her birth."

"Why did you not say her name was Lindsay?"

"When Papa made me take on a new name, I gave Lindsay her own new name. She reminded me of the heroine in the old Irish tale."

"Did you tell her that?"

"No, some things can still remain between you and me," she smiled.

"You still lied to me."

"Lloyd, listen to me. When Papa was forced to leave the land, the poaching, all of that is true."

"Your father didn't retrieve Lindsay when you left Ireland?"

"No, she was adopted by the Fitzgeralds."

"They truly lived in a castle? Am I really to believe this?"

"You must. It's an estate that has run in their family for centuries. However, they could no longer upkeep the estate, so they sold it and moved to England. Lindsay told me it was such a disgrace to their family. I don't know what happened entirely, but they lost so much of the money."

"I am certain their affluence came from the estate," I replied.

"Yes, I believe you are right."

"Lindsay must have been young when they left Ireland. When I met her, she was not known in most of society's circles," I replied.

"Yes, she had just turned thirteen when they left Ireland, that was the last time I saw her, when I went to visit the castle. That following year, when I found the castle barren, I thought that perhaps she had died, for she was so ill the last time I had seen her."

We both sat there with nothing but silence between us.

"Rose, I honestly don't know what to make of all of this. It is difficult for me to even say aloud, but how am I supposed to trust you?"

She did not answer.

"How can I trust you? Give me one reason."

"I was trying to protect you."

"What is there to protect, Rose? Is your name even Rose?" I exclaimed.

"My name is Rose. I have not lied to you about that. Papa made me change my name so that Lindsay would never be able to make contact with me ever again. He said our lives were ruined because of her. He blamed her for getting caught for the poaching amongst so many other things. The only reason I had any reason to believe he had some love for her was because of his paintings of her. Yet, when he did not succeed with his painting career, he blamed her once again, said he wished her more pretty. He spoke in circles. I never realised until I was older that my papa was not a normal man, that is why I chose to never remain in contact with him another day."

"You mean to say that you have had no contact with Lindsay for all these years, even after she moved to England? You had not once ran into her in the streets? None whatsoever?"

"You must remember that I never knew that she had moved to England. When I arrived at the castle just before my sixteenth birthday, they were all gone. If you calmed down for a moment and allowed me to speak, then you would understand how it all happened."

"You had no indication to where she was *all* these years?"

"I tried so many different ways. Perhaps my belief was the very reason why I spent so much time with Charlotte and her family in Ireland. I had dreams that one day we would be invited to a dinner and there would be Lindsay, seated beside the Fitzgeralds. I imagined we would make up for lost time and that her sickness of mind had been cured, but then one day, I grew up and no longer tried. Meeting Charles allowed me to forget it all. My life as a farmland girl with a father who couldn't even take care of his own self seemed like a lost memory of a past lifetime."

I listened as she continued to speak.

"When Charles first told me about Lindsay, about the girl whom you had loved and had left for Ireland, my heart had perked up. Every time her name was mentioned in conversation, I thought of her. Do you not think the same when Victor's name is mentioned, even if it is not your brother that is being spoken of?"

I just sat there and waited for her to continue.

"I knew it was a silly thought, and I knew that I was wrong to take such hope in such a thought, but I did want to learn more about her, so that's why I asked you about her so often. And, I knew you would not deny me for you were half in love with me then."

Her confidence roamed the room like a lurching lion. The Rose that I knew, the one who was unafraid to say what she thought and truly meant began to return to the room as she told the story, a story that seemed too much of a coincidence to even be true.

"I wanted to know what girl in this universe had the privilege to occupy Lloyd Fox's heart." A slight smile appeared on her face.

As she spoke, my heart began to soften at the sweetness in her voice.

"So, when you told me that one night about Lindsay's sickness, I was quite shocked because your stories were so similar to my Lindsay. Thus, I wrote the only man who knew of your Lindsay's whereabouts."

"Your father in-law." I said it before she could say so herself.

"Yes, Mr. Atwood. He had made light mention of being acquainted with the Fitzgeralds at dinner one evening. It was before Charles and I were ever married and long before I had ever known the severity of Lindsay's situation. Thus, after learning from you the information that the Atwoods had not enlightened me with that night, I asked of Mr. Atwood if he could contact the Fitzgeralds for me in request for Lindsay's address. I did not tell him why, but I did wait until after Charles and I were married so that Mr. Atwood would have not as difficult a time accepting such a peculiar request."

"How did you know that the Fitzgeralds would agree? Wouldn't it have been easier for you or Mr. Atwood to ask me? You would have saved yourself a whole lot of trouble."

"You and I both know that you wouldn't have given me Lindsay's address and I had objectively told Mr. Atwood not to include you in this, and as his daughter in law, he agreed with me. "

"I supposed that's true. But, the Fitzgeralds?"

"Mr. Atwood is a man of prominence. Had they refused him information, it would not look good on their family's part. There is such a thing as blackmail, you know."

"What story would he make up?"

"Oh, Mr. Atwood was quite proud that he had information on the Fitzgeralds that would give them no hesitation in offering Lindsay's address."

"But, you never wrote her?"

"No, I was on the brink of doing so, but you had agreed to go to Ireland. Had you not gone, I would have most certainly written her in the end."

"Why did you wait?"

"Because if she received an anonymous letter from a woman named Cherry, or even Rose, I doubt she would ever reply, but if she met a friend of Cherry's who she was already friends with, which of course is you, there would be a trust established between us that would encourage her to reply to my letters that I sent after your visit."

"Has anyone ever told you how intelligent you are?" I was amazed at the intricate way in which she had thought it all out, not even certain at the time that it was indeed her sister. Of course, if one had been disconnected from a relative and there was a chance of re-acquaintance, I am certain that one would go to the ends of the earth for such hope.

She smiled and continued. "When she finally replied, I knew that it was my Lindsay."

"How could you determine such?"

"I knew not only from the content, but I knew from her writing."

"Her writing? How ever are you to determine that?"

"Annabel reads me the letters."

"I figured so, but how were you to know that it was your Lindsay by her writing?"

"There is something peculiar about Lindsay's handwriting. She writes her f's and j's backwards. Mam used to tell her that she wouldn't get a decent job if she wrote like such, but of course, Lindsay never took no for an answer."

"I supposed that's a trait of the Ellis family," I smiled.

"Yes, we don't take no for an answer." She returned the smile.

"So, when I asked Annabel if Lindsay's f's and j's were backwards, I could tell that she thought it was such a strange question." Rose began to laugh and brought a hand to her mouth. "Little timid Annabel laughed when I asked it as well. But, then, her laugh quieted and she asked me how ever would I know such a thing. The f's and j's were indeed backwards. Oh, Lloyd, when she said those words…" She was choking up. "I burst into tears. I knew it was *my* Lindsay. To be separated from a sister for nearly half your life and then, in one moment, to know she is alive and living in Ireland and that I had contact with her once again, it was the most strange, yet wonderful moment."

"I cannot imagine."

"I am sure you can."

"So, you and Lindsay swore to a secrecy, not ever for a moment considerate of the fact that I would want to know?"

"We would tell you eventually."

"Once we were married?" I asked honestly. "Was this your scheme all along?"

"No, not at all. I didn't want you to think that once I found out who your Lindsay was, that I would push you back together for my sake, so that I could be re-acquainted."

"Well, wasn't it? Isn't that why you did it?"

"No, if that was the only reason I did it, then I would not have pushed you away," she paused, "from any physical affection."

"I am gladdened that you speak honestly."

"How long will it take for you to trust me again? I can't bear not having your trust."

"It's going to take a little time, Rose. I'm still trying to grasp it all."

"As it should be, as it would be for anybody."

"So."

"So?"

"Lindsay Ellis, not Lindsay Fitzgerald."

"Yes, Lindsay Ellis," she smiled.

"Does Lindsay know what happened to your father?"

"Yes, she was rather not surprised."

"I just can't get my head around the fact." I laughed harshly. "Of all the women in England, *my God*."

We sat there for a few minutes in silence before she finally spoke again.

"If I had to endure heartbreak through our friendship to be reunited with my sister then I must assure you that I am glad for it."

"It could have been done another way if you had told me the truth from the beginning."

"It is what is is, Lloyd. Besides, you went and saw Lindsay in the end. You gave us what we could not give ourselves on our own."

"Had I not gone you would have written her anyways, you would have cursed yourself to remain silent all these years."

"But, if you hadn't gone, I don't know if she would have

believed the letters, no matter what they said. She probably would have thought it a cruel joke. Lindsay is not like the rest of us. Do you think she would have replied?"

"That is something that we will never be able to answer."

"You are right. Well, this is the way that life has played out and there is no point in going backwards, we must both move forward with a life that now includes Lindsay."

"Which means you and I will forever be connected."

"Yes, but you love her."

"And, I love you," I said softly.

"No man can love two women," she replied hesitantly.

"I love you differently, just as you last told me." I paused. "I do *love* Lindsay, but you must know that it breaks my heart that Charles doesn't love you in the way that you deserve and I wish I could give you that."

"You have given that to me, Lloyd. You have given me back my sister. There are much more heart breaking circumstances on earth than ours. Let us count our blessings." She spoke with such grace.

"God knows I don't deserve either of you," I said.

"So, there is a God?" she laughed.

"Perhaps there is. If some intelligent mind went through all of this to bring Lindsay and us back together, then I must applaud him."

"Indeed, he does deserve such an applause, Reverend Lloyd," she smiled coyly.

"Why do you tease me so?"

"Because your pride is getting in the way of what you have come to determine as truth."

"Which is?"

"That there is a God and that religion isn't so tedious as you have always believed it to be."

"You and Thomas speak on similar terms."
"Because Thomas and I know what's right." She laughed and then her face softened upon my reply.
"You were right. You can't outrun the past."
"Yes, the past will catch up to you at some point, as it has done for us both."
I knew then that I could trust her again. She had done what any sibling would have done in her situation. I knew I would have done the same had it been Victor. Now, there was only one thing left to do: I had to purchase a train ticket.

Chapter 27
Cliffs of Moher

I had knocked on the door profusely, my feet tired from the two day journey. The night previous, I had arrived into town rather late, taking to the same pub that I had stayed at on my last visit to Fanore.

"What are you doing here?" Lindsay stood at the door, like the same awkward mouse that she had been when we were in my hotel room in London.

"I received your note." I held out the piece of paper that had been left at Mr. Abbey's desk.

"I wondered if he would give it to you." She still stood there, half her body hidden behind the door.

"May I come in, Lindsay?" I asked tenderly.

She nodded and welcomed me into the cosy parlour. Her aunt's quilts were spread out on a rocking chair underneath the beautiful landscape of Cornwall that Lindsay had painted.

"It is good to see that you arrived here safely," I said, eager for her to know that Rose had told me the rest of the story.

"I would have said goodbye, but if I had done so, you would not have let me go, and I needed to come back," she stuttered.

"But, why?"

"I don't want to go back to the asylum," she stated fiercely.

"You would never be sent back there."

"How am I to be certain?"

"Lindsay, stop fooling yourself. Why is it that you really left?"

"I saw how angry you were when I told you the truth."

"What man wouldn't be outrageous at finding out that he had been lied to for the past few months?" I softened my voice. "Look, Lindsay, it was all overwhelming, but I understand it now. It is a tale of fate if ever there was one. I've just heard nothing else like it. These things only happen in novels, the same ones that you read to fulfil the hours in your day. At first, I thought you were making it up, I don't know why, but I thought supposed it was done to receive a reaction from me."

"But, it wasn't, not in anyway."

"I know that now."

"Because Rose told you the rest of the story, and you trust her. You trust her, unlike me."

"Would I have made the trip to Ireland if I didn't trust you?" I raised my voice, but only slightly.

"In truth, I don't know why you are here."

"To ask for your forgiveness, to tell you that I am sorry that I am not the same man that I was before I left for France, to tell you I am sorry that Victor died and I didn't." The words came spiralling out of my mouth. I had never even said the words aloud to myself.

Neither of us had taken a seat; we were still standing in the parlour, still as statues on a summer day. She moved towards me and grabbed my arm.

"I am not sorry that Victor died and you didn't. Your music would have never brought my sister back to life had you died at war." Tears filled her eyes. She was rather forgiving, despite her lack of understanding sometimes.

"Your sister would have found another to do so," I commented, looking at the wall above her head.

"Lloyd, I love you." She said the words quietly, but then repeated them with a greater passion in her voice. "That is why I left in haste. For I couldn't fool myself any longer into believing that you would have me and the sooner I left, the easier the parting would become."

"What would make you think I would never have you?" And, just like that, the tension in the room was broken like the lake's surface in spring. Aunt Birgitta entered the small room with a handful of biscuits in hand. Lindsay backed away shyly, shifting her gaze to the window.

"Oh, Lloyd, it is you. We had no idea that you would be here. Would you care for a biscuit?"

My eyes that were fixated on Lindsay gave full attention to Aunt Birgitta now.

"No, ma'am, but thank you all the same."

"Are you in town long enough to stay for dinner?"

"I booked a room at the Black Panther, ma'am."

"What delightful news. Oh, Lloyd, it is so good to see you. I am grateful for your letters while my Lindsay was away."

"It was my pleasure to write to you," I smiled.

"I am going to start on the potatoes. Lindsay, dear, will you make sure our guest is comfortable?"

"Of course," she nodded at her aunt.

When Aunt Birgitta left, we stood still like statues once again. Of course, I always knew it, but for her to say it aloud was a feat that I could not have expected. I knew we wouldn't return to where our conversation had left off, so I eased the room with a few words that would brighten Lindsay's day.

"I drove a car here." I sounded like a newspaper reporter.
"How ever did you afford such a thing?" She did not
leave her gaze from the window.
"I told the bartender that I wanted to give a special girl a
spin. He and I, well, we got well acquainted during my
last visit."
"Should I trust your story?" she smiled.
"See for it yourself."
"Will we be back for dinner?" she asked, her arms still
crossed.
"With plenty of time to spare," I replied.

We told Aunt Birgitta who was more than pleased by
the idea, even though she reminded me on several
occasions not to get carried away by speed. I assured her I
was not a race car driver and that we would be back
before the sun had set.

When Lindsay saw the green rims of the vehicle, she
laughed at the sight of such a beautiful car.
"I didn't know you knew how to drive such a thing."
"We all learned after the war, most of us anyways."

I helped her into the car, and laughed as she let out a
squeal when the car shifted into the first gear quite
abruptly. Her brown curls floated in the wind, and for a
moment, I forgot how strange this all was. Just a few days
ago, we were together in London and now, here we were,
away from life as we had known it.

It was only a thirty mile drive to the Cliffs of Moher. I
had insisted that Lindsay see their majesty, something that
she had not yet been granted since moving to Ireland.
The fact of the matter had made me terrifically sad in a
way; so I decided to enrich her life with a trip to the cliffs.

When we arrived, Lindsay, dressed in a light blue dress
and a summertime's hat, echoed her awe. I couldn't help
but grin at the eagerness in her step to leave the car door

and walk on ahead towards the edge of the cliffs.

"I might burst from such happiness." Lindsay's excitement roared with the waves.

She lifted her hands towards the sky and closed her eyes. I simply sat there and watched her, like a man gazing at the most infamous of paintings. She was wildly enchanting.

"Does it not remind you of the White Cliffs of Dover?" she shouted in the winds.

"My favourite place to go as a boy," I replied.

"Mine, too. Of course, not as a boy."

She then ran over towards me and grabbed my hand.

"Come on, then. Let's run along the shore, like how we used to in Cornwall. You aren't too much of an old bloke now. Or, are you?"

I shook my head and laughed at her, reminiscent of those days in Cornwall, which seemed like centuries ago now. Her hair smelled like roses, her smile more endearing than the view itself, and it was then that I couldn't take it any longer.

Taking her in my arms, I gave her a kiss, the first in years. She ruffled her hands through my hair and touched my face as though it was the first time she had ever held it. There was a certain curiosity in her, just like the first time we had kissed, but this time, there was something different, perhaps a maturity that I had not yet been able to see since my first visit to Ireland.

"What's on your mind, Lloyd?" she smiled.

"Do you really want to know? I asked

She nodded, her eyes still closed, the waves sounding quieter than they had in years, for it seemed as though their song had drifted to a minor key, allowing myself to only hear my own heartbeat. She opened her eyes as I brushed her cheek.

"Lindsay, I am not one for elaborate speeches. That is why I compose music. So, without making a fool of myself over such, I want to ask you, will you marry me?"
There was a distant shock in her gaze and at first, she seemed gobsmacked by my proposition.
"Why did you wait to ask me? Why did you not ask me when we were in London? I wouldn't have left had you asked then."
"That's a loaded question, Lindsay. I cannot give you a simple answer."
Then, she asked what was really on her mind; a question that I undoubtedly expected.
"Did you really love Rose?"
She asked the question honestly. I thought of the time that I had sat with Rose and she had asked me the very same question of Lindsay.
Taking her tender hands into my own, I stared into her emerald green eyes.
"Your sister redeemed me and you, my sweet Lindsay, have given me a new life worth fighting for."

My forehead met with hers and we allowed the extravagant winds to intertwine between us as the distant sounds of an Irish folk song seemed to drift in and out of the waves that crashed below us. I had been afraid of this moment, but as it came, I knew that it was right; I knew that I wouldn't lose her, and I knew that we would be able to face the inevitable trials of life together. Whereas I used to hear Rose's voice in the wind, it was replaced by a sweeter one. Lindsay's pure vocals were unmatched by anyone walking this earth. I needed her to know that no matter how often she felt that her life was not worth living, it was all a lie, a lie that I would not allow her to live by. I had to convince her against the ways in which I used to also think. If it wasn't for Rose, perhaps I would have always remained there, entirely stuck with no purpose and no desire to move forward here on earth.

"Lloyd, but I am not, and will not always be as pleasant as you hope me to be. But, I do believe that I can change."

"You don't need to change, Lindsay."

I brushed her hair with my rough fingertips, and even though I believed the antithetical in my statement, I needed her to believe in herself as much as Thomas and Rose had believed in me.

Her upper lip quivered for she felt that by accepting me, she was denying my rights to freedom.

"I have refused until now, but I will accept you on one condition."

"Yes?"

"You will not deny my rights to an acceptable doctor," she almost murmured.

"Have you been denied one?" I was shocked.

"My family thinks I cannot be cured, and for so long I thought that nothing was wrong with me and that sending me to the asylum was foolish of them all, but I know now that it was for my benefit."

"It was not for your benefit. It was a selfish decision."

"Lloyd, let us not quarrel now. Let me say this, though." The waves roared below us as the sun's peek began its slow descent towards the horizon.

"I do not understand my illness, but I have accepted it. That is why I want help, but not in the ways that the asylum provided. They believe there is no hope for us there, for it was truly the most inhumane feeling."

"That is why I got you out of there."

"My papa didn't order you, then?"

"No, he forbade it."

"It was *you*, all along." Her whisper seemed almost a cry.

"Yes, did your family tell you otherwise?"

"Aunt Birgitta told me that my parents insisted on my leaving, blimey, why would they do such a thing?" the tone in her voice shifted.

She could not finish the sentence and felt betrayed by her own family for she realised that the best life that she could possibly have, in her current condition, was the opportunity that had been given only through her new life in Ireland. However, if I had not intervened, such would have never been the case. I had wanted her to believe that it was her family's doing all along, for betrayal by one's own family is a difficult matter. I, of all people, knew this so well.

"Lindsay, you cannot blame your family for the choices they did or did not make. You've admitted that your health, *my God*, your mind, was not in its right condition. You could not see the harm that you brought to those around you, surely you must try to understand."

She did not speak as tears glistened in her eyes. Even then, she was a beautiful creature.

"Yes, Rose finally came to believe the same thing."

"Rose chose to understand you," I replied. "Just as I have chosen to do the same."

"You will help me, then? I trust you, Lloyd. I trust that you want to give me a better life."

"Yes, of course, I will help you, but you must know that despite your illness, I love you. It does not make me love you any less."

"You love me?" She stood still.

"I would not ask you to marry me if I did not, Lindsay."

"You love me," she repeated. "And, I love you."

The sunset evoked a pastel sky over the triumphant sounding waves. She rested her face upon my chest, and together, we gazed out at the Western sky, knowing that this moment was a rare gift that we could not have predicted for ourselves.

"Yes, I will marry you, Lloyd. I thought I would never say such words."

Her soft and tender voice weakened my flesh, and yet I couldn't help but think of Rose in that moment. Rose had made me realise how foolish I had been, how I had allowed my cynicism to get in the way of ever believing that I would truly be given back the joy that Lindsay and life itself had brought me many years ago. I felt undeserving of such, and yet, here we were.

The temperatures had quickly dropped as the sun continued its descent into the sea. Kissing Lindsay's forehead, I told her that it would be best that we make our way back to the cottage. She nodded and took my arm, her head resting gently atop my shoulder. As we walked through the fields and made our way into the car, she began to sing the song once again, the one that Rose had written for her.

Seen though she is not seen
I just want her to know
That she is seen
Though she feels not seen
I just need her to know

Hidden behind glass walls
Secrets buried deep
Tears gone unnoticed
Fears never voiced

Seen though she is not seen
I just want her to know
That she is seen

Though she feels not seen
I just need her to know

Seen though she is not seen
I just want her to know

She sang the last note and took my hand as we drove away, the sun melting over the sea's horizon. Kissing her hand, I smiled as she lifted her other hand into the wind, believing that Lindsay knew all along that this moment would be forever ours.

"When are we to marry?" She laughed playfully and took another glance at me, trying to determine if it was indeed true.

"Tomorrow morning?" I asked unexpectedly.

"So soon? But, shouldn't we tell our family and friends?"

"Our family and friends knew that I was coming here to marry you. There would be no point in waiting another day. Besides, I don't want an extravagant wedding."

"Nor do I," she smiled.

"Will the local priest do it?"

"I don't know how much notice one must give, but I am certain it won't be a problem. Aunt Birgitta could be a witness. Oh, how pleased she will be."

"She will probably go into a frantic about baking a cake," I laughed.

"Oh, yes, how dare you leave Aunt Birgitta with such a task."

The sunset was a kaleidoscopic wonder of which a tint of red danced in Lindsay's hair, the first that made me realise that Lindsay and Rose truly did look like one another. Now, I would never be able to not see it.

The sun peeked its way into the bedroom. A bouquet of roses sat by the window. They had complimented Lindsay's pink dress wonderfully the morning before. Lindsay stirred in her sleep, her fair skin seemed to shine more brilliantly in the cool of the morning. For the first time since the war, life had felt perfectly right; for the moment, there was a happiness within myself that I could not describe.

"Did you really marry me?" Lindsay's sweet voice filled the air. She scooted closer to where I lay and I wrapped her in my arms, the smell of flowers still in her hair from our wedding the day before.

"Do you really think I seduced you into bed?"

"No, Lloyd Fox isn't capable of such," she smiled.

"Lindsay Fox." I said the words out loud for the first time.

"It's rather fitting, don't you think?" Lindsay asked, twirling her fingers in her hair.

"It's rather unconventional," I laughed.

"It is our new ordinary life," she smiled.

"Far from ordinary, but ordinary all the same."

Her head rested on my chest, her fingers softly played with my own, and her eyes danced like they always had, yet having her so close to me made me realise it all the more.

"It won't be easy," she sighed.

"Life isn't easy," I protested.

"Will you hate me for asking you for something?"

"We've been married for one day. I will not refuse my wife of something she may desire."

"*Your* wife? I don't think I will get used to that."

"Perhaps neither will I. So, what is it that you request?"

"When we return to London, I'd like to attend church with Rose."

"Why would you think that I would hate you for such? I would never be opposed to it."

"Are you more fond of the idea now?"

"I'm more fond of God." I kissed her forehead, her smile so incandescently happy.

"If I had known that this is what it would be like, I would have run away years prior to come find you," she laughed lightly.

"You wouldn't have wanted me then." I played with her hair and she smiled, completely satisfied with where we remained, no eagerness to start the day.

"Will they be happy for us?"

"They are happy for us," I corrected her. "All of them, especially Rose."

"I won't mention her again, not now. It's just you and me." She kissed me.

"It's just you and me," I replied and kissed her back.

"Do you have everything you need?" Aunt Birgitta was frantic whenever change took place. "Would you like to take some of the cake to go?"

"No, it wouldn't last us the journey." Lindsay kissed her aunt on the cheek. "Besides, I don't think you will have a problem eating it on our behalf. Celebrate us all week long if you must."

"I didn't mean to take her from you again, but at least you have the dog," I joked, trying to make our departure as light as possible.

"Could you not stay longer?" she asked for what seemed

the hundredth time.

"I told you, Lloyd has to get back to work." Lindsay held her aunt's hands in her own.

"Would you like me to drive to the train station with you all?" she asked.

"There is no need for that. We will walk to the pub and catch a ride to the station from there," I replied, giving the stout woman a kiss on the cheek myself.

"Take good care of her, buck," she said.

"You don't have to tell me twice." I grabbed Lindsay's hand and we both waved goodbye to the woman, Lindsay holding nothing but her suitcase and the Cornwall painting in hand. She had insisted that we take it with us, and Aunt Birgitta had reluctantly agreed in the end.

The walk to the pub was a short journey. When we arrived, I knew that we would only have about an hour or so until our ride was to take us over to the train station. As soon as we did, the clerk at the front desk made mention that a phone call had come for me just a couple hours ago.

"Did they leave a message?" I asked.

"Just a name and number. Said it was urgent," the gentleman replied.

I called the number that had been given and heard the click on the other line. Charles had been right to call here, for we both knew of no other place in Fanore.

"Charles, did you call to offer your congratulations?" I laughed when the click indicated that he had joined me on the other end.

"Lloyd, I don't know how else to tell you." His reply was sombre, instantly reminding me of the time that Charlotte had called me on the night of Rose's accident.

"What's happened?" I didn't hesitate to ask and turned my back from where Lindsay sat on a bench in the hall.

Charles breathed heavily on the other end and spoke so softly I thought I had misheard him.

"Cherry is dead. Cherry is dead, old chap."

Chapter 28
Jazz Riots

"I don't even know where to begin." Charles' voice was scattered as I remained quiet on the other line. "Are you there, old chap?"

"Yes, sorry, are you certain—"

He cut me off.

"Yes, my wife is dead, Lloyd." Charles' voice hardened. A silence that tested all of time then stood between us.

"When?" I finally asked, my voice shaky by the news.

"Last night."

"How did..." I couldn't get the words out.

"There was a riot, there at the nightclub in town. There's been a few riots here and there, a group of men, I don't know what they call themselves, but they haven't taken a liking to a band with a bunch of black musicians. The bloody ignorance of them." He was angry, yet there was also a deep sadness in his voice. "It was poison, old chap. Before the riot broke out, one of the men poisoned the band's evening drink. Cherry had asked for a drink while we were all still performing on stage. The waiter had then told her that a gentleman had just brought complimentary drinks to the table. It wasn't long after ..."

He couldn't get the words out.

"You don't need to tell the whole story now."

"She was murdered by a toxic dose of phosphorous. Old chap..." He couldn't say anything else, for he started sobbing. I too felt quite choked up over the most dreadful of news. Now, with a happy bride on my arm, I was going to have to pretend as though everything was alright in the world.

"God, help us," I whispered.

"I had to call you." He was nearly choking on his own tears.

"We are coming home now," I replied.

"I am sorry, old chap."

"I am sorry, too," I replied.

Charles then told me that the man who had killed Cherry had been locked up in jail. His trial was to come, yet justice would most likely not be served, just as it seemed to always be done. I put the receiver back in its place and stood there for a moment, staring at the wall before me, my entire being shaken by the news. I had never felt more numb in all my life.

I was breathing steadily, yet felt that I myself had been shot in the chest. Crikey, not Rose. I closed my eyes and felt as though the entire world around me had gone dark. I placed my hand against the coolness of the wall and just stood there, not knowing how I would be able to take the next step. I could feel a quiver in my lip and made it stop. "Sir, are you alright?" a bartender asked.

"Just feeling faint all of a sudden." I hid my face from him, my hair hanging loosely over my face. If any man was to glance a glimpse of my eyes than he would know that the most tragic thing that could have ever occurred in my life had just taken place. Cherry Rose Ellis was no longer alive. How could the world go on living without her? I felt that I lost everything in that moment and had to remind myself that I had a wife in the other room patiently waiting for me.

"Would you like a glass of water? I can fetch one from the bar." The bartender had remained in the shadows, careful not to move a step closer.

I nodded my head roughly and said nothing more. However would I tell Lindsay the news? She had nearly lost everything when she lost Victor, and now Rose? How would she take it? I decided that I wouldn't tell her until we arrived in London, for I myself didn't know how to cope with it all. I kept trying to tell myself that it wasn't true, but you can't reason yourself out of reality, no matter how many times you try.

The bartender brought me the glass of water, my hand still resting on the wall. My throat was dry, my pulse felt as though it was growing weaker, and my heart was hurting in a way that I had never imagined.

After taking a few minutes more to gather my thoughts together, I joined Lindsay in the pub's hallway. "Is everything alright?"

"Just received some news from the hotel, nothing to worry yourself about." I took hold of her hand, squeezing it harder than I had intended.

"Are you certain? You look as though you've seen a ghost."

"There's nothing that can be done now. Let's enjoy the journey back to London, shall we?" I kissed her forehead, although I knew that there would be absolutely no enjoyment on my part.

Charles' words rung in my head. "Cherry is dead. Cherry is dead, old chap."

I still had yet to tell her, for how I could tell her the very thing that I myself had trouble believing. Crikey, I couldn't wrap my head around it for it was more unbelievable than even Victor's death had been. When life expects the unbearable, it makes life more easy to bear, but when the very thing that would never be expected occurs, it almost becomes unforgivable. I closed my eyes while the train tracks below reminded me of the days us soldiers would return back to the trenches after our escapade on the English land.

I dreaded returning to London and returning to the hotel where Rose's laughter would never split the air again. How would I endure their faces again, the high and mighty dining at dinners too affordable for their pockets that made it all the more sickening for even those of the middle class. Thank God for Lindsay. I would have gone mad if it wasn't for her.

The pureness of her breath and the quiet manner of her chest brought a realisation that this accord would not last for that much longer. I wished I was ignorant of the information that awaited us at Belgrave Square. In a way, I wished we had found out together, but perhaps it was better this way, for me to grieve alone before being a support for Lindsay, for it would make it easier.

The train shifted violently all of a sudden and I grabbed the handle beside us, alarmed by the winds outside. My nerves were completely on edge. The movement jerked Lindsay out of her sleep.

"Are we almost there?" she asked.

"Yes, we are almost home, darling."

"What a life we will build together." She took my hand and kissed my cheek before laying her head on my lap.

I had to distract myself with the sweet pleasure of her company.

"What kind of life do you want to build?" I asked her, my voice just as quiet as though we were two young lovers who did not want to be caught by the headmaster that walked on by.

"I would like us not to live in the hotel forever, and I would like my own garden, like the one in Ireland."

"Do you suggest we move back to Fowey then?" I could barely get the words out without breaking into tears.

"I am quite fond of the sea, but I do not know if I want to build a life there. Besides, I want to see you succeed. London has changed you."

"For the better?"

"Yes, our children will be glad one day."

"So, there is children in this future life of ours?" My voice was still rough around the edges.

"Do you not want children?" She turned her face towards me.

"Yes, I want your children." I forced a smile, although it did not last long.

"By golly, I hope it's my children you want," she laughed.

"All in due time. There is no need to think about that now."

"Who will entertain me while you are away teaching during the day?" She was so concerned and I found it all terrible, concerning herself over matters that were so trivial. Was it wrong of me to keep her in the dark?

"You have friends," I replied.

"Who are all mothers," she stated.

"I didn't realise how much you wanted to be a mother."

"You had never asked," she defended herself.

We were on the outskirts of London now; Lindsay's head remained on my lap as the rest of England swept past us. She closed her eyes and continued to rest while I simply gazed out the window, my heart too numb to understand that I would never hear another note escape from Rose's violin. I dreaded the moment that I would have to tell Lindsay, for I knew that the sweet smile that now rested on her lips would be no more, not for a while anyhow.

As the train tracks echoed below us, I felt as though they hauntingly sang the lyrics to Rose's *Song for Somme*. I felt sick to my stomach. Closing my eyes, I only hoped that I wouldn't throw up the only meal that we had that morning.

It wasn't that much longer until we pulled into King's Cross Station. Lindsay, who had slept for the past hour, smiled upon our arrival.

"There is nothing quite like London, is there?" She gazed outside at the passersby.

"Nothing else like it." I grabbed our bags and beckoned for her to take the lead towards the train platform.

"Will you call for the hotel chauffeur?" she asked gleefully.

I should have allowed her one more night's sleep without hearing the news, but she needed to know. There was no point in waiting any longer for I would certainly burst into tears in the middle of the night and then she would ask me what was wrong then.

"We will take the bus to Belgrave Square," I commented.

"Are Rose and Charles expecting us?"

"Not entirely."

"Then, it's a surprise?" she smiled.

"Let's find the next bus to the square, shall we?" I could tell she was not pleased by my response, but she didn't ask any further questions. She took my arm, abiding by my lead.

When the car pulled up to their address, my legs became frozen to the seat.

"Lloyd, whatever is the matter?"

"Exhausted from the journey, that's all."

When we knocked on the door, it wasn't Annabel who answered, but the butler, Mr. Clark, like tradition would have it. This slight change in Rose's household brought about a sincere curiosity within Lindsay. For a slight moment, I was about to interfere and inform the gentleman that we would call tomorrow instead, seeing as it was getting late outside.

However, my words were frozen within my throat and I simply followed them into the main hallway of which the halls themselves seemed no longer vibrant or full of any colour.

Charles footsteps sounded in the upstairs hall, heavier than usual. Mr. Clark asked if we would like to take tea in the parlour but I insisted that we would rather remain in the hallway. We weren't going to be long anyways. Lindsay observed me closely, and yet, she decided to say nothing no matter how curious she was by the strange mannerisms in which both Mr. Clark and I carried.

It wasn't that much longer until Charles made his way down the spiralling stairwell. He greeted us in a monotone, which even the sight of Lindsay's smile could not uplift.

"Is Cherry already in bed?" Lindsay asked.

Charles and I made eye contact, and I dipped my head, indicating that I had not told her yet.

"What is it?" Lindsay looked at the both of us.

"Why don't we move to the library?" Charles asked in a rough manner.

We followed him in the room and I took a seat alongside Lindsay on the sofa.

"Is this a guessing game? What is it that you two aren't telling me? I'm not as daft as you think."

"Lindsay, we all know you are smart…" I was fighting my own emotions and dreaded the conversation that was to come.

"Well, what is it, Lloyd? Apparently, you have known of this for a little while and found no fancy in telling me." Charles was not as sensitive to her emotions. He wasted no time in telling her.

"Cherry is not in bed, Lindsay. Cherry passed away two days ago."

Lindsay, who had been staring at Charles as he said the words, turned towards me with misty eyes.

"Is he telling the truth?"

She didn't trust Charles for one moment. I didn't blame her.

"Yes, I am afraid so." I looked up at her, deep sorrow clearly written across my face.

I grabbed her left hand that was resting on the sofa. Her other hand immediately covered her mouth as she gasped out loud and began to slightly sob; she was trying her best to control herself and understand it all. And, then, it really hit her.

"Oh, God, it can't be." She buried her face into my chest. Her sobs could be heard by the entire downstairs staff no doubt.

Charles, who felt uncomfortable all of a sudden, rung for tea and sarnies; I wish he had given Lindsay a few more moments to cry in the absence of others, but he knew not what else to do. Besides, I didn't see the need to call for a plate of food at such a late hour.

There was a sympathetic gaze in Mr. Clark's eyes as he took Charles' request back with him to the kitchen staff, a small staff to say the least.

Lindsay had become ashen in the face, which made me believe that Charles' call for food and drink was probably a good one after all.

It took her several minutes before she finally spoke.

"You knew the entire time?" She looked into my eyes, her hand rested stiffly on my chest.

"Charles called me right before we left." I reassured her that I had not known for much longer than she had.

She nodded, but was not pleased, taking her hand away from my own.

"How?" she asked, staring at Charles through her tear-stained face.

"There was a riot at the club. Cherry was poisoned. By the time she arrived at hospital, there was nothing that could be done."

"Was it intentional?" Lindsay cried.

"Yes, but it wasn't meant for Cherry. They had intended to kill me, not Cherry." His hands covered his face.

"Oh, God." She let out another cry and then fell flatly into my chest once more.

There was nothing that I could do or say that would comfort her. She remained that way for quite some time. What could any man say to her, really?

One of the footmen arrived with the sarnies, and after a few failed attempts to get Lindsay to eat something, she finally took a sarnie.

"Has Annabel been dismissed?" I asked Charles, curious as to why Mr. Clark had taken to answering the door again.

"No, I still need someone to upkeep the household chores," he replied steadily.

"Of course."

"Perhaps, it would best if you two stayed for the night. I could have Annabel arrange a room for you both."

For as much as I despised him, in that moment, I was thankful for his suggestion and replied that this would probably be the best idea as it was a late hour. Lindsay needed to rest, if she could at all. I didn't want to take her back to the hotel, not at this hour anyways, especially in her condition.

Lindsay spoke no more and she neither accepted nor objected to Charles' suggestion. Charles rung for Mr. Clark and asked if Annabel would be willing to arrange a room for the Foxes. He nodded kindly; a few moments later, Annabel came to show us to the room.

"Actually, I am going to stay in here for a little while longer. Lindsay, darling, why don't you follow Annabel to the room?"

She didn't speak, not one word, and she refused to look at any of us. It was the most dreadful feeling. My thoughts kept circulating, bringing me back to the time after Victor had been pronounced dead. Would she relapse into such a state again? Crikey, I hoped not.

After Lindsay had left the room, Charles informed me that Charlotte and Allen were to come over in the morning to discuss arrangements for Cherry's funeral of which Lindsay and I could also be a part of, if we so chose, although I did not know how much Lindsay would be able to handle; and truthfully, I didn't know if I would be able to handle it all either. It was too soon. Rose's life couldn't be treated like a business transaction.

"Father said it would be best to sell the house," Charles stated after we had sat there in silence for quite some time, drinking the bottle of brandy that he had opened after Lindsay had left the room.

"What will you do?" I didn't care to talk about it all, but we had to talk. It was the only way any of us would stay sane.

"I'm going to move to America with the band. There are groups that are more accepting there, at least in some parts."

"Do you think that is what's best for little Rose?" I asked with slight discomfort.

"Rose is staying here," he said it with no emotion in his voice.

"Rose needs her father," I stated through gritted teeth.

"I am no father to her, you said it best," he stated again with no emotion. As he said the words, I thought of Victor and how Charles really was the greatest coward of them all.

"With whom will she stay?" I asked.

"I've already contacted the Carnegies. They agreed to take her in."

"Of which they are pleased by the idea? It is not done out of mere charity?" Suddenly I was interested.

"They seem to be," he stated and poured himself another glass of the drink.

We both sat there, silently waiting for the other to speak. "It's been a tiresome day, old chap. I'm going to say goodnight."

"Thank you, Charles, for letting us stay."

And, somehow, by no means did I intend to, I shook his hand.

After he left, I wandered throughout the library, trying to find something to read. And, there, beside Rose's chair was an open book. I imagined that Annabel read to her every morning and evening. By the binding of the book, I knew immediately what it was. It was her bible.

Although she was no longer here, it felt as though she was leaving behind the secrets that would allow those she loved the most to unlock happiness as she knew it. I drew my fingers across the words and didn't know how to feel. Crikey, I wish I could have another conversation with her. There were so many questions I had for her, now more than ever.

It almost felt as though she was in the room, her slim figure dancing through the soft glow of the light, her red hair wildly greeting the books on the walls that had become her closest friends, and her smile, so ever enchanting, painting the darkness that now filled our lives. Yet, even as I grasped for the memories, she was fading. I brought a hand to my mouth and let out a very small cry.

"Pardon me, sir. I thought everyone had gone to bed."

I turned slowly and found that Mr. Clark had come to clean up the mess that we had left behind. It wasn't his job to do so, and I wondered if the rest of the household had taken to bed early after such a dreadful spell to have spilt over the place.

"Don't mind me, Clark. I don't want to go to bed, not yet. Blimey, I'm sorry."

"There is no need to apologise, sir. All of us downstairs are very grieved by Cherry's death."

I couldn't remember if I had ever held a conversation with him before.

"Would you care to sit?"

"Not in your presence, sir," he smiled sadly.

"I am a musician, not a lord. Please sit with me."

He took a seat, most awkwardly, wondering if he should speak or not.

"You see, Clark, I really don't want to be alone. I've spent many hours with Cherry in this library and now, it doesn't feel right."

"You were good friends," he said.

"How will our lives ever be right again?" I looked up at him, my eyes glazed with hurt.

"Sometimes, life is unfair. We will grieve for now, but we will learn to keep going, we have to," he gently replied.

"I know someone who would agree with you."

I thought of Thomas then and wondered what he would have to say. I didn't want to hear what he would have to say, really.

We sat there for a few minutes longer to which Clark quickly stood up and said he must finish the last of his duties for the evening.

"Of course, I am sorry to have taken up so much of your time," I replied to the kind-hearted gentleman.

"She touched each of our lives immensely. This household will never be as it once was without her." He smiled, but it flickered away like a candle that had lost its light. It saddened me that Clark and the rest of the staff were now forced to find employment elsewhere.

As I left the library and walked down the long hallway, the eyes of dukes and duchesses following me as I walked by, my body felt suddenly more lonely than ever. It was a strange feeling to desire Lindsay all of a sudden, for I felt that I couldn't live without her now. And, if it hadn't been for Rose, I would have never had her. How different life would have been if I had decided to stay in America. Lindsay wouldn't be here either. It is interesting to think about our lives, all a series of decisions that lead us to the present moment in time.

I quieted my footsteps upon arriving at the bedroom that Annabel had put Lindsay up in. Annabel had come to the library after Lindsay had gone to bed and asked me if I would like for her to arrange another bedroom for myself, but I reminded her that we are married now to which the young girl had blushed and apologised. She was such a strange girl.

Quietly closing the door behind me so as not wake Lindsay, I began to undress.

"Lloyd?" her voice was but a whisper.

"I thought you were asleep, darling."

"I've tried, but I can't fall asleep. Oh, Lloyd." She started to tear up, silently at first. I climbed into the bed with her and took her into my arms, kissing the top of her head as she cried into my chest.

"I've tried to tell myself that it isn't true."

"I'm afraid it is." It's all I knew to say.

"I thought that if we went to bed and woke in the morning, she would be at the dining table like she always had been."

There was nothing that I could even attempt to say to make her feel better about the situation. All I could do was hold her as I held my own tears. Yet, no matter how hard I tried, I could not contain it. A few silent tears fell down my cheeks and met her golden brown hair. I kissed her forehead again and held her. We had one another, that I was comforted by. We had one another to make sense of this tragedy.

Chapter 29
Amazing Grace

As I stared at her coffin, I wondered how many secrets had truly died with Rose Ellis that day. Ever since Rose had died, I wondered if it was fate, some manner of coincidence, that had brought us together or if it truly was the intricate designed plan of God as she had believed before her death. However, this moment, her death, I did not believe was part of any plan. I had rather us never met. Yet, Lindsay reminded me that this was a statement that I didn't truly wish, for if it hadn't been for Rose, Lindsay and I would have most likely never been brought together again. Even so, I thought it. I didn't know how to deal with the grief.

Lindsay squeezed my hand as I then stood up and made my way to the piano stool. When Charlotte and Allen had come over that following morning when we had arrived in London from Ireland, funeral arrangements had been made. Furthermore, it had been discussed how important it would be for me to play *A Song for Somme* at her funeral. It was what Cherry would have wanted, they all had said. Even Lindsay had agreed, although she had been quiet most that morning and had said nothing more than a few words since she had cried in my arms that first night that she had found out about Rose's death. As we prepared plans for today, Lindsay had secluded herself from the rest of us, only to be found staring blankly at the library's shelves of books throughout the day. Even when we had returned to the hotel and I returned to playing in the dining hall the last few evenings, Lindsay preferred to eat a quiet dinner alone and then return to our bedroom on the second floor.

Now, as I glanced over at Lindsay sitting in the church pew, I was thankful to see that there was more life in her than there had been for the past week. Taking a deep breath, I reminded myself that I was doing this for Lindsay, just as much as I was doing it for Rose.

My fingers hovered and then began to play, all eyes fixated on the absence of Rose, my own ears filling the gap where Rose's violin should have met the notes from my piano. As I played, something broke within me, and I played with a fierce passion that I had never felt before. The pure transcendent notes floated through the room as I played the last of the third movement, dropping from C minor to A major, a confession of redemption and trust in something outside of my own self. And, then, it ended just as shortly as it had started, just like Rose's life it had seemed, just like all of our lives really, a mere vapour.

I returned to my seat, tears unable to form in my eyes; Lindsay took my hand, the softness bringing about a comfort beyond words. Rose knew I needed Lindsay and Lindsay, somehow, knew that I needed her.

Rose's death had been in the papers and had even been announced this morning through the British Broadcasting Corporation. I had asked Charles if it was really all that necessary, but he reminded me how much of a musical influence Cherry had been in the community. Besides, people would wonder why Charles Atwood's wife didn't attend his concerts anymore. "She hardly did so before," I had commented. He had ignored me. I had understood covering the story from a crime perspective, but nothing more. Rose lived a mysterious life; she didn't want everyone to know about her public and private affairs. Yet, now it seemed that all of Great Britain would now know. Rose's murderer was to be hanged, and what justice was there in a man losing his life with no consequences for his crime. It was the easiest way out. I tried not to think about it, for my voice would not matter in such a debate.

The vicar said a few more words to which I heard nothing. All I could do was stare at Rose's coffin. Taking a slight glance to where Charles sat, I was not surprised at how hard his face looked. He had not shown me, nor anyone else for that matter, any kind of emotion since he first told me the news over the phone. If he had not shown it then, I would have truly wondered if he had loved her at all. He seemed to have loved her out of convenience, more than anything else. I brushed the thought aside and held onto Lindsay's hand, slowly standing when they lifted Rose's coffin to take her outside to be buried.

As the men carried her coffin out the church, a set of bagpipes greeted us with the song that Rose had been entirely enraptured by. It had to be Lindsay's doing. Then, like a chorus of angels, people began to sing the words, people of whom I had never met. Even sweet Lindsay began to sing, although only a few words came forth. *I once was blind, but now I see*; the people echoed these words through the church's doors as the bagpipes played quite beautifully the melody to *Amazing Grace*. Rose would have been perfectly pleased.

Then, as Lindsay took my arm, something remarkable happened. There in that church, I felt something that cannot be explained, maybe it is what Rose spoke of all along, it was an absolute peace that I could not find the words for.

Lindsay curled up in bed beside me. Her hair smelled just the same as it had after the morning we had married.

"Thank you," she finally whispered.

"For what?"

"For allowing me to meet my sister in her final days. Don't you think it was God's gift to us?" She paused. "That's what Rose would have said."

I was silent.

"She's on your mind just as much?" she asked.

"Little Rose is on my mind. She needs her mother," I replied unexpectedly.

"Yes, yes she does," Lindsay said quietly.

"Charles is leaving for America, you know?"

"Yes."

"He's not taking little Rose with her."

"Why ever not?" she asked with alarm in her voice.

"You and I both know that Charles found her to be more of a burden than anything else."

Lindsay was quiet and said nothing; she played with her fingers like she always had.

"Lindsay, I believe we have one more gift that we could give back to your sister."

"What is that?"

"Little Rose. What would you think of adopting her for

our own?"

"Do you mean it?" She sighed deeply. "I thought you didn't want children, you got so quiet on me the last time."

"It's not that I don't want children. I just don't want to fail our children like my own father had done me. I didn't know if I was ready to face that."

"You aren't your father."

"Rose told me the same thing."

"Because, she meant it, as do I. If you are ready to face it, then I am too."

"I am."

"Oh, Lloyd, can we really? Little Rose is the only piece of family I have left."

"And, Aunt Birgitta?"

"Yes, but little Rose is much more pleasant." She slightly laughed and I returned her smile.

"Let's talk about it in the morning. It's been a rather draining day."

"I love you, Lloyd."

"I love you, too, my dear Lindsay." I kissed her forehead before she fell asleep in my arms, her voice now silent to the emotions that had changed our world forever.

However, it wasn't that much later when I heard Lindsay, it must have been two or three in the morning. I tossed over and found that she wasn't in the bed. Rather, she was curled up in a ball on the floor, crying, by golly was she crying.

Crikey, I wished I could have helped her, but it was entirely out of my control. We were to face a lifetime of this together and I would do whatever it took to make her realise that I cared. She had never had that, not all her life.

"Lindsay, why are you on the floor?"

"First Victor, now Rose, next it will probably be you. I'm

cursed."

"No, darling, don't say that."

"I cannot help it, Lloyd. At one moment, I feel fine and the next, I feel lost."

"You've lost your sister. Anyone would feel the same way."

"Don't say things just to make me feel better," she said bitterly.

"What else am I to say, Lindsay? It's so early in the morning. Let's go back to bed and talk when we are both more stable for conversation."

"You must be sorry you wed me."

"Yes, bitterly sorry," I smiled.

"Oh, don't try to joke, not now." She wiped her nose with her sleeve.

"I promise that I will allow nothing bad to happen to you."

"You say things that are too good to be true," she stated. "You can't promise me that. Look what happened to Rose."

"I can't promise things that we are uncertain about, but I can promise you that of which I am certain and that certainty is that I will never leave your side, no matter what scheme life conspires."

I grabbed her face in my hands, her eyes frantically searching for that which she would not be able to find, the peace in her mind that both her and I longed for.

"You will be okay."

"I don't know that," she cried.

"Do you trust me?" I asked.

She nodded, very slightly.

"There, that's all we need. We must trust one another."

She calmed down and wiped the rest of her tears aside. I scooped her up in my arms and her body relented, knackered and feeble by the emotions of the past week. Placing her in the bed, I stared at her with a new found love, a love that made me realise Thomas was right all along. I never knew what love was, not until this moment. Before, I would have been angry with her and I would have cursed a God I had not believed in, but what good would that have done any of us and what good would it do us now?

After wiping her tears and softening her lips, she gathered herself in my arms.

"Oh, Lloyd, are you not sad?" she asked.

"I've never been more grieved by anything in all my life," I whispered, fighting the tears. "I haven't been able to cry since her funeral, for I am afraid that if I do, it will be an acceptance that she is gone."

I had not meant to admit it to Lindsay, especially in her condition, but I had. She merely nodded, accepting the roughness to my nature for the past couple weeks.

"Lloyd, I don't know if I want to be a mother after all," she whispered in my arms quietly.

"You don't mean that." I brushed her hair with my fingertips.

"I do, I do mean it."

"You will be a wonderful mother for little Rose."

"She needs *her* mother, not me."

"You are the closest thing to her mother, and she will come to know you as her mother. I doubt she will remember Rose at all."

"As much asI do not remember my own birth mother and was later forgotten when I became too much of a burden for my adopted mother," she said.

Now, it all made sense. Lindsay knew what it was like to grow up with parents who were not her own, to be loved by them, but then to be tossed aside when she became too burdensome, something they had not accepted when they had first taken her as their own.

" No, it won't be like that. Remember what Rose told you?"

"Remind me."

"You are not the same as your mother, nor your father, nor anyone else for that matter. We are not our parents." I paused, "You are Lindsay Fox, and the world needs you, just as you are."

She nodded, and fell asleep to the comfort of my words, yet even though I had said them, I was not comforted in return.

After she had fallen asleep, I grabbed my coat and went for a walk, silently exiting through the hotel's back door.

I didn't care that it was in the early hours of the morning, it was better this way. As I walked, the hardness that I had felt ever since we had returned from the church had begun to melt away. I crossed the bridge at the park; grabbing the end of the railing, I felt the coolness, a reminder of when I had first received the news of Rose's death. It was real, she would never sing another note. And, without a thought, a cry birthed much deeper came forth.

"Why, God? Did you not consider the cost of taking her away from us?"

It was an unfair question to ask, I know. The tears were hot as I allowed only a few tears to fall down my cheeks. The anger that had billowed within erupted. I searched for the peace that I had felt at the church, but I found none.

"Why couldn't it have been me?" I asked, burying my hands in my face.

A month had passed since Rose's death. After my conversation with Lindsay, the Carnegies agreed that Lindsay and I would make fine parents for little Rose, especially after discovering the truth as to who Lindsay was. We had to tell someone else our secret, although we told them that we wished on keeping the secret that Lindsay and Rose were sisters just between the four of us. They seemed to understand the reason for secrecy, especially from all the hurt that had been caused from Lindsay's childhood.

Little Rose stayed with the Carnegies until we were able to make arrangements and process the adoption papers, which was by no means an easy process. We were patient, though, and went to visit the Carnegies every weekend.

Even though time had passed, it was still so difficult, especially for Lindsay. I refrained from drinking, a request made by Lindsay, and obliged, no matter how much I wished I could grab a bottle and ease the pain. However, I knew better than any man that it would not take it away. I feared I would end up like my father. Rose knew this and now, Lindsay, too.

"All I can do is think of Rose when she laughs, when she cries, when she smiles. I can't help it, Lloyd," there were tears in Lindsay's eyes.

We had just arrived back to the hotel on a Sunday, after spending the past two days in York.

"It will get easier, I promise." I kissed her forehead, although I wasn't certain myself that it would get easier.

"How are you able to just brush it all aside as though nothing has happened?" she asked.

"I don't, Lindsay. But, we must move forward now, for little Rose." I said the words, speaking to myself more than anything.

"I'm still grieving."

"As you should," I replied.

"And, you?"

"Yes, but in my own way. It would do you no good if I expressed that to you, now would it?"

She sat on the bed and stared out the window, her lips piercing the air, trying to find the right answers, yet finding none in the window's reflection.

"If we are to welcome little Rose into our family, I don't believe this hotel room will be a suitable place to raise her," I finally said.

"What do you have in mind, then?" She still gazed out the window.

"I have enough saved to buy us a home in West London."

"You've already looked into it?"

"I've already agreed to the down payment."

"Without telling me?"

"I didn't want to bother you and felt that it was the right decision to make on my own."

"You won't make that same mistake twice," she said.

I took a seat beside her on the bed and took her hand. "It has a music room and a small parlour for you to entertain guests and an extra room for additional children."

"Our children?" she looked at me.

"Yes, one day, Lindsay."

"Can we visit it tomorrow?"

"The house?"

She nodded.

"Yes, we most certainly may." I gently touched her cheek.

"Do you really believe Rose would think we are good parents for her little Rose?" she suddenly asked.

"I think she would have hoped for nothing more." I kissed her forehead.

Autumn 1925

JENNIFER MALECH

Chapter 30
The Eagle and the Child

We moved into the house in West London. Charlotte was eager to help decorate and teach Lindsay the proper ways in which a lady should prepare her home. I had heard them gleefully laughing from the kitchen while I organised papers in my office. Lindsay was happier than she had been in the past few months. I had convinced her to see a doctor; she was not eager to do so after Rose's death but then agreed after I reminded her about what she had told me on the day I had asked her to marry me.

The doctor who had been seeing her had said that there was nothing that can be done except surround her with good thoughts, so we did everything that we could to keep her by such. He had also prescribed Lithium salts to help stabilise Lindsay's mood after identifying her symptoms to be what Jean-Pierre Falret had called *la folie circulaire*. Lindsay had been terrified that they would send her to a psychiatric hospital upon such a diagnosis to which I only wrapped her in my arms and told her that as long as I had breath in my lungs, she would never see that day. The comfort was in the fact that we knew that

Lindsay was not the only one who suffered from the syndrome. Perhaps, one day, there would be a cure for such a sickness of the mind; even if everyone else didn't believe it to be true, for some reason, I did. Besides, the Lithium was helping tremendously. My thoughts were not voiced, not even to Lindsay, but I believed in the day when medicine would meet the mind to its greatest degree.

Perhaps, little Rose was also Lindsay's medicine. She was blossoming into a mum like no other, almost as though it was what she had been created for, an entirely unexpected realisation on all our parts. She would have despised me for saying the words out loud, for I knew that she was created for much more than motherhood. It just brought me, even me, an unexpected joy to see her like such. It was hard to believe that a few months had already passed since we had adopted little Rose as our own and now we were planning her first birthday party. The time was passing rather quickly.

It was now a beautiful autumn day and I was meeting with Reverend Thomas at the Eagle and Child.

He had not changed since the last time I had seen him, and I was surprised by how glad I was to see him again. "Ahh, it is good to see you, Lloyd. You look healthy! Is that wife of yours spoiling you?" He patted me on the back.

"No more than another man's wife," I smiled.

"Would you care for a drink? It's on me."

I reluctantly agreed and Thomas beckoned the bartender over.

"I was very sorry to hear of Cherry's death, but all the more glad to know that her daughter would grow up in good hands."

"Thank you for that," I replied steadily. It was still

difficult. I imagined that it would always be difficult, anytime her name was mentioned.

"You loved her very much."

"Yes." I tapped my foot on the barren floor, still lost in a way.

"When you love deeply, it makes the loss all the greater," he gently remarked.

"Yes, so I know," I replied.

What else was there to say?

"I am sorry that I have been absent, it's been a rather busy time. I should visit you and that new wife of yours."

"Yes, you certainly should."

"What's her name again?"

"Lindsay."

"Beautiful name."

"Most charming." I slightly smiled.

He thanked the bartender who brought our drinks and then raised his glass.

"Cheers."

I raised my glass and took a sip.

"How are things keeping up at the university?" Thomas asked.

"The University of London is different from Oxford, but it has been very enjoyable. I enjoy teaching much more than I did playing at the hotel every night." I paused.

"I've been asked to teach piano again in the spring."

"Have you given up music composition, entirely?"

"No, I will always have my music, but I discovered that it's not what I want to do for a living after all."

"Is this because of Cherry?" he suddenly asked.

"No, not entirely. It's more than that. It's the war. I thought if I wrote the music, it would erase the guilt from my bloody hands, from their bloody last breaths."

"The music won't take away the guilt, but it will most

certainly heal. It has healed you, and it will continue to heal others," he gently replied.

"Guilt can't be taken away in the blink of an eye," I replied.

"No, it will take time, but you are the only one who can make the choice to free yourself from that guilt." He paused and grinned. "Not even I am capable of such powers."

"Cherry tried to force me to understand that," I remarked.

"We never know the ways in which one will impact our lives for the better," he replied with a gentle smile.

"It's like a Latin teacher trying to get her English students to understand the language. That understanding and knowledge comes in time." I smiled then, thinking of the time Rose had told me the very same thing. "That is why I want to teach, I believe, to give my students that revelation."

"What revelation is that?" he asked.

"Music will not fulfil a man's ambition for success, but it will give light to the unexplainable circumstances in our lives."

"I always knew you would be a teacher. There is too much knowledge in that brain of yours. You might take to teaching a philosophy course as well."

"Perhaps, it is in my future. Are you prophesying such?"

"Just a note of observation," he laughed.

"How is Ted? Have you seen him lately?" I suddenly asked. "He is doing just as wonderful as ever. His sisters come to visit most often and the congregation that he oversees is rapidly growing."

"That is good to hear. We've written the occasional letter, but I must be honest that I haven't kept in close touch."

"Friends come and go, just like the seasons of life." He

took a sip from his glass. I smiled at Thomas's wisdom that he always seemed to offer in every conversation.

"Thomas, I really came here today to thank you."

"What for?"

I replied honestly, "For not condemning me, but for pointing me in the right direction. I fear I wouldn't have Lindsay nor little Rose without it."

"Lloyd, it is never a man's place to put judgement on another man. If that was the case, we would all be dead."

I hesitated, for I had sworn that I didn't want to mention her memory again, but I knew I would. Why else had I come?

"Rose said something similar once," I smiled.

"Rose?"

"I meant Cherry, of course. Rose is her daughter's name." He simply smiled which made me feel like somehow he knew, but he didn't say anything.

"Every man's journey is his own. I played a very small part in your own, but I am glad to have done so."

"As did Cherry."

"Yes, as did Cherry," he smiled.

"There's something that I realised at Cherry's funeral, something that I believe both you and her were trying to tell me all along."

I had not admitted the words out loud, not even to myself.

"By all means, I'm in suspense now," he remarked.

"God is just, man is not. Isn't that why you all sing about his grace? Amidst human suffering, there is somehow this God who surprises man with peace in his pain."

"It is why I never forced you on your knees. What good would that have done? It is the quest that man searches for, remember?" he smiled.

"Yes, there are few conversations that do not leave my

brain's memory bank." I smiled and then stated with a quizzical brow, "Yet, while I now believe that God exists, I rather have a difficult time understanding his relationship to man."

"Why did you marry Lindsay?" he asked suddenly.

"Because I love her, because it was the right thing to do."

"But, from your letters, you wrote of how she has brought pain at times. Why, then, do you still love her?" I knew this was another one of his queries to get me to understand something, rather than convincing me that I had no love for her at all.

"It is unexplainable," I finally said.

"It is not trivial."

"No, indeed far from it." I took another sip from my glass.

"That is where man has misunderstood the love of God. He views it as trivial, when in fact, it is far from such. This love is persistent and absolutely inescapable."

"If not for pain, would we understand love?" I asked rhetorically.

"My boy, you've nailed it right on the head."

"And, God?"

"God loves without impedance. When we understand that, we understand our existence."

"Which is why Cherry, who was even denied human love in the latter days of her life, was full of such joy."

"Yes. Cherry had a choice when it came to her pain, as does every man. After giving birth to little Rose, she could have been rebellious towards her husband and given into what she had always desired."

"Me?"

"To put it frankly, yes."

"But, she chose religion instead." I played with the rim of my glass coming to understand Rose's point of view.

"Cherry made an adjustment towards faith in order to overcome her pain," Thomas said, correcting my statement.

"Is all pain meant for such?" I asked sombrely.

"Not all, but I do believe that pain arouses something within man, draws him towards a greater good, recognising that it is only he himself who needs to change, not the world that surrounds him."

"That's a rather bold statement." I took another sip from my glass.

"I am not speaking for all circumstances, only Cherry's. She came to visit me, you know?"

"No, I did not."

"A few days before her death, in fact."

"Why ever so?"

"She wanted to thank me, I suppose just as you have done. She came with her maid, what's her name? I'm terrible with names."

"Annabel."

"Yes, that's right. Well, she told me she found life's truest contentment. Even in letting go of you, she said that she had never felt more at peace. She discovered that there is nothing on earth that comes close to it. There is no competing factor to such attribution."

"She was remarkable." That was all I could say.

"I believe our human idea of love is very selfish. When we identify with the love of God, it becomes the very opposite. For what does God attain in return from our love? If He is everything, what can he gain from our love? That, by definition, is selfless."

"A selfless love, that if reflected by man, moves our society towards goodness. In the same way that you spoke about man's free will, isn't it?"

"Yes. You've opened your heart, haven't you?"

"No," I laughed. "Not entirely."

"But, you have, which is why Cherry knew she had to let go of you and insist upon yours and Lindsay's marriage."

I was silent for a few moments.

"I can't believe she told you all of that, about Lindsay and me. Do you know the rest?"

"That they were sisters? Yes."

"Remarkably impossible." I smiled and took another glass of drink.

"Almost impossible. If you live long enough, you'll hear a story or two about such."

"Do you believe then that God had his hand in it?"

"I don't believe in coincidental appointments. Cherry believed that. Cherry wanted you to know that. Her husband, however, I believe she had given up on."

"I don't blame her."

"Forgive me if I've spoken out of place."

"No, Thomas, you have not."

"I do not know Charles, ha, there's a name I remember. Anyways, since I do not know him, I have no claim or judgment to his actions, only a one-sided understanding from Cherry."

"She told you?"

"About his short affair, yes. I believe she wanted to make sense of it, and make sense of how she was to continue living under the same roof as him while also being a submissive wife. That's why she came to me, really. She wanted advice from a friend, rather than her own vicar."

"Cherry, submissive? There's two words that would never be found in the same sentence," I laughed.

"In submission to God, she became a different person, a better person than she already was, which we all know was already quite splendid." He rejected my statement and added, "I imagined that Cherry wanted me to meet with both her and Charles, to offer counsel and guidance in their marriage. Though we never met, at least Charles asked for her forgiveness in the end."

"How could she give it?" I asked, though not expecting an answer.

"Though not easy, she forgave him because of a thing called grace."

We remained silent for a moment.

"Hmmm. You know that song *Amazing Grace*?" I asked suddenly continuing to play with the rim of my glass.

"Who doesn't? It's an ancient hymn," he smiled.

"They played it at the funeral. Cherry loved the hymn, she always said it gave her a certain joy, which I could never understand. When the bagpipes played the song as we left the church, I felt, call me a crazy man, that Cherry was there. That peace, the feeling that she had first told me about all those months ago, I believe I felt it. It was almost as if it was her parting gift."

"A gift that God gave mankind many years ago through his son."

"Was it God I felt? I do not know, but ever since that day, since that experience, I haven't felt the same."

"Impossibly remarkable," he echoed my words and smiled.

"She wanted me to love Lindsay and not to spare grace despite suffering."

"Which you will?"

"Yes. And, now, my choices are entirely dependent upon another with adopting little Rose."

"To be a father is a remarkable gift, especially to Cherry's child."

"I am a father now, Thomas, and perhaps, not until that moment occurred, when I asked Lindsay what she thought of the proposition, did I realise that I truly could no longer think of myself. What a fool I've been since the end of the war."

"At war, you never thought about yourself once, Lloyd. I believe you have given yourself less credit than you are."

"All that time wasted after the war, though."

"Not wasted. Give yourself some grace, just as Cherry would have done. Those years in America, even if you did think of only yourself, they shaped you and led you to where you are today, did they not?"

"No step taken by coincidence, right?" I closed my eyes and allowed the drink to wash down my throat.

"What's more is I believe you stopped thinking of yourself when you gave yourself to Lindsay, don't you think?"

"Yes, but this is something different."

"It is something different, but something different has happened in you."

"Yes," I took another sip from my glass.

"You've been surprised by joy. That's what Cherry told me last."

I smiled slightly and soaked up those words, "There isn't always joy, though. More sorrow as of late."

"As to be expected; if we were full of good spirits all the time, would we be truly human?"

"You seem to be," I stated.

"Don't think about it too much. Don't allow logical reasoning to out rule that surprise within. I learned that long ago and it's saved me a lot of time wasted from spinning unanswered queries in circles. There are some things that we must accept. Cherry's death is one of those things."

"Crikey, I've really shown too much emotion, haven't I?"

"Even man isn't spared from emotion. Women are just better at conveying it."

"That is very true," I replied steadily and then added, "Our conversation has reminded me of something Cherry said once."

"What did that wise girl say?" his eyes sparkled.

"That in a world of uncertainty, faith gives us hope."

"Faith in God is the only absolute truth, Lloyd. Man just tries to find it through other things," he gently smiled.

"As you have always said," I added and took another glass of drink.

"She was remarkable through all adversity," Thomas commented.

"Yes," I could feel the tears in my throat and didn't want to say anything more.

"Her life had a peaceful denouement in the end," he smiled gently.

"Cherry's life gave the war an understanding denouement," I replied.

"She opened your eyes to your pain," he remarked. "She answered the why queries that we can't seem to ever ignore, especially the war."

"As did you, Thomas. Our conversations have unexpectedly changed me."

"For the better?" his eyes sparkled.

"For the hope of a future beyond the life we've been given," I replied.

There was a dance in his eyes as I said the words aloud.

"To Rose," he lifted his glass.

"To Rose," I toasted and didn't know if the Rose he toasted to was my little Rose or the one who would always remain with me all the days of my life. His eyes continued to sparkle, and I asked no queries. There are some things that Rose, herself, would have preferred to remain silent among men.

"Taking holiday soon? It might be good for your new

family," Thomas then said after we both drank to Cherry Rose.

"Actually, yes, at the request of Lindsay. We are taking little Rose to Ireland once the spring term ends."

"By golly, I haven't been there since I was a boy. What are you to do there? Join the Irish Republic?" Thomas laughed and I, too, returned his laughter.

"No, we are going to introduce little Rose to her new family."

"What a marvellous decision," he smiled.

Summer 1926

After spending the morning playing with little Rose in the gardens, Lindsay and I once again left little Rose in the hands of Aunt Birgitta. It was hard to believe that it had almost been a year since Rose's death. We took to it as a family as anyone would. Charles never wrote, and we never asked about him. I had rather he be gone from our lives entirely, especially little Rose.

When we had arrived in Ireland, Lindsay had insisted that we return to the Cliffs of Moher, just the two of us. She said that it brought her great happiness and that the doctor had suggested she surround herself by things that made her happy.

"Am I not enough?" I laughed.

"You know what he means," she smiled.

"Yes, I do. Then, I must steal a car once again," I mischievously smiled. .

"Oh, Lloyd," she giggled, her brown curls once again chasing me in the wind.

We had walked hand in hand to the pub where we met with Tom, the bartender who had been a friend of Aunt

Birgitta's as well as my car lender every time we came into town. He had once again given into our plea and allowed us to borrow the car, as long as we returned it to him by sunset. I smiled and told him that it would be no problem whatsoever.

Lindsay hopped in the passenger seat and laughed, making me feel as though the worst of life was through. Everything that we had been through made these simple moments in life so much sweeter.

We arrived at the Cliffs shortly after, their majesty nearly bowing down to us upon our arrival. Upon exiting the car, she grabbed my hand, quite out of habit, more than anything else, and breathed in the salty air.

"Will you promise that we take holiday here every summer?" Lindsay asked me.

"What do I get in return?" I smiled.

"My company," she laughed.

"I suppose I could count that a fair trade."

"As fair a trade as you giving up alcohol for the church?" she smiled.

"It does more harm than good," I replied.

"And, I?" she laughed and then ran ahead of me.

My hands were in my pockets and I looked away, then back at her, playing into her small game of flirtation. It felt as though we were indeed in Cornwall again. I imagined us being old and grey, and still feeling the same way.

She stood there, her white flowery dress blowing in the wind, her hair in a braid that flowed like a waterfall down her back, and her smile as brave as the morning sun.

She needn't do anything at all, but just stand there. Her childlike joy, when it did come, I hoped it would never leave her, was unimaginably enrapturing.

Like a bird's mating call, she sang in the wind, glancing back towards me as she ran towards the edge of the cliff; I left my watch and answered her call. Before she could run any further, I grabbed her from the waist and held her closely. Kissing her affectionately, her lips warmed my body despite the chilly winds. Little Rose already adored her, and I adored her all the more.

"I've so much love for you, Lindsay Fox," I kissed her forehead.

"So much love that you are willing to bring me and our children here every summer, no matter the cost?"

"Little Rose for now," I replied.

"That is until next summer," she smiled.

"Lindsay?"

"Yes, Lloyd?" she smiled so brightly.

"Are you pregnant?" I asked with great shock.

"Don't be too surprised. You are the father," she laughed.

"How long have you known?" There was great surprise in my voice.

"For a couple weeks now."

"Are you pleased?" I asked.

"Oh, Lloyd, more than pleased. I am the mother of your child, what greater happiness is found in that?"

I swooped down on one knee and kissed her belly. Then, standing up, I kissed her again.

"I'm afraid I have no words," I held her in my arms and gazed out upon the waters, watching as the tides came and went, in the same way that our lives did the same.

Then, once again, as though it was our anthem to life, Lindsay began to sing Rose's *Song for Somme,* yet this time she made it her own.

Seen though she is not seen
I just want her to know

Seen though she is not seen
I just need her to know

Hidden behind a castle
Secrets buried deep
Father's Paintings forgotten
Her daughter's laughter eternal

Seen though she is not seen
I just want her to know
Her love goes on
That I finally know

After she sang the last note, I took her hand and we walked along the cliffs.

"I promise I will be the best father for little Rose and our child," I stated through the rush of the winds.

"You already are. I imagine Rose is smiling down upon us now."

"I hope so."

"Do you still think of her?" she asked.

"Every day," I replied, taking her in my arms.

"Me too. I don't know if I will ever be able to let go of Rose," she whispered.

"One day, we shall."

"Just as we've done with Victor, although I still miss him dearly," she said and then suddenly added, "If it's a boy, I'd like to call him Victor, what do you think?"

"I say that would be a wonderful tribute," I replied steadily, the winds agreeing that it would be a good thing.

"Do you ever think about how strange this all is?" she laughed.

"What? Our lives?" I asked calmly.

"Yes. All those years ago, in Cornwall, I never would have imagined that despite the tragedy in between, you and I would end up here."

"Life is funny, isn't it?"

She simply answered me by singing an old Irish folklore that her mam had sung to her when she was a little girl. Lindsay loved to sing, and it made her happy, so I never did stop her, even if I preferred silence from time to time.

I did not understand my own life timetable, but as I stood there, watching as Lindsay's insatiable voice greeted the evening wind, I realised something, something of which both Thomas and Rose had been trying to tell me all along; and, they were right. It was something that I had to learn for myself.

Our lives changed not because we were ordered to, but because our choices were then made by a love that could not be explained. We can't understand love just as much as we can't understand the battles we fight and endure in this world. That is what Rose meant. Rose knew this more than anyone else I had ever known. She told me that true love is sacrifice. I was still trying to understand it all and perhaps I would never fully grasp it, but Thomas was right, I was more open to a life that offered hope and peace instead of despairing emptiness.

As the sun descended beneath the clouds, I believed, somewhere deep within, that her words were true. Rose's legacy would always live on, as would every soldier who fought in the Battle of Somme.

Epilogue
Spring 1935
Rose's Song for Somme

"Papa, I don't want to wear these shoes. I want to wear my wellies. Look, it's raining outside!" The brown haired blue eyed boy, wild as ever, his hair an absolute ruffled mess, pointed his finger at the window beside his bed.

There was a layer of fog that melted over our back gardens as a light rain began to greet the barn's ivy covered walls.

"Your wellies aren't suitable for a concert. I don't believe your mum would be too pleased if we showed up to the music hall dressed like such, now would she?" I replied.

"We never get dressed up. I don't think Rose cares what I wear," he objected.

"Victor, do not make me force them onto your feet. You are old enough not to be dressed by your old man."

"I am eight." He stared at me.

"And, my favourite colour is blue." I placed the black dress shoes by his feet. He was not pleased by my flippant reply.

"It's just a concert."

"In honour of Rose's mum," I stated.

"My mum?"

"No, Rose's birth mum. You already know that."

Victor still had a hard time understanding how Rose could have two mums and he had only one. I loved his imagination. He would often tell me that his other mum was fighting the Sea Loch Ness Monster and was much too busy to take to dinner with us. Whenever he told us this at the dinner table, Lindsay couldn't help but laugh. No one could make up the things he said.

"Well, Mum wouldn't like it if I got my trousers all wet. You'd be happy I wore my wellies."

"You are to dress smart tonight, no queries."

Victor was impossibly stubborn sometimes. I rolled my eyes and left his bedroom, hoping that for once he would actually listen to me. He was a bright kid, but he rarely took to instruction. Victor reminded me of myself when I was his age, so I tried not to worry about him too much. Rose, his older sister, was the complete opposite. She was quiet and shy, yet took to herself in an entirely different way when she played that violin of hers.

I spied her red hair fly around the corner towards our music room, the one where we had spent many hours, her and I, entertaining guests that came to visit us. She loved it when I played the piano with her. Rose was the best pupil I had ever had, because she reminded me so much of her own mum, except much quieter. I wondered if that would one day slip away as well.

Rose had been playing since she was four years old, and now at almost eleven years old, she was my little prodigy, in the same way that her mum had been Lord Branston's prodigy. "Are you ready, darling?" I grabbed Rose's hand who sat at the piano stool, staring at her violin composition that she was to perform that night at the Café Royal.

"I'm nervous."

"Don't be."

"Were you ever nervous, Papa?"

"From time to time, all musicians are. But, you know what your mum used to tell me?"

"My mother, Rose?"

"Yes, that's right."

It was hard to believe that it had been ten years since her death.

"What did she used to tell you, Papa?"

"To close your eyes and act as if nobody else was watching."

"But, I thought she couldn't see?"

"Exactly that. Her everyday world showed you and I that it doesn't matter what they all think out there. What they see in you isn't as important as what you see in yourself."

"But, they do see me, Papa."

"Not entirely. They see you playing on a stage, but you yourself can close your eyes and play wherever you'd like. You could transport yourself to the Appalachian Mountains or set sail on the Atlantic's ferocious seas."

She smiled incandescently.

"Where did my mum like to play?" she said with widened eyes.

"York, she loved to visit there," I smiled.

"Where else?"

"A place called Queen's Hall. It's a music hall in London. That's where your mum and I first met."

"Will you take me there one day?"

"You might play there yourself one day."

She smiled and I echoed her smile.

"There we are. Should we see if your brother and mum are ready to walk to the hotel now?"

"Yes, thank you, Papa."

I kissed her cheek; there was never a day that I regretted the decision that Lindsay and I had made those many years ago.

"Lloyd, have you seen Rose?" Lindsay's voice echoed through the main hall.

"She's in here," I replied and took Rose's hand.

Lindsay was the bravest woman I knew. From time to time, her sickness would take her to a dark place, but then, as though she was switching gears in a car, I would remind Lindsay of the hope that her children gave her, and thence after, the darkness would soon fade away.

The doctor said that she had improved dramatically and that while he had other patients with a similar case as Lindsay's, she was the healthiest of them all. I believed that was due to her inner strength, a strength that could have only come from a childhood of uncertainty.

Rose and I made our way to the hallway where I heard Lindsay scolding Victor.

"What am I going to do with you?" she asked.

"Throw me in the barn," he replied.

She was angry with him, but couldn't help herself, and let out a slight laugh.

"Alright, you can wear your wellies, but once we get to the hotel, you are changing into your dress shoes. Do you hear me?"

"Yes, mum," he said, smiling that mischievous smile of his.

Her hands were on her hips and she just shook her head, still looking as young as ever in the dim lighting.

"You look lovely," I gave her a kiss on the cheek.

She smiled and grabbed Victor's hand, Rose and I following close behind. I glanced at the composition that she held in her left hand, holding to it like a jar of gold. It was our jar of gold, it always would be. My handwriting, although faded over time, read the words clearly to me, *A Song for Somme*. I knew then, more than ever, that Rose was smiling down upon us from heaven.

It wasn't until Rose had left us that I understood her change of heart in her last days. It is a hope that we are searching for, whether we realise it or not. For it is through man's unexplainable relationship with God that true happiness is found. We can't place it on the people we may lose or the success we may never achieve, for it will fail us every time. That is what Rose had been trying to tell me all along.

I smiled as I watched my family walk and laugh their way through the park, the magical colours of the leaves reminding us that a new season was springing into existence.

It was true. We never knew where life would lead us, but if we allowed the music into our lives, just as Rose had done, there would always be hope - man's greatest gift to life.

End.

ACKNOWLEDGEMENTS

This book would not have been possible without the love and support of so many people. To my editor, Toni, and the entire team at First Editing, thank you for your professional guidance and expertise that truly brought A Song for Somme to life.

To my friends, Charity Hall and Sarah Winkle, who were my sounding boards throughout the entire process of writing this book, I can't thank you enough. Charity, thank you for being the first person to read this story and reminding me of the power of redemption in each of our lives. Sarah, thank you for your extra help on the design cover and always offering good critique with your artistic eye.

Also, a special thank you to Samantha Solovieff who travelled with me to England and helped make this dream possible by visiting the Eagle and Child, Oxford University, and the Cafe Royal. Your encouragement and extra hand in the creative process made the editing process all the easier.

Lastly, thank you to my parents who financially supported this book to which this publication would not have been possible.To my father, Maverick Malech, who told me to keep following my dreams, for you never know where they will lead you, I am forever grateful.

ABOUT THE AUTHOR

Jennifer Malech graduated from Azusa Pacific University where she earned her Bachelor of the Arts in Communication Studies with a concentration in Journalism.

After graduating in 2016, she interned with World Vision, a non-profit organisation that provides humanitarian aid in more than ninety countries. During her time at World Vision, she had the opportunity to interview people all around the world, people who are making a global impact in providing health care and clean water for those in developing countries. This opportunity in journalism is what ignited her passion to continue in the writing field after college.

Jennifer currently works in Advertising in the Greater Los Angeles area, while writing and travelling on the side.

She also serves in ministry at Life Church Monrovia under the leadership of Pastor Rich and Tamara Brown, where she has helped with youth and college ministry for the past four years.

A Song for Somme is her second novel, published a year after her debut book, *Unkempt Secrets from the War.*